Sleep did not come easily. She saw his face each time she closed her eyes. She tried to drive him from her thoughts, but he always came back...tormenting...tantalizing...teasing....

....from: The River that Turned to Roses

She turned slowly and found him very close, smiling down at her. For an instant she hovered on the razor's edge between love and hate for igniting her sleeping passions—for tormenting her.

....from: Leap into Love

He turned and left her without another word, but his meaning was clear; the marriage that she so desperately wanted was to be had...but at a price. She stood where she was, rooted to the spot with shock and dismay.

....from: Design for Loving

A Heather Romance

Novel 1.

The River that Turned to Roses
by Susan Widdicombe

Novel 2.

Leap into Love
by Paula Lindsay

Novel 3.

Design for Loving
by Samantha Grantley

Wallaby, Ingalls & Peterson, Ltd.
New York   London

A Heather Romance

Volume R 114

The River that Turned to Roses
Copyright © IPC Magazines Ltd, 1975

Leap into Love
Copyright © IPC Magazines Ltd, 1978

Design for Loving
Copyright © IPC Magazines Ltd, 1978

Heather Library Series: USA
Copyright © Wallaby, Ingalls & Peterson Ltd, 1978

ISBN No. 0-933844-05-0
Manufactured in the United States of America

A Heather Romance

THE RIVER THAT TURNED TO ROSES

by
Susan Widdicombe

CHAPTER ONE

Stephanie Loman gazed across the open grass-land of the veld with sad eyes, for she knew that this small corner of South Africa, where wild animals found sanctuary, was in danger. The Van Dooran Game Reserve was fast running out of money. As far as the eye could see, the tall grasses rippled in waves as the breeze stroked them gently. The occasional clumps of thorn acacia trees, with their spindly trunks and umbrella-like upper branches, stood solitary and parched under a clear sky which was white with sunlight.

Stephanie bit her lower lip thoughtfully and

turned to look across to the complex of buildings which had become her home. Behind them, the blue mountains rose majestically. She didn't want to leave, for this part of the Orange Free State had captured both her heart and her imagination. As for the animals, she loved every one of them, from the largest down to the smallest. She even felt compassion for the jackals and hyenas. It was not their fault that Nature had endowed them with a scruffy appearance and discordant voices.

With a long sigh the girl strolled back to the jeep and headed for home. The sprawling, single-storey building where she lived with her father, the Chief Warden, looked as though it had been thrown together in a hurry. Nearby was another roughly erected structure where the other Wardens lived, some outhouses where the vehicles were kept, half a dozen pens which had been specially designed to hold large wild animals in need of treatment or care, and a couple of buildings where smaller animals were given shelter when necessary. Lastly, there were several strongly constructed pens for the pigs, chickens, and cows the household relied on for fresh food.

The Basuto housekeeper, whom everyone on the Reserve called Nancy, because her real name was beyond pronunciation for Europeans, greeted Stephanie with a wide grin and said: "Your breakfast's waiting—and your father was asking for you."

Nancy was like a mother to all of them. Her body was as wide as her smile, her skin as black and shining as coal. She was an excellent cook and was a friend rather than a servant. She had worked for the Van Dooran family for many years before coming out to the Game Reserve.

Stephanie walked from the kitchen and through the house to the shaded veranda outside the main living-room. As she sat down at the table she commented: "It looks very quiet this morning."

Jim Loman looked across at his beautiful young daughter and told her: "Just as well. We've got enough trouble here." He waved a letter at her.

"From the bank?"

"Yes." Jim nodded. "Paul drove into Welkom yesterday and stayed the night. He collected our mail and brought it back with him. This letter's very polite, but the bank manager says he can't lend me any more money, in view of my existing overdraft."

"Then what's going to happen?" Stephanie asked with a frown.

Her father paused for a moment. "If the worst comes to the worst, we'll have to go back to England. The Game Reserve will simply have to look after itself. We can't go on like this. I've already got a mountain of unpaid bills. My creditors have been very patient so far, but they won't wait for ever. Then there's our veterinary bill. Roger's been so kind that I can't take advantage of him for much longer." He looked across at Stephanie and forced a smile. "Wouldn't you like to go back to England? Don't you ever get homesick?"

He had sometimes thought that it was unfair to strand such a beautiful young girl in the wilds of Africa. She was small and slim, but her boyish jeans and shirt-styled blouse did not conceal her lovely feminine figure. Her long, fair hair was tied back with ribbon, but a few wisps softened the outline of her face. She had very regular features, with a neat, straight nose and delicately curved mouth. Her fair skin was tanned to a golden colour and her blue eyes shone like water reflecting sunlight. It was a happy and contented face. An innocent face.

She took a deep breath and her lips parted in a smile that revealed small, even teeth. "There have been times when I've felt homesick," she admitted. "When I first left school and came out here to you, I missed my friends. But now," her smile broadened, "my home is here and I have more friends than ever, even if they are mostly four-footed. I'd rather stay out here and stick it out with you. I could never live cooped up in a town again. And someone's got to look after the animals, even if I end up by eating grass!"

"What about Roger?" Jim asked.

He was referring to Roger Vincent, their veterinary surgeon, who came from a very wealthy family. Roger was an eligible bachelor in his late twenties, and he took a great interest in Stephanie. As well as visiting them when an animal needed his professional attention, he would drive the fifty-odd miles from Welkom at the slightest excuse, just to see her.

"What about him, then?" Stephanie answered evasively.

Jim sighed and got on with his breakfast. Stephanie's reply was just a polite way of telling him to mind his own business.

Stephanie admitted to herself that she liked Roger. They had a lot in common. They both loved animals and the wide open stretches of veld. He had taught her a great deal about African wild life and the local environment, but she really thought of him more as an elder brother than as a suitor. Although companionship was essential in any marriage,

there had to be more. Her heart would have to race at
the very thought of him and her mind be overpowered at the sound of his voice; but this did not
happen when she was in his company.

She had a secret obsession, which had begun
when she was sixteen and came out to join her
father on the Reserve, where he had been Chief
Warden for three years.

The land used for the Reserve had been owned by
an eccentric millionaire, Henry Van Dooran, whose
only son, Anthony, known as 'the wild one', had
disappeared just about the time the Reserve was
created. Anthony had been eighteen then and
Stephanie heard many tales about him from her
father when she came out to South Africa.

The more she'd heard about Anthony Van
Dooran, the more she had fallen in love with his
image. At sixteen, a girl's mind is prone to fantasies;
but as the years passed, Stephanie could not get 'the
wild one' out of her dreams. Even now ... at the
mature age of twenty ... her obsession for 'the wild
one' constantly tormented her. It seemed so foolish
that she had never told a single soul; not even her
father.

"Is there still no news of 'the wild one'?" she
inquired now.

"No," Jim replied. "The solicitors have scoured
England and Europe. He's vanished into thin air.
And there's no doubt about it, we shan't get any
money from old Henry's estate until they've found
out what's happened to Anthony. It sounds unkind,
but it would be better if they could prove he was
dead. So far, they haven't even been able to do that!"

"It's a pity the old boy left such a complicated
Will."

"Yes. I suppose he always hoped that Anthony would turn up and change his mind about helping with the Reserve. Just before he disappeared, he told his father that there was as much chance of his coming out to the Reserve as there was of the river turning to a bed of roses. And it looks as though he really meant it."

Jim's face saddened. He had never had a son of his own, but knew how Henry Van Dooran must have felt. Jim was thankful that Stephanie was a good and loyal daughter, despite her strong will and tomboyish ways.

"I'll have to speak to the Wardens," he went on worriedly. "Don't know how they're going to take the news, but they'll have to wait for their wages from now on. If they want to stay, they're welcome to free board and lodging, but I can't produce money out of a hat...and that's that."

"They won't let you down, Dad!" Stephanie smiled, trying to cheer him up.

"It's not just a case of loyalty, Steve. They're all good men, but some of them have families and they take their pay home at the end of the week. I shan't blame them if they leave to get other jobs. They're good men, but most of them have commitments."

The two sat in silence for a moment, eating their breakfast. Finally Stephanie asked: "What's the worst that can happen here through lack of money?"

"No money...no Wardens. Without Wardens to supervise the movements of the animals and keep them within the confines of the Reserve, whole herds can stray on to farming land and create havoc. I know this is a relatively small Reserve, but someone's got to patrol it and keep things in order.

So far, we haven't been troubled by poachers, but if word gets around that we haven't got enough Wardens to patrol the area, they could start sneaking in and there'll be no one to stop them."

"And that's only the beginning," Stephanie observed with a sigh. "What we need is someone with a helicopter. He could do the whole Reserve from the air and—"

"Steve!" Jim interrupted. "Stop dreaming! I can't even afford a few men in jeeps, and you start talking about helicopters!"

"I wish I could help," she said with quiet concern.

"I know. And you do help. You've been a great pal to me since you came out here. When your mother died, I don't know what I'd have done without you."

Stephanie smiled and hurried to finish her breakfast.

She had to see to the sick-pens first. These were where animals which had been injured or become lame were cared for until they were fit enough to fend for themselves. At present the inmates included a baby deer deserted by its mother; Stephanie had hand-reared it and was dreading the day when she would have to let it go, to take its place in the herd. There was also a young lioness which had been bitten in the shoulder whilst fighting. Although the wound had not been serious, it had caused the animal to limp. Roger Vincent had administered antibiotics so that the wound would not become infected, but the lioness had to stay in the sick quarters until she could catch her prey in the wild.

The young deer greeted Stephanie with affection when she let herself into its pen, which was protected by high, stout fencing and covered in heavy mesh netting so that predators could not attack the deer. This was only a precaution, because most wild animals keep well clear of human habitation.

In the second pen Stephanie was not greeted in such a friendly manner. The young lioness was fully grown and resented being held captive by mere humans. Stephanie fed a hunk of raw meat to the animal through a special trap in the surrounding wire, and the young lioness pounced on it and dragged it into the shade of the man-made den.

These two animals were Stephanie's favourites— the gentle deer and the angry young lioness. They were such opposites—and yet each magnificent in its own way! After feeding the remaining invalids, Stephanie made her way back to the house.

Her father was just making his way back from the Wardens' quarters, and his sunburnt face wore a look of disappointment and hopelessness.

"Well?" Stephanie asked as she walked towards him. "How did they take the news?"

"Badly," Jim replied. "We're losing four of them. The two who are staying are Tom and Paul. They haven't any dependants and they're devoted to their work. The others want to go at the end of this week and I've agreed. I can't hold them to their contracts, under the circumstances."

For a moment Stephanie didn't know what to say or how to console her father. Eventually she forced cheerfulness into her voice and told him: "Never mind! I'll work twice as hard for you. We'll cope somehow."

But they both knew that, however hard they slaved, they could not hope to do the work of four men.

They didn't have time to brood over their plight or go into a lengthy discussion. Stephanie had to go and replenish the salt-licks, and Jim had to investigate a complaint that a small herd of zebra had strayed from the Reserve and ruined a dozen acres of maize.

Stephanie took one of the jeeps that had been specially adapted for them. It had extra metal spars on the bodywork to protect the occupants in the event of being charged by elephant or rhinoceros. So far, this had never happened; but if it did, the outcome could be fatal in an ordinary vehicle.

It was a pleasant drive to the various points where Stephanie had to deposit the blocks of salt. There were no roads as such; mostly she followed tracks through the tall elephant grass.

Most of the animals were quite passive and viewed the jeep with indifference. The graceful giraffes paused for a moment, looked down on the vehicle with an expression of snooty disdain, and then went back to nibbling the upper branches of the thorn acacia trees. The various deer were more nervous and made sure that the jeep was not passing too close before they settled down to graze again. The elephants on the whole ignored the intrusion, but occasionally one of the old bulls would let out a roar which meant: 'I'm bigger than you, so watch it'. In which case, Stephanie would veer away.

The majority of the Reserve was grassland, relieved by clusters of trees, mostly thorn acacias, and outcrops of rocks which were reddish in colour; but to the east, where the boundary was a tributary of the Orange River, the mountains rose in tabular formation against a sky that was dazzling in the sunlight. This stretch of the Reserve which ran by the river was Stephanie's favourite, but she was usually too busy to visit it strictly for pleasure.

She had gone to three salt-licks and was making her way to the fourth when her attention was caught by a strange sight. At first she wasn't sure, but after slowing down the jeep and peering out of the window, she made out the figure of a man on a horse. He must be a stranger, and unaccustomed to the area, she decided, for no one in his right mind would travel across the Reserve on horseback, unaccompanied and unarmed.

Stephanie changed direction and headed toward the horseman.

"What on earth are you doing here?" she shouted angrily, stopping the jeep and getting out.

The horse was sweating and looked weary. He had obviously been travelling for quite some time. The rider was a young man, and as he dismounted Stephanie saw that he was tall, well-built and in his middle twenties. He had fair hair and his skin lacked the bronzed colour which the sun brought to the whitest of skins. It was clear that he had not been in South Africa for any length of time.

"Are you quite mad?" she went on angrily. "Didn't you see our notice, or can't you read?"

The tall young man walked up to her, leading his tired horse. Despite his fair skin and hair, his eyes were as dark a brown as Stephanie had ever seen.

"I've read the notices. They warn about wild animals, but they don't mention female wild-cats of the human variety. Tell me, were you born rude or do you have to practice?"

In that one brief exchange Stephanie knew that the stranger was not a man to wrangle with. She did not know who he was, or where he came from, but he had an unmistakable air of strength and authority. His face was taut and his mouth set in a dangerous smile.

"You're trespassing!" Stephanie announced determinedly.

"Am I?" he challenged. "And how do you know that I haven't got a valid reason for being here? You haven't even had the good manners to find out!"

Stephanie was a little panic-striken. She had never been faced with a stranger on the land before. Since the Game Reserve had been opened, the intruders they dreaded were poachers. These were not simply men who killed elephants for the ivory, or leopards for their skins; there were also those who killed simply for saleable meat. Was this man a scout? Was he spying out the land to find if poaching could be carried on with comparative ease?

"I've got a rifle in the jeep," Stephanie told him, opening the door of the vehicle.

"So go ahead and shoot me!" the young man laughed. "You'll have a lot of explaining to do to the police—for shooting a man in cold blood."

Stephanie stood quite still and made no attempt to reach inside the jeep.

"You haven't got a rifle!" the man goaded her. "Your object here is to preserve life, not to go around taking pot-shots at it."

He was right. Stephanie had no rifle in the jeep.

"All right," she conceded. "So what do you want here?"

"I was on my way to see the Chief Warden. I'm told his name is Loman. James Loman. I was told he might be able to fix me up with a job."

Stephanie relaxed and immediately changed her tone. "James Loman is my father," she said amicably. "But it's quite a ride back to the house. At least ten miles."

"Well," he sighed, looking at the tired horse, "we've come so far, we might just as well go the rest of the way."

"Where have you come from?"

"England."

"All the way from England on that poor horse?" Stephanie smiled. "No wonder he's tired!"

The stranger was not amused. He gritted his teeth and explained: "I came by plane to Welkom, via Johannesburg. From there I hitched a lift to a farm on the other side of the Reserve. The farmer very kindly lent me this horse. He hadn't got a spare vehicle. But he wants the horse back. All right?"

"The farmer must have been mad! No one in their right mind rides a horse through here."

"Horses can gallop, you know!"

"They can't out-sprint a cheetah."

"You've got an answer to everything, haven't you?"

"No. But I have learned to stay alive round here. No one takes chances unless they're suicidal." Having made her point, she stared at the young man and asked: "Why have you gone to so much trouble to come and ask my father for a job?"

"Whatever the reason, it seems I've wasted my time. Apparently, you don't make strangers welcome—even harmless ones," he answered scathingly.

Stephanie would not risk driving him away as they were so short of labour. "I'm sorry!" She sighed and held out a hand. "I'm Stephanie Loman."

The young man reluctantly shook the proffered hand. Stephanie felt the power of his grip and noticed that his hand was well cared for and had not been used for manual work.

"My name's John Kingsley," he told her, and released her hand.

"Well, Mr. Kingsley, my father could certainly do with some extra help here—but who sent you?"

"I bumped into a chap in Welkom. I told him I was out of work and wanted a job as far from civilization as possible. He said his brother had worked out here and it sounded like the sort of place I was looking for. So here I am. Is there a job going?"

"You'll have to speak to my father," Stephanie answered. She didn't want to put him off by explaining the financial complications involved. It was better to let her father explain. Right now it was important to snare this potential worker, so she said: "I have to drive back now. I'll take the shortest route and you can follow. But don't gallop that poor animal. If I drive slowly, he can jog along behind. If we do come up against a dangerous animal, you'll have to dismount and get into the jeep with me. The horse will have to take his chances. Is that okay with you?"

"Fine."

John Kingsley climbed back on to the horse and Stephanie got into the jeep. As she drove slowly back to the house she was very puzzled. It was possible that someone in Welkom had sent this man out to the Reserve, but it was highly unlikely. There were dozens of places where he could have found work in equally isolated areas.

There was a strange flicker of intuition in Stephanie's mind that told her this young man was looking for something more than a job.

Jim Loman was surprised and delighted at the prospect of having an extra Warden, and it was agreed that the newcomer should start on a month's trial.

"You clearly understand that I can't pay you anything at present?" Jim said in conclusion, "but you'll be well fed and I'll keep a tally of what I owe you. We're short of money just now. You should get your pay all right—eventually. But I can make no promises. You come on the understanding that you might never get your back-pay!"

"That's all right by me," the younger man said in his deep, educated voice.

"If it's not too personal a question, Mr. Kingsley," Jim asked politely, "may I inquire as to why you want to work out here, miles from anywhere?"

John's face tightened for an instant, then he said slowly: "I've been ill. A dose of TB. I was in a chest hospital for three months. My doctor suggested that I should find a job where I could work out of doors, and preferably where the climate is warmer and more consistent than in England. I hitched lifts to the South of France and worked there in the vineyards, picking grapes, until I'd saved enough for my air fare here. All I need now is plenty of peace and quiet, and all the fresh air I can get."

His story was feasible, but Stephanie when she heard it, doubted its validity. There were plenty of farmers in the area who would have hired him and paid him good wages, so why had he chosen the Van Dooran Reserve, seeing that it was the only place in the area that could not even afford to pay him? And if he had been picking grapes in the South of France, why was he not sunburnt? However, these were questions that would have to be shelved for the time being.

"Have you a special interest in wild life conservation?" she asked.

"No," John admitted. "I don't even care about animals very much. But I shan't let that prevent me from learning about them. As long as I can be useful—and by that I mean mending broken fences or running errands—I'll work hard. Just don't ask me to go and comfort a lion who's got raging toothache, that's all."

"Fair enough!" Stephanie smiled. "At least you've been honest about it. I don't think you need worry about lions with toothache. We have a very good vet for that purpose. He's also very good with elephants who've got colds in the nose and giraffes with sore throats."

John's mouth tightened and the natural curve of his lips disappeared. For a moment anger showed in his eyes.

After a brief, awkward pause, Stephanie said: "Well, lunch will be ready any time now. I'll show you to the Wardens' quarters. Life here is a bit frugal, but I think you'll be comfortable.

"The water from the stream is quite pure," she told him as they walked along together. "It's safe to drink straight from the tap. And we've got our own generator for electricity. You'll find it's quite civilized in the Wardens' quarters. The beds have all got interior sprung mattresses and there are plenty of blankets. It can get very cold here at night. We're nearly four thousand feet above sea-level, and however hot it is during the day, it can turn very cool once the sun's gone."

"What about food? Do we prepare our own?"

"No. Nancy—our housekeeper—sees to all that. She'll also do your washing and mending."

They had reached the Wardens' quarters—a long, narrow building constructed from wood. It had plenty of windows and was airy and clean. Each Warden had his own small room with a table and arm-chair, in addition to a single divan and wardrobe. There were two bathrooms and a large recreation-room fitted out with a billiard-table and a good selection of books. Also, there was a rather antiquated radiogram and plenty of records.

As Stephanie showed John the recreation-room, he remarked: "Well, no chance of getting bored here! I thought you said that life was frugal?"

"It is, compared with what was planned. There was to be a bar in here, so that the men could have a cold beer in the evening ... and each bedroom was to be fitted with a shower." She shrugged her shoulders. "But fate stepped in and we found we had little enough money to care for the animals properly, without affording luxuries for ourselves." Then she smiled as she told him: "And as for your getting bored, I promise that you won't have time for that. You'll only be fit to drop into bed when you've finished a day's work here. We start with breakfast at seven, and dinner is at eight in the evening. There's lunch at noon, but if you're working at the far end of the Reserve it's too far to come back, so Nancy will provide you with a packed meal."

Stephanie led him from the recreation-room to the dining-room. Some of the Wardens were already at the table, waiting for Nancy to arrive with the food. Stephanie introduced John to them, then led him to the far end of the room, where she showed him a small kitchen and explained: "You can brew up a pot of tea or coffee whenever you like, or make a snack." She pointed to a cupboard. "The provisions are in there, and Nancy keeps it well stocked. Just help yourself. If you feel hungry, you're quite welcome to fix yourself a plate of bacon and eggs."

"You scarcely starve here, do you?"

"No. We're lucky in that respect," Stephanie replied as she led him back through the dining-room. Well...I'll leave you to get acquainted. See you after lunch. Okay?"

When she took her place at the table on the veranda and waited for Nancy to begin serving lunch, Stephanie's face was creased with bewilderment and she began to twist a strand of her fair hair round her fingers. She had always done this when something troubled her, and her father was quick to notice.

"What's the matter?" he asked. "What's bothering you, apart from our financial problems?"

"I don't know," she replied. She stopped fidgeting with her hair and sighed. "I've just got an uneasy feeling about John Kingsley." She gazed at her father with candid eyes. "Don't you think there's something odd about him?"

"Depends what you mean by 'odd'."

"He's supposed to have been ill, but he doesn't look as though there's been anything wrong with him."

Nancy arrived with a tray and, after setting soup bowls before Stephanie and Jim, she took her own place at the table. She always ate lunch and dinner with them, at Jim's insistence.

"What do you think of our new Warden?" he asked her.

In her own version of English she answered:
"You mean the tall man with gold fuzz instead of
hair? The man what I see just now when I took
lunch to the Wardens?"

"That's the one."

"He just a man to me." She smiled broadly, her
white teeth gleaming against her near-black lips,
and added: "Apart from his pale skin, he just
another Warden."

They started to eat their tomato soup, but
Stephanie paused to ask: "Dad...did you ask for
references?"

"No. Under the circumstances, how could I? He
was prepared to take me on trust in regard to wages,
so I had to do the same in regard to references." He
paused and gave a brief smile. "To tell you the truth,
there's something I like about him. I've got a vague
notion that I've met him before...a long time ago.
I'm sure he's honest. He openly admitted that he
didn't like animals much, didn't he? I think there's
something odd about him being here, but I'm
certain he isn't a rogue."

"Dad," Stephanie persisted, "his hair! The way
it's cut! Doesn't it remind you of anything?"

"It looks a bit Germanic, come to think of it!"

Stephanie shook her head. "No, that's not what I
meant. It reminds me of a convict's haircut!"

Jim's humorous eyes widened. "You think he's
been in prison?" he challenged laughingly. "Come
off it, Steve! He's not the type!"

"How do you know what type he is?"

"Get on with your lunch," he said more seriously,
"and stop creating mysteries!"

For a while the conversation turned away from
John Kingsley, but as she discussed Reserve

matters, Stephanie's mind was still occupied with the mysteries that surrounded the newcomer. When Nancy had served ample helpings of apple-pie with fresh whipped cream, Stephanie said suddenly: "I suppose he isn't Anthony Van Dooran?"

Jim stopped eating and stared wide-eyed at his daughter. Nancy also stopped eating and her brow slowly became creased with thought.

" 'The wild one'?" Jim queried. "Yes... I see what you're getting at. He's about the right age, and he doesn't seem willing to talk about his background."

"And why did he single us out?" Stephanie added. "He could have got a job on any one of a dozen farms and been well paid."

"Yes, indeed." Jim paused for thought, then shook his head. "No... he can't be Anthony Van Dooran. His father always spoke of his son as having 'wild blue eyes'. Blue... not brown eyes. And young Tony was supposed to be quite mad. The old boy didn't know what he was going to get up to next. From what I've seen of John Kingsley, he's as sane as you or I."

Jim's gaze turned to Nancy, the Basuto housekeeper. She was still deep in thought.

"You were housekeeper to Henry Van Dooran when he lived in Welkom," Jim began. "You looked after the whole family until they decided to go and live in England. You must have known Anthony when he was a child?"

"That's right, Mr. Loman," Nancy agreed. "I remember when he was born, and I look after him until he go to boarding-school in England. Then I look after Mr. and Mrs. Van Dooran until she becomes so ill that they go to live in England. Mrs. Van Dooran... Mistress Elizabeth... was born in

England and she want to go home to die. And Mr. Van Dooran never come back here again. He sell the big house in Welkom and I go to work for another family until he write and ask me to work for him again, here on the Reserve."

"In the early days," Jim said, "you must have seen a lot of the boy during the school holidays."

"That's right. I knew that little boy well. He was a wild one, and him and his father not like each other at all. Elizabeth Van Dooran used to be very afraid when Master Anthony coming home for holidays. She was a very sick woman and all the bad quarrels make her worse."

"Go on," Stephanie urged.

"Well, it's not easy to say, after all these years. I not see Master Anthony since he was a boy, but I do remember he had blue eyes. They was bluer than the sky. And his hair was one mass of golden curls. When I used to wash him and put him to bed I used to tease him and say that with pretty hair like that he should be a girl."

"Is there anything vaguely familiar in John Kingsley?" Jim inquired.

Nancy shook her head. "No, Mr. Loman. I can't say there is."

CHAPTER TWO

Although the idea that John Kingsley could be Anthony Van Dooran had been dismissed, Stephanie could not rid herself of her interest in him. As soon as lunch was over, she set out to find him. She did not have to look far, for he was striding towards her. He had washed and looked fresh and somehow dignified, despite his well-worn clothes.

"Mr. Kingsley," Stephanie began, "Dad thinks we should get the horse back to the Sekker farm as soon as possible."

John towered over her, smiling and naturally dominant. "How do we get the horse back?"

"We've got an animal transporter; it's only a converted truck but it will serve as a horse-box. Do you want to come with me? I can tell you something about the work here on the way."

"Yes. Thank you. You can give me some idea of what I'll be expected to do. And I can collect my grip which I left with the farmer."

Stephanie led the way, pointing out the generator-shed, the henhouses, the piggery and the small enclosure where the cows were kept. Finally they reached the compound where the horse had been allowed to rest, and they had no trouble in getting him into the transporter for his ride home to the Sekker farm.

As Stephanie took her place behind the driving-wheel she was aware of John's penetrating stare.

"Mr. Kingsley," she asked tersely, "have I got a smut on my face or something?"

His stare mellowed until his face was wreathed in a smile. As the corners of his mouth tilted into a grin, the trace of a dimple formed in his chin.

"I'm sorry," he said. "I didn't mean to stare. Please forgive me. It's just that you seem so out of place. What's a girl like you doing here ... doing a man's job?"

Stephanie hardly knew how to answer. "I like animals," she told him coldly.

"Can you tell me why?"

"Yes." She changed gear. "I like animals because they're so much nicer than people and they don't ask a lot of personal questions."

"Bully for them!" he said, grinning.

They drove on in an uneasy silence for a while.

"You drive quite well for a woman," he commented finally.

"Look," she said with an angry sigh, "you're doing us a big favour by working here during our financial crisis, but it doesn't give you the right to be so familiar with me—or personal. So, if you don't mind, Mr. Kingsley—"

"John," he interrupted.

"Very well, John! Will you just accept that I'm here from choice and, despite my lack of size, I can work a fourteen-hour day alongside any man—and thoroughly enjoy it!"

"Will you be working alongside me?"

"For a few days, yes. Unless you make yourself really unpopular with me," she told him. She looked into his face and her anger ebbed.

He smiled down at her and seemed outwardly relaxed, yet she sensed that, deep inside him, there was a spring which was so tightly coiled it was ready to snap. She had seen the same haunted look in the eyes of animals which had suffered a traumatic shock.

"I won't ask any more personal questions," he said. "Would you mind if I smoke?"

"Not at all," Stephanie replied. "But I must ask you to be very careful where you throw matches and cigarette ends. The grass round here is as dry as hay at times and it would only need a spark to set it off."

John nodded. "I'll remember that." He took a tattered packet of cigarettes from the pocket of his jeans, and a box of matches. He lit up a cigarette and made sure the match was not burning before he flicked it out of the truck window. As he exhaled the smoke, a question formed in Stephanie's mind. Would a man who had recently spent three months in a chest hospital, suffering from tuberculosis of the lungs, smoke cigarettes?

The very definite answer came back—no, he would not!

"I'm surprised to see so much wild country, without a sign of man in sight," John remarked as they drove across the veld. "I always thought this part of Africa was full of gold mines."

Stephanie was driving steadily while keeping a look out for animals. "This used to be mining land," she told her companion. "Henry Van Dooran—the man who started the Game Reserve—was the owner. He and his family lived in a glorious mansion in Welkom, but he spent most of his time out here with his workers."

"There's nothing left to indicate that mining went on here," he observed as he cast a glance round at the landscape.

"Mr. Van Dooran had all the shafts filled in and sealed. He didn't want animals to fall down them. Then the buildings were flattened. They were only made from wood. The machinery was taken away and the place was generally tidied up. The gold was worked out, but he felt it was only right to leave the land as he found it. Nature soon covered the scars with vegetation, and now you'd never know where the mines were sited."

"Did Van-what's-his-name get much gold?"

"Enough to make him a millionaire several times over!" she laughed.

"If the old boy's rich, why is the Reserve short of money?"

"Henry Van Dooran is dead. The money's tied up for the time being."

"How's that?" John asked.

"It all began ten years ago," she explained. "Henry Van Dooran realised that the gold mines were exhausted and he decided to retire in England. He'd spent his whole life in South Africa, but his wife—Elizabeth—had been born in England and she'd always wanted to go home. She was an invalid and her condition was becoming critical. Well, the gold was exhausted and Elizabeth was dying, so he sold his house here, but kept the land, and they went to live in England. They had one son, Anthony, who'd spent most of his time at boarding-school in England. He and his father were always at loggerheads. He nearly drove his father out of his mind and, to make things worse, Elizabeth died within six months of returning home. Henry blamed it on Anthony...he said the worry of her son killed her. Anthony went on behaving like a young madman. He ran away from school several times. It was because he wouldn't fall in with his father's plans about his own future and about the Reserve that we are now in deep water financially. Old Henry Van Dooran is dead and the money we should be getting to run the Reserve is tied up."

"You seem to know a lot about the family," John remarked. "Did you meet Henry Van Dooran?"

"No. I was only a child at school in England at the time all this happened. But Mr. Van Dooran told my father the whole story. Naturally, Dad told me when I came out here."

"What do you yourself think of this Anthony Van Dooran?" John asked curiously.

"I think he was filled with a spirit of adventure—his own kind of adventure. He wanted to discover life for himself, not take over where his father left off. But the old man preferred to believe that his wild ways and daring exploits were evidence of an unhinged mind, and everyone else thought Anthony was just trying to scare his father into loosening the pursestrings in his favour. However, Henry Van Dooran had worked hard for his fortune and he was determined that it would be put to good use. He didn't want it to be squandered by his son."

"That seems reasonable," John commented. "So what did he do with his money?"

"For the next three years he did nothing. He was more concerned with getting his son on the right road. He wanted him to go to University and study ecology. Apparently, Anthony was brilliant at school, despite his wild behaviour. But he wouldn't listen to his father's plans. That was when Henry Van Dooran had the idea of turning his land into a Game Reserve. And this is where my father comes into the picture. He saw the advertisement for a chief game warden to take charge of a Reserve in the Orange Free State. The idea appealed to both him and my mother. Dad was a consultant in animal husbandry, so he knew all there was to know about breeding animals. At the interview, Henry Van Dooran took to him immediately and the job was his. As they planned the Reserve together, Henry told my father all about his family history...and Dad told me. I found it all very fascinating."

John grinned. "Yes, I suppose the idea of a wild, adventurous young man would appeal to your romantic proclivities."

Stephanie felt a flush rising to her cheeks. John was so close to the truth...and she had never told anyone of her obsession for 'the wild one'.

"Certainly not!" she denied. "It was the idea of coming to South Africa that appealed to me."

"But you didn't come out with your parents straight away?"

"No. I went to live with my mother's sister, so that I could finish my schooling in England."

"And what happened to the villain of the piece?" John asked.

"If you mean Anthony, his father told him that if he didn't settle down to serious study he'd be disinherited; he then made a Will, whereby Anthony could only inherit a share of the Van Dooran fortune if he took an active part in running the Reserve."

"And the plan misfired, I suppose?"

"Yes, Anthony simply laughed at his father and said he'd lead his own life. On his eighteenth birthday he left the house and has never been seen since, despite extensive inquiries."

"And the money's tied up, you say?"

"Indeed it is. Henry Van Dooran was so certain that sooner or later he could blackmail his son into doing what he wanted that when the Will was drawn up he made no provision for the Reserve to be kept going in the event that his son couldn't be found. Anyway, no one could have foreseen that Anthony wouldn't put in an appearance when he knew his father was dead. Last year, Mr. Van Dooran was talking about changing his Will, so that a certain amount of money would be available to us if he died suddenly, but he had a fatal heart-attack before he'd actually done so. Everything is tied up until the solicitors can trace Anthony—alive or dead. At present they can do neither. 'The wild one' has disappeared from the face of the earth."

"He must be quite a character," John said with a strange smile.

"I don't know about that," Stephanie replied with a touch of anger, "but he's a darned nuisance. He could at least show up, so that the executors could get on with the job of administering the Will. If he's alive, it's such a dog in the manger attitude. He can't claim his legacy, so he's hiding out and depriving the Reserve of the money it needs to keep it going!"

"Perhaps he doesn't know that! If he's made his way to the other side of the world, he might not even know that his father is dead."

"That's most unlikely. When Henry Van Dooran died, he was important enough to rate a notice in every leading newspaper throughout the world, I would think. He was quite a man ... one of the old mining pioneers. He started off without a penny to his name and worked like a slave to get his first mine established. I think that's why he didn't want Anthony to get his money. Henry had to work for it and he meant his son to work hard, too."

"And if Anthony Van Dooran is proved to be dead?"

"Then a Trust will be formed to administer the Reserve and start other wild-life schemes that Henry Van Dooran had been planning ..."

"How long can the Reserve hold out before it's in real danger?"

"That's hard to say. Strangely enough, it depends more on the animals than on us. If they take it into their heads to wander off the Reserve and cause a lot of damage because we're short of Wardens, the farmers will just have to shoot them."

John was taking in every word and obviously giving it deep consideration. "What happens at the present time if a farmer discovers lions near his livestock?" he asked.

"Well, if a farmer discovers a pride of lions settling on his land, he usually gets in touch with us and we transfer them here."

"That must take some doing?"

"Yes." She smiled. "You can't just call 'Kitty-Kitty' and hope they'll follow. It's a much more complicated procedure than that. The lions have to be tracked down, anaesthetised with drugged darts, and moved while they're sedated. It takes at least a couple of strong men to lift a lion on to the transporter, and all this takes time. Some farmers can't be bothered, so they shoot them instead. The lion population isn't too close to extinction yet, but we're very concerned about leopards. We were actually prepared to pay to have some of them brought here, so that we could encourage them to breed; but without money, we've had to postpone that part of our work."

"For heaven's sake!" John said airily. "Who really cares? Isn't it more important for mankind to survive?"

"Survive for what?" Stephanie flared. "If there's nothing left but human beings in a couple of hundred years time, what a dreary planet this will be."

"Don't be ridiculous!" John chided, as he gazed out of the window. "There are still thousands of square miles of land that haven't been touched. And who honestly cares if the greater spotted Mongolian whatsit becomes extinct?"

"I care! And so do a lot of people who've given it any thought."

"Why?"

"Because if all these animals become extinct, it'll upset the balance of nature!" she told him with rising indignation.

"Rubbish!" he laughed.

"And," Stephanie continued heatedly, "if our generation isn't going to stop destroying wild life by direct and indirect methods, we'll have a lot to answer for when our children grow up. Who knows what might happen if we upset the balance of nature."

John was staring at her with a mixture of humour and delight in his dark eyes. "My!" he teased. "It doesn't take much to get you going, does it?"

Stephanie had had enough. She turned to face him, bringing the truck to a standstill. "You've done nothing but interrogate me since the moment we met. Why?"

"I'm just interested."

"I don't believe you." She paused to stare at him, but found his gaze so disturbing that she had to give way and look straight ahead. She went on bravely: "I think that Anthony Van Dooran sent you here! He wants you to find out what's going on and see if there's a way he can claim his inheritance by unfair means. It seems highly unlikely that you'd go out of your way to work for a concern that couldn't even pay you, when you don't believe in what we're trying to achieve here. You're not the least bit interested in preservation."

John's smile increased until the dimple in his chin was clearly visible. "I must admit that the only life I'm interested in preserving is my own," he told her smoothly.

"That's easy to believe!" she said disgustedly. "But it doesn't explain what you're doing here. Who are you? Come on! Your name isn't Kingsley, so what is it? And what are you up to?"

"If I tell you who I am, will you promise to keep it a secret?"

She answered: "Yes," but had no intention of keeping her word.

John leaned towards her and for a moment a suggestion of panic touched her nerves as he came so close to her. Then he whispered in her ear: "I'm Father Christmas!" and sat back in his seat.

Stephanie had reached breaking point; she could stand his mockery no longer. She leaned across his broad chest and flung open the passenger door. "This is where you get out!" she stated firmly.

"Why?" He smiled, folding his arms and making it quite clear that he had no intention of climbing from the vehicle.

"Because I'm tired of you. Dad took you on and gave you a job, and already your behaviour towards me leaves a great deal to be desired." She stopped, took a deep breath and tried to control her temper. In a calmer voice she went on: "We've had several men working for us over the years, but never has any one of them treated me with such disrespect, and I don't have to tolerate it. So would you kindly get out?"

"It must be quite a few miles back to the house," he said quietly. "You've told me that it isn't very safe to walk...so how do I get back?"

"Seeing that you are Father Christmas, why don't you whistle up your reindeer and sleigh?" she demanded childishly.

"I didn't bring them with me...they're not used to such heat."

They had reached a stalemate, and now eyed each other angrily. She was trembling, and began to feel an acute sense of anxiety. Her anger began to subside. He reminded her again of an animal which was ready to spring in defence...not attack. She suddenly sensed that he must have been deeply hurt at some time. If this were the case, she must not injure him further; she must try, instead, to gain his confidence. With a sense of defeat, she started the engine again.

John was quiet and brooding for the rest of the outward journey and only spoke to thank Mr. Sekker for the loan of the horse.

On the way home he started to talk again, but Stephanie did not want to become involved in conversation. Although she had suggested earlier that the two of them should work together for a few days, the events on the outward journey had caused her to change her mind...

Within an hour they were back at the house. It was just after four o'clock and Stephanie suggested some tea before they resumed work. Normally she had very little to do with the hired hands unless it was in the line of duty, but she felt compelled to show kindness to John, despite his hostile nature.

She had intended to tell her father about how inquisitive the newcomer was during the journey to the Sekker farm, but something stopped her. She wanted time to investigate this interloper, for there was much she needed to know before finally passing judgment on him.

James Loman was not at the house.

"He drove north-west to see about the zebra that got out," Nancy told Stephanie, as the girl made her way to the living-room, accompanied by John.

Nancy then disappeared to prepare a tray of tea and sandwiches, and John walked to the window, staring out at the expanse of grass as he stood with his hands thrust deep into the pockets of his jeans. There was a distant yet disturbed look in his eyes.

"What's the matter?" Stephanie asked as she perched on the arm of a chair and looked at him with slight bewilderment.

"Nothing." John sighed. "I was just thinking over what you'd told me about the financial stalemate here. It seems a shame that the project should fizzle out, after you and your father have worked so hard."

This was a new John; he sounded positively sympathetic. "How did you manage to hold out for so long? If Henry Van Dooran died almost a year ago, where have you got the money from?" he inquired.

"Most of it came from my father's own pocket. He sold his house in England as soon as we realised we wouldn't be going back...and he had a small amount in savings. It kept us going for a few months. From then on, Dad arranged to have an overdraft, but the banks have put their foot down now."

John nodded. "Yes. Money is scarce all over the world at present," he remarked. He turned from the window and faced Stephanie. "Tell me, what would you do if you had unlimited funds? Apart from being able to pay off your debts, how else would you spend it?"

"That's easy. The first thing we'd do would be to buy a helicopter and hire a pilot to go with it."

"A helicopter, eh?" John grinned. "Your plans aren't exactly modest, are they?"

"The way I have it figured," Stephanie explained, "a helicopter would be more economical in the long run than our present system. As it is, we run four jeeps and the animal transporter, and they've all got to be kept in first-class order mechanically, because we can't afford to be stranded if they break down. We have to keep a good supply of fuel here, too. So if we had a helicopter, the pilot could do the work of half a dozen men, and fly to Welkom to fill up with fuel in a matter of a few minutes. He could pick up our mail and supplies daily, and transport animals. There's no end to the possibilities." She ended, on a very positive note: "One helicopter could work wonders for this place."

John shook his head and smiled. "You deserve ten out of ten for ambitious thinking! And I can see your point of view. All you need now is for the missing heir to turn up, so that the Van Dooran fortune can be handed over."

The mere thought of Anthony made Stephanie smile, and a wistful look came to her eyes. "Yes ... " She sighed. "But he won't show up. I get the impression that he doesn't need a share of his father's millions. He's the sort of man who'll get what he wants, even if he has to move mountains to achieve it."

John studied the small face that had become distant with dreams of 'the wild one'. "Don't tell me that you're in love with him?" he said.

So far, Stephanie had told no one of her secret longing to meet the elusive Anthony Van Dooran. She had always been afraid that she would make herself appear foolish.

"I wouldn't call it love," she admitted. "It's more a form of fascination. He creates such a romantic image ... at least, for a woman. I can't help conjuring up all sorts of situations when I think about him. With a personality like his, he must have women falling at his feet. He's not the type of man you'd meet every day."

"But an eccentric, from what you say."

"His father thought he was downright mad, as I

told you. But then, he was so different in temperament himself."

"Mad? If that were true, it would be quite a different thing," John said soberly.

Stephanie shrugged. "We're all mad in our own way. I'm mad about animals; you're mad to be working here, when I'm sure you've got the abilities for a much better job. I've known girls who were mad about clothes, and men who were mad about cars. We've all got our eccentricities."

John strolled over to an arm-chair and sat down. His eyes fixed on the coloured mat on the floor in front of him, he inquired: "So if young Van Dooran turned up here, you wouldn't condemn him as being mad without a fair trial?"

"If he came here, I'd be too nervous to think straight," she laughed. "Funny you should mention that! When you turned up this morning, I wondered if you were 'the wild one'."

"Me?" John's eyes widened. "That I should be so lucky! But just as a matter of interest, what made you decide that I wasn't?"

"Nancy. She used to look after Anthony when he was a child. She says there's definitely no resemblance. For one thing, your eyes are wrong."

"I'm sorry to disappoint you."

"I'm not disappointed. If you were 'the wild one', I wouldn't be sitting here talking to you like this! Tell me about yourself. Where did you live in England? And what are your parents like? They must miss you!"

There was a rapid change in John. The warmth vanished from his smile and his eyes turned cold. The hurt look was back.

"I would rather forget my parents," he said tersely. "Mine was hardly a devoted family. That was one of my reasons for leaving England. I want to forget my past life and everyone in it."

Stephanie was shocked by the sudden change in him. She had only tried to show polite interest, but he had reacted as if under attack. Why? Was she right about his convict hair-cut?

Nancy came into the room with a tray of tea and sandwiches. She placed it on the table between John and Stephanie and said: "Here you are, then!" She smiled down at John and added: "Mr. Loman told me I got to take extra care of you, 'cause you've been poorly." She gave him another wide grin, then left the room.

For a few moments neither John nor Stephanie spoke, then Stephanie sat down in the chair, picked up the teapot and began to pour out the tea. "Milk and sugar?" she inquired.

"Just milk, please," he replied. After a brief pause he asked: "Hadn't I better get down to some work soon? You're supposed to be short-handed, and yet I haven't done a stroke since I arrived."

"Can you drive?" she asked, handing him a cup of tea.

"Yes."

"Have you got a licence?"

"If you mean a driving licence...no. I lost it, together with my wallet and my passport. I had my pockets picked in Marseilles. The thief took the lot and they haven't been recovered. But I give you my word, I'm a capable driver."

Stephanie's brow creased and she could not hide her bewilderment. "If you had your passport stolen,

how did you get out of France and into South
Africa?"

The cup trembled in his hand. His eyes grew
angrier and his mouth tightened even more. Finally
he snapped: "Your father didn't ask all these
irrelevant questions when he interviewed me."

"Then he should have!"

John replaced his cup and stood up quickly.
Hovering over Stephanie in a hostile manner, he
demanded: "Who is in charge here? You or your
father?"

Stephanie shrank down in her chair. She did not
like what she saw in John's face. "My father's in
charge," she answered meekly.

"Then, if he wants to know more about me, I'm
sure he'll ask." He was looking down at her with
such anger and resentment that she dared not
pursue the argument. Without meeting his angry
eyes, she said: "There are several jobs you can do, if
you can drive. The licence doesn't really matter,
because this is all private property on the Reserve.
You could help with maintaining the fencing; it's
our biggest headache." Her voice trailed off as she
thought it would be prudent to let her father handle
John Kingsley in future. "I think you'd better ask
Dad, though. He ought to be back soon."

"Right. I'll go to my room and wait for him."

John strode from the house and headed towards
the Wardens' quarters. Stephanie felt strangely
depressed. He had told her nothing about himself,
but his attitude suggested that he had more to hide
than she had previously imagined.

When James Loman returned, he found Stephanie in an unusually quiet mood.

"Dad," she said, "have you asked to see John's passport?"

Nancy came out on to the veranda, where they were going to have dinner, and set bowls of iced melon in front of them, before taking her own place at the table.

"No," Jim answered. "We have a sort of gentleman's agreement. I don't ask questions and he doesn't ask for money."

Stephanie looked down at her slice of melon and cut out a small piece with her spoon. "Did you ask him how he came to be in Welkom?" she inquired.

Jim's face tightened a little. "He said he'd come by air. Why?"

"But he couldn't have done. Not officially!"

"Why not?"

"He hasn't got a passport. Earlier this afternoon he told me that all his papers had been stolen when he was in Marseilles, so how did he manage to get from France to South Africa?"

"Yes..." Jim said thoughtfully. "You've got a point there."

"Don't you think you ought to check up on him? To be on the safe side. We don't really know who or what he is. Suppose he's a crook on the run!"

Jim sighed. "Steve, you've made a very interesting point about the passport, but I can't afford to upset him. And you're letting your imagination run riot again. At first you thought he was Anthony Van Dooran, but Nancy says he most certainly can't be. So, now that theory is squashed, you want us to believe he's a villain." He leaned toward his innocent-faced daughter. "Shall we keep our heads for a while, and see how he makes out with the other

Wardens? At present I can't do without him. When the four men leave at the end of the week I'll be glad of any help I can get. If John Kingsley hasn't upset anyone, or given us any trouble...he stays. If you don't like him, Steve, keep out of his way. All right?"

Stephanie dug her spoon aggressively into the slice of melon in front of her. "I'm not afraid of him, if that's what you mean!" she said crossly.

Jim and Nancy looked at each other and smiled. They both knew this to be true. Stephanie was as brave and fearless as a young lioness.

CHAPTER THREE

Stephanie rose early the next morning and, as she washed and dressed, she became aware that she was taking more trouble over her appearance. She tried to make her hair look more feminine by tying it less tightly and, when she chose a clean blouse, she looked for one that was not too plain or severe. She even enhanced the curve of her mouth with lipstick, one which she had bought during a shopping trip to Welkom but had not used before. She tried to convince herself that she was doing all this because Roger Vincent was due to call that morning, but she had not bothered for his other many visits.

When she sat down to eat breakfast with her father and Nancy, she could not help but ask: "What about John? What's he doing today?"

"He's going out with Paul. They'll mend the fence, and then Paul's going to show him round, to help him get acquainted with the layout of the place. I don't expect them back until late this evening," Jim told her.

A sense of relief flooded through Stephanie. She would not have to go out of her way to avoid John! And yet a faint sense of disappointment tugged at her heart.

With a sigh, she said: "I'll stay near the house this morning, if you don't mind. Roger will be here soon."

...By the time Roger arrived, she had tended all her patients in the sick quarters and was waiting for him. She greeted him with more than usual enthusiasm. "Hello!" she beamed, and held out both her hands towards him.

As he took her hands in his, he kissed her briefly on the cheek. "My!" he observed. "You're in good spirits. How's my girl today?"

"She's much better," Stephanie answered, referring to the lioness in sick quarters. "She's not even limping now."

"I meant you," he smiled, gently patting her cheek.

"Oh, me...yes, I'm fine, too."

Together, they walked to the animal compounds. After observing the lioness for a moment, Roger nodded his head and pronounced: "You're quite right. She's ready to be released."

"I'll be sorry to see her go," Stephanie admitted.

Roger ruffled her hair. "That's your trouble.

You'd have every animal on the Reserve wrapped in cotton-wool, if you had half a chance. You shouldn't become so attached to them. You only get upset when they have to be set free."

She smiled faintly. "Yes...I worry about them. When they're here they become part of my family."

"Talking of families, Mother wants to know if you can come for the week-end?"

"I'd love to," she answered quickly. "Better check with Dad, though. We're going to be desperately short-handed. Four men are leaving on Friday."

"Four?"

Stephanie nodded sadly. "Yes. The bank's refused us further credit." She told him about the letter they'd received the previous day, and ended by making a casual reference to John. "He's going to give it a try...just for a month."

Roger's pale eyes searched her face with tenderness. "You know that my father would lend you money for the Reserve. As much as you needed."

"Yes. And he's very kind to make the offer. But you've already been so good to us that we couldn't possibly accept."

He slid an arm round her waist and pulled her close. "I'd do anything for you! I thought you knew that. And my parents think the world of you, too."

Stephanie pulled away. The subject was embarrassing; she was not the type of person who would take advantage of the situation, when all the time she knew she had no intention of marrying Roger.

To change the subject she said: "Dad's got two Wardens standing by to take the lioness back to her territory. We'd better not keep them hanging about too long. There's so much to do."

Roger soon had the animal sleeping like a

helpless baby. As Stephanie watched him, she was
aware of his great devotion to animals. It was so
tragic that she could not find one glimmer of love for
him. She and Roger would have made an admirable
couple. Their joint aim in life would be to conserve
and protect wild life. But there had to be more to a
marriage than that.

. . . Once the lioness was under sedation, the two
Wardens loaded the animal into the specially
constructed transporter, with Roger's help. Jim
came up, and Roger repeated his week-end invitation for Stephanie.

"Yes, you go, Steve. Do you good to have a
change. We can manage here," Jim said.

Stephanie nodded and smiled. "Lovely! My
thanks to your parents, Roger."

She climbed into the driving seat of the transporter.

The journey out to the river territory took about
half an hour. Stephanie drove quickly, so as to reach
her destination before the lioness recovered consciousness. She stopped where the grassland ended
and shrubby vegetation took its place. Various
palms and giant ferns flourished. Trees, mostly of
the eucalyptus family, towered up to forty feet amid
outcrops of red sandstone. The surrounding country
was greener and fresher, due to the presence of
running water, and animals collected in vast
numbers in this area for their daily bath.

It was an area that had always fascinated
Stephanie, and she longed for time to explore it. She
had a strange feeling that a part of Anthony Van
Dooran lingered unseen, for as a child he had played
here; it was his favourite spot. It was said that,
although he always had a guard with him, in case a

wild animal threatened him, Anthony had never shown any sign of fear. When he had stated that he would only come out to the Reserve if the river turned to a bed of roses, this was the river to which he had referred.

Stephanie indulged in day-dreaming while the two Wardens left the cab of the truck to lift the sleeping lioness out and lay her gently on the ground. Then one of them had to give the animal an injection, to speed up her recovery. After that, it was just a question of waiting until the lioness was on her feet again.

Stephanie stared out at the expanse of river...hoping, almost praying, that Anthony would turn up at the Reserve, whether the river turned to roses or not.

As soon as the lioness showed signs of recovery, the two Wardens climbed back into the cabin and waited until the animal was on her feet; then Stephanie started the engine and headed back to the house.

There was still plenty of work to be done, and for the rest of the day she hardly saw anyone except her father and Nancy. She did not mind the solitude; it gave her time for day-dreaming. But today her dreams kept being interrupted. John Kingsley persistently crashed into her thoughts.

Sleep did not come easily that night. She saw his face every time she closed her eyes. She tried and tried to drive him from her thoughts, but he always came back; and suddenly she felt choked with resentment that he should have arrived from nowhere and coloured her whole life...

It was pointless to lie tossing in bed, growing more restless every minute. She had to do something to take her mind off John Kingsley. She thought that if she took one of the jeeps out to the river area she could drive round for a while to see if the lioness had found her way back to her pride. If she had not, she would still be wandering about in a very sorry mood.

Unarmed and unafraid, the girl drove through the still night, occasionally catching a glimpse of an animal in her headlight beams before it scuttled away. When she arrived at the river area she drove slowly and carefully between the trees and shrubs, skirting clumps of acacias and aloes as she kept a constant watch for the young lioness. The vehicle bounced as she drove over rough ground strewn with red sandstone rocks, and frequently she had to slow right down as her headlights caught a pair of eyes and lit them up like stars amid the vegetation.

Stephanie covered the area where they had left the lioness, but there was no sign of the animal. She decided to end her search and head back home; but, as she swung the jeep round, a most unusual sight was illuminated by her headlights. It was another jeep, one belonging to the Reserve; but there was no sign of its driver. He must be hurt, Stephanie decided.

It took a lot of courage to climb from the safety of her vehicle. Not only was she putting herself at risk, where the wild animals were concerned, but she would also have to face her father, and he would be frantic with anger when he found out what she had done. She really should have gone back to the house for help, but it would have taken too much time. Moments counted if she were to help an injured Warden—and she dared not leave, in case he came to a very unpleasant end.

Standing close to her own vehicle and leaving the door wide open, in case she had to make a hasty retreat, she called out: "Hello! Who's there?"

Her only answer was a variety of animal protests.

"Who's there?" she shouted again. "If you can hear me, please answer."

There was still no human response.

Stephanie did not know what to do next. It was foolhardy to walk too far from the jeep, but if a man was lying hurt she ought to look for him. She did not have a torch and her vision was restricted to the two bright areas in the headlight beams.

She had only taken a few steps when she heard rustling in the undergrowth, then a dark shape appeared beyond the headlights. After an instant of panic she saw that it was human and, as she sighed with relief, she called: "What's going on out here? Are you all right?"

As the figure walked up to her and stood directly in the headlights, she saw that it was John. He glared down at her, maintaining an air of dignity, in spite of the faded and well worn lumber-jacket that he wore.

"Do you normally take midnight rides?" he asked crossly.

She looked up at him and answered in a sharp voice: "No . . . and no one with his head screwed on the right way would wander about out here without some form of protection."

"Why were you following me?" he demanded.

"I wasn't following you. I drove out here because I couldn't sleep. That's all. I thought I might as well check up on the young lioness that we released here this morning," she explained. Then it was her turn to ask questions and she inquired: "But what are you doing here? Does my father know?"

"No. Why should he? Do I have to get his permission every time I want a breath of fresh air?" His dark eyes had taken on a hard glitter and he was not in the best of humours. "If you must know, I was looking for poachers."

"Poachers?" she queried, knowing full well that there had been no evidence of such activity recently.

"That's right. Poachers! I spent the day with Paul, and when we'd done the fence he showed me round and explained that there could be a danger from poachers, once it became common knowledge that the Reserve was so short-staffed. It occurred to me that they might make their first bid from across the river. No one would expect them to come from that direction."

"No," Stephanie agreed, then added with a smile: "But I'm just wondering how they'd manage to swim back with an elephant tucked under each arm?"

He turned to face her, his eyes blazing with annoyance. He was a man who did not like a joke at his own expense and it showed in every line of his face as he clenched his jaw tightly. He leaned toward her and, through tight lips, asked: "Is making people feel foolish your sole ambition in life?"

"No, John, it isn't," she told him in a very forthright manner. "But I get the distinct impression that I'm the one who's being made a fool of. I don't seem to have had one single straight answer from you since the moment we met. And if you drove all the way out here at dead of night to stalk poachers, then I'm the Queen of Sheba!"

As she turned to get into her jeep, John lifted a

hand and gently touched her cheek. "What's made you so cynical?" he asked quietly.

Stephanie began to tremble slightly. She was not afraid of him, but she was resentful that he should touch her in that manner. He took his hand away, and yet she could still feel the warm imprint of his fingers.

Facing him, but lowering her gaze, she replied: "I'm cynical because you've told me such a load of absolute rot. I don't believe a word you've said since you arrived here. Your story's got more holes in it than a collander. I'm sorry if my attitude offends you, but you can hardly expect me to show you respect unless you offer some in return."

"You were following me?" he persisted, ignoring her reasoning.

"No, I certainly was not," she told him dogmatically. "And if you'll kindly get out of my way, I'll go home and leave you to get on with whatever you were doing. It's of no consequence to me! If you want to deliberately put your life at risk, that's your business."

She reached out to grab the side of the jeep, but John closed his hand over hers and stopped her.

"All right," he said in a more friendly manner. "I guess I have been flippant with you. Suppose we start again?"

"There's no point," she said sadly. "There are things that I'd like to know about you, but it would be impertinent of me to ask. You'd be quite within your right to refuse to answer me."

"You never know!" He smiled. "I might be persuaded to tell all!"

"Hm!" She laughed. "Yes, when the river turns to roses!"

His face straightened and he paused for a moment before asking: "What a strange expression! Wherever did you pick that up?"

Whenever Stephanie spoke of Anthony Van Dooran her face grew gentle, whilst her eyes had a dreamy look. " 'The wild one' used to use it. Or so I was told."

" 'The wild one'?" John queried.

"Henry Van Dooran's son."

"Oh, yes!" He grinned. "Your secret hero."

Stephanie felt herself blushing a little. "Yes..." she admitted coyly. "But it doesn't do any harm to dream. It doesn't hurt anyone."

"Is that why you've never become romantically involved with a real man?"

"That's not fair!"

"A man like me, for instance?" he persisted.

"I could never trust a man like you." It was said before she realised the sentence had been framed.

"But why?" he demanded.

"The story you told doesn't ring true," she brought out reluctantly.

"Oh? You'd better get down to details!" His voice was steely.

"Well," she began nervously, "you said that you'd flown to Johannesburg from the South of France...then you said that previously all your papers, including your passport, had been stolen in Marseilles." She bit her lips, then asked very quietly: "How did you get through Immigration?"

He forced a smile and told her casually: "A slip of the tongue. I should have said that my pockets were picked in Welkom. Did I really say Marseilles?"

"You know you did! I queried it at the time and you flew into a rage. Why didn't you explain then?"

"I was just being awkward. I didn't see why I should answer you. After all, it's your father who runs the place—not you."

"Oh..." Stephanie said, although she was far from satisfied. "Did you report the theft to the police?"

"No, I didn't get round to it. I was going to the police station when I met this chap in a bar and he told me about your Reserve here." He studied Stephanie's innocent face and asked: "Is that all you want to know?"

"No," she replied. "There's something else that puzzles me. You said you'd been in a chest hospital, yet you smoke the occasional cigarette. Don't you think it's rather foolish? Smoking's bad for health, anyway!"

He eyed her with a strange smile. "You're very astute!" he commented. "You're quite right. I ought not to smoke."

Stephanie smiled uncertainly. "You must admit," she reasoned, "it did seem unlikely that you'd come to work for us unless..." She hesitated, not knowing how to phrase her suspicions without causing offence.

"Yes?" he urged. "Unless what?"

"I wondered—" she lowered her gaze—"perhaps you're hiding from something?"

"Such as?" he taunted, as if daring her to put her uncharitable thoughts into words.

"I did wonder if perhaps you'd been wrongly accused of some crime? I thought you needed somewhere to hide out, because you'd become the innocent victim of—"

He was grinning and shaking his head. "No,

Steve! No! Nothing like that!" Then he threw back his head and laughed outright before remarking: "No wonder you've been suspicious of me!"

"And I've no cause to be?"

"No." He stopped laughing but went on, in a good humour: "I'm not 'wanted', I promise you. I've done nothing against the law. I've never even broken a traffic regulation."

She instinctively knew he was telling the truth. He had been so relaxed as he spoke. No one could utter untruths with such jocularity. She was also very relieved that he had taken her accusation so lightly, and she was oddly pleased that he had called her 'Steve'.

There was a brief pause as they looked at each other. Stephanie could not help but stare at the strong face that was but a hand's breadth away from her own. John was not simply gazing at her, but seemed to be looking right into her soul. A strange yearning, a tightening round her heart, started to develop and she wanted him to touch her face again. When he had touched her before, it felt as though he had infused her with the magic glow of warmth.

He finally lowered his eyes, turned his face away and said quietly: "Your intuition's not entirely wrong. I am running away. I did come out to your Reserve because it's so remote." He added with a touch of bitterness: "I'm hiding out. I'm also trying to recover from a soul-destroying experience. Do you need to know all the details before you'll leave me in peace?"

A moment earlier she had been so happy; she and John were communicating at last! Now her spirits plunged again and her anxiety rushed back, filling her with despair. "Not unless you want to tell me," she replied.

He sounded choked as he mumbled: "It's not my favourite subject."

"Then let's leave it," she suggested. "It's time we drove back now, before someone misses us and thinks there's something wrong. You'd better go back to your jeep—but make sure there aren't any animals about first. As for our conversation, I think we'd better forget what's been said. As long as your secret doesn't bring any unpleasantness to the Reserve, we'd best forget you ever mentioned it."

John could not help but notice the hurt in her voice, as if she had suddenly become totally indifferent.

"Listen," he said, turning back to her, "I'm simply here because I want to put as much distance as possible between myself and a certain woman. She won't look for me here, and if I can stay for a few months I might get over her."

She didn't believe him. It seemed such a poor excuse that she retorted: "If that's all it is, you should have gone to the big city and found someone else. That's usually what men do when they want to forget! They say anyone will do—for consolation!" Her scorn was withering.

He grabbed her arm tightly and said angrily: "Stop trying to make a fool of me, or you could end up by being very sorry!"

Although he was hurting her, she replied bravely: "If you want to keep your job, don't threaten me!"

"Do you know something?" he said, his voice and his eyes hard and cruel, "You and Pat have a lot in common. She wasn't the most charming person in the world, either. Perhaps I won't stay here, after all."

"That's your decision."

He gave a short, disgusted laugh and let go of her arm. "No . . . I'm not going to let you get the better of me. At least I've got one advantage here—I'm not married to you!"

"Married?" Stephanie gasped as she rubbed her arm where he had held it.

"That's right. I made the mistake of marrying Pat, so it doesn't matter where I go . . . I've got that hanging over me like a thundercloud."

Married! That was all Stephanie needed to know. From now on she would avoid him at all costs. She would neither comfort him nor argue with him. Her anxiety for his well-being would have to be overcome. Even though his marriage was unsatisfactory, Stephanie could not allow herself to become involved with him. She must go back to her illusion of love for 'the wild one' . . . at least it was safe to dream.

The week-end in Welkom was just what Stephanie needed to take her mind off John Kingsley. Roger's parents treated her as if she were their own daughter and were always overjoyed to have her pay them a visit. She spent Saturday afternoon shopping with the family. She liked Welkom. It was such a clean, open town. It was comparatively new and the shopping area had been built in the shape of a horseshoe, with a beautiful park in the centre. At times Stephanie could almost imagine that she was back in England, except for the perpetual hot sunshine.

In the evening, Roger took her to the cinema and

afterwards they had a superb supper before returning to his home. On Sunday she lazed in the garden, which was more like a park in itself than any back garden she had known in England. She and Roger splashed and swam in the pool. Iced drinks were always at hand, and Stephanie was given royal treatment.

Lunch was served on the shaded patio. Exotic food from the most expensive delicatessen almost made the wrought-iron table buckle under its weight. Stephanie knew that all this luxury was hers for the asking, for the rest of her life. Roger was an only child, and if Stephanie married him she would one day become mistress of the house, and everything in it.

At seven o'clock that evening, Roger said that it was time they were leaving, if he was to drive her home to the Reserve.

They were taking one last stroll round the magnificent garden, hand in hand like two children and just as full of happy innocence, when he said: "I hope you've enjoyed yourself? We don't seem to do very much when you come for the week-end."

"I've had a glorious time!" Stephanie told him. "I always do. Your mother spoils me so much that it's almost embarrassing."

"Yes, well, she thinks of you as the daughter she never had. I know she fusses too much, but she means well."

Roger put his arms round her and pulled her close. He kissed her on the lips, then said with a disappointed sigh: "I don't see you often enough. Will you come again next week-end? Please?" He kissed her again.

Stephanie shook her head. "I can't leave Dad to

cope on his own too often. Next week we'll only have three men working for us, and one of those isn't really trained for the job yet. So I honestly don't think I could spare the time. I'd love to, but—"

They searched each other's faces for some time, then Roger pulled her close again and said passionately: "Marry me, Steve. Marry me!"

He kissed her lingeringly, caressing her hair and gripping her slender shoulders. But Stephanie could not return his passion or enthusiasm. He was an ideal companion, but there it ended.

"I'm tempted to marry you," she answered evasively, "but I would like a few more months to decide." She smiled innocently. "You're ten years older than I am. You've had time to set the course for your life. I'm still not sure what's lined up for me."

She looked up at him with tenderness, but there was no adoration in her eyes.

"Is there something wrong between us?" Roger asked.

"No, of course not. You're sweet and kind and wonderful, but—" She could not tell him that there was no love in her heart and that love could not be forced.

"You could have anything you wanted," he pointed out.

"I know," she answered humbly. "In fact, there are times when I think you offer me too much. I become almost frightened by the idea that there would be nothing left to wish for and hope for."

She eased herself from his arms and began to walk through the wooded part of the garden. The week-end had been pleasant; she wanted nothing to spoil it at the last moment. She had relaxed with the Vincents but was ready, now, to go back to work again. The pale green dress which she wore made her feel very feminine, but she longed to get back to the comfort of a pair of jeans. The novelty of trying to be glamorous soon wore off. There were so many things that were more important to her than luxuries and high living, and although an occasional taste of them was good for her morale, she did not think she could endure such a way of life for any length of time. Even if she did decide to marry Roger, her work on the Reserve would have to go on. She could not give it all up just to be a 'lady of leisure'.

Roger caught up with her and walked by her side, but did not speak for a while. But as they turned to make their way back to the house, he hesitated and then held her arm to halt her progress.

"Steve, I don't really know why, but this weekend I feel that something's come between us. I can't explain it, it's too elusive, but you've been so strange and distant. At times I've felt that you were miles away. Is there something on your mind?"

"I'm worried about the Reserve," she replied. "I try to put it out of my mind, but it's there all the time...like toothache. I'm sorry if I haven't been good company."

"I'm not complaining," Roger said with a smile. "You've been wonderful company—you always are. It was just that, a couple of times, your thoughts seemed to wander." He paused, then became more serious. "As far as the Reserve's concerned, Dad would lend you the money, as I've told you. I've discussed it with him and he's quite prepared to lend your father as much as he needs for an indefinite period."

"No," Stephanie refused politely. "It's overwhelmingly kind of you and your father, but we couldn't. I know Dad wouldn't even think of it."

"He borrowed from the bank?"

"A bank's different. Money is their business. My father says the surest way to end a good friendship is to lend or borrow money. He thinks far too highly of your father—and of you—to risk that." She looked up at him earnestly. "Dad and I have discussed it. Believe me, we couldn't impose. We're already in debt to you for your veterinary services for which you won't submit a bill, and that doesn't rest too easily on our consciences."

Roger shrugged his shoulders and his pale eyes darkened with a shadow of disappointment. "Well," he sighed, "the offer's always there!"

...Stephanie arrived back at the Reserve too late to see anyone except her father. The Wardens had retired to their quarters and Nancy had gone to bed. Roger said a brief 'Hello' to Jim, but did not stay as he had to drive the fifty miles home.

Stephanie leaned back in one of the tatty armchairs and felt good to be home. Roger's home had everything, but it was too palatial to be cosy.

"Had a good time?" Jim asked, drawing on his pipe.

"Yes, thanks," Stephanie answered with a grin. "Roger's parents send their regards. They want to know when you can spare the time to go and stay for a week-end?"

Jim gave a short laugh. "I wish I could!"

"How did you cope this week-end, without proper staff?"

Jim took his pipe from his mouth and held it by the bowl. "It wasn't too bad. I was surprised at John Kingsley. He did the job as if he'd been trained for it. No problems there."

Stephanie wished he had not mentioned John's

name. That uneasy yearning was stirring again in the region of her heart.

She took a deep breath and changed the subject, asking abruptly: "What do you want me to do tomorrow?"

"Whatever you usually do on a Monday," Jim told her, noticing her sudden tenseness.

"I usually drive out to the river area. The elephants are playing havoc with some of the vegetation there. I've been keeping an eye on it and it's worse every week. I think we're getting over-stocked with elephants, and they and the other animals are going to suffer. I'd better take a quick survey, to see if we ought to get some of the young cows transferred to another Reserve...a bigger one."

"That won't be easy," Jim observed. "We haven't got a big enough transporter."

"We'll have to hope the other Reserve will help over that."

"We can try." Jim nodded, knowing that his daughter was anything but faint-hearted when it came to asking for help with the animals. "You're quite right about the elephants. We do seem to have a lot."

Stephanie got up from her chair. "Well," she said, walking towards her father, "if you haven't anything else lined up for me, I'll drive out there as soon as I've had breakfast."

She leaned over and kissed his bronzed forehead before turning to walk to the door.

"Did Roger ask you to marry him again?" Jim called after her.

"Yes," she replied.

"And?"

Stephanie shrugged her shoulders. "I said 'no' again."

"You could do a lot worse!"

She nodded and smiled. "There's already one man in my life, and in regard to him I couldn't do better."

Jim looked surprised and demanded: "And who's he?"

"You!" She grinned and, screwing up her innocent face, blew him a kiss.

It was hot and airless as Stephanie drove out to the river area the following morning. She had risen at six o'clock, tended the animals in the sick quarters, eaten a light breakfast and rushed off to her favourite part of the Reserve. Once again, she had taken more care over her appearance, enhancing her lips with a touch of lipstick and brushing her long, fair hair until it shimmered like wild silk. This time she did not tie it back, but let it flow round her shoulders. Her father had smiled with delight as the young lady who was emerging from the high-spirited tomboy, but he had not commented, in case she took offence and reverted to her old self.

The river was dark blue under a bright sky, and it ran swiftly and silently between dense green banks. Stephanie took the jeep as close to the river as the vegetation and sandstone rocks would permit, before leaving it to make the rest of the journey on foot. At the insistence of her father, but very much against her will, she had armed herself with a rifle, which was slung round her slender shoulders. She knew that she would not need it. She had a rare understanding of animals. However, as she had to spend most of the day in the open, and the river area attracted more animals than the rest of the Reserve, she had armed herself—but only to humour her father.

She needed a good vantage point so that she could observe the elephants and begin her survey. About a hundred yards down-river was a high outcrop of rock which would serve this purpose ideally.

With binoculars slung round her neck and a pad and pencil sticking out of the pocket of her jeans, Stephanie began her climb. Brilliantly coloured birds flew into the air as she disturbed them, looking like pieces of coloured tissue paper caught by a breeze. An occasional small lizard moved jerkily away from her path.

She knew that about half-way up there was a natural platform where she would be partially shaded from the relentless sun yet would have a clear view of a good stretch of the river. She had only about ten feet to go when she heard a loud roar. There was a lion near by! Was he sunbathing on her special platform?

Slowly and carefully she pulled herself up the next two slab-sided rocks, which took her to a narrow ledge. So far, there was no sign of a lion. She sidled carefully along the ledge, which broadened and led to the platform. As she turned the last corner, the sight which met her eyes made her head spin with panic for a moment.

At the far corner of the platform, his back pressed hard against the sheer rock behind him, John Kingsley stood, white and trembling, his eyes fixed in a glassy stare on a huge lion which had him well and truly cornered.

Stephanie froze. Even at that distance she could see tiny beads of perspiration shining on John's forehead, and a vein in his neck stood out, throbbing violently.

The lion was quite the largest on the whole Reserve—a magnificent beast with a huge ginger mane which he wore like a cape round his solid shoulders. He snarled at John again and displayed large teeth which glinted like ivory daggers. His tongue was pink and moist. John, unarmed and quite defenceless, just stared as if transfixed.

Stephanie had to think quickly. She deplored the idea of shooting the lion, but it was his life against John's. She edged a little closer and pulled the rifle from her shoulder. The lion sensed her presence, turned briefly to view the new intruder—then, with another long snarl, turned his attention back to John.

John could not have been more helpless if he had been caught in a snare. There was no way of escape. When he saw Stephanie, his lips moved, but no sound came from them.

Bringing the rifle round in front of her, she slid the safety catch off, raised it and, with the butt hard against her shoulder, took careful aim. It would be a difficult shot, for if she missed the lion or he suddenly moved as she fired, the bullet would probably hit John. There was only one chance.

John, still frozen with fear, watched Stephanie as she closed in behind the lion. He could not understand why she had not already used the gun. Every second counted, yet she seemed to be more concerned with examining the animal than shooting it.

Then the massive beast lifted his arrogant head and slowly turned to face Stephanie. As the seconds passed, John thought Stephanie was never going to pull the trigger. Or had she lost her nerve?

CHAPTER FOUR

To John's amazement, Stephanie lowered the rifle, slipped the safety catch on again, and slung it back over her shoulder. Then she sighed, shook her head and said calmly: "Don't be so unsociable, Murphy. That's no way to behave!"

As she walked towards the lion with one hand extended, she called to John: "Don't move and don't speak. I'll handle this."

The lion began to saunter towards Stephanie with a gleam of recognition in his eyes. When he finally reached her, he lowered his head and brushed it hard against her, just like an overgrown tabby cat greeting his owner.

65

Stephanie touched his mane and said gently: "There, there! How's my baby, then?"

The lion continued to rub against her with the gentle affection of a domestic cat. Stephanie looked down at his massive paws, then asked: "How's your foot now? Better?"

The lion was all but purring. He almost knocked her over with his display of affection.

"Steve—" John said nervously.

"It's all right," she called. "Just stay where you are and don't move. He's got more cause to go for you now than before—he might decide that I need to be defended."

She leaned down and kissed the soft velvet fur on the lion's nose. "Where've you been?" she cooed. "I haven't seen you for days. Looking for a wife, are you?"

John's fear had quickly turned to anger. "I gather you know this creature?" he called resentfully.

"He isn't a creature," Stephanie corrected. "This is my friend, Murphy. We got to know each other a few weeks ago. But please don't move until he's gone."

"I thought he was a wild lion," John said with a great sigh.

"He is a wild lion," she explained, carressing the animal's mane. "Earlier this year I found him with a badly torn claw. He could hardly walk, so we took him home and Roger operated. Roger had to remove the claw. That's why I recognised him. He's one toe short. We became friends while I was nursing him. He was with us for over a month." She gave John a gentle smile. "I'm very proud to have such a magnificent friend."

"Do you make friends with all your patients?"

"No, Murphy was an exception. I didn't realise he was so fond of me until we came to release him. When we opened the transporter, he'd already recovered from the drug Roger gave him and he jumped out at me. There was a terrible panic and I nearly died of fright, but Murphy only wanted to be with me. He chased the two Wardens back into the cab. I was very flattered."

"I thought he was going to kill me," John said.

"Yes—" Stephanie replied awkwardly. "You are a stranger to him, and you're on his territory. I couldn't guarantee that he wouldn't harm you. I really think you should avoid this stretch of the river in future."

Murphy stopped fussing round Stephanie. He gazed up at her with a positive grin on his regal face, then sauntered off.

As soon as the lion had climbed down from the platform, John strode towards Stephanie. "Thank goodness you came!" he said. He took a handkerchief from the pocket of his jeans and wiped the perspiration from his forehead. "Phew!" he added. "I thought I'd had my lot. I'll never come out unarmed again."

Stephanie looked up into his face as he towered over her. "If you do as you're asked in future," she pointed out, "there'll be no need for you to be armed. We don't hand out guns just for the fun of it. In fact, this is the only weapon we possess . . . and it's only been fired in practice."

Resentment showed in his face. He did not like the reprimand, but he took it, for he knew only too well that he had been in the wrong and she had saved his life.

Stephanie sat down with her back against the

rock. John hesitated, then sat down beside her.

Looking out over the river, she asked: "Just as a matter of interest, what are you doing here? Dad asked you to take over the maintenance of the boundary fences, and this is the one place where you won't find any!"

As he turned to face her, she was suddenly self-conscious. She could feel her soft hair about her shoulders and she knew that her face was glowing with a strange warmth. She wanted John to look at her and find pleasure in what he saw...and it was wrong!

John's dark eyes avoided her and there was a suggestion of embarrassment in his manner as he explained: "I suppose I was a bit off course. I did set off for the west boundary, but I'd only driven a couple of miles when I saw what I thought was a white rhino—"

"A what?" Stephanie interrupted in a startled tone.

"A white rhino! I know you're particularly interested in them. Your father said they're almost extinct."

"That's quite true. They're very rare now. But what made you think it was a white rhino?"

John was staring out across the tangle of trees and undergrowth which lined the river bank. His voice was curiously hollow as he answered: "It was a much paler colour than the common rhino, so I followed it until it disappeared into the jungle...down there." He pointed to the dense greenery beneath them, then continued: "Having gone so far out of my way already, I didn't see that spending another half an hour out here would do any harm, so I climbed up these rocks to get a better view. I was hoping to see it again and find out if it had a mate."

Stephanie knew that what he had told her was a pack of lies, but she chose to humour him. "It's very commendable that you're so conscientious. I'm sure Dad will be delighted to hear you've sighted a white rhino. I wonder how he got into the Reserve?" She had only said this in order to find out just how far John would go with his fictitious reason for being by the river.

He turned to her, smiling as he said: "I expect he got through a break in the fence somewhere. From what your father told me, animals are constantly damaging it."

"The elephants do, but then nothing will stop them."

She stared into his dark eyes, wondering what could be his real motive for being near the river again.

"Thank you for saving me from Murphy," he said in a quiet and very sincere voice.

"It was sheer good luck. But until you know more about the Reserve and the animals here, you really mustn't take chances."

Whether it was something in her eyes as she gazed up at him, or a hint of deeper feelings in her voice, she suddenly knew that she had unconsciously laid her soul bare for an instant, for he put his arm round her and kissed her.

She fought, pushing against his shoulders.

It had never been like this when Roger kissed her. It was then that she realised that it was not John she was fighting but her own secret desire for him to go on kissing her.

She pushed back her hair and stood up. "You

aren't free, so please never do that again!"

"I don't know why you bothered to save me from your friend Murphy," he said bitterly.

"Neither do I!" she flared.

John got to his feet and walked to the ledge which led from the rocky platform. "I'll get back to my fences," he told her. "It seems to me that all you women are best left alone."

...Stephanie tried to drive John from her thoughts as she sat high on the outcrop of rocks and made notes about the elephants. She had a packed lunch of sandwiches, fruit and a flask of tea in the jeep, but when the time came to eat, she had no appetite.

It was only with great difficulty that she managed to record the number of herds, the number of elephants in each herd, and finally assess the number of baby elephants and expectant mother elephants. When she eventually decided that there were too many for the Reserve, she was glad to get back to her jeep and drive home.

During the evening she was so restless that her father could not help but notice. "Whatever's the matter with you?" he asked, putting his pipe in the ashtray and staring at his daughter. "Can't you sit still for two minutes? I'm trying to concentrate on this lot." He flicked through a wad of bills on his desk.

Stephanie sighed and put down the novel she had been trying to read. "I'm sorry, Dad. I didn't realise I was disturbing you."

"Well, you are, and it's not like you. You're supposed to be reading, yet I haven't seen you turn over one single page in the past half hour."

Jim stood up and went to sit opposite her, leaving

the clutter of papers on his desk. "Come on," he urged, "What's unsettled you?"

She could hide nothing from her father—not that she had any desire to—so she admitted quietly: "It's John. The more I know about him, the more concerned I am."

"What's happened this time?"

"I don't like to be a tell-tale—" she stared at the floor—"but..." She looked up at her father with eyes that were begging for reassurance.

"Come on," he said. "Get it off your mind!"

"John's reason for being near the river the first time was a load of rubbish. Then this morning I found him there again, and he told another whopping fib."

Jim showed more interest. He said: "Go on—tell me the rest."

"He claimed that he'd seen a white rhino and followed it to the river bank. When I asked him to describe it, he said it was a much paler colour than the common rhino."

"Did he, indeed? I gather you didn't enlighten him?"

Stephanie shook her head. "No. I didn't want to make him appear foolish. He obviously doesn't know that the word 'white' has nothing to do with colour. I didn't tell him that it's thought to come from the Afrikaans word for 'wide', because the species has a much wider jaw. Nor did I tell him there aren't any white rhinos in this area."

Jim scowled. "You were right to tell me, but I shan't confront John."

"I don't want to make trouble for him," Stephanie said with deep concern. "I think he's a very lonely and unhappy man, but twice I've found him by the river and both times he's made up foolish excuses for being there."

Jim leaned back in the worn arm-chair. "It certainly is a mystery!" He sighed. "But I'm quite certain there's no harm in the man. He's most eager to please and I haven't got a good reason to sack him."

"That's the last thing I'd want," she said.

She did not tell her father that John had kissed her. She would not allow it to happen again or show John the faintest sign that she was attracted to him.

"Don't send him away," she said, trying to sound casual. "If he stays, we might find out what he's up to."

"Yes," Jim agreed. "I'm sure there's a good reason for his strange behaviour."

"Have you any special jobs for me tomorrow?"

"Nothing out of the ordinary. Why?"

"I'll go round the salt-licks," she said with an odd gleam in her eyes, "and take John with me. He ought to know something about animal behaviour before he lands himself in real trouble. Lions and elephants might not be as understanding towards him as you and I!"

Before Stephanie and John began their tour of the salt-licks next morning, she had made up her mind not to ask him any personal questions.

John was reasonably sociable and said a pleasant 'Good morning', but once they were seated in the jeep and were driving across the veld, he asked: "Have you decided that I'm not to be trusted to work without supervision?"

Stephanie had gone back to her old image; with her hair tied back and no trace of make-up, she felt

less likely to attract attention. A strange fight was
going on inside her, one part of her keeping him at
arm's length, the other yearning for just one kind
glance from him.

She tried to sound as pleasant as possible as she
told him: "No. Dad and I just thought you needed a
few lessons on behaviour."

"And what's wrong with my behaviour?"

"Not your behaviour!" She smiled. "Animal
behaviour."

She was becoming agitated by the nearness of
him. Perhaps it had not been such a good idea, after
all, to go out alone with him.

"You mean like meeting your friend Murphy?" he
asked with an answering smile.

"Yes. We don't notice it ourselves, but we humans
have our own distinctive scent, just as animals have
theirs. There is a theory that the human scent is
quite unpleasant to animals and their natural
reaction is to turn away and avoid us. Both Dad and
I have been in situations where we've found
ourselves too close for comfort to various animals
and each time the animal has been curious, but after
taking a good sniff has gone away."

"So what went wrong when your friend Murphy
cornered me?"

Stephanie glanced at him and smiled. "You were
frightened, to put it bluntly. Fear changes one's
scent, and when Murphy realised that you were
afraid, he was ready to defend himself. You see, fear
does strange things to people. It can turn a normally
docile person into a hostile enemy. When you
became terrified of Murphy, you transmitted it in
your scent, but he didn't know why you were afraid
and he interpreted it as aggression so he was ready

to do battle with you. That was all. I'm certain he wouldn't have attacked you without real provocation. He wasn't angry."

"Wasn't angry!" John repeated with amusement. "And how would you know that?"

"When a lion's cross he flattens his ears and wags the tip of his tail very briskly. That's when you know you're in real trouble. You can ignore his growling. That doesn't mean a thing. Just look at his ears and the tip of his tail."

John gave a quick, caustic laugh. "I'll remember that, the next time I come face to face with a lion. If I have time!"

"The idea is to avoid the animals, if possible, not go out looking for trouble."

"So what about the other animals? Is it ears and tails with all of them?"

Stephanie was approaching the first salt-lick, but seeing that the blocks of salt were only half-used she decided to drive on to the next one.

"Ears play a large part in the warning system, but there are other factors. For instance, an elephant will hold its ears out at right-angles to its head to make itself appear even larger and more ferocious than it is. But with a bull elephant it's mainly bluff. Cow elephants are a very different matter. They really mean business when they're angry. And don't be misled into thinking they're slow creatures. Keep away from elephants, especially if they have their young with them. All right?"

John was still watching her, studying every move as she drove to the next salt-lick. She was aware of his dark eyes examining her and, although he did not attempt to touch her or speak out of turn, there was a strange, silent communication between them.

"I don't intend to get in their way," he said. "I'm not looking for adventure."

"That's just as well. There's precious little adventure here. Only lots of hard work, and sometimes it can be monotonous."

"Tell me," he said thoughtfully, "what you see in it, to get so involved."

Stephanie shrugged. "It's difficult to explain. I enjoy animals because I get pleasure out of watching them. I feel our society could learn a lot from animals, if we hadn't become so civilised."

John gave a scornful laugh. "Are you trying to tell me that the world would be a better place to live in if we all behaved like animals?"

"I hate that expression!" she flared. "Lots of people use it, and they mean it in a derogatory sense. If you study animal behaviour you'll find that they don't fight needlessly. There are precious few who kill indiscriminately. They are very devoted parents, they don't over-eat, and they're seldom ill. They are also very loyal to their own group and, once they've established their own small territory, they don't go around trying to take others. You can't say that about mankind!"

She turned to glare at him and found him smiling at her with a contemptuous expression on his face. He looked downright superior! It was as much a part of him as his bristly crew-cut.

"Human beings are more highly developed than animals, thank goodness," he said. "As we increase in numbers, we naturally need more land. Isn't it logical that we should better ourselves as we progress? The ambition to own more land than the next man isn't a crime."

"Perhaps not," she agreed, glancing at him occasionally instead of watching the grassland ahead of her, "but I don't call it ambition; I call it greed. I've never met a greedy man who was happy. Have you?"

"That depends on what you mean by happy!"

"You know full well what I mean! To be contented with life, able to get up every morning with a carefree heart and go to bed each night without a guilty conscience to keep you awake."

His face darkened, and he leaned towards her. As he spoke, she felt his warm breath on her cheek.

"You know your trouble?" he said venomously. "You live in a dream world! To you, everything is sweetness and light. You've been so coddled by your father and kept apart from everyday life by living out here that you don't really know what life is all about."

"I know enough," she said quietly. "I did live in England until I was sixteen. I did meet people."

"But obviously not the right kind!" He smiled enigmatically. "I think it's time you learned a few plain truths. Someone should teach you about the human race—and it rather looks as though that teacher is going to be me."

Stephanie looked at him. His face was as hard as a rock and his dark eyes unyielding. What a mistake she had made in bringing him out here, where they were alone! Under the circumstances, how unscrupulous would he be with her?

"You're the one who's the pupil!" she reminded him sharply.

For answer, he put his arm round her shoulders.
"And kindly take your arm away!" she added.

John behaved as though he had not heard her.
Instead, he tightened his grip.

"This is foolish and dangerous when I'm driving," she complained. "Take your arm away, or I'll be forced to stop the jeep."

"Then do just that!" he said with a laugh.

She had no other choice. He was gripping her so tightly that she could not steer the vehicle properly. As she braked hard, they both lurched forward and John was obliged to take his arm from her shoulders.

Stephanie had had enough. Her nerve gave way and she leaned towards the steering-wheel and curled her arms round it as she said with a sob: "Please—please stop this! I don't know what sort of a girl you think I am, but your attentions are neither wanted nor appreciated." There was no way out of the situation and she gave way to more tears as she went on: "We're miles from anywhere and it isn't at all safe to get out and walk back, so please—please leave me alone!"

John did not move, did not utter a single word. Stephanie raised her tear-stained face from the steering-wheel and looked at him. He was sitting facing her, with his back pressed against the passenger door. He could not have pushed himself farther away.

"What do you want with me?" she asked tearfully.

A second before, John's face had been as hard as rock, and with his severe hair-cut he had looked very menacing. But the trace of a smile softened his expression and his eyes were kinder as he said: "I'm sorry. I didn't mean to upset you. I've been used to girls who weren't so sensitive."

"Girls? I thought it was your wife who'd been the faithless one?"

"She was. But since I left her there've been a couple of girl-friends." He looked sheepish, lowering his gaze as he added: "I'm only human!"

"Perhaps you are, although there are times when I doubt it. But as for girl-friends," she went on in a stronger voice, "I have no wish to become one of their number. If you think I'm after a whirlwind romance you couldn't be more wrong."

John nodded. "Okay. You've convinced me. I won't harass you again. I thought you'd be only too eager to receive a little attention. You lead such a solitary life here. It seems I was mistaken."

Stephanie had stopped crying and she now felt a surge of relief. John was being sincere. She had no further need for anxiety. She raised her eyes to his and there was a flicker of gratitude in them. John acknowledged it with a brief smile. "Friends again?"

She nodded.

"Sorry I'm not to your taste!" He took a deep breath and asked: "What would you do if the missing heir to the Van Dooran millions turned up? Would you fall at his feet... or throw yourself into his arms?"

Colour rushed to Stephanie's cheeks at the mere thought of 'the wild one'.

"I don't know," she admitted shyly. "I've never given it any serious thought. But I'm not the sort of girl who would throw herself indiscriminately at any man's feet, even the elusive Anthony Van Dooran's."

John laughed. "You're lucky! You're in love with a dream, and you can make it end however you choose."

"I'm not in love with him. I'm just intrigued."

"If he turned up here, it would make him eligible for his inheritance. Doesn't the idea of his potential wealth appeal to you?"

Stephanie turned her face up to his and, with honesty radiating from her eyes, said: "No, John. Money would be the last thing I'd want. In fact, it would work the other way with me. I'd be put off by the idea of wealth."

"You really are a dreamer," John said with a curious smile. "I suppose it's quite harmless unless..." He paused, began to frown, and then turned quickly away and stared into space.

"Unless what?" she inquired, wondering why his good humour had suddenly deserted him.

"Dreaming is harmless, unless someone wakes you up." He swung round to face the windscreen and gazed out at the vast expanse of rippling grass. "Life can be very cruel, Steve. And if something cruel happens, no amount of dreaming can help."

Without thinking, she put her hand on his arm and said: "I wish I could help you."

He gave a brief smile and told her throatily: "I believe you do." He took her hand, lifted it to his lips and kissed it. Then he placed it gently back on the steering-wheel.

Stephanie dared not pursue the subject. She started the jeep again and said: "I suppose we ought to get on with our work. We're almost at the next salt-lick."

"You do everything you can for the animals here, don't you?" he observed with sincerity.

"Yes. I'd be quite content to spend the rest of my

life looking after them."

"Does that mean you've no wish to get married? Wouldn't you like a husband and a couple of children?"

Although he was being too personal for Stephanie's liking, he was in such a congenial mood that she was loath to spoil it.

"I've considered marriage," she replied. "In fact, I received a proposal of marriage only last weekend." She thought that if she gave him the impression that she was seriously considering marriage, he might be less ardent in future.

"Was that while you were staying with the Vincents?" he inquired.

"Yes!" she exclaimed. "But how did you know I was there?"

"I asked where you'd gone to, and Paul told me. He said he thought you and Roger might get married eventually."

"That's very possible," she confirmed, without showing the indignation he had sparked off by openly admitting that he discussed her with other Wardens. "Now—shall we get back to animal behaviour? Did you know, for instance, that rhinos are terrified of birds? One dove fluttering its wings above a rhino can send it into a state of frenzy!"

"How very interesting!" John said, with a note of boredom.

Stephanie went on with the lesson. It was much safer than discussing either his private life or her own.

. . . For the rest of that week, whenever Stephanie saw John, their conversation and manner towards each other were very formal. It was hard work on the Reserve without a full complement of staff, so there was no chance of Stephanie going to Welkom again at the week-end. Roger visited the Reserve twice during the week for the release of two more animals, but that was all Stephanie saw of him.

CHAPTER FIVE

It was during the third week of John Kingsley's employment that Jim Loman said to his daughter: "I've found out something rather alarming about John. I've asked him to come over after dinner to discuss it, and if he doesn't mind your sitting in on our conversation, I'd like you to stay—since it was something you said which put me on to it. But I won't say any more now."

"All right, Dad."

Stephanie's eyes had grown wide with speculation, but she knew it was pointless to press for details. Her father could be just as stubborn as she was herself. She would have to wait.

Nancy came in just then, to serve the evening meal. Stephanie was abstracted as she ate, thinking over what her father had said and wondering what he would have to say to John.

When the meal was finished, she and her father went into the living-room and Jim told Nancy that he would be having a private conversation with one of the Wardens very shortly and did not wish to be disturbed.

Stephanie watched from the window and presently saw John strolling towards the house. He was self-assured and held his head high with pride. The fear and distrust that she had occasionally seen in his face were not evident. He was as arrogant as an uncrowned king.

He came up the veranda steps, and Jim called: "Come in, John. Sit down, please!" he added, as the younger man regarded him quizzically.

Stephanie walked from the window and stood between the two men. "If you'll excuse me," she said, "I think I'll leave you to talk in private."

John looked bewildered. "I don't know what this is about, but you are welcome to stay, as far as I'm concerned." He sat in an arm-chair next to Jim.

"This is a very personal matter," Jim said.

"I don't know what's wrong, but Steve is bound to find out sooner or later, so she might as well stay."

"Very well," Jim agreed, and waited for his daughter to sit down.

"So?" John inquired. "What have I done?"

Jim was embarrassed and obviously loath to broach the subject, but he faced John and began: "You've been with us for almost three weeks and I've never known a man to work such long hours and so uncomplainingly. As far as your work here is concerned, we're permanently indebted to you."

"If it's not my work that's at fault—" John glanced suspiciously at Stephanie for an instant, wondering if she had complained about his behaviour toward her.

Jim took out his pipe and filled it with tobacco as he continued uncomfortably: "Ever since you showed up here, there's been an air of mystery about you. I've tried to ignore it because you're such a good worker, but a couple of things have played on my mind and I would be grateful if you'd offer a more detailed explanation."

John's fair skin began to colour slightly and his mouth tightened, but he remained silent.

"Firstly," Jim went on, between attempts to light his pipe, "you're a very clever young man. You could find a far more worthwhile job with a very high salary, yet you choose to work for me without any certainty of remuneration. Steve told me about your wife and how you came out here to forget this soured marriage, but it strikes me that you could have gone anywhere in the world to start your new life, and I feel it difficult to believe that you found us by chance."

John remained silent, but his face was growing harder every minute.

"The other point I have to raise with you," Jim continued, "is far more serious." He paused. He was not enjoying this confrontation any more than John. "Steve told me that you'd had your wallet and papers stolen in Welkom; so a few days ago when I went into Welkom to try and persuade the bank to lend me more money—which was a waste of time, incidentally—I took the liberty of calling on a good friend who's in the police. I asked him if he would look into the theft."

Alarm showed in John's eyes, and Stephanie tensed.

"It's all right," Jim assured them. "No cause for alarm. There's nothing official about this. But I do feel that I have a right to know how you got into South Africa, because you haven't got a passport. My friend checked with Immigration in Johannesburg, and no one by the name of John Kingsley has passed through—at least, not recently. I was suspicious from the very beginning about your story of having flown here from Marseilles. You told me you were recovering from TB. What you obviously don't know is that it's very difficult for anyone who's recently suffered a serious illness like that to get into the country."

John was staring at the coloured mat under his feet. He took a deep breath, shrugged his shoulders and sighed. "I knew this would happen eventually. Can't say that I really blame you for checking up. You've been very kind and patient so far."

"We're not exactly condemning you now," Jim interrupted, and added with deep concern: "If you're in some sort of trouble, we'd try to help you."

John looked up at Jim and smiled with surprise. "Yes, I'm sure you would. I've been very foolish in trying to deceive you. I'm sorry, genuinely sorry." He sat back in the chair and looked straight ahead, his gaze distant as he explained: "I didn't arrive by plane. Please don't ask me how I got here. I can't explain that just now. I hoped to come into this country and leave without anyone noticing. And as for the Reserve, I did know about it. My coming here wasn't pure chance. When my marriage turned sour, I blamed it on not having enough money. Pat would've been quite happy if I'd been able to keep up with her extravagant habits. She craved for things I could never hope to buy, however much I earned by sheer hard work. So, when I left her, I came here deliberately, in the hope that I might find gold. That's why I've been searching the river area. I've been looking for traces of gold. So far, it's been a waste of time but I've good reason to believe that there is still gold here."

Jim's face was a picture of incredulity. "Gold! You've been looking for gold! But, John, if you'd found any," he reasoned, "you would have had no right to it. It would have belonged to the Van Dooran estate." He shook his head and added: "Anyway, the gold that was mined here was six thousand feet underground and all the mine shafts were blown up, filled in and levelled off—years ago."

"I didn't want much." John smiled vaguely. "A few thousand pounds' worth would have been enough. I thought there might be some in the river bed. This was once a very rich gold area."

"If you'd found any," Jim asked, "how would you have got it out of South Africa?"

John gave a short laugh. "I came here without anyone noticing me, no doubt I could have got back to England with my gold dust by the same route."

"I don't like the sound of that," Jim said, straight-faced. "So far, I've gone along with you and I've even said I'd help you; and if you're involved in anything illegal, the sooner you leave here the better."

He looked at John and sighed. "I don't know what to do about you. My instincts told me you were honest and dependable. I didn't really go for your story about running away from your wife. You seem too much of a man for that. But if you came here to steal gold so that you could keep up with your wife's demands, then I've no alternative but to ask you to leave immediately. No doubt you'll find employment elsewhere...providing your new employer doesn't ask for references."

John was clenching his jaw, more in desperation than anger. He said quietly: "I've been very happy here, away from pressures and responsibilities, and you've been kind and patient with me. If I gave you my word that I wouldn't attempt to look for gold again, would you give me another chance? I've no idea what would happen to me if you turned me out."

"Let him stay, Dad. Please!" Stephanie begged.

"Only if he'll tell me how he got into South Africa!" Jim decreed.

"I can't do that," John replied, shaking his head. "I can only give you my word that there'll be no come-back on you as a result of it. Whatever you may think, you're not harbouring a criminal. If that's your main worry, I assure you that you can forget it."

Jim was anything but convinced. His naturally good-humoured face was uncertain. "I don't like being a party to this," he complained. "Not one bit, I've already got enough on my plate."

Stephanie had other things on her mind. With a strange look she asked: "John—you admit you came here to find gold, and you knew all about us. Would you mind telling me where you acquired all this knowledge? We're not a big Reserve, we don't encourage the public to visit us, and we don't get any publicity. We're not even listed in holiday guides."

John smiled directly at Stephanie and replied: "I don't mind telling you. I've nothing to lose by it. I

heard all about the Van Dooran Reserve when I was
still at school. My room-mate told me. He and I were
the best of friends. In fact, we went right through
school together until we were eighteen; then he went
his way and I went mine. But I remembered all that
he'd told me, especially about the gold. He claimed
that if you stood on the rocks above the river,
sometimes you could see it shining up through the
water."

"What was your school-friend's name?" Stephanie asked in a daze, already suspecting the answer.

John looked at her with steady eyes and smiled as
he told her: "Yes, I've got to admit it. He was
Anthony Van Dooran!"

Stephanie's eyes grew wide with excitement.
"You were at school with 'the wild one'?" she
gasped.

John nodded.

"Tell me about him!" she pleaded. "Was he really
wild? Did you think he was mad? Did he have lots of
girl-friends?"

Jim interrupted. "There are more important
questions, Steve. For goodness' sake control your
imagination for once!" He turned to John and went
on: "I knew there was more to you than you
admitted. There had to be! So tell me, were you with
him just before he disappeared?"

"Yes. We'd just had our A Level results, and he
should have gone to University," John explained.
"Tony was very angry with and bitter about the
Reserve. He resented the fact that his father
thought more of a few wild animals than he did of
his own son. Tony wasn't quite as greedy as you
were led to believe. He didn't want to get his hands
on his father's fortune; he simply wanted enough

money to enjoy life while he was still young and adventurous; but his father had this obsession about the Game Reserve, and Tony didn't want to know about it. He said he'd keep in touch with me but I never heard from him after we finished school. He had told me that he was going to live rough on the Continent until he was due to start at University. That was the last I heard of him. I half-hoped to find that he'd turned up here."

Jim nodded. This was the best explanation so far. "You have no idea where Anthony might have ended up?" he asked.

"No." John shook his head and looked despondent. "I don't think he even knew where he'd end up himself."

Stephanie had been growing more and more agitated. She asked again: "What was he really like?"

John smiled. "I'm sorry to disappoint you, Steve, but he was quite ordinary. He had ambitions and he dreamed of adventures, but no more than any other lad of his age. He wasn't the gay, reckless youth you've made of him. It was rather the opposite. He was shy and reserved—a rather lonely sort of person. He didn't mix easily, and I only became a close friend because we shared a room. He was clever—he never had trouble passing examinations—but he had no 'wild' ambitions. I suppose he might have changed; it's over six years since I last saw him. "He'll be twenty-five now—same as me."

"Was he very handsome?" she asked.

John looked embarrassed, "It's difficult for me to answer that. He had very fair hair and incredibly blue eyes. I can't say whether a woman would consider him handsome, but he certainly wasn't ugly or disfigured or anything like that."

"Did you think he was mad?"

"No. I think a more apt description would have been 'sad'."

"Why sad?"

"I've told you. He was a very solitary sort of chap. A loner. He'd always been at boarding-school. His parents hadn't much time for him and I got the impression that he felt a bit of an outcast."

"This isn't getting us anywhere," Jim put in. "Our most urgent problem right now is what to do with you. Let's forget Anthony Van Dooran for the moment and decide on your future."

"If I give you my word that I won't look for gold, or even think about it again," John urged, "will you let me stay? If only until your financial problems are settled."

Jim looked at Stephanie, who was glowing with quiet excitement at the thought of knowing someone who had been close to the 'wild one'. "Let him stay, Dad," she pleaded.

"I'll give you one more chance," Jim finally decided. "But if you put a foot out of line, or if any officials from Immigration come here after you, that's the end. You must understand, John, that I will not tell lies for you or help you in any form of deception and neither will Stephanie."

"I understand!" John smiled. "And I'm most grateful. Thank you."

Stephanie stared at him with a wistful smile and for once in her life was bereft of speech.

John worked unceasingly after that, and his eagerness to make up for his previous behaviour was boundless. He did not take time off at week-ends and he never even mentioned the pay that was owing to him. Stephanie spent many happy hours with him, chatting as they worked and teaching him all she knew about animals and their environment.

She bombarded him with questions about Anthony, and he supplied most of the answers.

A new Anthony rose from the ashes of the old one. He was still a strong, attractive man, although rather quieter than she had previously envisaged. To her surprise, he was even more attractive to her than the wild, adventurous idol, for now he had become flesh and bone and his solitary nature offered more of a challenge.

Jim Loman was not totally happy at having John stay on at the Reserve. The mystery of the missing passport and John's entry into South Africa had left the older man with an uneasy conscience. One evening, when dinner was over, he confided to Stephanie: "After I tackled John about his passport and he told us about being at school with Anthony, I decided to check up on him."

Stephanie's eyes widened as she listened, and at first she felt uneasy. It was clear to her now that she loved John very deeply. She could not show it or speak of it, but he had come to be her first thought on waking in the morning and her last thought before falling asleep. The idea that her father might send him away made her heart ache.

"I was writing again to the solicitors in London," Jim went on, "and I suggested it might be profitable if they found out who was Anthony's best friend at school, with a view to tracing the heir through him. The answer came this morning." Jim waved a letter.

"Paul brought it from Welkom. It says that Anthony Van Dooran was at Heathbridge college, and his closest friend and room-mate was John Charles Kingsley. They have tried to trace John Kingsley, but have been unsuccessful. He was married but has left his wife, and she has no idea where he would be."

By now Jim was smiling, and so was Stephanie. John Charles Kingsley had told the truth! But that was only a passing ray of sunshine in the general gloom which now so frequently descended on father and daughter. Despite their efforts, the Van Dooran Game Reserve was becoming more and more difficult to run.

One farmer, who maintained his own stretch of fencing along the boundary, had written formally to Jim complaining that he had been obliged to mend his fence in three different places, and saying that if this continued he would have to submit an account to them. Jim did not blame him for his attitude; the whole situation was getting out of hand. Paul, Tom and John could not have worked harder, and Jim and Stephanie did little else but work. All of them rose at dawn to make the best possible use of the daylight hours and they did not stop until the pink dusk had given way to nightfall.

The climax came when Tom Fletcher, their most experienced Warden met with an accident. He got too near a cow elephant, not knowing that she had her baby near by. He retreated to his jeep, but she charged. The man had been injured and the jeep damaged. It was only when he didn't report in after the day's work that Jim and the others found him.

Jim arranged for an ambulance to be rushed from Welkom, and he himself followed in one of the jeeps, in order to hear the doctor's report on the injured man's condition and make all arrangements for Tom to receive medical care.

After Paul and Nancy had been persuaded to go to bed, Stephanie made a big pot of coffee, and she and John sat sipping mugs of the hot beverage while they waited for a radio message from Jim.

Finally, John broke the silence by saying: "I suppose you'll have to make some sort of financial gesture towards Tom? His medical treatment will have to be paid for."

"Yes, I know," Stephanie replied, with a surge of desperation, "but we haven't any money, and Dad's had to let the insurance lapse. The men knew. They agreed to take the risk. I expect he explained the position to you when you joined us. We certainly must try and help Tom, yet it's all so hopeless!"

John was silent for a moment, then he said disgustedly: "Money! I think we'd all be better off without it. It's money that's got you and your father into this mess, and it was the scent of money which brought me here. I can't say it's done any of us much good."

"Money's all right if you know how to handle it. We'd know what to do if we could get our hands on some of the Van Dooran fortune."

"I bet!" John said quietly. Then he asked in a strained voice: "And what exactly would you do?"

"I've told you a dozen times already. We'd pay off our debts and get a helicopter."

"Then what?"

"I don't understand what you mean?" she replied, bewildered.

John threw out his arms and said airily: "Surely there are a few things you'd get for yourselves?

Have you never thought of yourself behind the
wheel of an expensive sports car? With no one here
to dictate how you spent the Reserve money, you
could do anything you liked with it. Look at this
place—it's a dump! Admit it! You wouldn't live in
this way under normal circumstances. If you got
your share of the money, you aren't going to tell me
that you wouldn't build yourselves a splendid home
and live like lords. I'm quite sure some of that
fortune would find its way into your pockets, one
way or another. No doubt you'd look after the
animals, but if you didn't they'd hardly be in a
position to complain."

Stephanie could not believe her ears.

"How dare you? How despicable to make such
accusations! Did you know that my father gave up a
wonderful house and a highly paid job to come out
here? He didn't have to take this job. He came here
from choice! He's already given every penny of his
own money to the Reserve. If we did buy ourselves a
few luxuries, they certainly wouldn't cost what
Dad's already given. Anyway, we wouldn't dream
of squandering the Van Dooran money on our
selves! How dare you accuse us of such mercenary
intentions? We've given more in work and hard
cash than we'll ever get back. And money doesn't
buy dedication."

John did not apologise or back down. "There are
a lot of people who don't care much for money—until
they get their hands on it."

"I don't know how you came to such an unpleas
ant conclusion!" Stephanie blazed. "Is it a result of
your wife's greed? Do you think everyone is like
her?"

John turned away and could not look at the girl'

ndignant face. "I'd rather not talk about Pat. As far s I'm concerned, she doesn't exist any more. But er attitude toward money did leave a very bitter aste in my mouth. I'll not deny that. After my xperience with her, I'm entitled to be suspicious."

"Your suspicions are totally unfounded, so far as ve're concerned. Dad and I are only interested in elping animals. I don't see that it's any of your usiness, anyway. Don't tell me that you still have leas about making an easy fortune here?"

"Hardly!" he answered in a sarcastic tone. "As hings are, it doesn't even look as if I'll get my back ay."

The radio set began to emit a call sign. It was Jim, nd he had news of Tom Fletcher. He told Stepha-ie: "His right arm is broken and he has several racked ribs. He's in a deep state of shock and has st a lot of blood, but he'll be okay. He won't be back t work for several weeks, though, and he won't be ble to cope with manual work for some time."

Without Tom, their fight to keep the Reserve was ver.

"You heard that?" Stephanie asked John, not ooking at him because of the tears which were tinging her eyes.

"Yes." John nodded. "And I'm very sorry. Tom's good sort."

"We're really in a mess now. Right up to our ecks."

Was this why John had turned sour—because it vas less likely than ever that he would get his back vages? Sickened with disappointment that he hould have turned out to be so worthless, she said: You might as well go and pack your bag right way. Things can't get any worse, so you might as

well clear out. You have such a low opinion of Da
and me that I can't imagine why you've stayed s
long, as it is."

"Neither can I," John said as he stood up.

Stephanie tried to be brave and not give way t
tears in his presence. Yet even in the currer
atmosphere of anger and distrust she still felt tha
there was an invisible thread linking him to he
which could not be broken by words or deeds.

John was so close that she could feel the warmt
of his breath on her cheek.

"I've worked here for weeks without pay an
without even a half-day off, and that's all th
thanks I get!" he blazed. "I was only teasing, if yo
must know. But you never could take it, could you?
only wanted to take your mind off poor Ton
However, as you've sacked me, Miss High-an
Mighty Loman, I'll go! I'll leave first thing in th
morning, and you and your Reserve can rot for all
care!"

That night, when she'd at last gone to be
Stephanie made a vital decision. There was only on
solution to all their problems. It seemed that she ha
been forced into a corner and could take no othe
action in order to save all that she loved. Not tha
marriage to Roger Vincent would be all that terribl
She told herself that she was fond of him. They g
on well together and she would be a good wife t
him.

She awoke at daybreak as usual, although sh
did not feel rested. She would have liked to turn ove
huddle down under the bedclothes and go back t
sleep for a week. The dawn of this day was not th
happiest of her life.

She washed and dressed quickly, tormented by the thought that John might have left without even saying good-bye.

John was on her mind the whole time she was tending the sick animals. She had briefly explained the position to her father last night when he had eventually come back home.

"Well, Steve, you were no doubt justified in sending him packing," he'd said ruefully, "but I have to admit that I wish he'd stay on for a bit. I need him."

When she made her way to the house for breakfast she saw that her father was already seated at the table, looking drawn and tired. He gave her a welcoming smile as she joined him, but there was an air of defeat in his manner.

Stephanie sat down and began to eat her grapefruit. She wasted no time in telling her father: "You can stop worrying. After I went to bed last night, I decided to marry Roger. It's the only solution."

Jim noticed that his daughter could not look directly at him while announcing her sudden decision. "Steve," he challenged, "you're not doing this just for me, I hope?"

"No, I'm doing it for several reasons and they're all good ones. Roger's a fine man; one of the best. He and I share the same interests, he's attractive in a shy sort of way, and I'd be a fool to go on rejecting him. He won't wait for ever, and he could have any young woman he chose, so I might as well be the lucky one. But I only hope he doesn't expect me to go and live with his parents."

"I thought you liked his parents," Jim said, still dazed.

"I do. But his mother never stops fussing. I don't want to be treated like one of her priceless ornaments. I want to keep my own identity and go on with my work here."

"Yes...you would!" Jim smiled. "And, if I know you, you'll get your own way. Roger will agree to it because he worships you and always has." He paused, then went on with a hint of suspicion in his tone: "All our problems will disappear, won't they? We'll have money to burn."

Stephanie raised her eyes to his. "I'm not marrying Roger just for his money. I'm very fond of him. You know that."

"Yes. I like him, too. He's a kind and dedicated man and I'll be quite happy to hand you over to his care. There's only one thing that the Vincent money won't buy for you."

"And what's that?" she asked sharply. "You know I'm not the greedy type!"

"Nobody suggested that you were. What I had in mind was a very small thing, but I'm sure that without it you'll find life heartbreaking and intolerable."

"I don't know what you're talking about," she said, frowning.

"It was something your mother and I had. Money can't buy it, but no marriage is complete without it," he told her sadly. "It's called 'love'."

Stephanie had no come-back to this, so she ignored the remark. "Roger mentioned that he might drive out this afternoon, if he hasn't too much work on hand," she said in a matter-of-fact voice. "I'll suggest we choose the engagement ring next week-end."

Jim looked at her. "I hope you know what you're doing," he said. When she did not reply, he went on, in a different tone of voice: "Oh, by the way, I had a word with John this morning. He's agreed to stay on for a day or two, till we've got Tom's damaged jeep in and done one of two other urgent jobs. I'm sorry, Steve, but I just had to ask him."

"Oh, Dad!" Stephanie was contrite. "I'm the one who should be apologising. I ought not to have told him to clear off, but he can be so exasperating!"

"No need to apologise, Steve. And no need to say more than's necessary to him. But will you run him and Paul up to the damaged jeep after breakfast?"

"Yes, of course," she said. "I'm going round the salt-licks, anyway."

Once John and Paul had recovered Tom's abandoned vehicle and got it home, Jim was going to overhaul all the transport, in the hope that he would get a good price for them. He was dependant on the money to pay for Tom's medical treatment and he hoped the vehicle that had been overturned by the cow elephant would not be too badly damaged.

As soon as breakfast was over, Stephanie wasted no time in driving her jeep round to the storage sheds so that she could load the salt-blocks. While distributing them, she intended to check as much of the chain-link fencing as time would allow, and report any weakness or breakages to her father.

She finished loading the rock salt into the back of her jeep and waited for Paul and John to join her. Presently she grew impatient and decided to walk over to the Wardens' quarters to find out what was delaying them. She was only half-way there when Paul came striding toward her.

"Sorry about being late, but I can't find John!" he said.

"Can't find him?" Panic raced through Stephanie's eyes. "But he'd promised Dad that he'd stay on for a couple of days!"

"I know," Paul replied anxiously. "He was in a very bad mood this morning though."

"What about his belongings? Have you been into his room? Is it empty?"

"No. His odds and ends are still there, but he didn't have much."

Stephanie could not believe that John would simply take off without saying a word to anyone.

"There's something else," Paul continued. "One of the jeeps is missing."

"No!" Stephanie murmured incredulously. "John wouldn't steal one of our jeeps and creep off without a word. I'm certain he wouldn't. Come on—we must tell Dad."

Jim Loman was as shocked as his daughter and could not believe that John would do such a thing. The three of them went into the house.

"I ought to radio the police in Welkom," Jim said with reluctance. "I should report it. There's always been something odd about John. Perhaps I was wrong to keep on trusting him."

"He got on all right with the other Wardens," Paul offered. "He was a bit of a loner, but not unlikeable. There was only one thing that really puzzled us...he always kept his room locked. Nancy discovered it first when she went to make his bed and clean his room. When she asked John if she could go in there once a day, he said he'd see to it himself. We thought it was strange; he's got nothing worth pinching! Not that anyone would have stolen from him, anyway."

"But you went into his room this morning?" Stephanie queried.

"Yes. It wasn't locked." Paul looked down at the floor and shook his head. "That could mean he doesn't intend to come back! Whatever he was hiding in there, he's taken it with him."

"I wonder," Jim said thoughtfully. "I have my own private theory about John. I believe young Van Dooran might have sent him to spy out the land. John admitted that he knew Anthony . . . perhaps he knew him better than he let on. And now that John's discovered that the Reserve is finished, he can go back to Anthony and tell him the whole project is a failure. If Anthony hangs on for a bit longer, until this place is a real shambles, he could contest the Will and get the entire fortune. If he can prove that his father's wish to leave the money to a Reserve was a waste of time, with a bit of ingenuity and a good lawyer he could inherit everything. All very clever—sending John here to make sure things weren't going well." Jim started to walk toward the radio transmitter. "I'm going to report the stolen jeep to the police."

"Dad, no!" Stephanie said uneasily. "Your theory's very sound, but you haven't convinced me. Please give John a chance. Wait a while—please?"

"Wait for what?" Jim argued. "For him to get clear away?"

"He's not running away," she reasoned. "If he'd wanted several hours' start, he'd have disappeared during the night, when we were all asleep. He could have been miles away before that jeep was missed. Will you give me a couple of hours to look for him before we involve the police? I think John's still here; and if he is, I know exactly where to find him."

Jim was reluctant to condemn John untried. "All right. Two hours!" he said.

CHAPTER SIX

Stephanie had almost reached the limit of the Reserve in her jeep and was beginning to think that she had been wrong in suspecting that John would be in the river area, when she noticed the missing jeep—unoccupied. She had not brought the rifle, and clearly she was going to have to leave the protection of her own vehicle to follow John's tracks. It was a most perilous area, with towering outcrops of sandstone rocks where leopards could lie in wait for unsuspecting prey and numerous huge fig trees harboured snakes and baboons.

Ignoring everything she had ever learned about

safety measures, Stephanie parked her jeep and got out. She had learned not to be afraid of animals, but she knew she was taking her life in her hands as she followed John's tracks.

As she had suspected, he was heading for the river. When she at length emerged from the jungle fringe, she looked across the river—serene at this point—towards the blue mountains that rose in the distance. It was a beautiful sight. There were animals everywhere. Hippos bathed in the river, elephants gave themselves shower baths, crocodiles slept in the shallows at the edge of the water, and several species of deer were quietly drinking, but ever alert for predators.

It took Stephanie several minutes to pick up John's tracks in the sandy mud at the edge of the river. She sighed, looked round at the abundance of wild life, and wondered if she should go on. She was alone, unarmed, and very vulnerable. It was madness to put herself in such a situation, and John Kingsley must be even madder to take such risks.

The footprints led her down the river-bank to a huge outcrop of rocks that towered against the sky and hung over the river on a wide and very deep stretch. She had not explored this area before and had no idea what might be lurking amid the slab-shaped boulders. John had definitely climbed them, for there were muddy footprints leading upwards from the lower slabs.

Stephanie looked up at the sky, which was becoming clouded. She hoped it would not start to rain before she found John, because rain could wash away the faint tracks that he may have left in the dry, sandy grit between the boulders.

Half-way up, she found herself on a large

platform. Most of the rock slabs formed a solid wall encircling the platform, but in one place, right at the back, one slab had crumbled and subsided, revealing a small cave.

A shaft of light from a crack in the overhead slabs enabled Stephanie to look into the cave without entering it. In the far corner, huddled together in a mass of soft fur, were three lion cubs.

Stephanie backed away from the cave and made her way quickly towards the farthest point, from which she could continue her upward climb. But she was too late, and long before she reached this one and only exit upwards, a lioness leapt down from the upper slabs of rock and gave an almighty snarl.

Stephanie took a deep breath and remembered that a calm voice could soothe an upset animal. "It's all right," she said quietly, "I'm not going to harm your babies."

As she finished speaking, she tried to sidle forward, but her first step sent the lioness into a fury. Stephanie closed her eyes to the horror that faced her. She prayed that she would faint before the lioness actually pounced on her. But as she waited for those brief seconds which lasted a lifetime, a voice from nowhere shouted: "Run, Steve! Run!" A rock hurtled through the air and struck the lioness on the shoulder.

The lioness was too quick for him. She jerked her head to one side and the rock landed with a thud beside her. John had missed, and it had been his last chance. The enraged animal crouched in readiness to leap.

Stephanie closed her eyes, let out a long scream, and felt as though her life was held in suspension. John, who had been the object of all forms of suspicion, was giving his life without question. Only a very brave man or a complete fool would have acted in this way, and John was no fool.

An even louder roar filled the air and, as Stephanie opened her eyes in panic, she saw another animal hurtling through the air from the upper rocks. This second animal was a lion, a massive beast which made the lioness look small by comparison. Stephanie recognised him—it was her friend Murphy. He landed on top of the enraged lioness. In the struggle that followed, Stephanie had time to race across the platform to John, and together they made a hasty retreat.

As they climbed down, Stephanie panted: "Good old Murphy! He must have been following me."

"I never thought I'd owe my life to a lion," John said shakily, still shocked from his terrifying experience.

They climbed to the base of the rocks and sat down, panting and trembling. For a few moments neither spoke as John mopped his forehead with a handkerchief and Stephanie sat with her head bowed in her hands. When they had got their breath back and recovered from their ordeal, they turned and gazed into each other's eyes.

"Oh, Steve!" John said quietly, and with a sudden impulse he put his arms round her and pulled her close, holding her so tightly that she could not move.

Stephanie began to cry with relief. She could not stop herself from winding her arms round John's strong waist. She pressed her cheek against his firm shoulder and held on to him as if she were a frightened child. But presently she moved away.

"Dad thinks that Anthony sent you here to find

out what was going on, so that he can contest the Will. You have asked some very personal questions... is Dad right?" she asked brokenly.

"No, Steve; Tony didn't send me here as a spy. But if he had done so, I would have told him that the Reserve is a very worthwhile venture and that you and your father are as honest as the day and would never misuse the money."

A brisk wind was now rippling the surface of the river. As Stephanie watched the water, she asked: "Why did you keep your room locked? Paul told us this morning... he went there to look for you. He was surprised. Had you forgotten to lock it?"

"No." John turned away from her. "When I set out this morning I had no intention of coming back. I was going to drive into Welkom and leave the jeep outside the police station. Your father would soon have got it back."

"You were leaving without saying good-bye?"

"I didn't want to see you again—in case you made me change my mind." He became shy and admitted quietly: "You see, I've become very fond of you."

"Why did you come all the way out here?" Stephanie inquired.

"Gold!" John smiled. "I thought I'd have one last look. Tony was right. You can see gold in the river, but unfortunately it swims about. The gold that you see is nothing more than yellow fish. When you came snooping, I hid for a while, until I heard that lioness snarling and I knew you were in trouble. I can't leave now, Steve. I want to be near you— always. Seeing that I saved your life, can't I stay on indefinitely?"

Stephanie paused for a moment and avoided his eyes when she finally answered: "No, that wouldn't be a good idea. I'm going to marry Roger Vincent. I decided last night."

"Why?" John gasped, his eyes wide.

"To help the Reserve—and because Roger and I are two of a kind. It will be a good marriage."

John sighed heavily and looked out at the river again.

"And what about being in love?"

Stephanie stood up. She wanted to go before the situation got out of hand. She brushed the sand from her jeans and started to walk to where the vehicles were parked.

John caught up with her and asked: "When will you be seeing Roger? How soon will you be setting a date for the wedding?"

"The sooner the better," she replied. "I'm hoping he'll come to the Reserve this afternoon, and I expect we'll buy the engagement ring this weekend."

He caught her by the arm. "Can't I say anything to stop you?"

Stephanie pulled away from him. "No. Everything that could go wrong has gone wrong. There's nothing that anyone can say or do to alter things now."

They walked in silence to the place where they had left the jeeps.

A friend was waiting for them. He sat between the two vehicles, smoothing his ruffled fur with long, slow strokes of his pink tongue. When he saw John and Stephanie he stopped and gave them a smile.

"Hello, Murphy!" Stephanie glowed with affection for the animal as she walked to him and put her arms round his huge neck. "Are you all right?" As she patted him, she examined him for bites and scratches.

Without fear or hesitation, John also walked up to the lion and patted him on the head. "Thank you, Murphy. Your arrival couldn't have been better timed."

"He's not hurt," Stephanie observed. "Not even a scratch. And he's too much of a gentleman to have hurt the lioness. I expect he just gave her a mild lesson on manners and sent her back to her cubs."

John smiled. "With a friend like Murphy, who needs to be afraid?"

It was such a tragedy that John had grown to trust and understand animals when it was too late. "You will leave today?" Stephanie asked.

"Yes." John sighed. "No point in staying where I'm not wanted. Shall I go right now—like this?"

"I think you'd better." Stephanie said. She kept her gaze fixed on the ground. "Take the jeep in lieu of wages. I'll explain everything to Dad. And, if you need references, write to us. Dad'll see you right."

As she moved towards her own jeep, John followed her. He took her by the arm and pulled her close to his chest. "Does it have to be so final?"

Tears glistened in her eyes as she struggled from his grip and said: "Yes. Please—it's difficult enough as it is." She paused, looking up at him for the last time. "Good luck!" She stood on tiptoe, kissed his cheek and then climbed quickly into her jeep.

With a roar, she drove off as quickly as she could, and all John could see was a cloud of swirling dust as the vehicle disappeared.

With a sigh he patted Murphy again, went to his own vehicle and climbed in. He knew exactly what

he had to do. John Kingsley must disappear for
ever.

...Stephanie drove recklessly, her heart aching
and tears pouring down her cheeks. When she
arrived back at the house she found her father, told
him that John had gone for good and, unable to
control her tears, rushed to her bedroom and cried
her heart out.

At last, she started to feel guilty that she was
neglecting her duties. She washed her face in cold
water in the hope that it would soothe her eyes.
When she went outside, she discovered that Paul
had distributed the salt-blocks, and the damaged
jeep had been brought back.

At lunchtime Paul ate with the family; there
seemed no point in having Nancy walk to and from
the Wardens' quarters to serve the only remaining
Warden.

Stephanie was very quiet, and the air of unrest
made Jim, Paul and Nancy edgy. Jim tried to
persuade Paul to drive into Welkom to make
inquiries about another job.

"But I don't want to leave," Paul said dogmatically. "I know things are pretty hopeless now, but I'll
stay till the end."

"It wouldn't do any harm to have another job
lined up," Jim argued.

"All right. We'll see about it when the time
comes."

The group ate in silence for a while. John's
departure had upset all of them, in one way or
another.

"What are you going to do this afternoon, Steve?"
Jim asked at length.

"I don't know. Roger's supposed to be driving over, so I'd like to stay close to the house. Have the cowsheds been cleaned out this week?"

"No," Jim answered. "No one's had time."

"Then I'll do that." She sighed as she pushed away her unfinished meal.

...She had just finished cleaning out the cowshed with savage thoroughness when Nancy came across from the house. "I got a radio message for you! Mr. Vincent radioed in. He's very sorry but he won't be coming to see you this afternoon. He's been called to a farm right the other side of Welkom."

"Oh..." Stephanie sighed. "Any other messages?"

"No, Miss Stephanie. Was you expecting one?"

"Not really."

Perhaps Fate had intervened. Perhaps she was not meant to marry Roger. From the way things had happened, it seemed the Reserve had been doomed from the start. In her heart, Stephanie knew she could never make a success of marriage with Roger...not now that she knew John Kingsley loved her.

When her father returned home that afternoon, Stephanie told him that Roger had not been able to come—and that she now realised she had made a mistake in thinking she could make a go of marriage with him. "I'm sorry, Dad. I always seem to be saying I'm sorry lately. But I've thought it over and it wouldn't be right. It wouldn't be fair to him. Can you forgive me?"

Jim smiled. "Nothing to forgive. I think you've made the right decision. You were marrying for the wrong reasons. Fact is, we both of us seemed dogged by ill-luck. I don't think this place was meant to succeed. But we've had some good times, Steve, haven't we?"

Stephanie nodded. Jim glanced at her sharply, then resolutely changed the subject. "We're going to have rain," he said.

It was late afternoon and the whole sky was turning pink. The small white clouds, spurred along by a rising wind, had pink edges to them and looked like oyster shells.

"You'll miss South Africa," Jim couldn't help saying wistfully. "Especially the river."

Stephanie's mouth curled. "No. I put too much faith in this place and that silly river. Do you know, until recently I really believed that Anthony Van Dooran would come here and that the river would somehow turn to a bed of roses! I've stood on the rocks and looked down and seen it . . . the water gone and the riverbed strewn with pink rose-petals." With tears forming and a choked voice, she ended: "If I ever took lessons in stupidity, I'd get a first-class degree!"

"Don't," Jim said, laying a weatherbeaten hand on hers. "Don't torment yourself, Steve. We'll go back to England and make a new life. It'll be all right. You know what they say about it always being darkest before the dawn."

"The people who say that," she mocked, "are even more stupid than I am."

"You haven't been stupid. You've been an angel."

She looked at him and smiled. "If I had been stupid, you'd never admit it." She choked as a lump rose in her throat. "Could I tempt you with a cup of tea?"

Jim grinned back. "That's one temptation I've never refused in my whole life!"

Stephanie made a pot of tea, but before they had finished drinking it the radio began to give out a call signal and Jim went into the living-room to acknowledge it. When he returned to the veranda he wore a very puzzled expression.

"It was the police in Welkom. The message was actually for you. They said that if you'll drive out to the river you'll find John Kingsley's jeep!"

"John's jeep?" Her eyes widened. "But what's it doing by the river?"

"They didn't know. They received a telephone call from John...he asked them to relay the message. Apparently, he said he didn't need the vehicle again, then he hung up on them. But I can't think why he left it down by the river instead of bringing it back here."

Stephanie laughed briefly. "I suppose he suddenly decided he was too proud to accept it. But he didn't have to come back to the Reserve. He could have simply left it outside the police station."

"He always was odd," Jim said. "I suppose we'd better drive out there and pick it up before a couple of rhino decide to play football with it."

Stephanie stood up. "Come on then."

They did not have to search for the jeep. Stephanie guessed that John had left it near the rocks where he had first encountered Murphy, and sure enough it was there.

Jim climbed from the passenger seat of Stephanie's vehicle and got into the other jeep. "See you back at the house."

"Coming in a minute," Stephanie called after him. "I want to take a quick look round."

"All right. But don't be too long, and don't take any chances with the animals."

Jim started the engine and drove it away.

Stephanie looked round, a strange sensation tugging at her heart. John was near! She could feel his presence. He was watching her from the outcrop of rocks on the river bank.

At first she sat in her jeep, wrestling with her conscience. Her common sense told her that she ought to drive away and never see him again, but a strange intuition told her that John would not have lured her out to this spot unless he had a very good reason.

She left the jeep and headed towards the rocks. There were animals about, but they did not take much notice of her. As she climbed there was no sign of John, but something led her upwards. The wind was very brisk by now and caused the water to ripple. The clouds were growing a deeper shade of pink as the sun sank in the sky.

As she looked up she saw the figure of a man silhouetted against the pink sky. She was not sure that it was John Kingsley. The clothes were not John's. She climbed to the same level and took a closer look at the man. He looked very like John; he had the same face and short, brittle hair, but this man was surely not the one to whom she had said her farewell earlier that day?

"John?" she called.

"No," the man called back. "John's gone. You'll never see him again."

Stephanie became slightly afraid. She did not know what was happening. The voice was John's, although stronger and more authoritative. She walked nervously up to the stranger and studied his face as he stood gazing down at her. Her heart began to pound as she stared into John's face—but in place of the dark brown eyes, two of the bluest eyes she had ever seen looked back at her.

"You are John!" she murmured. "But what's happened to you?"

The stranger extended a strong hand and smiled. "Allow me to introduce myself. I'm Anthony Van Dooran."

Stephanie was speechless. She could not shake the hand he offered. All she could do was stare into the wild blue eyes that held her captive. She had no doubt that the man who faced her was the missing Van Dooran heir. She tottered slightly as if she were going to faint.

Tony smiled, put out an arm and steadied her round the waist as he said: "I think we'd better sit down, don't you?"

He held her as they walked to the back of the rock ledge and found a sheltered spot. They sat looking out across the jungle and the veld beyond, to where the sun was setting in the west and turning everything pink.

Stephanie was so confused and shocked that she wanted to cry. She had always wondered how she would feel if confronted by 'the wild one', and now she knew. He was sitting right beside her, and she was seized with panic. She wanted to stand up and run, but her legs were too shaky to support her weight.

A strong arm was laid gently round her shoulders. She tensed, petrified.

"I didn't mean it to be such a shock," Anthony said quietly. He inclined his head toward hers and spoke softly into her ear. "Come on, Steve. Pull yourself together." He tightened his grip round her shoulders and stroked her hair with his other hand. "Come on—at least look at me!"

She took several deep breaths and finally had enough strength and courage to look up at 'the wild one'.

"You..." she said slowly. "You are John, but your eyes and your clothes... You're John, yet you aren't John!"

"I was John...I borrowed his identity."

"You borrowed his identity?" she repeated incredulously. "But your eyes? A person can't change his eyes!" She was looking into them again. They were so blue, so determined and steady...she was overpowered by them.

"I knew that my eyes would give me away, especially if I came face to face with Nancy, so before I left England I bought special contact lenses. I heard of them from a friend at college; his father owned an optical firm which made lenses. Occasionally they had orders from television and film stars who needed to change the colour of their eyes for a certain role. These cosmetic lenses change the colour of the iris without interfering with the vision, and I thought a set could come in useful, so I sold my gold watch and had them made. They were very expensive, but they've been worth it. That's one reason why I kept my room locked. I kept the lenses box and special eye liquid in the drawer there. I must say, it's a relief to be rid of them."

Stephanie gazed up at him, still in a maze of incredulity. She found a thread of voice to ask: "But I was told that you had fair, wavy hair."

"I have," he admitted shyly. "I used to get teased unmercifully when I was younger. That was why I had to disguise it while I was here. I'm sure Nancy would have recognised it. I kept it trimmed to a crew-cut and touched it up with a hair-colour preparation I bought in town."

He gazed down at her and slowly drew her close to him. "Steve," he said passionately. "Oh, Steve, how I've longed to do this!" He kissed her on the lips, the ears, the eyes and the throat.

Stephanie was still suffering from shock and could not believe that this was happening with the man who had been her secret hero for many years. She began to tremble, and a dull warmth in her veins surged until it became fire. It was like a dam bursting in her heart. All her feelings for both John Kingsley and 'the wild one' flooded over her. It was just as she had imagined it...total commitment. But so dangerous! She realised that she was being swept away by this flood of emotion and suddenly she struggled away from him.

"No! Don't do that!" she gasped.

"What's wrong?" he asked. "I'm not married, if that's what worries you. John Kingsley is...or at least he was, the last time I heard from him. Just before we left college John was very much in love with this girl named Pat. He used to see her when he went home for the holidays. Pat lived next door to his parents. When I did my disappearing trick I kept in touch with him for a time. He married Pat, but it didn't work out. She turned out to be a worthless wife, and eventually he left her. It gave me a unique opportunity to borrow his identity. I knew that if anyone checked up on John Kingsley, the story would fit. The last time I heard from him, he said he was going to follow in my footsteps and flee to the Continent. He hasn't been seen or heard of since, so it was a perfect cover for me. If he couldn't be found, I was in no danger of being exposed."

"Why did you go through with this outrageous pretence?" Stephanie challenged.

"I had to." He went on, although he sounded ashamed as he spoke: "My father had left several million pounds to be shared between myself and this Game Reserve, and I was quite certain that it would be misappropriated. Steve, there is so much greed in the world today and so many thoroughly mercenary people. That's why I tested both of you...I had to!"

"Tested us?"

"Yes, I deliberately told lies to see how you'd react. I know that white rhinos aren't white, and I know that anyone suffering from TB would find it almost impossible to come into South Africa. But neither you nor your father got nasty about it. Curious, yes, but not unpleasant. I tried so hard to make you lose your tempers with me...but you didn't. You just kept turning the other cheek. There aren't many people who are as kind and loyal as you and your father. Even when you thought that I was a criminal on the run, you were prepared to give me one last chance. If anyone deserves to have a share of the Van Dooran fortune, it's your father, and I intend to see that he gets it! I've already sent a cable to the London solicitors...no doubt I'll have to fly over there."

Stephanie's jaw dropped a little and she ran her tongue nervously along her lower lip. Then she asked: "Do you really mean that?"

"Yes." He grinned at her. It was such a captivating grin, full of mischief, that it rocked her senses. He went on: "I've been into the bank in Welkom, and

I promise you they're ready to help your father. You can buy that helicopter."

"But—" She paused. "How are you going to get out of South Africa to visit London, if you haven't got a passport?"

Tony was still smiling down at her and it sent ripples of fire through her veins. "I've been here in South Africa for over five years." He reached into the inside pocket of the jacket he was carrying and took out a passport. "I've got a passport...I've always had one. That's another reason why I had to keep my room locked." He handed the document to Stephanie.

She opened it and looked inside. It was a South African passport in the name of Anthony Van Dooran. "So you came here under your real name?" she said.

"Of course I did. I haven't committed any offences. I told you that."

"It's incredible!" Stephanie said, her voice growing stronger. "You're been here for over five years and no one knew? I wonder why your father didn't suspect that you'd come home?"

Tony looked straight at her. "Tell me, if you wanted to hide a tree, where would you put it?"

"I've no idea." Stephanie paused for thought. "Trees are usually so large and conspicuous."

"Not if you plant them in a forest." Tony smiled. "The last place anyone would search would be the most obvious. Father would never have dreamed that I'd come back here. Once I'd arrived in Johannesburg, I took on a false identity again...I became John Kingsley. I didn't use the cosmetic contact lenses, though. I saved those until I knew I'd meet someone like Nancy. She'd have recognised my eyes and hair immediately if I hadn't disguised them. When I read about my father's death, I let things ride for a while, but eventually my curiosity got the better of me. I didn't want his wretched money. I had quite a bit of my own by then; I'd earned it by sheer hard work."

"Where had you been working?" Stephanie inquired, remembering how pale he had been when he arrived at the Reserve.

"My last job—" he laughed—"was down a gold mine. There's no chance of getting sunburnt down there. There isn't much that I don't know about gold."

Stephanie frowned. "Then why did you go out of your way to make Dad and me believe that you were after gold on the Reserve? You must have known all along that there was none in the river!"

"I'm sorry, Steve," he said, shaking his head. "I was trying you both out. I thought you might want to join in my illicit activities. I tried to convince you that there was still gold to be found, in the hope that you'd start looking for it, too. If you'd been greedy or mercenary, you might even have asked me to help you smuggle it out for you. Gold does strange things to people . . . it can become an obsession. I gave your father every opportunity to suggest a partnership designed to rob the Van Dooran Reserve; but I was so wrong. Your father wouldn't know how to be dishonest; he wouldn't even know where to start. As I said before, he deserves all the help he can get."

He reached over and took Stephanie's slender hand in his. "Don't look so worried," he said gently.

She raised her eyes to his face and gave a nervous smile. "Tell me one thing?" she asked. "Why did your father hate you?"

Tony looked quite desolate as he explained: "My mother ought never to have had a child. The doctors thought that we'd both die, but I was a normal, healthy baby and eventually my mother pulled through; but the birth left her so weak that she never recovered her health. My father blamed me, and spent the rest of his life hating me. He condemned me from the moment I was born. It would have been kinder if he'd had me drowned."

Tony stared out at the jungle and veld. The sky was an even darker shade of pink and the entire view reflected it. Stephanie felt a lump come to her throat; no wonder she had seen the look of a tormented and suspicious animal in the face of this man when he had borrowed John Kingsley's identity.

"Mr. Van Dooran," she asked awkwardly, "look...I'm very sorry about all this. I didn't mean to pry into your past."

"Can't you call me Tony?" he said with an impatient sigh.

"No! It wouldn't be—"

"Try it!" he interrupted curtly. "I don't suppose your mouth will burst into flames."

The man she remembered flashed back for an instant, sharp-tongued and dominant; the man that she had known and loved as John Kingsley. A man whose bark was much worse than his bite. She forced herself to say: "All right...Tony!"

"There!" He smiled briefly. "That didn't hurt, did it?"

"No. But it feels strange."

"You'll get used to it." He went on in a different tone: "I hope you aren't going to feel sorry for me. I'd hate that! I've got over my bitterness towards my father. He was wrong about most things, but he was right about animals and conservation. You and your father have proved that to me. I'll stay here and help, if you'll let me—not because it makes me eligible for my inheritance, but because I want to work here." He stopped and smiled. "You can thank old Murphy for that. He helped to change my view about animals. He's quite a character!" Then his voice turned cold as he inquired: "How's Roger? Did you see him this afternoon and have you set a date for the wedding? I suppose that is why little Miss Prim didn't want me to kiss her, though no one is going to convince me that my kisses weren't welcome!"

She flushed and turned deathly white. "Roger didn't come," she replied. "He was called out to see some sick animals on one of the farms. But I'm not sorry. I've decided I don't want to marry him. It wouldn't be right—for either of us."

Tony looked down at her and asked with an air of suspicion: "So now that you've got the Van Dooran money, you don't need his? Is that why you've changed your mind?"

Stephanie glared back at him defiantly. "Certainly not!" she said crossly. "I decided earlier today that I couldn't marry him. Dad and I had made up our minds to pack up and go back to England, just before we got your radio message from the police."

"Oh ..." He seemed genuinely contrite.

"Come to think of it, why did you come back?" Stephanie challenged.

"I didn't realise you loved me until we had that encounter with the lioness. I gave you the chance to run for your life, but you wouldn't go. After that, I realised my life meant more to you than your own. If you remember, when we were talking afterwards I did beg you to let me stay, but you got on your high horse and, before you'd given me a chance to explain who I was, you'd announced that you were going to marry Roger Vincent. You made me so hopping mad that I thought I'd go through with my original plan."

"And what was that?"

"I was going back to London to see my father's solicitors. You would have got your share of the Van Dooran fortune, and mine as well. I wouldn't have qualified for my legacy, because I didn't intend to stay on here; but I didn't want my father's money. When you drove off and left me this morning, I thought: 'Right, you little madam! Go ahead and marry Roger...spend the rest of your life tied to a man you don't love. In a few weeks, when you get the Van Dooran money, you'll find out what a silly, impetuous decision you've made, but you'll be stuck with it'." He paused, then ended on a caustic note: "And it would have served you right!"

"I would only have married him to save my animals...and I wouldn't have hurt him or been indifferent. I'm really fond of him. Even so, I couldn't go through with it." Then she asked: "You still haven't explained why you did come back."

He shrugged his shoulders. "When I got into Welkom, my conscience began to play up. I couldn't let you marry Roger, so I decided to drive back here and tell you who I was, after all. Anyway, I wanted to say good-bye properly, and have a word with your father."

"I see. Thank you for coming back. At least, I don't have to worry about my animals now."

He looked toward the skyline. "You're too good to

be true!" he said sarcastically. "You can't think of anything except your animals! It might be all right when you're young, but when you get older, won't you regret not having a husband and children of your own? Are you so involved with your animals that you're prepared to ignore human beings ... human emotions?"

Stephanie stood up quickly and started to walk away. Tony leapt to his feet and followed. As he caught up with her he said with a little snarl in his voice: "I might have guessed that you wouldn't marry me. You're too good for me, aren't you? There's as much chance of your becoming my wife as there is of the river turning to a bed of roses!"

Stephanie stopped. Marriage? He hadn't mentioned marriage before. He had only talked of love. To a man of his roving disposition a tie like marriage would surely be a form of slavery?

"You still use that silly expression about the river?" she remarked, not daring to look up at him.

He stood over her, towering, dominant, smouldering with anger.

"Well, you're right about the river," she sighed, as she started to pick her way upwards through the rocks. "Rivers can't turn into roses."

He followed her, angry that she had not commented on his backhanded offer of marriage.

As they reached the rocky summit they looked down at the river, and then stood motionless with wide eyes and incredulous faces. Murphy was sitting a little way away, and he, too, was staring down at the river.

The brisk wind had rippled the water into small, leaf-shaped waves and the sky, now an intense shade of pink, was reflected in the water. This

unique combination of brisk wind and deep pink sky
had emptied the river of flowing blue water and
filled it with what looked like millions of shimmer-
ing rose-petals.

Tears filled Stephanie's eyes as she stared down
at the incredible phenomenon.

"Look!" she said softly. "The river ... it's turned
to a bed of roses. I've never seen it do that before.
Isn't it beautiful?"

Tony was speechless but nodded his head.

Stephanie went on: "Well, you did say that there
was as much chance of your coming back here as the
river turning to a bed of roses ... and it's obliged you.
Who says miracles never happen?"

"I also said there was as much of a chance of your
becoming my wife ..."

For a moment, Stephanie was too stunned by the
sight of the river to react. But then she turned to
Tony, put her arms round his broad chest and said:
"Well, we can't argue with the river, can we?"

THE END

A Heather Romance

LEAP INTO LOVE

by
Paula Lindsay

CHAPTER ONE

There was a stranger in the village.

Inskip was a small place where everyone knew everyone else. It was quite impossible for a newcomer to escape notice—and this was a particularly interesting newcomer.

Waldo McKinnon was not only a famous writer and television personality, although that was exciting in itself for a quiet little village like Inskip. He was also the man whose name had been linked with the lovely and tempestuous Dorian Leigh, the much-married film star who had died so tragically in a recent car crash.

There was a great deal of curious speculation about the tall man who leaned heavily on his stick as he made his way about the village, occasionally in the company of his cousin with whom he was staying for the summer, but very often alone. He gave the impression of being rather unapproachable and he was already described as unsociable.

Inskip was a little awed by the fame and brilliance of the celebrity in its midst, faintly embarrassed by the hint of scandal which still clung to him and somewhat shy of claiming his attention. Colin McKinnon, his cousin, was popular in the village and had many friends who had hoped he would bring his famous relative to the functions that had been hastily organised by ambitious hostesses. But it seemed that the writer was refusing all invitations on the plea of convalescence and the pressure of work. He had been badly hurt in the accident which had killed Dorian Leigh, and he had come to Inskip to regain his health and to do some writing.

Although he had been about the village on several occasions, there were still certain interested parties who had not set eyes on him. So when he slipped into a pew at morning service on that first Sunday, there was an immediate ripple of excited interest and the discreet craning of several necks.

Marian Cope, the Vicar's eldest daughter, smiled across the aisle at him. She was one of the few people in Inskip who had already been introduced to him, having the advantage of a long friendship with his cousin.

She was not deterred by the much-publicised affair with Dorian Leigh that had only ended with the film star's death. She thought it would be odd if a famous, personable man had not been involved in some kind of scandal at some time—and a rake was always more interesting, anyway. She seldom bothered about a man's past if there was the slightest possibility that she would figure in his future; and she expected to see a great deal of Waldo McKinnon in the coming months. It would be a sparkling feather in her cap if she could claim him as a conquest—and she had every intention of doing so.

Her sister, Lucy, resisted the very natural temptation to peep at the writer. She thought he must be embarrassed by the stares and the unmistakable murmur that had greeted his unobtrusive entry, and she would not add to his discomfiture for the world.

She had seen him from a distance, walking in the village, and recognised him immediately. She would have been neither human nor feminine if she had not felt a swift stirring of excitement as he made his way with painful slowness down the main street. It had seemed to Lucy that he conveyed bitter resentment in the very handling of the stick that he obviously still needed, although Colin had told them that he was recovering remarkably well from the accident.

The Reverend Michael Cope waited with quiet patience for the murmur to subside. The entire village seemed to be alive to the presence of Waldo McKinnon in the community; but Michael ruefully accepted that it was not because of the books he had written. The people of Inskip were not great readers. But they did read their newspapers avidly and delighted in all the current gossip about their television favourites; and Waldo McKinnon was a familiar figure on the small screen.

Michael felt that the recent scandal involving the man was most unfortunate and quite unworthy of a gifted writer whose books were so intelligently and sensitively written. The Vicar had met him one day in the week when he had found Waldo McKinnon exploring the churchyard. He had paused to introduce himself, and had enjoyed a brief and interesting conversation with the writer. He was pleased to see him at morning service but not so pleased to notice that Marian was showing a marked interest in the man. While he could wish that a man with his reputation had not come within flirting distance of his beautiful daughter, he admitted that it would be most unreasonable to expect her to avoid him. Colin was a family friend, and his cousin must be welcomed and entertained for that reason if for no other.

Michael had four daughters, and he loved them all dearly. Marian was the eldest: beautiful, talented, confident and self-possessed, apt to take what she wanted from life with both hands. At twenty-eight, she was still unmarried, but it could not be for want of asking, her father thought wryly: she delighted in seeking and making new conquests and she fell in and out of love as though it was just a game. But one day she would, no doubt, surprise them all.

Helen and Clare were twins and both were married. Helen lived in London with her successful barrister husband and three children. Clare was in Wiltshire with her doctor husband, and expecting her first child.

His eyes softened as his glance turned to Lucy.
She was the youngest, and Michael thought her the
loveliest of his girls with her thick, curling chestnut
hair, hazel eyes and clear skin. She was very like the
wife he had loved and lost soon after Lucy's birth.
He knew that Lucy was generally cast into the
shade by her beautiful, extroverted sisters; but that
suited her, for she was a shy, modest girl who
disliked the limelight. Her appeal lay in the candour
of her expression, the lingering sweetness of her
smile, the shy gentleness that made her the
delightful, thoughtful daughter he loved.

They had been enchanting little girls, the pride of
his heart and a constant consolation for the loss of
his wife. All too soon they had grown into young
women attracting admirers as a honey-pot attracts
insects. Marian and Helen had, from their teens,
thoroughly enjoyed a light-hearted, flirtatious
existence. Then Helen had met and married Spenser
Lewis, all within a few weeks. She appeared to be
extremely happy. Clare had set her heart on one
man when she was eighteen, and waited patiently
for him to qualify as a doctor and obtain a practice,
but she had never lacked for escorts in the
meantime. Lucy was twenty-two and not yet
thinking of marriage. Michael cherished a secret
hope with regard to her future, and thought it likely
that he would see it fulfilled in due course. She was a
sensitive and vulnerable girl and it was important
that she should marry the right man. Michael had
just the man in mind.

Waldo McKinnon was not unaware of the stir he
had created, but he was too used to attracting
attention to regard it. He was still wondering what
had prompted him to enter the church. But as he

made the responses and raised his voice in the
singing of the hymns, he was unexpectedly conscious of a quietude within him that eased the
turbulence of past weeks. There was a rare peace
within this ancient church of St. Edmund the
Martyr with its simple beauty, its quiet dignity and
the attentive country folk.

Tormented by an all too familiar depression, he
had left the Lodge to go for a walk, turning towards
the village without much caring in which direction
he went. Lost in thought, he had scarcely known
where he was until he was brought out of his reverie
by the slightly irascible voice of an elderly gentleman. Waldo discovered that he was standing by the
church gate and impeding the man's passage. With
a word of apology, he had moved aside, but
remained to study the church thoughtfully. He
recalled his meeting with the Vicar earlier in the
week, and remembered that he had been impressed
by the man's gentle dignity and quiet charm, the
warm sincerity of voice and manner. Waldo knew
that he had been recognised, and yet there had been
no hint of a mention of his books or his television
appearances or the recent revelations about his
private life. That kind of sensitivity was rare and
very welcome. On an impulse he had walked
through the gate and followed the elderly gentleman down the gravel path to the door of the church.

On his way to the village, he had been a seething
mass of impotent fury and bitter despair. Emerging
from the cool shadows of the old church into
brilliant sunshine, he felt that he had gained
something from that brief communion with God
and his fellow men and there was the first faint
stirring of hope in the depths of his being.

The past few months had been very black for
Waldo. There had been all the unwelcome publicity
of the accident, the shock of learning that Dorian
was dead, the heaviness of guilt and the darkness of
despair, the pain of his own injuries and the terrible
fear that he might never walk again. That fear had
proved groundless, but his recovery had been slow
and painful and he was still far from fit. He did not
need the doctors to tell him that a full return to
health was prevented by psychological rather than
physical causes.

He had agreed to Colin's suggestion that he
should spend the summer in Inskip without any
belief in the therapeutic qualities of a country
village. He was merely thankful to escape from the
reminders and the demands of town. Colin was a
friend as well as a cousin and understood him better
than most.

It had seemed the ideal set-up for a writer whose
publisher was anxiously awaiting delivery of his
next book. Colin taught at the private school which
occupied the near-by Manor House and his time was
very full. So Waldo would have long days to himself,
peace and privacy and the opportunity to work
without interruption. But things were not working
out as planned.

He had felt immediately at home in the old,
rambling house with its large and airy rooms and
its comfortable, well-worn furniture. Colin's housekeeper was a rare treasure, and she took Waldo
under her motherly wing, evidently touched by the
marks of suffering on his handsome face. He fell
easily into the habit of wandering into the kitchen
on some pretext and lingering to while away half an
hour in conversation with Mrs. Hunsley. She was a

small, bustling dumpling of a woman, talkative always cheerful, hard-working and happy and she had a fund of stories about the village, her neighbours and the ways of the country.

He also found it very pleasant to stroll along the lanes and through the fields, to explore the village or to find shade from the hot sun in the small copse that brought him so unexpectedly to the quiet lake in a sunlit glade. He liked to walk along the banks of the stream that ran through the fields to join with the river that cut the village in half. It was many years since he had given himself up to the simple delights of life in the country, and he took pleasure in discovering them all over again.

In fact, he found it much more to his taste to talk to Mrs. Hunsley than to turn his thoughts to the book he was supposed to be writing: far more attractive to explore his new surroundings than to sit at a desk and stare without inspiration at his typewriter. He had blamed his previous failure to write on the distractions of town life, the demands of his many friends, the attractions of a full social life the pain which still troubled him and the inability to forget the past—only to discover now that the fault lay within himself, and that the rot had set in from the first moment of his longing for the lovely desirable and demanding Dorian Leigh.

So much seemed to have been destroyed by the disastrous enchantment of a woman's possessiveness—his peace of mind, his self-respect his concentration, his very desire to write. All had been lost in the fierce, passionate flame of longing for Dorian. Love it had never been. He shrank from the thought that her untimely death had brough him release—but it was true, none the less. He was

ucky to have escaped with his life—he seemed to
have salvaged little else. Even the work which was
so important to him had suffered badly, becoming
an unwelcome, difficult, meaningless chore instead
of a stimulus that mind and spirit needed for well-
being. Without the compelling incentive of his
writing and the satisfaction it had always brought
him, there seemed to be very little purpose to his life.

It was not enough that there had been several
books, that many had been published in other
countries and in other languages, that one of them
had become a very successful film with Dorian
Leigh as its star. He was only concerned with the
next book—and all the books he had once believed
himself capable of producing. Now he doubted if he
would write again, if there was another book in him.

Those and like thoughts had brought him to such
a pitch of depression that he had found it impossible
to remain in the house.

Now he was glad that he had followed his
impulse and entered the church. The familiar
rituals had soothed him, and his heart was a little
lighter. Perhaps he needed the peace and the
harmony that this small village seemed to provide,
and Colin was the easiest and most undemanding of
companions...

Waldo received a warm handshake from the
Vicar who reminded him of their meeting earlier in
the week. There was little time for conversation, but
Michael threw out a casual invitation to him to call
at the Vicarage whenever he was passing.

Waldo nodded, smiling. "Thank you, I'll take you
up on that," he said. "My cousin tells me that you
have an excellent library."

"Entirely at your disposal," Michael assured

him, and turned to shake hands and exchange
greetings with a waiting parishioner.

Marian, surrounded by friends, called Waldo's
name as though she had known him for years, and
beckoned to him in the careless assumption that he
would leap to her bidding. But he merely smiled and
gave her a friendly, casual wave of his hand before
turning away.

Lucy stood by the church door, having joined her
father just too late to share in that brief exchange
with the writer. She looked after him as he made his
way slowly and heavily down the gravel path. She
wanted so much to meet him. She had known and
loved his books for years, and whenever she saw
him on the television screen or read yet another
article about him, she felt a familiar glow of
admiration and longed to know him.

Lucy was delighted that he had come to spend the
summer at the Lodge but, unlike her sister, she did
not suppose that their friendship with Colin gave
them an automatic right to intimacy with his
cousin. Waldo McKinnon did not seem to be in a
sociable frame of mind, and that was understandable when one recalled that he was convalescing
from a car crash. He had every reason to shun
company, Lucy decided, thinking of the woman he
had loved and lost and obviously mourned.

It was impossible for her to have been ignorant of
that affair and its tragic sequel but she had always
refrained from comment. She had no right to judge
others, she felt, and she firmly believed that every
act, good or bad, reaped its own harvest. She was
more concerned for the suffering that must have
followed that accident.

...The all-too-familiar depression stealing over

him, Waldo abruptly abandoned the typewriter. He had foolishly allowed optimism to overrule instinct and had sat down at the desk with the hope that the words might flow once more.

Stiffly, awkwardly, conscious of pain in his leg, he rose for his stick and made his way to the window. Opening it wide, he leaned out to take a deep breath. The sky was very blue and almost cloudless. The sun was high and golden on this lovely afternoon. It was very still, very peaceful.

Beneath the window there was a bank of flowers that permeated the air with perfume. Waldo could hear the soft humming of insects, and he was suddenly startled by the loud chirrup of the cheeky blackbird who seemed to be a permanent tenant of a near-by tree.

His spirits might have lifted as he surveyed the beauty of his surroundings if he had not suddenly been aware of the approach of his cousin and a young woman whom he particularly wished to avoid. He did not deny her beauty; she looked very well in the white linen suit she was wearing that afternoon. No doubt she was a very attractive girl and used to instant admiration from every man she met. But Waldo was in no mood to be drawn into polite conversation with anyone just then, least of all with the girl who had made a determined attempt to flirt with him at their first meeting. She seemed unable to appreciate his complete lack of interest in her or any other woman at this particular time.

He admitted that Colin must be expected to entertain his friends as usual; and he realised that some degree of effort would be required of him as Colin's house guest and cousin. But he had hoped for very little contact with people, and that included the beautiful girl who had obviously lined him up as her next victim.

He drew back from the window, hoping he had not been seen. The silent typewriter taunted him and he stared at it for a moment, frowning. Then he left the room that Colin had so optimistically offered to him as a study, and decided to go for another walk. His innate restlessness and dissatisfaction with himself could only find ease in walking for miles. It made his leg ache, but it tired him so that he slept at night without the pills which he had been alarmed to discover were rapidly becoming a habit.

He slipped out of the house and down the drive.

If only one could turn back the clock. If only he could go back to the time of that untroubled existence when he had worked at his books and articles with single-minded dedication, found pleasure and delight in the company of his friends, and considered himself to be a happy and fortunate man. If only he could re-live that first meeting with Dorian—and alter the outcome...

They had met at a party to celebrate the sale of the film rights of his book to the company which had the beautiful actress under contract. Waldo had been drawn by the magnet of her beauty, the famous allure, the fatal fascination that she wielded for almost every man. A warm and sensual and thoroughly spoilt young woman who took what she wanted without a care for the consequences, she had always considered the world well lost for love. She wanted Waldo McKinnon; and he had proved to be an easy conquest.

Dorian wanted marriage. It did not matter that

she was still legally tied to Joel Young. One
married—one became bored—one divorced—one
married again. But Waldo knew that while his
passion for Dorian might temporarily chase everything else from his mind, he did not love her; and the
very fierceness of the flame indicated that it would
swiftly burn itself out.

Marriage to Dorian would be a disaster, he
realised. She was hungry for attention, greedy in
her demands, jealous of everything that encroached
on the time or interest that she believed to be hers by
right of loving. She was like a greedy, selfish child,
wanting to own him completely.

The day finally dawned when he knew that he
had neglected his work for too long and must make
an effort to get back to it ... and quickly found that
he was lacking in all desire to write. His obsession
with Dorian had apparently drained him of all
inspiration and enthusiasm for his work. He
struggled to recapture the former enjoyment of
writing, but found it impossible. Then he began to
resent the demands that she continued to make on
him. She accused him of neglect, and the ugly
jealousy was unmistakable. It was how it would
always be—and he knew he must break with her
before she completely destroyed his ability as a
writer.

She could not bear to lose him. She had stormed
at him, struck at him and, finally, beside herself
with rage and fear, she had wrenched at the wheel of
his car and sent it spinning off the road in an
attempt to destroy them both. She had been killed
instantly; and Waldo would carry the scars of that
tragic accident for the rest of his life, both mentally
and physically.

He had emerged from the affair a saddened man, lame in mind and body. He was also burdened with a sense of guilt.

He knew only too well that he had never loved Dorian. He had been bound to her by the fierce demands of the senses; and he had been a fool and a rogue to allow the affair to go on for so long. It was true that he had never expected her to care for him with such jealous and lasting passion, for he had not supposed her capable of anything more than a fleeting attachment to any man. But he should have heeded the danger signals early in their relationship and broken with her long before he was so important to her.

He had so much to regret but he had learned an important lesson. It would be a very long time before he allowed another woman to play havoc with his emotions, and then he would be extremely cautious in his choice.

Towards evening, Waldo wearily made his way back to the Lodge, longing for a hot bath, a meal and a quiet evening with the books and music he loved. He limped along the narrow lane, his leg aching badly, admitting the need to lean heavily on the stick which was a constant and intolerable reminder of the past...

Dreaming, Lucy cycled along, with a parcel of parish magazines in her basket. It was a quiet lane, seldom used by traffic; and she carelessly allowed her cycle to wander in common with her thoughts. As Waldo McKinnon unexpectedly rounded the corner, appearing directly in front of her, she swerved violently, wobbled dangerously for a moment or two and then lurched into the ditch, landing among the brambles that scratched and nettles that stung.

"Of all the stupid idiots!" Waldo flared involuntarily, having wrenched his leg quite painfully as he leapt to one side to avoid a collision.

"I'm so sorry!" Lucy cried in distress, too thankful to have avoided him to care for his outburst or her own predicament. "Are you all right?"

"Yes, of course...I wasn't thinking." Lucy struggled to extricate herself from bike and brambles and was scratched all over again for her pains. She looked up at the tall man who still regarded her with angry eyes. "I do hope I haven't hurt you," she said anxiously.

"You missed me by some miracle," he told her curtly. "It's no thanks to you that I'm not sprawling in that ditch!"

Furious with herself, she suddenly flared: "Well, I am sprawling in this ditch and it would be to your credit if you made a move to help me out of it!"

Waldo stared at her in astonishment; and then his anger gave way to amusement. "The infernal cheek of the young!" he exclaimed but he went towards her. "Here, give me your hand."

Momentarily, Lucy had forgotten his disability. Her face flamed as he moved to assist her and betrayed an inevitable awkwardness. "Oh, do be careful!" she exclaimed anxiously—and could have bitten out her tongue as he stiffened in swift resentment.

"Why? Do you bite as well?" he demanded dryly. He held out his hand and she took it after a momentary hesitation. She scrambled to her feet.

He was a tall man and her head came just level with his heart. Waldo looked down at the youthful, flushed face, and the obvious distress in the wide hazel eyes made him regret his sharpness. She was very young and she had meant well; and he must learn not to bridle at the least reference to his lameness, he thought wryly. He retained the small scratched hand within his own for a moment and said with concern that atoned for his first fury: "How about you? No bones broken, I hope?"

"Oh, I'm fine," she assured him hastily. Heartened by his tone, she added gently: "I'm afraid I frightened you."

Waldo was surprised by the soft words. For he had been frightened, taken by surprise and knowing the swift fear of going down and injuring his leg all over again and putting back his recovery by heaven knew how long. It had been fear that found its vent in anger, combined with relief that it had been merely a girl on a cycle and not a speeding car that had rounded the corner. He was partly to blame—he should have known better than to walk in the middle of the road. But he was not a man to admit how near her words came to the truth, or to reveal his astonishment at her perception.

"Oh, out of my wits," he said dryly. He looked down at her with a faint smile. There was a slight trickle of blood oozing from a scratch on her cheek. Almost absently, he produced a handkerchief and wiped it away.

Lucy stood still and unprotesting, and hoped he did not sense the tumult within her startled heart. "It's only a scratch, isn't it?" she asked as she stepped back.

He nodded. "You'll live," he told her lightly. "But that was a nasty tumble; you must be feeling shaken."

Lucy shook her head. "No, I'm all right," she said cheerfully. "I've no one to blame but myself." She bent to rescue her cycle from the ditch and regarded it ruefully. "Just look at that wheel! Thank goodness I'm not far from home!"

"Where is home?" he asked curiously.

"The Vicarage. I'm Lucy Cope, the Vicar's daughter." She looked up and saw laughter dawn in his eyes and she smiled suddenly, radiantly. "It does sound rather like Happy Families," she agreed lightly—and again Waldo was surprised by a perception that lifted the very thought from his mind so swiftly.

He was also surprised to discover that this was the sister of the beautiful Marian.

Lucy stooped to gather up the scattered magazines—and wished she was not wearing what must be the oldest dress she possessed, a shabby cotton that she had chosen for its coolness, having changed on reaching home that evening. Pottering happily in the garden, she had reluctantly recalled her promise to deliver the parish magazines, and she had not bothered to change her dress before setting out. Now she felt grubby and untidy and could not rid herself of the conviction that Waldo McKinnon supposed her to be a mere schoolgirl. It was very natural in view of her old dress and sandals and dishevelled appearance.

Waldo studied her thoughtfully, knowing a faint stirring of interest. She was very young, about seventeen, he supposed, an appealing child with a swift, warm smile and clear, candid eyes. She still bore the bloom of innocence and that was rare in this day and age.

"I've met your father and your sister—but where have you been hiding?" he asked lightly.

Lucy looked up, and the hint of warmth in his gaze caused her heart to beat faster. "I wish we might have met in happier circumstances," she said, and she smiled at him with an easy friendliness that did not betray the tide of emotion he had so unexpectedly evoked.

"But I haven't introduced myself..." he began.

"No need," Lucy said lightly. "Everyone knows who you are and..." She broke off, feeling that the words she had almost uttered might have been tactless.

"...And all about me," he finished. "I suppose that was to be expected."

"This is a small village," Lucy reminded him. "We would be interested in any newcomer; and you are a more exciting newcomer than most, you must admit. It isn't every day that a celebrity comes to stay in Inskip. Of course it was to be expected that your arrival would cause a flutter of excitement and a great deal of talk."

"You are right," he agreed, amused by a faint reproof in her tone. "And I should like it even less if no one recognised me or talked about me—as you are burning to point out!"

Lucy laughed. "Perhaps, but I've been nicely reared as becomes a Vicar's daughter," she told him demurely, and turned her bike to face the way she had come.

He fell into step beside her as she began to walk

towards her home, pushing the damaged cycle; and they talked lightly of Colin, of Waldo's intention to stay for some weeks, of the village and, briefly, of his books. Lucy discovered that he was even nicer than she had anticipated.

Very shortly, they reached the gates of the Lodge. "Are you sure you feel all right?" Waldo asked, smiling down at her. "Why not come up to the house with me for a cup of tea? I'm sure that Mrs. Hunsley has something for those scratches, too."

"Old-fashioned iodine—and I'm a terrible coward!" Lucy told him, laughing. "I'm fine, really—and I shall be home in five minutes."

He held out his hand and she placed hers within it, a little shyly. "We shall meet again," he said, a certain promise in his dark eyes as he looked down at her.

Lucy nodded. "I imagine so," she returned lightly, although the warmth of his smile completed his all-unconscious conquest of her heart. "Inskip is a very small place!"

Waldo looked after her, wondering if she was so inexperienced that she did not recognise the implication in his words—or if the reputation which had probably preceded him made her wary of granting them the importance they deserved. For he meant to know much more of Lucy Cope. The shy, pretty girl possessed an appeal that the tempestuous and lovely Dorian had lacked. And at least Lucy was not setting her cap at him at first sight!

Dreading a repetition of the kind of affair which had already caused so much havoc in his life, he had instinctively erected a barrier to protect himself from Marian Cope's bewitching beauty. But Lucy did not represent any threat to his peace of mind and he believed that they could be friends without fear of complications.

CHAPTER TWO

It was another golden day. Bright sunshine had replaced the early morning mist and there was not a cloud in the very blue sky. The brilliant rays of the sun streamed through the curved window of the little antique shop, highlighting the dust that rose as its youthful occupant busied herself with the morning routine, finding every hint of gold in the warm chestnut of her hair, brightening every corner of the crowded yet orderly room.

Lucy loved her work, and handled each item with loving care and conscientious attention to dusty nooks and crannies, but on this lovely morning she

could not help glancing wistfully at the bright world
beyond the shop window.

It had been a lovely spring, holding so much
promise—of what she had not been sure, but deep in
her being hugging to herself the premonition that
something wonderful would surely happen soon.

And now, with the advent of summer, it had
happened.

Like every girl, Lucy had cherished a dream of
the one man in all the world who was destined to
sweep her into the ecstasy of loving and take her
into a new life as his bride...and her dream lover
had worn the handsome face of Waldo McKinnon
long before they met.

But dreams so seldom came true, and even in the
wildest flights of fancy Lucy had known that this
was one dream that could never know fulfillment.
For while she realised the possibility of meeting
Colin's cousin one day, she faced the fact that he
would not consider her attractive or interesting. She
was too young, too inexperienced, too
unsophisticated—far from beautiful or glamorous;
and Waldo McKinnon chose his women friends
from the ranks of stage and screen stars.

There had been a dream-like quality about their
encounter. She had almost pinched herself to
discover if she was asleep, but she had been too
conscious of her smarting face and arms to doubt
that she really had tumbled into that bramble bush.
Nor did she doubt that she had tumbled into love; for
the new, bewildering, tumultuous and breathless
delight still remained with her.

If she were younger and less practical, she might
be tempted to snatch at the golden opportunity of

his friendliness and even attempt to throw herself at his head. She might even be foolish enough to imagine that she could catch him 'on the rebound'. But Lucy had her feet firmly on the ground, even if her head and heart were full of sweet, impossible dreams.

She knew by instinct that he hoped for her friendship. But she must come to terms with the feeling he had evoked so swiftly and so surely before she committed herself to any degree of association with him. She must discipline herself into absolute contentment with the very little he would offer—for only a fool would expect more than casual, light-hearted friendship with a man who had known and loved the beautiful and fascinating Dorian Leigh . . .

The forgotten duster clutched tightly in her hand, eyes full of stars, Lucy re-lived the magical moments of her encounter with Waldo. It might have been painful, embarrassing, humiliating and fraught with emotional tension, but it had still managed to be wonderful. Her eager heart had leapt in swift response to the smile which lingered in his eyes long after his lips had ceased to curve. She recalled the sudden tingling of her body at his touch as he had dealt with her scratched face—much as he might have tended a child, she knew, but that did not detract from the impulse that had moved him. She was confirmed in her belief that he was a gentle, kindly man with a warm heart and a swift under-standing.

She had fallen so suddenly, so swiftly in love with him, and she knew that he would be her love for the rest of her life. She understood that there was no future in loving him, but it was much too late to retrieve her heart. She had always known that love, when it came, would be like this for her; but she had never supposed that it would mean the end rather than the beginning of a dream...

She almost jumped out of her skin at the sound of a man's voice behind her. It was not unexpected of course—it was simply that she had been lost in that enchanting world of her own.

Daniel Pegrim smiled indulgently. "Dreaming again, Lucy," he said gently. He understood her as few people did, and she was very dear to him although she might not appreciate the full extent of his affection. He was just Daniel—friend and confidant, good-natured, reliable, sympathetic— and he was content that she should regard him in that light. For there were too many years between them for him even to indulge the hope that she might marry him one day.

He was tall and lean with ascetic features and a natural reserve in his manner that belied the warm passion of the man beneath. His hair was just beginning to silver at the temples and there were faint lines about his eyes and mouth.

He had never married, partly because he had never been in love, and partly because he had always devoted too much time to his beloved books and antiques and neglected the social side of his existence. Now that he realised the lack in his life he considered himself too much of a bachelor and Lucy much too young to be tied to a serious-minded man like himself. His feeling for her did not consume him with passion. He was content to care for her in his own quiet way without expecting anything in return but the easy, light-hearted affection that she had bestowed on him since her childhood.

"Oh, is it coffee time? The morning has flown!" She tucked her duster into the pocket of her yellow overall. "No customers today, I'm afraid," she added blithely, knowing his indifference to such practical considerations. He welcomed callers who shared his own feeling for lovely things: he loved to show off his treasures, to explain their history, to describe their beauty and marvel at the craft of earlier times; but he seldom cared to part with a possession. He was a collector above all. He did not need to earn his daily bread, and he could well afford to add to his collection of beautiful things. The shop was simply part and parcel of his hobby.

He did not really need an assistant. But Lucy's presence in the shop left him free to visit sales in search of more treasures, to attend meetings of the local antiquarian society, to spend long hours poring over his books and writing his 'History of British Porcelain'. Lucy dusted, kept the accounts and enjoyed talking to those who came to the shop, some to look and some to chat and, more rarely, some to buy.

On leaving school Lucy had declared her intention of getting a job. Marian was then working as a designer for a textile company in the near-by town: Helen was secretary to the headmaster at the Manor School—hence the family's close association with Colin—and Clare was helping to run the local riding-stables. Lucy did not want to stay at home, although she was invaluable to her father in many ways; at the same time, she did not know what kind of career she wanted. Daniel and her father had put their heads together and hit on a solution which pleased everyone.

Lucy had been delighted. She was fond of Daniel,

and he had taught her to love and cherish beautiful things. She enjoyed looking after the shop, and Daniel was ridiculously generous in the matter of salary, especially when she had so little to spend it on.

Daniel went to the shop door and turned over the large printed card that hung there. The side with the word 'OPEN' was now visible to the world.

Lucy bit her lip. No wonder there had been no customers.

"I'm sorry," she said, knowing that her head and heart had been too full of Waldo McKinnon for mundane details. "I don't know how I came to forget!"

Daniel smiled. "How about that coffee?" he suggested. "I'll hold the fort." Lucy went through to the rooms behind the shop. A moment later the shop door opened and Daniel looked up from the catalogue he was studying.

Marian swept in, smiling, and Daniel reflected that it was impossible for her not to make an entrance.

"Don't be anxious, I haven't come for any of your treasures!" she announced. "I just thought you might like to give me a cup of coffee."

"Well timed," Daniel said. "Lucy is making it this very moment." He went to the open doorway. "Make that coffee for three, will you?" he called. "We have a visitor."

"How formal!" Marian drawled as she settled herself in a carved oak chair. "I'm not a visitor, Daniel." She smiled at him with all the confidence of a beautiful woman who does not consider any man too old to be stirred by her golden loveliness— and anyway Daniel was not very old.

Her bright, blonde hair, cut short in a sleek, boyish style that enhanced her femininity, was a gleaming cap of gold in the sunlight that fell across her chair. She was cool and elegant in the brown linen dress that left her arms and throat bare, and was short enough to reveal the slender shapeliness of long legs.

"We don't see very much of you," Daniel said, perching on the edge of the old desk that dominated a corner of the room. "Not working today?"

Marian shook her head. She had left the textile company to try her hand as a free-lance designer and she was enjoying a certain success. She worked at home and she worked when she wished—which suited her well, for she enjoyed a full social life and the earlier nine-to-five job had cramped her style considerably.

"It's much too hot," she returned carelessly, rummaging in her handbag. She found cigarettes but no lighter. She looked across at Daniel expectantly and, a fraction too late, he produced a box of matches from his pocket. As he held the match to her cigarette, she placed her fingers lightly over his hand to steady the flame and smiled provocatively into his eyes.

Daniel extinguished the match and returned to his safe corner; and Marian smiled faintly as he put as much distance as possible between them. She smiled—but she felt annoyed. Did he think she might throw herself into his arms if he gave her but half a chance? She was not such a fool! She wondered for the thousandth time if he had ever held a woman in his arms. It was hard to accept that any man could be as cold as he pretended, as indifferent as he seemed to an appeal that other men

found irresistible. It irked her—and not for the first
time. For years, Marian had been trying to break
through the cool, austere reserve of this man; and
for years he had been holding her at arm's length,
treating her with an avuncular indulgence that she
found infuriating.

It was strange how he sapped her confidence. He
seemed to offer some kind of a challenge that she
always failed to meet, and she invariably left him
with the uncomfortable fancy that she was not as
enchanting or as desirable as she believed herself to
be. But there was always another man—more than
one, indeed—to assure her that the fault lay with
Daniel and not herself.

Daniel regarded her thoughtfully. Flirting came
as naturally as breathing to Marian—and he
wished he could dismiss it as lightly as it deserved.
He was never wholly at ease with her, for she made
unwelcome demands on him, evoking thoughts and
feelings that he swiftly suppressed. He did not mean
to make the mistake of letting her know that he was
as vulnerable as any other man; he did not doubt
that she would compare him unfavourably with the
younger men who swarmed about her. She thought
him dull and unattractive, he knew—she practised
the art of flirtation on him merely because she was
so sure that there was no risk of burning her fingers
at that flame.

"You look very cool," he said, a little abruptly.

"Do I? I don't feel cool," she said. She kicked off
her high-heeled sandals and wriggled her slender
toes with a little sigh of relief. "I hate shopping," she
added.

"Is that what you've been doing?"

She nodded. "That's the biggest drawback to working at home, you know. If anyone is rushed for time they take it for granted that I can drop whatever I'm doing and help out."

"You said it was too hot to work," he reminded her, smiling.

"So I did. It's also too hot for shopping. I should love a dip in the lake right now. In fact I'm tempted to do a little trespassing this afternoon," she said lightly.

It could scarcely be called trespassing for the lake was part of the Lodge grounds, and Colin McKinnon was a friend who would never object to anyone making use of the water. But Daniel frowned, convinced that Marian was not so interested in a cooling swim as in the possibility of meeting Colin's cousin. She made no secret of her interest in the man.

Reading his thoughts, she wrinkled her shapely nose. "I might run into our celebrity," she said with deliberate provocation. "One never knows."

Daniel moved impatiently. It seemed to him that every woman in the district was ready to run after a man who had already set the village by its ears. And all because he had been involved in a highly unpleasant scandal. Any girl with sense would surely take care to avoid a man with such a reputation—but he knew enough about Marian to realise that the man's past only enhanced his attraction in her eyes.

It was none of his business, of course—and he was quite indifferent to Marian's many affairs. But this was rather different. The man obviously had a way with women, and Marian might so easily lose her head over him and find herself in serious trouble. Daniel could not help feeling a natural anxiety.

"I understood that he came here to rest and recuperate," he said, rather stiffly. "It would be a kindness in us all to leave the poor man in peace."

Marian laughed, not at all deceived by this spurious concern. "Actually, I suspect he had heard of the legendary charms of the Cope girls and came here to find out for himself if we really exist. He's a little too late to see Clare or Helen, and Lucy is really too much of an innocent for him; but I'm ready and willing to restore him to health if that's what he wants," she said.

Daniel smiled humourlessly. She was teasing, of course. But that laughing confidence jarred him a little. Oh, it was not really her fault. She was a beautiful woman, and she had never lacked for someone to tell her so; but Daniel sometimes felt that beauty could be shadowed by the very realisation of its impact.

Lucy was refreshingly unaware of her own quiet loveliness, he thought, as she came in with the heavy tray which he took from her with a word of reproach. She was so very different from her sister and perhaps her very appeal lay in that. He smiled down at her with warm affection.

Marian noticed the tenderness in that smile, and although she was familiar with their affection for each other she felt an odd little pang as she realised it once more. She could not help comparing that warm intimacy with the cool, courteous indifference in his manner towards herself. Oh, well, there were plenty of men in the world, and most of them were more interesting and certainly more responsive than Daniel Pegrim.

Lucy had recognised her sister's voice and she was a little surprised for Marian seldom came to the shop, frankly admitting to being bored by old things. Daniel bored her, too—but she could never resist trying to flirt with him, claiming that he was a dull dog who needed stirring up a little.

It never seemed to occur to Marian that she might stir him up too much and make him unhappy. After all, he was a man like any other, and men seemed to find Marian very attractive. It was surely not impossible that Daniel might fall in love with her. He was just a little too distant with Marian most of the time, and Lucy often wondered if that was his protective barrier against an attraction he refused to admit. She would never make the mistake of suggesting that possibility to Marian, of course; because her sister would laugh with delight and set out to achieve the final conquest as though she needed further proof that she was lovable as well as lovely.

Lucy did not envy her beautiful sister. She loved her and was a little saddened by the restless pursuit of a happiness that continued to elude her. For beauty and vitality and popularity did not automatically secure the lasting love of any man. Marian might declare that she was wedded to her work, and did not want to be tied down to one man and the humdrum domesticity of marriage, but Lucy was not deceived. She knew that at heart Marian was as eager as any woman for a husband, home and children of her own.

Marian constantly sought love, and Lucy felt

that she looked too hard and might never find it. For
herself, she had not thought seriously about love
and marriage. Her dreams were a youthful indul
gence with little connection with reality. The men in
her life were merely friends. She had not believed
that she was ready for the demands of loving. She
had certainly not expected to fall in love so suddenly
with a total stranger. But it did not occur to her to
doubt the feeling that had sprung to life at a smile, a
touch, a word. Although deep in her heart she knew
that she could never mean anything to Waldo
McKinnon, she also knew that she could never cease
to love him...

Daniel was the most hospitable of men, but he
was impatient for Marian to finish her coffee and
leave. She seemed to be idling away the morning
because she had nothing better to do—and he was
convinced that she was aware of his discomfiture
and enjoying it.

He found her very irritating that day as she sat in
the old chair, making idle conversation, smoking
too many cigarettes. He did not pause to analyse his
annoyance with her. If he had, he might have been
forced to admit that it was her golden beauty and
the hint of sensuality in her slender, long-limbed
body that compelled him to an awareness of a desire
that he fought to ignore and struggled to control.

Their eyes met once more across the room.
Holding his gaze, she blew a smoke ring, and smiled
slowly through the wreathing blue haze.

Daniel replaced his empty coffee cup in the saucer
with a sharp clink and rose to his feet. "I'm going
out now, Lucy," he said abruptly. "There's a sale at
Hippingham Hall today—I told you I meant to go

idn't I? I think it will be as well to make an early tart. You can manage on your own, can't you?"

"Yes, of course I can," she assured him. She often id, she thought dryly, a little startled by his nusual brusqueness. She had known about the sale ut this sudden decision to 'make an early start' was oth unexpected and out of character. Daniel was ot prone to impulses, being a man who liked to rganise and plan, and he usually stuck to his ecisions. She knew that he had arranged for an arly lunch at home before driving the few miles to he Hall, but she knew better than to make any nention of the fact. Daniel obviously had a reason or changing his plans so suddenly, and Lucy ancied that she could guess at it.

Marian leaned forward to stub out her cigarette. You might drop me off on your way," she said. "I'm aving clutch trouble with the car. I've left it with larry at the garage to be checked—and these andals weren't made for walking in."

"Oh, Marian!" Lucy exclaimed. "You only came o cadge a lift!"

Marian laughed. "True! I heard you mention at reakfast that Daniel meant to go to Hippingham oday and I thought he might be leaving about this ime. You don't mind, do you, Daniel?"

"Not at all," he said coolly.

She rose and went to him, tucking her hand in his rm and laughing up at him. "You do, actually. ou're just too polite to refuse me—and I traded on hat! You should know by now that I'm quite nscrupulous about using people."

Detaching her hand from his arm, he moved way, ostensibly to pick up the catalogue that lay on the desk. "Don't be silly, Marian," he said in a tone that would have crushed a more sensitive person. " don't mind being used. The Vicarage is on my way after all."

"Oh, I'm not lunching at home," she said blithely. "I'm meeting Nevil Joslin at the Cap and Bells." She referred to a man whom Daniel had met once and disliked on sight, and to a roadhouse that was currently popular with her set. She glanced at her watch. "I'll be a little early, I expect; but that will give us time for a drink together before you go on to the Hall."

There was nothing that Daniel could say to extricate himself without being rude; but he was determined not to be pressured into drinking with her until her escort arrived.

He looked at her with reluctant amusement in his eyes. She did not even pretend to subtlety, he thought, and if he allowed himself to be used, then he had no one to blame but himself. "You really are an outrageous minx, Marian," he told her without censure.

She beamed. "I know. You won't mind if we stop briefly at home—it's only to unload the groceries?"

"Where are they?" Lucy asked, looking in vain for a basket or shopping bag.

"Still in the boot of the car—but I don't think ought to leave them there, do you? I don't know what time I'll be back, and the frozen foods would probably melt. By the way, I told Harry that you' pick up the car this evening—is that all right? I'll leave the keys with him."

She swept Daniel out of the shop and across the road to the garage where she took the groceries from the boot, exchanged a few words with Harry and then accompanied Daniel to his car. Lucy watched and waved as they drove away, scarcely knowing whether to be amused or exasperated by her sister. Heaven help the man she decided to marry, Lucy thought, smiling. He would find himself at the altar long before it even crossed his mind to propose! Poor Daniel had tried to escape from Marian only to be caught more firmly in her coils; and now he was on his way to Hippingham hours before he had planned to go.

Lucy went back into the shop to carry on with the interrupted chore of dusting. She was reluctant to leave the warm sunshine, and she felt ridiculously forlorn at having been abandoned so abruptly. The rest of the day stretched before her, seemingly long and lonely; and she could not be sure of even a glimpse of Waldo McKinnon to cheer her.

She was quite unaware that he was at that very moment coming out of the small tobacconist's shop on the other side of the street.

Waldo stood still for a moment or two, leaning on his stick, looking up and down the village street with interest and the beginning of affection, absorbing its atmosphere and discovering in himself a desire to 'belong'. It was many years since he had spent much time in the country, and it was only now that he was aware of having missed all that it could offer a man like himself.

Inskip was a gentle, charming village with a warmth and personality all its own. Its people were plain and simple folk who went about their work and enjoyed their quiet pleasures and lived with each other on reasonably good terms for the most part.

Waldo was beginning to feel that he knew the

village. Each day, as he went about and encountered its people, he felt that he was gradually becoming accepted, and the earlier suspicion and disapproval were giving way to a hint of friendliness.

His glance encountered the antique shop with its old-fashioned bow window. He had seen it before and made a mental note to explore it. Now was as good a time as any, he decided. He needed a birthday present for Rowena. She collected antique jewellery and there might just be something of the kind in that small shop.

Entering, he stopped short as Lucy turned with a swift smile for a customer—a smile that faded with the shock of seeing him and returned with greater warmth at the tide of pleasure that flooded her being.

"What are you doing here?" Waldo asked, smiling back. The question required no answer—it was perfectly obvious from her overall and the duster in her hand that she was working in the shop. Or perhaps owned it, he thought. For she was certainly not the schoolgirl he had assumed her to be. The pretty overall gave her a demure dignity that the child in the cotton frock had lacked. "You look very efficient," he said.

Lucy thought wryly that she did not particularly want him to regard her as just an efficient shop assistant. "I'm the practical Cope," she returned lightly. "There has to be one in every family."

He grinned. "The smudge on your cheek rather ruins the image."

Her hand flew to her face, and she looked instinctively for a mirror. "Where...?"

Waldo went to her, put his fingers beneath her chin and turned her face towards the light from the window. "It's a bruise!" he exclaimed in surprised concern, gently touching the faint shadow.

"Oh, that! Yes, I must have hit my face on a stone or something when I fell," she said, silently marvelling that he could be so close and seem so unaware of the noisy pounding of her heart. She was both alarmed and excited by the careless intimacy in his manner. She stood very still, conscious of his nearness and hoping he would not sense the tumult of her emotions.

Waldo was a little disturbed by the trust that allowed a virtual stranger the easy familiarity of friendship. He was to be trusted, but she could not know it—such innocent unawareness of the dangers that might threaten an inexperienced girl was rare and made her very vulnerable. Perhaps her very innocence gave her protection, however. It would certainly deter the average man from betraying the shining trust in those hazel eyes. For himself, it was not desire that stirred as he looked down at her, but an odd little surge of tenderness.

"How are the scratches this morning?" he asked, releasing her and moving away.

"Better than the bike," Lucy returned.

Waldo laughed. "It was on its last legs, anyway—admit it!" he said with perfect truth. "Due for retirement."

"Yes, I know, but it is useful!"

"Which is more than can be said for most antiques," he agreed, his eyes twinkling.

Lucy smiled. "It isn't that old! It only needs a new wheel, and the garage over the road will see to that for me." She hesitated and then added, a little shyly: "How about you? No ill effects, I hope?"

"I'm fine, and all the better for seeing you, anyway," he said promptly and not very seriously— and was astonished when a delicious warmth stole into her face. It had been a careless enough remark. But she had undoubtedly blushed.

The words had been uttered too lightly for any sensible girl to attach importance to them, but Lucy was not feeling very sensible at the moment. She was in love—and the more she saw of Waldo McKinnon the more convinced she was that she had been born to love him. With every word, every gesture, every smile, he seemed to penetrate farther into her heart. And perhaps the warmth in his eyes and voice meant that he liked her a little, she thought hopefully.

Waldo picked up a miniature in a frame. "This is charming!" he exclaimed. "I came to find a present for someone, but I must have this for myself." He studied it closely. "Yes, it's good! Now, I want a piece of jewellery, I think—women always like jewellery, don't they? Something old and good— rings, brooches. Can you show me something?"

Lucy's heart plummeted. But she brought a tray of assorted jewellery and talked intelligently of designs and stones and fastenings while a part of her mind worried at the implication in his words.

A present for a woman...and the care he was taking over his choice implied that she played an important part in his life. Well, he was attractive and wealthy and famous, and he must have many women friends.

Lucy reminded herself that they were virtual

strangers and that he could feel only a passing
interest in her. It was impossible that he should find
her attractive or interesting, and it would be
dangerous to misinterpret the charm in his smile,
the warmth in his eyes, the friendliness in his voice.
But though she knew it was folly to want him, she
could not help aching for him.

His dark head bowed over the jewellery, Waldo
was unaware of her intent gaze or the wealth of love
in those hazel eyes as she regarded him. He could
not guess at the thoughts that chased each other
through her mind; and when their hands met
briefly, with the exchange of a ring or a brooch, he
could not know the fierce throb of excitement that
his touch evoked. Physical longing was very much a
part of loving, but Lucy had never known desire for
any man before and the feelings that he aroused
within her were a revelation. At last she understood
how it was possible for a woman to count the world
well lost for the sake of a man she loved.

"Help me out! Which would you choose?" Waldo
demanded at length, quite unable to decide. Some of
the pieces were quite lovely: one or two were
exquisite. But which of them would a very feminine
woman like his sister really appreciate?

Lucy reached for a cameo ring, delicately
wrought and particularly beautiful. "I like this,"
she said quietly, a faint wistfulness in her tone. "But
I mustn't influence your choice. Your friend may not
share my taste."

Waldo smiled. "I think you've chosen just what
she will like," he assured her, deciding in that
moment to make it a present for a 'friend' rather
than Rowena, after all.

At some suitable moment in the future, Lucy Cope should have the cameo ring that she so obviously liked and admired—and Waldo accepted the implication that some kind of meaningful association must develop if he could anticipate making this girl a present of an expensive piece of jewellery. He liked Lucy Cope with her candid eyes and shy smile, and he felt confident that she was ready to like him but would not make unwelcome demands on him.

Lucy found a ring box and tissue paper and wrapped the ring and the miniature with a care he found touching. "Thank you, you've really been most helpful," he said warmly, writing a cheque to cover the cost of his purchases.

"I'm glad you managed to find what you wanted," Lucy said.

Waldo paused by the door and looked at her with a faint smile in his eyes. "We can't go on meeting like this," he said. "Couldn't we arrange something a little less dependent on chance?"

Her heart lifted abruptly. He was lonely, of course, and still missing the woman he had loved. She knew it would be foolish to attach importance to his words, to feel flattered or to leap to romantic conclusions when she probably owed his friendliness to the mere fact that his cousin had known her family for so many years.

It did not matter that she might give him much more than friendship and know little in return, that she might suffer heartache when he went away, as he eventually must. She wanted his happiness above all else—and if she could supply a certain need within him then she would do so gladly and with a loving heart.

"Yes, I think we could," she said lightly, careful not to imply eagerness but merely an easy acceptance of mutual liking and casual friendliness.

"Perhaps you would meet me for a drink this evening," Waldo suggested. "What time do you close the shop?"

"About six o'clock, usually."

He nodded. "Then shall we meet at the pub across the road just after six?"

"I'll look forward to it," Lucy assured him, smiling at the man who had taught her in a moment what it meant to love.

The warm sincerity in her voice, the sweetness of her smile, stirred some unexpected response that was neither the leaping of desire nor the mere kindling of interest, but something that he simply could not analyse in that moment. She looked at him with such shining eyes and the glow in those hazel depths puzzled him. Many women had smiled on him with admiration, with frank interest, or with warm and friendly invitation; but there was so much more in the smile that gave her small face a sudden and striking beauty.

She was quite enchanting—and yet he left her with a vague feeling of disquiet, for he was far from being the knight in bright armour on a white charger that she seemed to think him. He wondered if it was wise to devote any attention to her, after all. She was very young and probably impressionable, and he did not want any complications. He realised that he must appear a romantic figure to an inexperienced girl, and he suspected that she was very vulnerable. It would be a pity to hurt her—but perhaps it was foolish conceit to suppose that she already liked him too much for her peace of mind.

He was thinking of friendship rather than flirtation, and it seemed to him that Lucy Cope could prove to be a valuable friend. For a tiny seed of an idea had begun to germinate, and he realised that a shy and gentle girl had provided him with the inspiration he needed. In a moment there was clarity where there had been nothing but despair.

His steps quickened with unconscious urgency as his thoughts chased each other in rapid succession, filling him with a feverish anxiety to capture ideas which might prove as elusive as all the others if he waited a moment too long.

CHAPTER THREE

Waldo missed lunch. He was too excited, too inspired to feel hungry or to notice the time and he waved Mrs. Hunsley away with an impatient gesture when she dared to put her head around the door.

At last he rose from the desk, fairly well satisfied with what he had done so far. He gathered the pages of typescript together, knowing they were neither perfect nor complete—but it was a beginning, and that was of supreme importance. Those few thousand words might seem little enough to anyone else; to Waldo they meant that he had the whole shape of a new book firmly in mind.

He felt elated, and very grateful to the girl who had so unexpectedly inspired him with the desire to

write once more. He had begun to believe that he
had lost the gift which had always been so precious
to him. He was relieved and thankful to find that he
still possessed it, that it had only needed the right
key to unlock that door in his mind.

Dorian had stifled his urge to write; but now Lucy
had revived it, and he sensed that he would find all
the inspiration and encouragement that he sought
in the affection and friendship she so generously
offered.

She had been much in his thoughts while he
worked. He was not consciously writing her into the
book: at the same time, he knew it would not be
written at all if he did not concentrate on a mental
picture of the shy, pretty and appealing girl who
had impressed him so much. She might never know
what she had done for him and it would probably
sound like a fantasy if he tried to explain. But he
would always be grateful to her . . . and he already
admitted and accepted that their lives must be
linked in some way in the future. For he needed the
warmth and the sweetness and the unselfish
generosity of heart that he sensed she had in full
measure.

He smiled, thinking of the small, slight figure in
the yellow overall, a splash of sunlight in the
shadows of the little shop.

His bruised and battered emotions needed the
balm of her sweetness. Her gentleness and shy
modesty invoked a protective instinct he had
scarcely known he possessed. The affection and
trust that she offered seemed to restore his confidence and renew his entire outlook on life.

He felt like a new man, for Lucy had not only
restored his desire to write, she had revived his early

belief in the innate goodness and sweetness of a woman. He had been an idealist and a romantic until he had known too many women who knew how to take all that a man offered and give as little as possible in return. Lucy reminded him that a woman could add a great deal to a man's appreciation of life without demanding the usual reward.

He found himself looking forward to the months he would spend in Inskip. He felt a new confidence ... the book would be written and well written, and he would be completely restored in mind and being, thanks to Lucy Cope.

He was not the kind of man to suppose himself in love on the strength of two meetings, a little conversation and an undeniable sense of affinity. He did not make the mistake of confusing warm liking and interest and gratitude with the deeper and more demanding instincts of love, an emotion he doubted if he would ever experience. He simply accepted the realisation deep within him that Lucy would come to mean much to him and was already important to him ...

Leaving his study, he almost collided with Colin. His cousin, not so tall and more stockily built, but bearing a definite resemblance to him, instinctively put out a hand to steady him, and Waldo realised with a tiny shock that he had forgotten to pick up his stick.

"I'm all right," he said swiftly, almost wonderingly. "In fact, I think I'm more all right than I knew," he added, smiling.

Colin accepted the cryptic remark without comment. "You've been working. Mrs. Hunsley tells me that you refused lunch."

Waldo grinned. Colin could never quite shake off

the air of authority that branded him as a successful schoolmaster, even in the casual, easy-going atmosphere of his own home. It amused rather than irritated Waldo, for he was very fond of his cousin. He laid an affectionate hand on Colin's shoulder and said cheerfully: "Very true—and now I'm ravenous! I was just going to the kitchen to beg a cup of tea and a sandwich."

"No need. Mrs. Hunsley has read your mind," Colin said, as his housekeeper pushed through the door with the tea-tray.

"Nonsense! She heard you come in and that's always the signal for tea to be brought in," Waldo retorted and moved to take the loaded tray despite Mrs. Hunsley's protest.

"Am I in disgrace?" he asked her. "I'm sure it was a delicious omelet, but I really couldn't leave my work just when it was going so well, you know."

"It's rest and plenty of nourishing food you need," she told him with mock severity. "Time enough for work when you're well."

"But I am well—never felt better," he returned, carrying the tray into the sitting-room and walking with scarcely a trace of a limp.

Colin lowered himself into an armchair. "How is the leg?" he asked, his eyes dancing.

"It seems to be fine," Waldo said slowly, suddenly realising with surprise that the familiar dull ache was missing.

"A miraculous recovery," Colin remarked lightly.

"Perhaps it's because I've been too busy to think about it." Waldo laughed suddenly. "A case of mind over matter—and the doctors were right, after all."

"Miracle indeed!" said Mrs. Hunsley briskly,

pouring tea. "You've been sitting down for once instead of tramping the countryside for miles, and it's rest that leg needed!"

Colin met his cousin's rueful eyes. "I think she may be right," he said quietly.

Waldo nodded, accepting a cup of tea and helping himself from the plate of sandwiches. "I suppose I've been overdoing it," he admitted, smiling. "But I've actually got down to some work at last, so I think my leg will be getting all the rest it needs for some time."

Colin, studying him thoughtfully, noticed the evident change of mood and was relieved. For too long, Waldo had been depressed and bitter, brooding on the past. Colin had hoped that the peace and privacy of the Lodge might prove beneficial, but no one could have foreseen such a rapid lifting of depression or such an early and obviously satisfactory return to work.

They were very close: Colin knew exactly what had troubled Waldo all these weeks, and that the failure to write had been a heavy burden on his mind and spirits. Now he was evidently writing again—and for Waldo that took priority above everything else and coloured his entire outlook on life.

"I met your Marian's sister in the village this morning," Waldo commented lightly, discovering a need within himself to talk about Lucy with someone who knew her better than he did as yet.

"She isn't my Marian," Colin retorted with cheerful resignation. "We are just good friends."

Waldo laughed. "That chestnut!" he jeered.

Colin smiled. "True, nevertheless. I am just a

convenient comforter when she is currently without an admirer. I cherish no illusions about the beautiful Marian or her motives." He reached for his pipe and busied himself with filling the bowl. "And what did you think of Lucy?" he asked.

"I thought she was charming," Waldo said warmly, making no attempt to conceal his admiration.

Colin busied himself with lighting his pipe to hide his surprise. He had supposed that if any woman could rouse Waldo from his present aversion to the fair sex, it would be Marian who was beautiful and vivacious and not likely to expect more from him than an amusing and short-lived flirtation which was just the kind of therapy he needed. So far he had shown little interest, but Colin had believed that he would appreciate Marian's attractions more as he saw more of her in the weeks to come. He dismissed this sudden, surprising interest in her sister as meaningless. Lucy was a dear girl, but not the type to attract Waldo.

"She's a general favourite," Colin said lightly. "A very nice girl."

"Tell me about her," Waldo demanded.

Colin looked at him, perturbed. "What do you want to know?"

"Everything," Waldo returned.

Colin was disturbed by the evidence of an interest that went deeper than he liked. There had been many women in Waldo's life and no one could deny that he was very attractive. If Lucy were as mature and as sophisticated as her sisters, it would not matter if Waldo paid her some attention; and it was very possible that her gentleness, sweet nature and quiet personality appealed to him after the blatant charms and vibrant temperament of Dorian Leigh. But Lucy was unused to the light-hearted affairs that her sisters had enjoyed from their teens, and she might easily take Waldo's interest much too seriously.

Colin said slowly: "That's a tall order and rather difficult to fulfil. She's a shy girl, very reserved, very quiet—something of a dreamer with a practical streak, if that makes sense. Head in the clouds and feet on the ground..." He hesitated briefly and then went on: "She's a serious child and she's inclined to take things seriously. Frankly, Waldo—not your type!"

Waldo smiled. "Warning me off?"

"I hope that isn't necessary. She's just a green girl and you are a man with a great deal of experience—a rake, in fact," he said, smiling to remove any suggestion of offence from the words.

"Too many willing women turn a man into a rake," Waldo returned, a little grimly. "It's refreshing to find that girls like Lucy Cope still exist. I'm sick of women who think that every man is natural prey. No man in her life?" he added abruptly.

Colin blinked. "Not to my knowledge. No one serious, anyway."

"Would you know?"

"Oh, I think so," he said confidently. "Lucy isn't a dissembler—and Marian tells me all the family news, you know. Lucy has had men friends, of course, boy and girl stuff, all very innocent, one imagines. She isn't the type to throw her bonnet over the windmill."

"Every woman is the type," Waldo retorted. "Given the right kind of temptation, of course."

Colin shrugged. "There is very little temptation

of that kind in Inskip for a girl like Lucy. She's intelligent, sensitive and very shy. She has been overshadowed by her sisters. Compare her with Marian and you'll understand why."

"There are a great many Marians in the world," Waldo said. "I think I've met most of them. Lucy has a very different appeal, you must agree."

"Not for you, surely!" Colin exclaimed sharply.

"Why not? I'm a man like any other," Waldo said, an imp of mischief lurking in his eyes as he realised his cousin's swift apprehension.

Colin rose, knocking out his pipe. "You are not serious," he said slowly. "You hardly know the girl!"

Waldo raised an eyebrow, smiling. "How long does it take to recognise a friend?"

Colin looked down at him as he sprawled in his chair, handsome, masculine and extremely sure of himself, in high good humour after the long weeks of depression. His brief encounter with Lucy seemed to have restored him to his old self, and perhaps he would gain from seeing more of her; but she might be in danger of losing her heart and her happiness like many another woman before her, Colin thought. He said quietly: "Friend—or potential mistress, Waldo?"

Waldo sat up swiftly, glaring—and for a moment there was anger in the air. Then he relaxed and laughed softly. "Your suspicions are probably justified—one must expect to be judged by one's reputation. But I don't anticipate that kind of affair with Lucy—if it's any of your business!"

It was true that he did not blame Colin for his suspicions, for it was inevitable that he should be judged by past performance. But he was furious that anyone should suppose Lucy capable of entering into a liaison. He himself had recognised the virginal quality which comprised part of her appeal, and Colin could not be blind to it.

"This concern for Lucy—is that just the protective instinct of the male coming out? Or do you happen to fancy her yourself?" Waldo asked, his smile just failing to conceal the challenge in his eyes.

Colin gestured impatiently. "My concern is for you. You've had a hard knock, and I want to see you over it. It will be a mistake to get involved with an intense child like Lucy Cope. Amuse yourself with someone like Marian, by all means—she knows all the rules of the game. Lucy doesn't, and she's the marrying kind, believe me."

Waldo glanced at his watch and rose, a faint smile on his lips. "What's so terrible about marriage? I know—you never thought to hear that sentiment from me. But a man can change his mind." He moved towards the door. "I'm meeting Lucy at the village pub, but I'll be back for dinner. Don't look so anxious—I'll be discreet and I'll take good care of her, you know." He grinned. "I'm not really as black as I'm painted!"

Colin was not at all happy about the situation, but there was nothing he could do. Lucy was not a child and it was not his business to warn her against his cousin. Besides, in his experience, no woman took kindly to warnings of that nature—and he did not doubt that Lucy would react with typically feminine perversity. Because he could not interfere, he could only hope that Waldo would be sensible and keep the affair on a light and friendly footing—and that Lucy would not make the mistake of becoming too emotionally involved with a man who would dismiss her when he became bored, as he inevitably would.

For Lucy, in her innocence, would look for a proposal of marriage—and Waldo was not a marrying man, even if he chanced to fall in love with a girl who was so different from his other women. Colin could not visualise him settling down to one woman, and he was not the kind to take a wife only to amuse himself with a succession of mistresses, for he was a compassionate man and it was probably his soft heart that had led him into too many love affairs. Only compassion had held Waldo long after his first wild desire for Dorian Leigh had died a natural death.

Colin asked himself if it was a mere coincidence that Waldo had begun to write again after that encounter with Lucy Cope. He did not need to wonder how Lucy had reacted to Waldo—she was a woman and they all seemed to find his cousin irresistible, Colin thought wryly...

Waldo whistled as he descended the stairs some half an hour later, newly showered and shaved. He put his head round the door of the sitting-room where Colin was marking exercise books.

"Give that a miss and walk down with me," he suggested impulsively. "It's a lovely evening—too good to waste!"

Colin looked up, smiling. "No, I won't come with you, thanks. Two's company, you know."

"Nonsense! I'm only meeting the girl for a friendly drink," Waldo retorted impatiently.

"Another time." Colin turned back to his books.

Waldo lifted his shoulders in a slight shrug. "As you wish!"

He was whistling again as he walked down the
lane towards the village, using his stick to slash at
the nettles that lined the ditches, delighted to
discover the new strength and sense of well-being
that seemed to be surging within him, and beginning to feel for the first time that the past might be
left behind him, after all...

Marian wandered aimlessly about the house and
garden, bored and unsettled and strangely restless,
filled with an odd kind of yearning for something
she could not even describe.

It had been a most unsatisfactory day, she
thought crossly. First, that trouble with the car so
that she had been forced to beg a lift from Daniel in
order to keep her date with Nevil; the journey from
Inskip to the Cap and Bells with the man who made
no effort to conceal his indifference and refused to
join her for a drink while she waited for Nevil;
lastly, a long, dull afternoon spent with a man she
had suddenly discovered to be boring and much too
possessive.

She had found it more and more difficult to
tolerate Nevil's attentions and at last, on the plea of
a headache, she had persuaded him to bring her
home earlier than he had wished.

Having sent him away, she scarcely knew what
to do with herself. Her father was in his study, busy
with his sermon; and the aunt who kept house for
them all was making pastry and had no patience
with Marian's admission of boredom when there
were so many household chores waiting for attention.

She settled herself in a deck-chair on the lawn
and tried to read, but the book could not hold her
interest. Her thoughts kept turning to Daniel and

the new light in which she had suddenly found
herself regarding him.

Sitting beside him in the car that morning, she
had studied him covertly, and wondered why she
had never noticed before that his nose was slightly
irregular as though it had been broken at some time,
or that there was a tiny, white scar at the corner of
his mouth. She had known a sudden, foolish
impulse to lean forward and trace the crescent
shape of that scar with her lips; but there was
something very forbidding about Daniel and his
cool, faintly contemptuous attitude to her light-
hearted, breezy outlook on men and their place in
her life.

The silver in his dark hair and the hint of
weariness about his eyes had reminded her that he
was not a young, impressionable man who would
amuse her with a mild affair. She had flirted with
him because she flirted with every eligible man.
Daniel had always been unresponsive, even disap-
proving; and she would probably have backed away
in alarm if he had responded when she was an
experimenting girl in her teens, just learning how to
cope with the emotions she aroused so swiftly in
men. But now, mature enough to appreciate the
qualities which had once seemed dull and unattractive, Marian realised that she was hurt rather than
piqued by his disapproval and disdain. It suddenly
seemed very important that she should penetrate
that cool reserve, if only to discover what kind of
man lay beneath.

Men like Nevil were amusing, good for the ego
with their extravagance of admiration and flattery.
A girl might fall light-heartedly in and out of love
with the Nevils of this world, but would never

seriously contemplate marrying one of them,
Marian thought wryly. She wanted to be married—
but only to a man of character and integrity, a man
who would regard her as the centre of his universe,
loving and cherishing her beyond all others.

She rose abruptly, suddenly impatient with
herself. She rarely indulged in that kind of sentiment and it was the height of folly to suppose that
Daniel could fill that role or that she could ever
compete with his beloved books and antiques. She
decided to walk down to the garage to collect her car
in Lucy's stead, and resolutely refused to admit that
the hope of seeing Daniel had anything to do with
her decision.

The car was not ready. An apologetic and very
heated Harry was still working on the clutch when
Marian called at the garage. Rather than wait in its
hot, greasy atmosphere, she set off for the antique
shop, her steps quickening unconsciously as she
saw Daniel at the door. Her heart began to race and
she felt oddly breathless at the sight of him. It was
not a new experience, but it staggered her that it
should be associated with a man that she had
known for so many years and had scarcely
considered in a romantic light until now.

Not looking where she was going, she almost
collided with Waldo at the door of the Dog and Duck.
He put a hand on her arm to steady her. "There's
something about your family!" he exclaimed,
laughing. "Always in a hurry—and always in a
dream! People like you should wear bells round their
necks."

Marian laughed, responding instinctively to the
friendliness and undeniable charm of the tall,
handsome man; but she looked beyond him to the

figure in the shop doorway. She sent Daniel a swift, warm smile and a slight wave of her hand. To her dismay, he turned away, ignoring her. Marian felt ridiculously hurt and suddenly angry with herself for wasting time and energy in wanting such a man. She slipped her hand into Waldo's arm and smiled up at him. "How nice to see you!"

Waldo had not bargained for a meeting with Marian; but she was Lucy's sister and for that reason, if for no other, he was prepared to be friendly. He glanced at the little shop, but there was no sign of Lucy who was probably getting ready to meet him. He looked down at Marian. "Come and have a drink," he invited.

At that moment Lucy, having finished work in the shop, happened to glance out through the open door—and felt a sudden spasm of pain.

Marian had not made any secret of her interest in Waldo McKinnon, and it had been inevitable that she would make a play for him. It had been equally inevitable that he should respond, Lucy thought despondently. The ease with which her sister acquired any man she wanted made Lucy feel very unsure of herself; and suddenly she wondered if she owed Waldo McKinnon's invitation to the fact that he had already met and admired Marian, and hoped to meet her again through his friendship with her sister.

Daniel said abruptly: "Isn't that the McKinnon man with Marian?"

"Yes, it is. Marian met him at the Lodge a couple of times, I believe," Lucy replied as calmly as she could, her heart sinking even lower as she realised that Marian had all the advantages, all the opportunities of meeting friends and enjoying a full social life while she herself was tied to the shop.

She frowned as Marian slipped her hand lightly into Waldo's arm and accompanied him into the pub. Surely he had not forgotten that she was meeting him at six o'clock, Lucy thought, apprehension bringing a sudden sickness to her stomach. Then it occurred to her that it was probably a chance meeting between Waldo and Marian, and that he had naturally mentioned their appointment. Which would be all the encouragement her sister needed to invite herself to join them!

"I knew they'd met, but I didn't realise they were already on intimate terms," Daniel said, moving away from the door.

"But they're not!" Lucy exclaimed. "That's just Marian's way—it doesn't mean a thing," she added, reassuring herself rather than Daniel. "Oh, you know Marian! She greets every man she meets like a long-lost lover."

"Not every man," he said, a little grimly. "Merely every new man who happens to catch her interest— someone more exciting than the last. She'll never settle down. I suppose she knows that she's playing with fire where McKinnon is concerned—he has quite a reputation." He laughed shortly and without humour. "But of course she does—that's the attraction, isn't it?" The words were born of a sudden, aching jealousy. He had seen Marian with a host of men, but it had never hurt so much until now—when he saw her smiling up at someone who seemed more of a threat than any of his predecessors.

Lucy stared in dismay, for the tone rather than the words brought sudden enlightenment. Something she had always feared had actually come about—Daniel was in love with Marian. She did not question how or when it had happened. She knew for herself that love could come unbidden and unexpected. The first dismay began to turn to optimism; perhaps it was the best thing that could have happened. Perhaps Daniel was the ideal man for her butterfly sister, if only Marian could be brought to realise it. Daniel was a marvellous person, so strong, so understanding, so reliable— and he desperately needed someone like Marian to bring out all the warmth and sweetness and tenderness dormant in his nature.

He said abruptly: "It's gone six—time you were going home, my dear."

Lucy nodded, her thoughts busy. It would seem odd if she failed to keep her date with Waldo, but she shrank from the thought of playing gooseberry. She was afraid that he would have eyes only for Marian—and that would hurt. But supposing she took Daniel with her? It would seem perfectly natural—and perhaps she could manage to imply that Daniel and Marian were already more than friends.

"I'm not going home yet," she said. "I'm meeting Waldo McKinnon for a drink."

He turned quickly. "You're meeting him? But he's with Marian!"

"Yes, I know; they must have bumped into each other when he was on his way to meet me. It was only natural that he should ask her to have a drink with him while he waited for me." She smiled at him. "Why don't you come over with me, Daniel? I want you to meet him—and you can do me the favour of distracting Marian a little, if you will. I've decided not to let her have Waldo McKinnon as easily as she's had all the others."

Daniel laughed. "Good for you!" he exclaimed. "It's about time you showed a little fight. Yes, I'll come with you, Lucy. I should like to meet the man who shows such uncommonly good sense in preferring you to your sister!" He put an arm about her shoulders, gave her a quick, affectionate hug; and almost wished that it was she who had taken such fierce possession of his heart instead of the beautiful, wilful and hopelessly fickle Marian.

Lucy had spoken confidently but she did not really think that she could compete with her sister. If Marian had decided that she wanted Waldo McKinnon, then she would be almost certain to get him.

Marian herself was convinced that she had made another conquest. She had supposed that she did not interest Waldo at all, but now she decided that he was attracted but cautious. She appreciated that no man would want to rush into an affair, however light, after the kind of experience that he had recently gone through with Dorian Leigh.

It was flattering to bask in the warm friendliness of his approach, and it was comforting after that deliberate snub she had received from Daniel. The writer might even fall in love with her, Marian thought, with the unconscious defiance of despair at the knowledge that Daniel would not—and she could not think of any reason why she should not settle down happily as the wife of a famous and wealthy man. She thrust away the swift, piercing desire to settle down even more happily as the wife of a virtually unknown antique dealer, and turned with a brightly provocative smile to the man who rejoined her carrying their drinks.

Marian did not know that he smiled upon her because she was Lucy's sister—or that he admirably concealed his fear, as the minutes ticked away, that Lucy did not mean to keep their date.

Waldo was quite clear in his own mind that he did not want to expose a girl like Lucy to the kind of speculation and gossip that any woman in his life had inevitably incurred in the past. She was young, she was shy and she was certainly inexperienced, and he fancied that she was a little uncertain of herself and him. He did not want her frightened away by the kind of publicity that he had so far been unable to avoid in his personal life.

Marian Cope would be a convenient smokescreen for the development of his interest in her sister; and would probably ignore or even enjoy local gossip about their association. He did not want to rush anything—he certainly did not want to rush Lucy into any kind of relationship. He needed time to be sure how deeply involved he wished to become, or to decide if it would be wiser to avoid becoming involved at all.

One day, he might want to know that Lucy cared for him—but he would need to be very sure of the depth of his own feelings when that day dawned.

"I suppose it will be some time before you are really fit," Marian said, as Waldo retrieved the stick that an unwary movement had sent flying.

"Oh, I can cope with most things now," he returned easily. "I'm not an invalid, by any means."

"Of course not," she agreed quickly, recalling that Colin had warned her that his cousin was rather sensitive about his lameness.

"I ought to appreciate the sympathy and concern that everyone shows towards me, but I'm afraid I find it very difficult not to resent the need for it," he said wryly.

"I can understand that," she assured him warmly. She smiled at him. "I promise not to show the least concern in the future!"

Waldo smiled absently. Their table was by the window, and his eyes were on the little antique shop across the road. Lucy had finally appeared, accompanied by a tall man who paused to close and lock the shop door while she waited for him.

"There's Lucy," he said, more to himself than to Marian.

He had already mentioned his date with Lucy; and Marian had been rather surprised, for Lucy had not mentioned having met the writer at any time. But there had been plenty of opportunities for her to have done so, of course.

Marian observed that Daniel had taken Lucy's hand and drawn it gently beneath his arm. He was looking down at her with an expression in his eyes that wrenched abruptly at Marian's heart.

It was no news to her that Daniel cared for Lucy—everyone knew it. It was generally agreed that he wanted to marry her, but felt himself too old to be a suitable husband for her—but that was ridiculous! Lucy would be very happy with Daniel. She was so generous with her affections, so innocent and trusting; it was frightening to think that she might give her heart to quite the wrong kind of man. She needed the protection of marriage with someone like Daniel. He would know how to ensure that her youthful dreams were fulfilled through him and not trampled on by some callous stranger who might play havoc with that loving heart.

Marian knew she was foolish to indulge even briefly in her own impossible dreams. It was natural that Daniel should want Lucy, who was loving and loyal and very sweet—all she herself could never be. She must not even think of loving Daniel, who was so perfect for Lucy.

But there were other men in the world, and among them was Waldo McKinnon who might have been sent by a kindly Providence for her special benefit.

CHAPTER FOUR

Lucy paused on the threshold of the crowded bar, looking hesitant. Waldo rose from his seat with a murmured excuse to Marian and went to meet the younger girl.

He felt as foolishly excited and eager as any callow youth in the throes of first love. Those days were long gone, he reminded himself wryly. Lucy could not be his first love; he did not suppose that she would be his last, and he was not yet convinced that he meant to love her at all. But he experienced a sudden springing of an already familiar tenderness as he made his way to her side, realising only as he reached her that she was not alone.

She had turned to Daniel, standing just behind her. "There he is," she said, indicating Waldo.

"Lucy!" he said, smiling; and it seemed that her name had never sounded so pretty until he used it for the first time. Her heart lifted at the promise for the future in his voice.

A little breathlessly, she apologised for being late, and hastened to introduce the two men who shook hands, assessing each other warily before deciding on a swift, mutual liking.

Lucy went to join her sister while the men paused at the bar for drinks. "I thought you were out with Nevil," she said lightly.

"Only for lunch," Marian replied. "As I was home early I came down for the car, but it still isn't ready. I ran into Waldo as I left the garage." She regarded her sister with faint amusement. "You're a dark horse," she accused. "You never told me that you knew our local celebrity."

Lucy shrugged. "There wasn't much to tell."

Marian raised a sceptical eyebrow. "Not much to tell!" she echoed mockingly. "Why, you must have been over the moon! Waldo McKinnon of all people making a date with you!"

"He was just being friendly," Lucy demurred.

Marian studied her naïve sister with amused tolerance and affection—and almost envied her innocence. Then it occurred to her that perhaps Lucy was right and she was leaping to the wrong conclusion. Waldo was probably merely making overtures of friendship because they knew Colin so well, and were likely to meet his cousin again and again while he was in Inskip. She turned to look at him as he stood at the bar. For the first time she saw that Daniel was with him.

She turned to Lucy. "What is your boss doing here?" she inquired.

"I brought him with me," Lucy told her.

Marian smiled. "Not for protection, surely?" she said with faint mockery.

"Don't be silly!" Lucy spoke with rare sharpness. "I happened to see that you were with Waldo and I thought we might as well turn it into a foursome."

The two men approached, talking in apparent amity. Marian felt ridiculously shy as she met Daniel's eyes. She waited with a thudding heart for his greeting, but it was so careless, so indifferent, that she felt it like a physical blow and turned to Waldo with more warmth than she had intended, in consequence. Daniel, observing the radiance in her smile and the coquetry in her beautiful eyes, felt all his first instinctive liking for the writer melt in a rush of anger.

Lucy took the glass that Waldo offered and looked up at him with a swift smile. The warmth in her expression almost took his breath away; and he knew again the conviction that she was ready and eager to give her heart. He must not allow her to rush her fences, he thought; he must not encourage her to suppose that he was equally ready to love.

Just then Marian claimed his attention; and briefly he wondered if he would be wise to follow Colin's advice and enjoy a flirtation with the more experienced sister, stifling the ache for the girl who hesitated to make any claim on him at all. Lucy sat quietly sipping her drink, while Marian monopolised his attention—and Waldo swiftly realised that Marian was so used to claiming the limelight that she was quite unaware that in doing so she cast her sister into the shade.

Lucy could not really compete with Marian and she was too sensible to try. She listened and smiled and responded whenever she was addressed. But for the most part she observed Waldo's interest in her sister and Marian's easy confidence in the rapid development of their relationship. There was a dull ache somewhere in the region of Lucy's heart. It was not the first time that a man had abruptly transferred his interest from her to Marian—but it had never really mattered before. Now it did matter.

It became more and more difficult to conceal the misery that welled in her breast, to behave as though all was well when suddenly everything was terribly wrong. She heard Waldo and Marian making plans for the days ahead—plans that could not include her and Daniel, because their free time was so limited by the shop.

A little later, Daniel rose to leave, excusing himself on the plea of having a great deal of work to do. Marian's heart sank. She could not know that he was leaving because he could no longer bear to listen to the plans for the long summer days that she would spend in another man's company.

She stared through the window until Daniel came into sight, paused at the kerb and then strode across to let himself into the little shop. He closed the door with a snap of finality that could not be heard but was none the less unmistakable. Marian fancied it was yet one more indication that he had closed the door years before on any sentimental regard for the woman who had once foolishly believed him to be the last man in the world she could love.

"Another drink?" Waldo was puzzled by a faint suggestion in the air that the party had fallen flat. He rose to his feet, gathering empty glasses.

Lucy said quickly: "Not for me."

He rested his hand briefly on her shoulder. "Sure? Marian, how about you?"

Marian accepted, and he left them to go to the bar.

Lucy pushed back her chair. "I know you won't want to rush away," she said, forcing lightness into her tone. "But I must go home."

"What's the matter?" Marian asked.

"I'm tired and I'm hungry," Lucy pointed out with a hint of impatience. "I've been working all day, you know. Besides, I hate playing gooseberry," she added, managing a little laugh. "You obviously have a lot to say to each other, and I shall only cramp your style."

"I don't know that he's so interested," Marian said slowly; and indeed she did feel that something was lacking in Waldo's response. It was as half-hearted as her own, she thought wryly; but whereas her lack of enthusiasm was due to wanting another man it was very likely that Waldo was merely amusing himself out of sheer boredom.

"Nonsense!" Lucy returned brightly. "You only had to lift a finger, as always."

Marian laughed. "It takes a little more than that!" She thought unhappily that Lucy was mistaken where Daniel was concerned—she could lift half a dozen fingers and each of them would be ignored by him. It was ironic that she should have discovered a need for the one man who did not respond immediately and reassuringly to the beauty and charm that other men found irresistible.

"Will you make my excuses?" Lucy said.

Marian patted her sister's arm. "Don't rush off without me," she urged. "I'll come as soon as I've finished this last drink. Waldo is expected at the

Lodge for dinner, anyway—we can drop him off on our way home."

Lucy hesitated. "I'll go down to the garage and check if the car is ready. You can meet me there," she suggested.

Marian wondered at her obvious anxiety to escape, and decided that Lucy had had enough of the pub's stuffy atmosphere. "Yes, all right. We'll be five minutes—no more, I promise!"

Waldo caught sight of Lucy as she pushed her way to the door. He went after her impulsively and caught her by the arm. "You aren't leaving?"

Lucy looked up at him, startled by the vehemence in his tone. "I'm going to the garage for the car, Marian's car," she told him. "It's getting late—I'm expected home for a meal."

"I see." Suddenly his eyes softened. He knew that she was shy with him, a little unsure of the wisdom of having anything at all to do with him, a little confused by feelings he unmistakably evoked—and he knew that he must tread very warily for he did not need Colin's warning that she was extremely vulnerable. "This was meant to be our evening," he said quietly.

A man pushed against her and Lucy was thrust forward unexpectedly. Immediately Waldo's arm was about her, and he turned with a swift, angry rebuke for the man. Lucy's heart was thudding and her entire body seemed to melt with love and longing as she stood in the shelter of his arm—his nearness could banish all her pride, all her knowledge that it was folly to want him, all her awareness that his light words and careless actions were born of his habitual attitude to women rather than a real interest in herself.

She smiled shakily in response to the man's apology and drew herself from Waldo's embrace, knowing she must avoid such physical contacts or else admit to wanting him to a frightening degree.

With an incoherent murmur, she left him—and Waldo looked after her, only slowly recovering from the unexpected impact of that brief moment when she had been so close to his heart.

He went to collect the drinks he had left on the bar counter, and carried them over to where Marian was sitting. She greeted him with a smile. "It's been fun, but I ought to take Lucy home," she said reluctantly. "It's a long day for her and she must be tired. She likes her job, but I wouldn't want to be cooped up in that shop all day—particularly in this kind of weather."

It was only a little more than the promised five minutes before they joined Lucy. She was chatting to the mechanic, who hastened to assure Marian that the car was in perfect working order at last and to apologise for the delay. Waldo declined the offered lift although Marian assured him that they could easily squeeze him into the sports car; and they said good-bye, reminding each other that they were to meet the following day.

Lucy glanced up and Waldo was troubled by the hurt he recognised in her hazel eyes. He knew and understood her reaction to his seeming interest in Marian, but he could scarcely point out to Lucy that it was for her own good that he did not sweep her off her feet.

Without conceit, he knew that it would need little encouragement for her to tumble into love—and that must not happen unless and until he was quite sure of his feelings for her. It was better that she should know a little hurt now rather than a great deal of heartache in the future, he thought with real concern...

Despite the promise that had seemed implicit in Waldo McKinnon's smiling words and her conviction that something had sparked between them when she stood in that brief, accidental embrace, Lucy was swiftly forced to the conclusion that she had foolishly attached too much importance to a fleeting interest and the easy manners of a man who was well aware when a woman responded instinctively to his charm. In fact, she soon decided that he was merely an accomplished flirt and very much the rake he was reputed to be; but that did not stop her from wanting him.

He was spending much of his time with Marian and her friends. Lucy had to be content with an occasional encounter that left her with little more than a smile or a casual word to cherish. For the most part he treated her with a light, careless ease of manner that virtually amounted to indifference. She did not want him to know that she ached for more, but it was hard to pretend a mere light-hearted liking for a man she loved so deeply.

She told herself that she ought to be glad that he could forget the tragedy of the past in her sister's company; and she did try to set self aside and wish wholeheartedly for his happiness. But it was painful to watch the gradual progress of an affair which seemed to indicate that he was falling in love with Marian...

Every Wednesday Daniel closed the antique shop at midday, and went off to the near-by county town for the meeting of the local Antiquarian Society. Lucy looked forward to that free afternoon, and she

welcomed it even more now that she was beginning
to chafe at the restrictions of her job and to envy
Marian's freedom to spend her days much as she
pleased.

Colin had decided to give one of his rare dinner-
parties, and conveniently chose a Wednesday
evening. Lucy meant to spend the afternoon in
washing her hair, doing her nails and putting the
finishing touches to the dress she had made for the
occasion; and she was particularly impatient for the
morning to pass. Perhaps it was foolish to indulge
in a dream that Waldo would suddenly discover her
to be beautiful in his eyes and far more desirable
than her sister. But a girl in love is entitled to her
dreams.

As twelve struck, she slipped out of her overall
with an audible sigh of relief. Daniel looked up from
the accounts, smiling, perfectly aware that she had
been watching the clock for some time.

"Anxious to get away? I expect you want to make
yourself beautiful for tonight," he said. "I'm just
coming," he added, for he usually dropped her off at
the Vicarage on his way to the Antiquarian Society
meeting in Melbury.

Lucy waited, thinking that Daniel looked a little
fine-drawn these days. She suspected that he was
not sleeping well—but who could on these warm and
airless nights, she thought a little wryly. He seldom
mentioned Marian, and had never attempted to
discuss Marian's friendship with Waldo McKinnon;
but she was convinced that it was as painful to
Daniel as it was to her.

They went out to the car together, and she settled
herself in the front passenger seat, wondering if the
long years of friendship and affection gave her the

right to comment on her conviction that he loved and wanted Marian.

As he inserted the ignition key and switched on the engine, she said carefully: "How long is it since you took a holiday, Daniel?"

He glanced at her, smiling at the faint reproach in her tone. "Too long, I expect," he said smoothly. "But what should take me away from Inskip, Lucy? My life, my interests, my friends are all centred in the village and the neighbourhood. I don't feel any need to get away."

But that was not strictly true. For Daniel had been thinking for some time of leaving Inskip altogether. He was tormented by the constant reminders of Marian's involvement with yet another man, and he was finding it difficult to shake off the heaviness of depression. Always honest with himself, he admitted for the first time that he was a lonely man with a desperate need for the happiness that a woman could bring into his life. Looking back, his life was very empty; looking forward, the future was bleak indeed.

He was resentful and jealous of McKinnon and found it hard to hide his feelings. Marian was different these days—quieter, more thoughtful, more mature. He could not ascribe the change to the seriousness of her affair with McKinnon, and he feared that she meant to marry the man if she could...

It took only a few minutes to reach the Vicarage. As she got out of the car Lucy said a little anxiously: "You are coming to Colin's party tonight, Daniel?" She had a feeling that she might be glad of his support.

"I accepted the invitation," he reminded her lightly.

"Yes, I know, but I feel that you'd get out of it if you could," she said bluntly.

He shrugged. "Perhaps it's a sign of old age that I don't care much for parties these days."

"You know very well that Colin doesn't throw the kind of parties you're talking about," Lucy said tartly. "You really mean that you aren't looking forward to seeing Marian in Waldo McKinnon's pocket. I know I'm interfering, but if you are so fond of Marian then you ought to make it more obvious."

He stiffened. "It appears to be sufficiently obvious already!"

"How can you say that? Marian hasn't a clue—and that's what really matters, surely? Why don't you give her the occasional hint of how you feel about her?" Lucy demanded.

"I wouldn't provide her with that kind of satisfaction," he said harshly. "She has enough men in tow without me."

"But none of them seem to make her very happy," she said quietly; then she shut the car door and stood back.

She watched as Daniel drove away. Sighing a little she turned towards the house.

Her father was calling out to her aunt that they had an unexpected guest for lunch. Passing the open door of the study, Lucy looked in with faint curiosity and a smile at the ready for her father's guest; but she stopped short as she recognised the tall man by the desk. He was using the telephone, his back to her as he explained to Mrs. Hunsley that he would be out for lunch after all.

Lucy's legs seemed to turn to jelly. Her heart foolishly missed a beat with the unexpected delight of seeing him. Unable to move or to speak, she could only stare, consumed with love and longing.

Sensing her presence, Waldo turned, and knew a swift impact on his emotions as he met her hazel eyes and saw the smile that trembled on her lips.

He had not expected to see her when he decided to call at the Vicarage that morning. He had reached an impasse with his new book; he found he had to check certain facts and he lacked the necessary reference books. Since he was always welcome at the Vicarage as a friend, and Michael Cope's excellent library was at his disposal, he went along there. Michael was at home and wrestling with his sermon; he was only too pleased to welcome an interruption.

They had so much to say to each other that the time had passed rapidly, and Waldo had been glad to accept an invitation to stay for lunch. He knew that Marian had gone to London with a folder full of new designs and an appointment with a famous fashion house. Forgetting it was Wednesday and early closing day in the village, he had not expected to see Lucy who was always so involved with the antique shop that she did not come home for lunch.

Swift delight flooded him now as he looked at her. Without pausing in his telephone conversation, he held out an impulsive hand. Briefly, Lucy hesitated, then she went into the room and put her hand in his. He looked down at her with a smile, the very smile that had first startled her heart into loving.

Ending his call a little abruptly, he replaced the receiver. "This is nice," he said warmly, still retaining her hand. "I didn't expect to see you."

She laughed softly. "But I live here," she pointed out.

"I was beginning to think you lived at the shop," he said dryly. "I hardly ever see you!"

It was not so much the words as the look in his eyes that sent the blood coursing swiftly through her veins. He was an incorrigible flirt, she reminded herself hastily; but it was hard to believe that he was not sincere when he looked at her in just that way.

"You know where to find me," she returned, marvelling that she could sound so cool and composed when both head and heart were in tumult.

"The atmosphere would cramp my style," he returned smoothly. "Besides, Pegrim wouldn't like it if you mixed business with pleasure. Has he given you some time off at last?"

"It's Wednesday—early closing in the village," she reminded him.

He smiled. "Yes, of course," he said. "I'd forgotten. Which makes it all the more clever of me to have chosen the right day to get myself invited to lunch!"

A delicate and very becoming warmth stole into her face. Waldo knew a sudden desire to kiss the mouth that slowly curved into the sweetness of her smile. Instead, he contented himself with carrying her hand to his lips, pressing a light kiss into the palm and closing her fingers tightly over it.

A little flustered, she murmured an excuse and escaped to her room. She sat down on the edge of her bed and raised both hands to her burning cheeks. Was he merely amusing himself in Marian's absence? Or did he find her attractive as she had suddenly believed, her heart lifting at that glow in his eyes, that warmth in his voice, that urgency in the clasp of his hand? It was beyond all her wildest dreams, but she indulged herself in the fancy that he cared for her; and there was hope in her heart and dancing delight in her eyes when she went down to join Waldo and her father in a glass of sherry before lunch.

She had not heard the sound of Marian's car, and she paused on the threshold of the sitting-room, surprised and dismayed and heavily aware that her brief moment had fled.

Waldo was very fond of Marian. She was amusing and intelligent and very good company—and undemanding. They had fallen into an easy, comfortable relationship within a very short time. In fact, they were friends; and it did not occur to Waldo that Lucy could seriously suppose that her sister represented a real threat to her happiness. Waldo was too experienced not to realise that Lucy was a little in love with him. And of course every woman knew intuitively when a man was on the verge of loving her, he told himself.

But Lucy did not know. She saw only the warm affection in his manner and heard the genuine interest in his voice as he demanded to know if Marian's trip to town had been successful. With a pang, Lucy understood that they were friends. Every other man had been a conquest, but Waldo was a friend who was already dear to Marian, and it was probably an indication that she was ready to love at last.

With an aching heart, Lucy slipped into her usual place in the background, knowing that Waldo's interest and attention were all for her beautiful sister—and wondering how she could have deceived herself even for a moment into believing that he regarded her with anything more than casual liking and acceptance.

Michael Cope had seen that stricken expression in her eyes and he was very shaken to discover that his darling had grown up. He had cherished certain hopes for Lucy, and it would have delighted him to hand her into Daniel Pegrim's safe keeping. But it seemed that it was not Daniel who had taught her to love. The glow in her eyes, so swiftly banished, had been for a man who was little more than a stranger. Michael liked Waldo McKinnon and admitted his ability as a writer—but suddenly he regretted that the man had ever come to their village.

After lunch, Michael returned to his sermon. Marian took Waldo out to the garden while Lucy helped her aunt to clear away and wash the dishes. Glancing through the kitchen window, her busy hands were abruptly stilled as she saw Marian and Waldo emerge from the seclusion of the small orchard, walking hand in hand like lovers. Pain stabbed ruthlessly. She longed so much for just a little of the affection he seemed to feel for her sister—and knew that nothing less than his eternal loving could really satisfy the insistent hunger in her heart.

CHAPTER FIVE

Waldo whistled blithely as he moved about his room, dressing for the evening. It was amazing how well he felt these days, he realised with a faint shock of surprise. It was not just the physical improvement. He had left the dark valley of depression behind him and the future seemed bright and very satisfying.

Mrs. Hunsley in her kitchen below smiled with satisfaction as her keen ears caught the sound of his whistling. He was certainly a changed man in a short time, she thought—and wondered what really had brought about that lifting of his spirits and renewed interest in his work.

She fancied that Mr. Colin was looking forward to the evening almost as much as his cousin. And at this point she stood back, surveyed the results of her labours and nodded in silent satisfaction. Mr. Colin seldom entertained, but when he did everything had to be just right—and she did not imagine there would be any cause for complaint this evening.

"Anything I can do?" Waldo asked, appearing in the open doorway of the kitchen.

"Not a thing—'tis all done!"

Waldo glanced at his watch. "Our guests will be arriving at any moment."

Mrs. Hunsley shook her head. "Don't expect Marian Cope to be on time for anything and you'll not be disappointed," she said dryly. "Now Lucy will fret if she's a minute late, for she'll do her best to please...she's her mother all over again—loving and giving and the sweetest nature you could hope to find."

Waldo regarded her quizzically. "You give her an excellent reference, I must say. You're very fond of Lucy, aren't you?"

"I'm fond of them all," she hastened to assure him. "Like a second mother I was to those girls when they were small—many's the time one or the other has run to me with a grazed knee or a torn frock. Their Aunt Alice is a good woman and a just woman, but she never knew much about rearing children with love." She sighed suddenly. "They grow up too soon, and you miss their loving little ways when old friends aren't as important as new. But Lucy doesn't change and she doesn't forget."

Colin came in to have a word with Mrs. Hunsley; and a few minutes later the first of the guests arrived—the Head of the Manor House school and his wife. Waldo was cornered almost immediately by Felicity Hughes, who had done a little writing and had met him at a literary luncheon in town. She recalled the occasion very well, but Waldo could not remember her at all; and he needed all his charm and tact to disguise the fact. He was rescued by Daniel Pegrim's arrival. It appeared that Mrs. Hughes was a fellow-member of the local Antiquarian Society but had been unable to attend the meeting that afternoon. As she was anxious for a blow-by-blow account of it, Waldo found himself deserted for Pegrim—and did not mind at all.

Marian was late just as Mrs. Hunsley had prophesied; and Waldo suspected that it was a deliberate policy. She swept in, profuse with apologies and very confident of instant forgiveness if only because of the vital and glowing beauty that seemed to brighten the room as she entered. In the long, black gown that was the ultimate of sophistication, she was a slender, golden goddess who commanded the admiration of every man.

Momentarily, Waldo thought she had arrived without her sister and he knew swift disappointment. Then Lucy appeared on the threshold, and he felt a familiar little surge of tenderness for the girl in her long, gold dress of some softly clinging material.

He began to cross the room to her side, deciding that she looked very sweet, very charming and utterly lovely. But he found himself forestalled by Daniel Pegrim who had shaken off the talkative Mrs. Hughes with an adroitness born of practice.

Waldo checked, annoyance in his dark eyes; then he turned as Marian spoke his name and placed her hand lightly on his arm.

Marian deliberately implied some claim on him

in the foolish hope that Daniel might notice and feel some stirring of jealousy. But Daniel had spared her no more than a glance and a brief smile as he made his way swiftly towards Lucy—and all Marian's pleasure in the evening was suddenly destroyed. She had taken such pains to look her loveliest, knowing that Daniel had been invited. But her beauty could not pierce the armour of his indifference, she thought bleakly, and clutched at the small comfort of Waldo's attentions so that none should suspect how hurt she was by Daniel's preference for her sister.

Daniel had been quite startled by the eager warmth in Lucy's greeting, the sparkle in her hazel eyes, the hint of coquetry in her manner. But he decided that this was only due to the constricting shyness that she fought so hard to overcome.

In fact, Lucy was very near to tears—and she almost fell on Daniel's neck in gratitude for the support that he offered. She had taken such care with her appearance and felt that she looked her best. Daniel was not a man to pay verbal compliments, but the appreciation in his eyes had assured Lucy that she looked pretty and that her dress was a success.

But there was little satisfaction in Daniel's approval when Waldo had eyes only for her sister. Her heart had lifted eagerly when he began to cross the room towards her, but he had turned to Marian. How swiftly he had responded to her voice, how warmly he had smiled on her, and how ready he was to devote his entire attention to her! How could anyone doubt that he was in love with Marian, like so many men before him?

At dinner, Lucy found herself seated between

Waldo and Colin, and felt a momentary panic that she had lost the comforting nearness of Daniel. But he faced her across the oval table, and he sent her a swift, reassuring smile as their eyes met.

Intercepting that exchange, Waldo was irritated without reason. He turned to Lucy, glad of an opportunity to talk to her, for they had exchanged only the briefest of greetings since her arrival. "You're looking very pretty this evening," he said softly.

Lucy smiled absently, refusing to betray the pleasure that the compliment brought. "Thank you, Waldo," she said, and turned to Colin to ask him a question.

Waldo waited until Colin's attention was claimed by his other neighbour, then he turned to Lucy. "What happened to you this afternoon?" he asked. "You're a very elusive young woman, you know. I wanted to see you, but you had simply disappeared."

Indignation suddenly sparked in her hazel eyes. "I didn't know you meant to give me the pleasure of your company or I should certainly have kept this afternoon free for you," she said.

"Ouch!" he murmured, his eyes twinkling. "It seems I made the fatal mistake of taking a woman for granted. Do forgive me! But I did hope you might have an hour to spare for a friend. After all, I abandoned my book for your sake!"

"Well, it all ended quite happily," said Lucy sweetly. "Marian told me that you and she met and went for a drive."

He held her gaze, a smile deep in his eyes. "Jealous, Lucy?"

She laughed softly, convincingly. "Well, of

course! Doesn't every woman want you?" she mocked lightly.

She turned to Colin and began a light-hearted, almost flirtatious conversation with him.

Waldo felt that the girl at his side was suddenly a stranger. He had never seen her like this... bright and sparkling and vivacious, gaily flirtatious. Abruptly he wondered if she was just as skilled at flirtation as her beautiful sister—and clever enough to appear innocent and unawakened...

Lucy suddenly realised that all her efforts to convince Waldo that she cared nothing for him had only misled him into thinking that she enjoyed light and meaningless flirtation as much as Marian did. For he was almost embarrassingly attentive, and she was increasingly aware of the disturbing magic of the man.

She tried to keep him at a distance but he refused to recognise any coolness in her manner and was determined to monopolise her attention. It was desperately hard to remember that it was no more than warm and teasing flirtation in his eyes when he smiled at her, murmured ridiculous compliments in her ear, provoked her to laughter with his nonsense and talked to her in low tones that hinted at an intimacy that did not and never could really exist between them.

She reminded herself bleakly that he was Marian's lover even if he was a shocking flirt, and she must give up the foolish dreams that had lived in her heart for weeks and had sprung to new life because he had paid her a little attention that evening.

She was glad to escape from the dinner-table, and immediately sought refuge in Daniel's reassuring presence. Marian, separated from Waldo during dinner, was swift to claim his assistance in choosing records for the radiogram.

Everyone relaxed over coffee and liqueurs. Music played softly in the background, and the conversation flowed with an ease appropriate after such an excellent dinner. The sliding windows which opened on to the terrace and the garden were pulled back, for it was a very warm night.

Suddenly, the tempo of the music changed and Marian decided that she wanted to dance. She pulled Waldo to his feet, brushing aside his protest with the reminder that he had danced perfectly well at the Cap and Bells earlier in the week. Within moments, the rugs had been taken up, furniture pushed into corners.

Colin grinned at his cousin as Waldo waltzed past him with Marian in his arms. His leg seemed to be slightly stiff but he was managing tolerably well; and Marian appeared to be content.

Waldo was looking well and relaxed, Colin thought with satisfaction. The long, lazy days had obviously been beneficial to his health and spirits. He was pleased that his cousin had taken his advice and transferred his disquieting interest in Lucy to the sister who could handle it so much more competently. Marian was the type of woman Waldo had always found attractive, and she was just the kind of feminine company that he needed at this particular time.

Marian, dancing past in Waldo's arms, felt her heart twist as Daniel bent to speak to Lucy, and she glanced up quickly with that eager, shining light in her hazel eyes.

She had always known that Lucy cared for him,

of course; but it came as a shock to realise that her little sister was so deeply in love. Could Daniel be blind to that glow? Surely no man could be—and yet he still hesitated to claim the happiness he must surely find with Lucy as his wife. He was held back by a foolish consideration for her youth, obviously—but the years between could not matter when two people loved each other tenderly.

The record finished, and Marian was claimed by Colin for the next dance. Out of the tail of his eye, Waldo saw Lucy slip out through an open window and walk to the far end of the terrace. He went quietly after her and stood behind her, checking the impulse to sweep her into his arms.

He said softly, close to her ear: "Moonbeams are dancing in your hair. Promise me that you'll always wear them!"

She turned slowly and found him very close, smiling down at her—the man who had become so incredibly dear to her in so short a time. For an instant she hovered on the razor's edge between love and hate. She loved him so much, but she hated him for tormenting her and not even knowing he did so.

With admirable composure, she laughed and said easily: "But they aren't always available, and they melt in the warmth of the sun."

"You shouldn't be so practical, Lucy," he said gently.

She wanted to cry that there was nothing practical in the way she felt about him or in her aching need to have his arms about her. Instead, she said lightly: "All right! I'll wish for the moon— and where will that get me?"

Waldo laughed. He looked up at the sky and said suddenly: "I'll get the moon for you!" He stretched a hand high into the air and made a swift, darting grab, just as the moon slid behind a cloud and disappeared. He brought down his clenched hand and held it out to her and in the sudden shadows she could only just see the smile that lurked in his dark eyes.

"Take it, Lucy, it's yours!"

Entering into the game, she placed both her hands carefully over his clenched fingers as though she meant to take what he held, and she smiled at him with that rare, spontaneous sweetness.

Waldo caught both of her hands in his and held them very tightly, gazing down at her with the blood storming through his veins in a tumult of longing.

Lucy's heart began to leap like a wild thing as she met the intense, smouldering glow in his eyes. She said shakily: "Now you've made me drop it, Waldo."

He slipped an arm about her slender waist. "You haven't danced with me yet, you know," he murmured as music swelled out through the open windows.

Her heart thundered and her senses swam as she moved in his arms. The music was slow and sensuous and he was holding her much too close— so close that he surely could not fail to notice the fierce throbbing in her breast or to sense the sweet flood of desire that swept through her veins. His arms about her were hard and muscular and determined. His magic was irresistible, compelling—and she cared for nothing but his nearness and the promise of ecstasy in his embrace.

The music went on but they had stopped dancing. Lucy looked up at him with a shy question in her lovely eyes. Unsmiling, Waldo looked back at her,

wanting her more than he had ever wanted any
woman in his life ... but wanting her for always and
not just to satisfy a fleeting passion.

Lucy waited, torn between the desperate longing
for the warm touch of his lips and the fear that she
might surrender too eagerly to the magic when he
kissed her, and so betray that she loved him.

It was inevitable that he should kiss her, but
Waldo hesitated. Her happiness, her security, her
peace of mind were suddenly so much more
important to him than anything else. He believed
that his feeling for Lucy went very much deeper
than anything he had known before. He believed
that it would last for the rest of his life—but suppose
it did not? Suppose he was mistaken? Suppose he
were to break that gentle heart?

He hesitated a moment too long ...

Lucy drew away in a confusion of thought and
feeling. She was ashamed of wanting him, and even
more ashamed that she had embarrassed and
disconcerted him by her readiness to melt into his
arms. She was desperately hurt by his failure to kiss
her, and she knew all the angry dismay that was
natural to a woman set on fire by a man's embrace
only to realise his lack of response.

The moon sailed out of the clouds to illumine his
face. Abruptly he moved away and stood by the
stone balustrade of the terrace, struggling with the
turmoil of his emotions. Lucy thought how cold and
remote he seemed, and how much he must regret the
meaningless flirtation which had aroused such an
unexpected and unwelcome passion.

He turned to smile at her, a little tensely. "The
moonlight and you—a dangerous combination," he
said, a little ruefully.

"Oh, don't pretend!" she said sharply. "It didn't mean a thing—and we both know it!" She forced a soft little laugh. "Everyone flirts at parties!"

He looked at her steadily; and suddenly his feeling for her crystallised and strengthened into swift resolution. The longing for her could not be denied, and he would never be free of it. He needed all the warmth and sweetness and loveliness that was Lucy—and if such a need was loving, then he must admit to loving at last.

He went to her and caught her face between his hands, gazing down at her with his heart in his eyes. "Oh, my dear..." he said helplessly, very much in love and unable to find the words to say so. The careless lover of the past had never imagined such an intensity of longing or such a foolish inability to express it in words. He bent his head and kissed her, so fleetingly it was scarcely a kiss at all. But there was a wealth of tenderness in the touch of his lips.

Lucy did not know that loving inspired that brief kiss. She did not sense the yearning within him or hear it in the quiet endearment or see it in his eyes. Dismayed and angry, furious with herself and with him, she felt that she hated him for knowing that she loved him and for having nothing to give her but compassion.

"Please, don't!" she said fiercely, knocking away his hands. Then she turned and fled back into the safety of the room and the company.

The sun was high in a brilliantly blue sky, reflecting a myriad of sunbeams in the clear water of the lake. It was quiet and peaceful and very, very hot.

Waldo stretched out on the sun-drenched grass with his hands beneath his head, idly watching Marian. She wore a brief bikini that emphasised the perfection of her slender body. Her golden cap of hair was bright in the sun, and her lovely face glowed with health. She was really very beautiful, he thought dispassionately—and very much like too many women he had known in the past. Marian could not stir him to anything more than mild liking and affection. He needed something that a woman like Marian could not give him.

He turned his head to look at Lucy. She was lying on her stomach, her chin propped on her hand, lost in thoughts which excluded him completely.

Daniel emerged from the trees, came towards the group by the lake, and dropped on the grass by Lucy's side. Lucy glanced up at him and smiled, and the pair of them began to talk in an easy, friendly fashion that left Waldo feeling jealous and resentful.

Within a few minutes, using the heat as an excuse and the coolness under the trees as temptation, Daniel persuaded Lucy to walk with him—and Waldo watched them with a frown in his eyes as they strolled off, still talking. He turned to Marian and made some casual comment on the close relationship between Lucy and the man who was both friend and employer. There was nothing in his tone to betray any objection to that closeness, for he was a proud man who had not given his heart lightly or easily; and he was far from ready to reveal his innermost emotions to an outsider—even to Marian who was more sensitive and understanding than most.

"He's known us all since we were children,"

Marian said carelessly; and did not look at Waldo for fear he saw something in her eyes when she spoke of Daniel. "Of course, Lucy was tiny when he first came to the village. I suppose that's why he finds it so hard to accept that she's grown up." She gave a brittle laugh. "It's astonishing that any man can be so blind. There's Lucy under his nose almost every day, fretting terribly, making herself ill with wanting him—and he just can't see it. There are times when I want to shake him!"

It was the last thing Waldo had expected, and a bitter blow to him. "I didn't know...I hadn't realised...I suppose I've not really thought about it," he said, when it became essential that he make some kind of reply. "Lucy really cares for him, does she?"

Marian was surprised by his lack of perception. She had not supposed that she would need to spell it out for Waldo. After all, Lucy had been wearing her heart on her sleeve for days. "She adores him!" she exclaimed; and her voice rang with the sincerity of her conviction.

Waldo was furious with himself. He had been so intent on his own feeling for Lucy, so intent on supposing her to care for him, that he had not considered the significance of her obvious affection for Pegrim.

Colin had assured him that there was no man of importance in Lucy's life—and he had believed him. He had looked on Pegrim as a family friend of the Copes, more brother than lover in Lucy's eyes. But Marian spoke too confidently for him to doubt that she knew the truth of the matter, and he was forced to accept that Lucy's sister was more likely to know than anyone else.

"Yes, it's obvious now that I do think about it," he said quietly. "One tends to think of Lucy as younger than she is; it's a deceptive quality."

Marian nodded in understanding. "She's such an innocent—that's the trouble," she said wryly. "She just doesn't know how to handle a man like Daniel."

Lucy stood at her bedroom window, watching the heavy raindrops as they spattered against the panes. The sky was streaked with purple and black and gold, and the low rumble of thunder in the distance warned of the approaching storm. Shivering, she drew her dressing-gown more closely about her slight body. There was something of a threat in the sudden stillness, the slow, splashing drops of rain and the rapidly darkening sky, she fancied—and wondered if it was an omen for the evening.

It was Marian's twenty-eighth birthday. As a rule she paid little heed to birthdays, but this year she had chosen to throw a big party to celebrate the occasion, taking over the Cap and Bells for the evening and inviting a host of people.

Lucy's dress lay across the bed together with filmy under-things. A new pair of evening sandals stood ready. Everything waited, and time was slipping by; but Lucy remained at the window, watching the rain. Her heart was as heavy as the sky, and she wondered bleakly if she would always live with this incessant longing for a man she might never see again.

For Waldo had gone back to town ten days ago, with scarcely a word of regret and only the vague explanation that he had various people to see—his agent, his publisher, friends who thought he had been away from town too long.

Lucy knew that Colin had been surprised by hi.
cousin's abrupt departure; and she knew tha
Marian had been deeply hurt and disappointed
although she was adept at hiding her feelings. Fo
herself, it had torn her to pieces to discover that h
had gone away without seeing her to say good-bye
and she had known then just how little she meant i
his life.

A knock on the door brought her out of he
reverie, and she moved towards the dressing-tabl
with a slightly guilty expression as Marian cam
into the room.

"I knew you wouldn't be dressed!" Maria
exclaimed reproachfully.

"I can be ready in ten minutes," Lucy protested

"Yes, indeed—if you don't mind looking a
though you've been thrown together!" Marian sai
with sisterly scorn. "This is a special occasion, m
girl; and you are going to do justice to it! Come alon
now; I'll help you!"

To please her, Lucy allowed herself to be take
over by her dominant sister who wanted everythin
to be perfect for her party. She sat meekly whil
Marian did her hair and face. When Maria
pronounced herself satisfied, Lucy stared at hersel
in the mirror—and saw a stranger.

She looked older, more mature, and there was a
unexpected character in the face that did not loo
like her own any more. Marian had created a ver
different person who looked as though she might b
much more interesting than Lucy Cope.

"What a night!" Marian exclaimed as the rai
hammered with renewed efforts against th
window-panes. "The experts are forecasting tha
this is the end of our glorious summer. But I wish i

ould have stayed fine for just one more evening!"

Lucy turned over her few pieces of jewellery, wondering what to wear with her dress. "How can ou grumble?" she reproached her sister. "We've had weeks of wonderful weather. You're as brown as a berry to prove it."

"Almost every inch of me," Marian agreed, her eyes twinkling. "So might you have been if you'd taken a holiday from the shop! Silly girl! Daniel ould have spared you and you might have had a lot f fun."

"Playing gooseberry?" Lucy asked dryly, selecting a strand of pearls and letting them run through her fingers.

Marian thought that she would gladly have changed places with her sister. Lucy might have had Waldo with her compliments if she could have spent her days with Daniel. But a Daniel who smiled on her with affection, who talked easily to her, who welcomed her company, who loved her as she loved him—not the Daniel who was so cold and remote and painfully indifferent.

"The weather really changed when Waldo went away," Marian said thoughtfully. "It rained on that last evening, do you remember? If he brought this storm with him tonight then I'm going to tell him ff."

The pearls slipped from suddenly nerveless fingers to clatter on the glass top of the dressing-table.

"Is Waldo back?" Lucy asked, trying to sound nconcerned, but the words came out unevenly from suddenly dry lips.

Marian did not notice. "Oh, of course you don't now!" she exclaimed. "Colin rang to ask if he could

bring Waldo to the party. He'd arrived unexpectedly. As if he needed to ask!"

"That's a birthday present that you didn't
expect," Lucy said, a little tremulously.

"Yes, indeed! A lovely present!" Marian said
lightly. "The party wouldn't have been the same
without him. Any more than the summer would
have been. Indeed, this has been quite a summer,
Lucy, a summer to remember."

A summer to remember. The words caught at
Lucy's heart. For the golden summer had brought
Waldo into her life, too—a brilliant, handsome
celebrity who was also a warm-hearted and wonderful man. She had leapt swiftly and impulsively into
loving him. Perhaps it had been her destiny to love
the man who seemed the hero of all her dreams. But
these dreams, so strangely fulfilled, had not
prepared her for the pain and despair of loving a
man who did not want her, of wanting a man who
loved someone else—and that someone her own
sister. Now it seemed that he did love Marian. He
had come back on the day of her birthday, surely
with the intention of asking her to marry him.

Marian reached for Lucy's dress with careful
hands and held it out to her; then noticed with
dismay that her sister's eyes were wet with tears.
She was abruptly reminded that Lucy also cared for
Daniel; but she had no need to cry, for she was
fortunate in loving a man who had loved and
wanted her for many years.

Marian was a perceptive young woman but she
was laying the blame for Lucy's heartache at the
wrong door. For weeks she had known of her sister's
unhappiness—and, to Marian, only a man could

cause that kind of despair. She was convinced that there was only one man for Lucy, but Daniel was infuriatingly slow to realise it, and stubbornly blind to the fact that Lucy had acquired maturity through loving him.

Lucy was shy, unsure. She did not know how to force the pace as another woman might. Perhaps she was even beginning to wonder if Daniel cared for her at all. Whereas Marian did not need to wonder. She knew only too well that Lucy's gentle, modest loveliness had always been dearer to Daniel than her own vivid beauty and flamboyant personality.

She zipped Lucy into the lovely, slim-fitting gown. Then she turned her round, smiled her approval and wiped away a tear from her sister's cheek.

Lucy said swiftly, defensively: "It's the mascara—it makes my eyes water."

Marian accepted the blatant untruth without argument. "You'll soon get used to it," she said lightly. "I can't take it off now, because it would mean doing your face all over again, and there just isn't time." On a sudden impulse she planted a kiss on Lucy's cheek and then laughed softly at the look of bewilderment in her sister's eyes, for she was not particularly demonstrative as a rule.

"Don't worry, darling," she said. "You look lovely—and he must think so, too. This might be the start of something you've always wanted."

Lucy stared at her, sudden panic clutching at her throat. "I don't understand..."

Marian smiled with faint reproach in her eyes. "You don't have to pretend with me, Lucy," she said quietly. "I am your sister and I'm not stupid. You really know what it's all about at last, don't you? You really do love him."

Lucy's hand flew to still her suddenly plunging heart. For if Marian had guessed, then so could others—and that included Waldo. She would not be able to bear it if he were to discover how she felt about him. He might cherish some suspicion—but that was not knowing.

"I might have thought so at one time," she retorted. "But I was mistaken. Anyone can make a mistake, Marian. As you should know! How many times have you thought you were in love?"

"Too many times," Marian said wryly. "But we're talking about you—not me." She smiled with warm understanding in her eyes. In recent weeks Lucy had taken very few pains to hide her feelings, and only someone as stubbornly blind as Daniel could have remained so unaware of the truth. Marian suddenly decided that something had to be done about Lucy. Even though it meant an end to her own dreaming, she must do what she could to secure her sister's happiness and peace of mind.

"Be as proud as you like with other people but don't shut me out," she said gently. "I know you care for him, Lucy; and I want you to stop worrying! Everything will come right for you in the end; and that's a promise."

Lucy stared in astonishment. How on earth could Marian make such a promise? Lucy was quite sure that her sister was in love at last—and with the one man, the only man, that Lucy herself could ever love. Marian was warm-hearted and generous, but no one could expect her to sacrifice her happiness even for a sister. And it would need a miracle indeed

for Waldo to discover that he preferred Lucy to the
beautiful, bewitching Marian.

She said with sudden impatience: "Oh, Marian!
You mean well, but it's just ridiculous to talk as
though he's ever really given me a second thought!"

She was about to point out that only a fool would
suppose that Waldo had come back to Inskip for her
sake, when it had always been obvious that he
wanted Marian. But her sister exclaimed in swift
irritation: "Now you're just being silly and defeat-
ist! Sometimes you have to make an effort to get
what you want from life, you know!"

"All the effort in the world wouldn't get me a man
who doesn't want me," Lucy returned. "Now don't
encourage me to start dreaming all over again,
Marian. It's a bad habit and I'm trying to give it
up."

Marian might have persisted, but there was very
little time left; and she still had to add the final
touches to her own face and hair. So she merely said
with a hint of tartness: "You'll never give up
dreaming—and if you aren't careful you'll end up
with nothing but dreams."

But as she went back to her own room, Marian
admitted the awkwardness of the situation. For
Daniel was a proud, reserved, reticent man who
could seem strangely remote for all the long years of
friendship. If he chose to say nothing, then it was
impossible for Lucy or any other woman to assume
that he cared. The whole world might suspect that
he loved Lucy; but if he stayed silent then she could
do nothing. A woman needed the right kind of
encouragement to reach out for what she wanted,
and the kindly, affectionate indulgence in Daniel's
attitude did not even hint at loving.

Supposing everyone was mistaken and he felt no
more than ordinary liking and affection for Lucy?
She would never recover from the rebuff he would be
compelled to give her, for Daniel was not a man to
marry on the strength of mere liking. Suddenly
Marian was torn between a natural concern for her
sister's happiness and the urgent desire to discover
that Daniel felt merely affection for Lucy...

He looked particularly well that evening in the
crisp black and white of formal clothes. He was not
handsome as other men were handsome, but there
was something very distinctive about him.

Marian's heart somersaulted as he greeted her
with smiling warmth, held her hands a moment
longer than necessary, bestowed a rare kiss on her
cheek and told her that she was much too beautiful.

She laughed and returned a light answer, her
heart very full and, ridiculously, leaping with hope.
For she did not think he had ever before told her that
she was beautiful. He was not given to paying easy
compliments, and he had always given her the
impression that he disapproved—not of her beauty
but of its impact on people and her blatant use of it
to get what she wanted. His words might have
indicated disapproval with the claim that she was
'much too beautiful' if it had not been for the
surprising warmth of his tone and a certain smile in
the eyes which so seldom betrayed the real man
behind the cool, confident façade. Did he mean
'disturbingly beautiful'? Had he meant to imply
that she disturbed him with her beauty?

She could not help the eagerness of hope—but
then he went to Lucy with outstretched hands and a
warm exclamation of admiration, and Marian knew
that her heart was much too quick to mislead her

and that she must force herself to accept that she had discovered her love for Daniel much too late.

For while he might not be deeply in love with Lucy, he was a man like any other, and he could no doubt be persuaded into linking her with thoughts of marriage. The look in his eyes as he went to her sister indicated that he had been jolted to a sudden awareness that she was very much a woman.

For suddenly Lucy was no longer an immature girl with her hair tumbling on her shoulders and soft freckles powdering her nose. Nor was she the neat, efficient and easily overlooked assistant in a prim overall.

She was a woman, slender and lovely and surely desirable in the flowing dress that clung to her slight, feminine figure, a dress designed in varying shades that rippled from brightest flame to palest gold and back again, complementing the gleam of gold in her hair and the gold flecks in her hazel eyes.

She was unexpectedly beautiful in her brief moment of delighted awareness that every eye was upon her, but suddenly she was the Lucy everyone knew, as she gave Daniel her hands and smiled at him with enchanting sweetness and raised herself on her toes to give him a kiss before everyone.

CHAPTER SIX

Waldo paused in the act of tying his tie. He studied his reflection in the mirror, frowning. For despite the tan he had acquired during those long, lazy days in the sun, he looked tired and far from well, and there were shadows beneath his eyes. His nerves were ragged, too.

He had been overworking, overdoing the social round, imagining himself completely fit a little too soon—that had been his explanation to Colin who had told him bluntly that he looked ghastly.

His mouth twisted wryly as he admitted the truth to himself. Who would have thought that a woman could cause him to lose sleep, could possess his every waking thought, could tear him to pieces with longing, could humble his pride to the point where nothing mattered but the need to see her, speak to her, touch her hand and hear from her own lips that it was hopeless to love her?

He had gone back to London believing he could put her out of his mind and heart if he accepted that she cared for Pegrim and so was out of his reach. He had told himself that he would soon forget her, but he had discovered that he needed her too much to walk out of her life so completely. Lucy was a delight he could not deny himself even if he had to be content with no more than her friendship, even if he must endure the sight of her in the company of the man she wanted to marry.

He knew that he loved her with all his heart. He loved her as he had never thought it possible for him to love—and it was hard to accept that she had been lost to him long before he entered her life. He had committed himself completely to loving, despite all his resolutions—and he had chosen to love Lucy of all the women in the world. Although it did not seem to him that there had been much choice about it, he thought wryly. He had not meant to love her. He had fought it from the beginning, knowing instinctively that he would love more deeply than most men if he ever loved at all. But he had fallen beneath the spell of her enchantment, and finally allowed himself to love with all his being, in the confident belief that he had only to speak to have her secure in his arms for ever.

He had been deceived by that yearning he sensed within her, a yearning to love and be loved. He had failed to realise that while she was eager to know all the sweet ecstasy of loving it was not his arms, his kiss, his passion that she ached to know. He had been so blind, so arrogant, so cocksure! It had simply not occurred to him that Lucy might be committed to loving another man.

At last he had reached full understanding of how it had been for Dorian who had loved him and wanted to die when she discovered how little he really cared for her. He was stronger than Dorian, and he did not wish for oblivion as a release from futile loving and longing. But when he thought of a future without Lucy, he could understand the agony of mind and heart that had driven Dorian to that desperate act.

He had never wanted marriage. Now he wanted to marry Lucy, to love and cherish and look after her, to have and to hold her for the rest of his life. He wanted her warmth and sweetness and integrity for his own. He wanted her love and her trust as he had never wanted anything in his life. His need for her had brought him back to Inskip with the determination to discover if his love was truly in vain. For he could not meekly accept defeat when he had not even attempted to fight.

Looking back, he knew he had handled everything with incredible clumsiness for a man of his experience—and all because he had been afraid of loving, afraid to give himself wholly and irrevocably to an emotion which must alter his entire outlook on life.

Meeting Lucy, he had been instinctively drawn towards loving her—and then retreated in foolish alarm. He had played fast and loose with her friendship, encouraged her and everyone else to suppose it was Marian he wanted, ignored golden opportunities to win Lucy's lasting affection if not her love—and seized the most inopportune moments to make love to her. It was not surprising that she had taken to treating him with cool reserve and faint wariness—or that she had fled to Pegrim at the very moment when he himself had been about to speak of his love for her.

He was too experienced to doubt that desire had leapt in her when they stood together beneath the moon. But physical attraction could leap to life between a man and a woman without owing anything to mutual regard. There was some kind of chemistry that could spark an immediate reaction between two people—even strangers—and perhaps it was only that kind of response he had sensed in Lucy which had encouraged him to suppose that she cared for him. However it was, he would not rest until he heard from her own lips that she loved Daniel Pegrim.

Marian greeted him with eager delight. He took her hands and smiled down at her, knowing he had missed her as he had missed the village and all the friends he had made during the weeks he had spent in Inskip.

"How are you?" he said warmly.

"I'm fine! I am glad you came back; my party wouldn't have been the same without you, Waldo!" She searched his handsome face, a tiny frown in her eyes. "But you don't look well," she said bluntly.

"Perhaps I've been burning the candle at both ends," he said. Still clasping her hands, still regarding her with that glow of affection in his eyes, he suddenly bent to kiss her—and it was a kiss between friends. "Happy birthday, Marian," he said softly.

As he straightened, he looked beyond her—and

met the coldness in Daniel Pegrim's gaze. He felt the shock of unmistakable antagonism that emanated from the man. The original amity between them had been quickly lost and never recaptured, and in the light of later knowledge Waldo had understood the dislike and resentment in the other man's attitude. It was obvious that Pegrim would not welcome his unexpected return; but this was something more. This was a flash of actual hatred, and Waldo was shocked and alarmed.

However, he smiled and moved towards Daniel Pegrim with outstretched hand, ignoring the hostility in his eyes. "Good to see you again!"

Daniel was innately courteous, and wholly unaware of that betrayal of his innermost emotions. He shook hands, murmured something polite, and struggled with the cold anger that consumed him. When McKinnon's attention was distracted by the warm, surprised delight in Michael Cope's greeting, Daniel turned away, searching instinctively for Lucy who had possibly witnessed that tender exchange between Marian and McKinnon. His anger was born of his concern for Lucy, who was very dear to him, and aroused all his protective instincts. If McKinnon had kept away, then Lucy might have forgotten him in time, even if she had continued to cherish a tender memory of her first love.

He saw her and hurried across the room to her side, and she turned to him with a swift smile.

"McKinnon is here, Lucy," he said quietly.

"Then he did come!" she exclaimed with betraying eagerness, scanning the crowded room for him. "Where, Daniel? I can't see him!"

"He's talking to your father."

She caught sight of Marian's blonde head. Slightly to the left of her sister stood the tall, familiar figure of the man she sought, and her heart stopped for a moment. She gazed at him longingly, willing him to look her way, but he was intent on his conversation with her father.

When Waldo did look in her direction and saw her for the first time, she was clinging to Daniel's arm and laughing up at him as though she did not have a care in the world. He stopped in the middle of a sentence, struck by the change in Lucy, and not sure that it pleased him. She was suddenly so mature, so confident, so much more of his world—and yet farther out of reach than ever.

Watching the way she clung to Pegrim's arm, hung on his every word, Waldo knew it had been a mistake to return to Inskip, to obey that foolish impulse and heed the insistent hope that he could wean her away from the other man. It was obvious that the quiet, reserved, somewhat austere Pegrim, so much older than Lucy, was the axis of her small world.

Watching with the eagle eye of a lover, he knew swift concern for Lucy who gave so generously of her sweet self to a man whose devotion did not seem to him to be the kind of loving that she sought and merited. He knew instinctively that there was something lacking in Pegrim's feeling for Lucy. Perhaps he meant to marry her, but Waldo did not believe that he loved her. He was undoubtedly fond of her. He was affectionate and attentive, but there was nothing of the lover in his expression or his attitude. Or so it seemed to Waldo—but he was honest enough to admit that he could be blinding himself.

He was silent, studying the couple across the room, unaware that Michael Cope was regarding him with kindly understanding.

At last Michael said quietly: "A father shouldn't have favourites, but Lucy has always been the dearest of my daughters. Her happiness is very important to me."

Waldo turned to look at him, steadily. "And you think she will be happy with Pegrim." There was a faint challenge in his tone.

Michael hesitated, reluctant to hurt a man he liked and admired and called friend, but determined to protect Lucy from possible pain and disillusion in the future. Daniel was reliable and trustworthy, a staunch friend, loyal in his affections. He would look after Lucy with tenderness and loving concern, and shield her from all harm. He was a little old for her, perhaps; but that did not matter when weighed against all the other advantages. What could Waldo McKinnon offer Lucy? His way of life was so utterly different from anything she had ever known. His reputation with women was a poor recommendation for her happiness. He was wealthy, brilliant, famous and he moved in sophisticated circles. Lucy was shy and sensitive, a girl who preferred the company of friends and neighbours she had known all her life. She could not know lasting happiness with a man from a different world. In all sincerity, Michael thought that Lucy would be making a disastrous mistake if she married this man. Perhaps she would not marry Daniel if McKinnon disappeared from her life; but in time there would be another man for Lucy, someone more suitable than this handsome, distinguished writer.

Michael said firmly: "I know she will be happy. She may be young but she is very sensible. Falling

in love is all very well, but Lucy needs to feel safe—
and Daniel can supply that need, you know." He
added, more kindly: "I'm afraid you don't know
Lucy very well, but—"

"I love her!" Waldo broke in brusquely. "I'm sure
he doesn't!" He turned on his heel and strode away,
knowing he had been discourteous but in no mood to
regret it. Without hesitation, deciding to burn his
boats, he forced his way through the press of people,
impatient to get to Lucy.

She saw him approach, and her heart contracted
as she thought how proud any woman would be to
know herself loved by such a man. For he was not
just a good-looking charmer with a smooth tongue.
He was all that any woman could want—and she
wanted him with all her heart, she thought wistfully.

She had tried so hard to hate him, but it was
impossible. She loved him dearly and nothing he
said or did could ever alter the way she felt about
him. Suddenly she knew that loving could outweigh
all pride. It no longer seemed to matter that the
world might guess at her love for Waldo McKinnon.
It no longer seemed to matter that Waldo himself
might discover that she loved him. For where was
the shame in loving?

Lucy saw that his eyes were blazing with anger
and her heart missed a beat. But he could not be
angry with her, for he had no cause. So she held out
an eager hand to him as he reached the spot where
she stood with Daniel, and as he clasped her fingers
she said warmly and impulsively: "You did come
back—I'm so glad!"

He looked down at her. "Where can we talk?" he
demanded without ceremony.

Lucy looked into that unsmiling face with some

misgiving, and racked her memory to think what she could have done to displease or offend. She glanced at Daniel a little uncertainly, and saw that he regarded Waldo with cold dislike and un-disguised hostility.

Misinterpreting that glance, Daniel stepped in swiftly. He took Lucy's hand in his and drew her to him—a protective gesture that looked very much like a proprietorial declaration and caused Waldo's mouth to tighten ominously.

"Bad timing, I'm afraid," he said lightly, smooth-ly. "Lucy has just promised to dance this one with me."

Waldo glowered. Lucy stood irresolute for a moment, and then she detached her hand from Daniel's clasp. "May we postpone our dance for a while?" she suggested quietly. She smiled at Waldo, rather shyly.

"What is it, Waldo? Is something wrong?"

"Come with me and I'll tell you," he said brusquely.

Waldo's rudeness was so out of character that Lucy knew he must be under strain.

"Daniel," she said, "I'd like to hear what Waldo has to say. Why don't you dance with Marian—she's looking this way." She smiled up at him with a plea in her eyes. "Go on, Daniel."

He hesitated but there was an unexpected confidence about her, and it suddenly occurred to him that he was very much in the way. For Waldo McKinnon, instead of attaching himself firmly to Marian, had made a beeline for Lucy and seemed very determined on some private conversation with her. And if one correctly construed the look in his eyes as he waited impatiently for Lucy's attention, it might not be too difficult to guess at the reason for his urgency.

Daniel was astonished, but delighted for Lucy if McKinnon had returned so unexpectedly for her sake. She was a dear, sweet girl who deserved all the happiness she could find; and if she was so sure that she could find it with McKinnon then everyone must want her dream to come true.

Marian was certainly looking their way and Daniel wondered if she was aware of this unexpected turn of events. As their eyes met across the room, Marian smiled.

He fancied there was a certain encouragement in her smile, and he suddenly knew that the love he felt for her, alarming in its intensity, left no room for pride. Perhaps he would be merely one more conquest to be discarded when she was bored; but perhaps he could persuade Marian into loving him if he tried. Nothing ventured, nothing gained ... and it was time that Marián discovered that he was not the dry-as-dust old bachelor that she imagined him to be.

"I believe I'll take your advice," he said to Lucy, smiling. Then he made his way round the swirling dancers until he reached the spot where Marian stood with her friends. He touched her lightly on the arm and she turned—he saw a swift, leaping delight in her beautiful eyes. But it was hastily concealed, so hastily that he almost believed he had been mistaken.

Marian smiled with the cool confidence of a beautiful woman, but her heart was unsteady. She said lightly: "Hello, Daniel, have you come to dance with me at last?"

"If you care to risk it?" he returned, smiling. "But

I was born with two left feet, you know."

Faint colour stole into her face at the reminder of an accusation she had thrown at his head so long ago that she was surprised he should remember the incident. "Oh, that was years ago," she exclaimed, laughing. "Let's forget it!"

"By all means," he agreed.

He danced well, so well that she wondered that she had once taunted him with being awkward. Perhaps he had seemed stiff and unresponsive then, and that coldness in him had infuriated and baffled her. Now he held her close and with a startling, unexpected tenderness; but now it was Marian who held herself stiffly and did not dare to melt into his arms. For she had surely forfeited all right to Daniel years before, and now he loved Lucy.

So she held back from the invitation in his embrace, and knew that she danced badly. She wished with all her heart that she had not been so foolish in the past...

Lucy turned to Waldo who waited with ill-concealed impatience, a nerve jumping in his cheek and his eyes very dark. She felt swift concern for him, wondering if he was ill. He did not look well, and it was most unlike him to behave so strangely.

"Shall we find a table?" she asked.

"It would be impossible to talk in this noisy atmosphere," he said impatiently, looking around the crowded room.

"The bar?"

"Much too public!" He took her arm and drew her through the press of people towards the exit. "It will have to be my car," he said firmly.

The rain had stopped, leaving enormous puddles, and Lucy had to step very carefully in her thin sandals. The air struck cold, and she shivered slightly as she waited for Waldo to produce the car keys and open the doors.

Waldo said swiftly: "It's too cold for you, Lucy. I'm so thoughtless. I'll go and get you a wrap."

She checked him hastily as he turned to go back to the roadhouse. "It doesn't matter—I shall be warm enough in the car," she assured him. "You might run into someone who would keep you talking for ages!" She slipped into the front passenger seat of the car and smiled at him.

Waldo went round to the other side and got in behind the wheel. He stared at the flickering neon sign above the building, thoughts and feelings in turmoil. For now that she was beside him and they were alone and he had all the opportunity that a man could wish, he could not muster a single coherent sentence to tell her how he felt.

The silence was puzzling. At last, Lucy said gently: "Are you in some kind of trouble, Waldo?"

He looked at her then. "It depends what one means by trouble, I suppose."

"You...you aren't ill?" she asked with a tremor of apprehension in her voice. She could not bear to think of him hurt or in pain.

Waldo smiled wryly. "Not ill, exactly," he said slowly. "Sick at heart, perhaps."

Impulsively Lucy laid a hand on his arm. "Tell me, Waldo," she invited gently, warm compassion in her eyes. "Perhaps I can help."

It surprised her that he was unhappy; but perhaps Marian had found it impossible to love him, after all. Perhaps that explained his abrupt departure—and perhaps a reluctance to give up all hope of marrying Marian had brought him back so unexpectedly. Loving him, Lucy knew only too well the terrible sickness of heart in wanting someone who did not care, and she ached to comfort him.

Waldo looked at her steadily, loving her, knowing the impulse to take her in his arms then and there, dispensing with all need for words. She was incredibly sweet in her obvious concern for him and he loved her all the more for the compassion she offered. She could not know how little it seemed to a man who longed desperately for her love.

He had been so determined to tell her of his love for her, to ask her if she was so very sure that she wanted to marry Pegrim, to beg her to think again and give him a chance to prove how much he loved and needed her, give him a chance to teach her to love him. Now he knew that he must say nothing. For she did not know that she was the cause of his heartache, and it would distress her too much to be told. Lucy was the kind of person who dreaded to inflict pain on anyone, and it would not be fair to let her know how much she had hurt him merely because she loved another man.

"Pegrim's a lucky man," he said quietly, trying to keep all trace of bitterness from his voice.

Lucy stared in astonishment. The words were so unexpected. He must mean that Marian was in love with Daniel, after all, and her heart lifted with sudden delight for she could wish for nothing better for either of them. Daniel would be perfect for Marian who needed his steadiness, his strength of character, his integrity and the kind of lasting love that he would bring to their marriage.

It was marvellous news, she thought happily, and wondered that Marian could have kept it to herself for so long. She obviously did not realise that

Daniel cared for her; and Lucy devoutly hoped that he would take her advice and reach out for his happiness that very evening. Oh, Marian was so much more fortunate than she knew, she thought wistfully...

"Daniel isn't the only lucky one," she said lightly, remembering as she spoke that the good fortune that Daniel and Marian shared in loving each other had brought unhappiness to the man by her side. But her heart leapt with the sudden awareness that now she could begin to dream again; for who could tell what might happen if she just went on loving and hoping and trying to be all that a man like Waldo could want?

"You're very sweet," Waldo said quietly, breaking into her thoughts.

She looked down in sudden, shy confusion. "I'm very tactless," she said ruefully. "I'm so sorry, Waldo. I didn't mean to hurt you."

"Then you do know," he said slowly, almost savagely.

Lucy nodded. "I've known for a long time," she said, recalling the pain of past weeks.

He uttered a harsh laugh, mocking his own stupidity. "And I brought you out in the cold to tell you something you already knew!"

He was suddenly racked with the torment of love and longing and wondering how he could go away and forget her when he needed her so much. But he could not stay. He had foolishly supposed he could be content with her friendship, could endure the daily witnessing of her love for another man. But he would not be content with anything less than having Lucy for his wife, and that was impossible.

"No, you didn't mean to hurt me, Lucy," he said

dully. "It isn't your fault that I was fool enough to cling to an impossible dream."

Lucy turned to him and put her arm about his broad shoulders, her heart tearing with grief that he should be so unhappy and she should be so powerless to comfort him.

At her touch he stiffened. Then abruptly he turned and took her in his arms, impelled by the urgency of his need. Perhaps he would never hold her again, but this would be one moment to recall, to cherish, to treasure—and her warm generosity of heart would not deny him this brief comfort.

Lucy gave a little gasp. Her heart seemed to stop, and then plunged with breathless delight as she saw the wealth of longing in his eyes. She smiled tremulously and raised a hand to the lean, smooth cheek. He turned his head swiftly to kiss the slender fingers, and she moved her hand to caress the back of his neck. Drowning in the sweet, fiery flood of wanting that tumbled in her veins as she met his gaze, she waited for the touch of his lips.

Waldo held back. His control was near to breaking-point and he knew he could not surrender her to any man if he once allowed himself to know the sweetness in her kiss. She was young and impulsive and generous, and he ought not to take advantage of her reluctance to refuse him these few moments of happiness.

Lucy loved him, and she wanted him. She did not think about her pride. Because he would not kiss her, Lucy murmured his name with her lips against his—then she kissed him, and all the magic she had dreamed of was in the swift ardour of his response.

At last, with an effort that left him weak, he released her, smiling shakily and leaning forward to kiss the tip of her nose.

"Waldo?" she whispered, consumed with longing or him.

He laid his fingers on her lips, and smiled when he kissed them impulsively. "You give too much of ourself, Lucy," he said, sighing. "It makes it very hard for a man."

"I love you," she said softly, scanning his face for he merest flicker of response to her words. "I love ou so much."

He caught her hands and held them very tightly. 'At this moment, perhaps; or you think you do, Lucy," he said. "You are such an innocent. You want me, that's all, because I made you want me. But that isn't loving."

"I do love you," she said stubbornly. "I've always oved you. It isn't just wanting you—that's only part of the way I feel about you. I won't pretend any more, Waldo—why should I?"

"Lucy, Lucy, you don't know what you're saying," he said ruefully, kissing her lightly. "You're in love with Pegrim and you're going to marry him—remember?"

She pulled her hands free and sat up abruptly. 'Marry Daniel—me? What are you talking about? You said that Marian was going to marry him!"

"No, I didn't."

"Yes, you did!" she declared emphatically. "You said Daniel was a lucky man."

"Because you love him!"

"But I don't! I love you!" she said angrily. "I've never even thought about marrying Daniel!"

Waldo suddenly threw back his head and laughed softly. "We've been at cross purposes, Lucy!" He put an arm about her shoulders and drew her against him, resting his head against the soft hair, framing a face that was luminously lovely in the pale glow of light that invaded the car.

She was suddenly very, very happy. There was a closeness between them that she had never sup posed to be possible even in her wildest dreams, and she knew instinctively that it would last for eve and beyond. She felt very safe, very protected, an very much loved. He did not need to tell her in s many words that he cared, but she was feminin enough to want to hear it.

"I was so afraid you loved Marian," she said.

"I was afraid you meant to marry Pegrim," Waldo returned, a faint smile playing about hi mouth.

"Poor Daniel, you were very rude to him," Lucy said.

He nodded. "Extremely! I must make him a handsome apology."

"I think he understood," Lucy said softly. "H loves Marian very much, you know. I hope things d work out for them both." She looked up at him with a swift, sweet smile. "I want everyone to be as happy as we are, Waldo."

"Impossible! No one could be as happy as w are," he said, touching her lips briefly with his.

"I do love you so," she sighed.

His arm tightened about her. "Lucy, there hav been many women in my life," he said quietly. "To many, and I'm not going to pretend otherwise. Bu I've never told any woman that I loved her and th words don't trip lightly off my tongue. I don't thinl you'd want it to sound too practised, anyway. No have I ever asked any woman to marry me, unti now.

"Lucy, loving you is the most wonderful thing that ever happened in my life. Marry me, m darling, because I can't do without you!"

For answer, she kissed him, and he tasted salt on his lips from the tears that ran down her cheeks. Tears of happiness, he knew; and he vowed that she would never have cause to shed any other kind, if he could help it.

They eventually went back to the party, glowing with the kind of radiance that told its own story. Marian stared, and turned so swiftly to Daniel that she sent her glass of champagne flying across the table. Without heeding it, she reached for his hand and pressed it hard, offering a silent understanding of the way he must be feeling as Lucy and Waldo McKinnon moved through the crowd, his arm about her shoulders, her face tilted towards him and declaring her love and her happiness for all the world to know.

Daniel smiled at her with warm understanding and swift compassion, gratified that she had turned to him for comfort at that painful moment. Marian was faintly puzzled by the sympathy she found in his eyes, but there was no time to question it for Waldo and Lucy had reached them. The next few moments were a confusion of explanations and exclamations and swift congratulations.

Later, Daniel saw that Marian was alone, watching her sister and Waldo making the rounds of their friends and well-wishers. He went to her and laid a hand briefly on her shoulder and she looked up swiftly, startled. "You're a brave girl, Marian," he said quietly. "You always had courage, of course; but it takes a special brand of courage to smile in these circumstances."

She looked up at him steadily. Then she said quietly: "Sit down, Daniel." When he was seated,

she took a deep breath and plunged. "I suppose you
aren't the only person who thinks I've lost the man I
want to my sister, Daniel. But it isn't true, you know.
I like Waldo immensely and I'm delighted that he
means to marry Lucy. She couldn't have given me a
nicer brother-in-law."

"You really mean that," Daniel said slowly.

"Of course I do." She suddenly held out her hand
to him. "Hold my hand, Daniel. I want to say
something and it won't be easy," she said impulsive
ly.

He took her slim fingers and clasped them firmly,
his eyes on her beautiful face, wondering at the
doubt and hesitation he saw in her expression and
surprised by the strength with which she clung to
his hand. "What is it, Marian?" he asked.

She was silent for a long moment. Then she said
breathlessly: "Perhaps if you didn't look at me,
Daniel..." She did not look at him, either, keeping
her gaze on the broad, well-kept, very masculine
hand that covered her own on the table between
them.

"I've never done this before—I've never needed
to," she said, blurting out the words before her
courage failed her. "Daniel, I'm not just flirting—
and I'm not piqued because Lucy's going to marry
Waldo. Daniel, I know how you feel about Lucy, and
I couldn't hope to mean anything like as much to
you. But I would try to be like Lucy. I'd try to be the
kind of woman you want."

She broke off, knowing that she must sound
incoherent and very foolish.

"I don't want you to be like Lucy," Daniel said
gently. "I love you just the way you are."

"I know what a bad impression I've alway

made—" As his words registered, Marian stopped short, staring at him in wonder. "What did you say?"

He laughed softly and touched her cheek with gentle fingers. "I love you just the way you are," he repeated and his eyes held all the loving tenderness that any woman could wish.

She caught his hand and held it close to her cheek, rubbing her face against his fingers. "Oh, Daniel," she said helplessly. "Oh, Daniel!"

And Waldo, glancing at them from across the room, suddenly smiled and bent his head to whisper to Lucy. She followed his glance and recognised the radiance in her sister's face which must resemble so much the radiance in her own—and Marian's obvious happiness made her own complete.

THE END

A Heather Romance

DESIGN FOR LOVING

by
Samantha Grantley

CHAPTER ONE

Mim put the phone down, a puzzled look on her face. Why had he phoned now? She had last heard from him six months ago. And yet, Richard had sounded as if only an hour or two had elapsed, as if he had never stood her up all that time ago. And, she could not deny, it was all too easy, now, to forget about it herself.

She recalled that day, when she had last heard from him. "I'll be round for you at eight," he had said. "Be ready, because I won't be able to park anywhere."

She had been ready. As always, she had bent over backwards to do his bidding, no matter what it had

been. Just to see him was such a joy, she would have
done anything to please him.

But he hadn't been there at eight. Nor at eight-
thirty, nor at nine. He hadn't rung later, either, to
explain, or apologize. In fact, she had never heard
from him again—until today.

Not that she had been surprised. Richard did that
sort of thing all the time. He would say he'd ring,
and then never do it. Or he would ring three days
later, and never mention the fact that he had
neglected to do as he had promised. Still less would
he say he was sorry about it.

It was simply that when he had actually stood
her up, actually not appeared for a date that he
himself had arranged, it had been the last straw.
Before that, on so many occasions in the year that
they had known each other, Mim had finally rung
him to see what had happened. She had always
worried about him: perhaps something terrible had
happened to him; how unfair it would have been of
her to be angry with him, when in actual fact he
might have been ill, or had an accident. Never once
had it occurred to her that he simply hadn't cared
enough about her to be bothered about the fact that
she would be miserable and worried.

That last time, though, she had had enough. For
once she would save herself the humiliation of
running after him. Had she not, after all, done all
the running since she had met him? Of course he
always sounded as though he thought a lot of her,
and enjoyed her company, but it had hurt her
beyond words to have to admit to herself that she
was obviously one of the people in his life whom he
saw when he had nothing better to do.

In the end, she had convinced herself that she

was better off without him. Being tied to Richard meant that she had no opportunity of building up a relationship with any other man, and once she could get over him, she would be much better.

Even so, it had taken her all of six months. It had taken her all this time to get him out of her system.

Why hadn't he stayed away longer? Why couldn't he have waited until she was in love with someone else, until her heart was strong and able to withstand his persuasive charm? Because she knew, with a certainty that was irresistible, that if he started again to call her sweet names in his soft, warm voice, she would be lost all over again.

Mim went to her bedroom and looked at herself in the mirror. She hadn't exactly let herself go since she had last seen Richard, but she couldn't in any way fool herself into thinking that she looked as smart and attractive as she had made herself seem when he was around. She had put on a few pounds and, as she was only a half-inch over five feet tall, even a few pounds made a difference. Her hair, formerly worn short and almost boyish, she had allowed to grow to an indeterminate length.

She nodded at her reflection in affirmation of her thoughts. She wouldn't be seeing Richard for three days, which would give her time, if she had nothing but two apples and a few ounces of cheese in the intervening days, to take off the weight. And she would get her hair done. Even if Richard had come back into her life for one day only, she was darned if he was going to see that his absence had made any change in her.

Would the other people in the office know that he was back? Mim wondered. It was through the advertising firm for which she worked that she had

met him. She had been much impressed by Richard.
A free-lance artist, he was in and out of the office
frequently, his portfolio loaded with drawings. Tall
and dark, his almost craggy good looks had
attracted her from the first; and when he had asked
her out, she thought that she was the most
honoured, favoured person in the world.

It was through the firm that she had heard that
Richard had been out of the country. One of the
other artists had mentioned it casually one day,
almost a month after she had last seen Richard.

"Have you heard about Carlson?" the artist had
asked Mim's boss. "Went to Europe, evidently
hoping to take the art world by storm. Good luck to
him, I say," he had added, his tone implying that
Richard would need every bit of luck he could get.

At least Mim had learned that he was all right.
From then until now, she had set about trying to
force herself to forget him, to tell herself that now
was the time to begin looking for someone who
would care about her in the same way that she had
cared about Richard.

The question now was, why was he back, and
how long did he expect to stay? Hard as she tried to
stop herself, Mim could not help wishing that he
would have realized in their long separation that
she was the only girl for him, and that he had
missed her fully as much as she had missed him.

The three days seemed interminable. Mim dieted
strenuously, had her hair done, and spent far too
much money on a new outfit with which to dazzle
him. If he was only in town for a flying visit, at least
she would be able to make him believe that by jilting
her he had not bothered her one jot, and she had
done very nicely in the interim.

She was grateful, too, that no one in the office

seemed to have heard of Richard's reappearance. At least she wouldn't have to put up with having her leg pulled by the rest of the staff.

Finally, and with almost perverse sluggishness, Friday afternoon arrived. Mim straightened her desk hurriedly and ran from the office.

At home, she bathed and perfumed herself, and then applied her make-up carefully, remembering Richard's penchant for glamorous women. It was through him, in fact, that she had learned about good grooming. Whereas he was very sparing indeed with his compliments, he would always let her know if the way she looked was not quite perfect. "Too much colour around the eyes," he would say, or: "That lipstick is far too bright for your face." Yes, Richard had taught her a lot.

Mim prided herself on the fact that she was quite calm and collected by the time Richard was due. He was late, of course, but she had expected that. When the doorbell rang, however, she had to take a few deep breaths to steady herself. Then she was opening the door, and there he was. As handsome as ever—no, handsomer. Richard had the kind of good looks which always appeared carefully groomed, while in reality he was casual about his appearance. Well, he can afford to be, Mim thought. He's got all the necessary equipment.

He held out his hands to her, and smiled at her with his eyes.

"Mim, darling! It's so very good to see you."

"Would...would you like a drink?" she stammered, suddenly tongue-tied when confronted with those black, magnetic eyes. "Is there time?"

He walked in easily, as though he had never been away. "Plenty of time," he said. "The table's booked for eight-thirty."

Still holding her hands, he stood back and looked at her. "You've changed," he said quietly.

"Is something wrong?" she asked, worried.

He smiled slowly and drew her to him.

"Of course nothing's wrong. You're even more beautiful than I remembered you, that's all."

She stood absolutely still, praying that her knees would not give way, and that soon she would be able to breathe again. It was hard to believe that she was not dreaming, that he was actually there, and she could feel the strength of him, the warmth of his arms around her. She had dreamed of this for so long, how could she be sure it was really happening?

"What about that drink?" he said, moving back.

"Oh, yes, of course." Mim moved to the sideboard where she kept her small stock of liquor, counselling herself all the time to stop behaving like a teenager. Calm and collected! she thought with an inward laugh. The best I can hope to do, it seems, is to keep him from noticing that I'm really nothing more than a love-struck kid, despite my twenty-four years and supposed sophistication.

He accepted the glass of whisky and water—Mim did not have to ask him what he wanted—and held it up to her.

"To us," he said, and it was difficult for Mim to make herself believe that he didn't mean it.

He took her to a charming, expensive restaurant, and that in itself was something of a landmark. When she had known him before, either she would cook for him, or it would be fish and chips on the way to a film or a party. What had happened to him in those six months, she wondered—and what was going to happen now?

It was a splendid evening. He told her all about

what had happened to him while he had been away. No, of course there was no hint of apology about the last time, but at least he seemed genuinely pleased to be with her now, and made her feel, perhaps for the first time, that she was the one person in the whole world that he wanted to be with.

Yes, Richard had certainly changed. And Mim was simply swept off her feet.

After their leisurely, delicious meal, Richard announced that what he wanted to do most was to walk.

"I haven't had a chance to see London since I got back," he said. "I've been rushing around, fixing up a place to live, making contacts. And there's nothing to beat London at night. I've found that out if, nothing else."

As they walked, hand in hand, he told her more about what he had been doing. He had been all over Europe, evidently. He had made new friends—and here Mim had to fight off a sudden irrational stab of jealousy—and experienced life in a way that he had never done before. Most important of all, he knew now what he wanted to do with his life.

"Textile design," he said. "That's what I want to concentrate on. There's something about marrying design with rich fabrics that... well, I can't completely describe the feeling it gives me. Let's face it love, I'm no artist. Not one that's going to shake the world. It's true that I could go on for the rest of my life making a satisfactory living from commercial artwork; but this is different. This is real, deep pleasure. And there's a fantastic market for it. I'm good at it, too, Mim. I really am. Wait till you see some of the things I've done."

He went on to tell her about the studio he had

rented, with a flat at the back. It was ideal, from what he said, and he could hardly wait to get started in earnest.

They walked along the South Bank, stopping occasionally to look at the Thames as it drifted by, unhurried, uncaring. Mim listened dreamily to Richard's words, hearing the sound of his voice more than what he actually said. At that moment it didn't seem to matter why he had come back into her life, or how long he intended to stay. Just being with him was enough. She hugged the moments to her, savouring them, storing them up in case they would be the last for a long time to come.

And yet, nothing about him was giving her the impression that this would be a once-in-a-lifetime happening. He was somehow including her in his plans, placing her firmly in his future. He didn't actually speak about 'us', but the tone of his voice implied it. He had only been home for a few days, and yet he had made a point of ringing her, of seeing her. It was the kind of heaven that Mim had almost stopped believing she would ever know.

They walked for hours. Richard talked most of the time, but they were silent, too, just enjoying being together. Now and again he would stop and take her face in his hands. Not a passionate kiss, no, just his lips brushing against her nose, or her eyelids, and the unspoken promise of more loving moments to come.

"I'm going to take you home now," he announced suddenly. "We've both had a long week, and I can tell that you're as tired as I am."

Then he did kiss her. Right there on Hungerford Bridge, with the Thames sweeping on beneath them. Mim almost fainted from the pure joy of it.

"Oh, it's so good," he murmured, his face buried in her hair. "It's so very good to be with you again."

They stood together for an eternity, just being together and holding each other. Then Richard gently pulled away, took her hand and led her down the steps to Charing Cross Station. Without knowing where he was taking her, or caring, Mim followed Richard to the Strand. He hailed a taxi, and somehow she heard him giving the man her address, and then saying that he would be going on to Fulham.

Then, all too soon, she was home, and Richard was opening the door for her. He kissed her gently on the cheek, and told her that he would ring her very soon.

Mim watched the taxi pull away, her hand raised in farewell. But Richard did not look round...

The next days were like some strange, unpleasant dream from which Mim thought she would never wake, until Richard rang again.

It was not until Monday night that she finally heard from him. He apologized for being so long—in itself a milestone—and told her in detail what he had been doing for the past three days.

For the first time, his plans didn't sound wild, like fantasy schemes dreamt up on the spur of the moment. Richard had evidently gone into this project carefully, finding out in advance how much money he would need, what materials and equipment were necessary, and where he could sell his finished designs. From what he was saying, a few firms and individuals had already promised to take some of the work, and so he had the chance of recouping some of his expenditure before he even started.

"I won't be able to see you for the rest of this week," Richard said, and Mim's heart sank with a thud. "It's really exhausting, getting this sort of thing going."

"Yes," Mim answered, anything but wholeheartedly.

"How about the week-end, though?" he asked. "I'm free on Saturday. What about you?"

Her spirits soaring, Mim tried not to let her excitement show.

"Saturday? Yes, I'm sure I'm free."

"Great. What would you like to do?"

Be with you, she thought. Just be with you. On the moon, if necessary.

"Whatever you'd like, Richard. After all, you're the one who's been away."

"Fine. What would you say to me picking you up at about seven? We'll have a meal, and then perhaps go to the theatre. Is there anything you'd particularly like to see?"

The theatre! Mim loved the theatre, and it thrilled her to realize that Richard remembered that.

"No, nothing in particular. I don't think I've seen anything that's on in the West End at the moment. You choose, Richard. Whatever you say will be marvellous."

And so it was arranged. Richard said that he would not have time to ring her before Saturday, but promised that he would be on time.

Then came the interminable days between Richard's call and Saturday evening. Because she could think of nothing else but the forthcoming date, Mim threw herself into her work during the day, and at night got on with the play she was writing.

She had wanted to be a writer since she was ten years old, and had never completely stopped writing in the fourteen years since then. Plays, short stories, poems, even a novel had come from a series of pens and pencils—so far without any kind of success whatever. She still had high hopes, however, and she could not have stopped, even if she had wanted to. Writing was in her blood, it was her life. It helped her through difficult times, and gave her a sense of purpose.

Richard had always laughed at her efforts. He had said, on several occasions, that it was a sheer waste of time. Mim had never managed to convince him that the satisfaction she derived from the actual writing was worth while.

Saturday came at last. Once again Mim took great care in getting herself ready for the date. She had allowed just the right amount of time for her preparations, so that she would not be left with an hour to spare, all made up and ready, and afraid to have a drink or a cigarette in case she might spoil her carefully applied make-up, or get anything on her dress.

When he did arrive, Richard was carrying a beautiful bunch of flowers. He handed them to Mim, kissing her lightly on the cheek at the same time.

"I hope you like them," he said. "I spent hours in the shop, picking out each and every bloom."

She beamed. "Of course I like them. They're perfect. Thank you, Richard."

"It was a pleasure, darling," he said.

Mim turned away, suddenly almost overcome with emotion. While she searched for a vase, she kept hearing his voice as he had said 'darling'.

They went to the same restaurant as before, and

enjoyed a wonderful meal. When Richard announced that he had not actually bought tickets for the theatre, having decided instead to see how they felt at the time, Mim was conscious only of being glad that they would not have to be among people, and trying to concentrate on the stage, when her thoughts, she knew, would be on him.

There was a niggling little voice at the back of her mind that suggested, nastily, that if they were going to be eating after seven, there would be precious little time to get to a theatre; but she studiously ignored it and concentrated instead on the man she was with, the man she could never help loving.

Richard said more than once how beautiful Mim was looking, and how deeply happy he was to be with her again. He talked of his business venture, and made it sound the most exciting thing she had ever heard of.

"Of course, there's a bit of a money problem," Richard remarked at one point. "But that will sort itself out, I'm sure."

Mim looked at him dubiously. "Are you having trouble with money, Richard?" she asked. "I thought, from the way you were talking, that you had worked that side of it out."

He smiled warmly and covered her hand with his. "It's close to being sorted out," he said, squeezing her hand. "Don't worry about it. I just need a bit more than I've got, that's all. But I'll be able to manage it somehow."

Mim chewed her lip thoughtfully. "Can't you get a loan from the bank?"

Richard laughed. "My darling, I'm in debt to the bank already! No, they've given me the limit that they're willing to part with. The fact of the matter is that I need a bit more, that's all." He looked into her eyes and grinned. "I don't suppose you have any dealings with a millionaire who's looking for something to put his money into, do you?"

Mim shook her head. "No, I'm afraid not." She hesitated, trying hard to fight that nasty little voice that was telling her to keep quiet, to hold her tongue. Then: "How much do you need?" she asked him.

He looked up, his eyes wide, a small frown between his eyebrows. "Darling, let's not talk about it, okay?" he asked. "It's my problem, not yours."

She took a deep breath. Ignoring her better judgement, she went on quickly: "No, let me know. I've ... I've got a bit of money, as it happens."

Richard raised his eyebrows and asked innocently: "Oh? That's something new, isn't it?"

"My father died while you were away, and ..."

"Oh, I am sorry," he cut in. "Was it a terrible shock?"

"It wasn't unexpected. He had been ill for some time."

"You poor darling, how did you manage to cope?" Richard cried.

"As I said, I did have some warning. And I have an aunt who was a tower of strength. But I'd rather not discuss it, Richard, if you don't mind. It was a loss, a sad loss, but it's over now. The thing is, my father left me some money. About five thousand pounds, in fact."

"But you must need that for yourself," Richard said. "Surely you want to do something with it."

"I haven't decided yet. It's quite a lot of money— to me at any rate, so I've put it in the bank while I think about it. I was toying with the idea of buying a flat, or a new car, but I haven't made up my mind.

Anyway, how much do you still need?"

"But my dear, I couldn't possibly ask you..." he began.

"I know that. And you haven't asked, have you? I've simply inquired how much money you need before you can get going with your project. Come on, don't be coy with me, Richard. How much do you need?"

"As a matter of fact," he said slowly, "it's just about five thousand pounds. So you see, you couldn't possibly lend me everything you've got."

Mim said with a little smile: "If I lent you the money, I wouldn't be any worse off than I am now, would I? I've still got my job, and I haven't needed my legacy until now, have I? There's just one thing, though, darling," she went on, daring herself to use the word, "I would like to see what you've done so far, before I actually lend you the money. Would you think that terrible of me?"

"Terrible?" Richard asked, his eyes lighting up. "I think it's extremely sensible, my love. Of course you must see what you're investing in. But please, Mim, don't feel that I'm forcing you into this. I hadn't intended to ask you for a loan. I swear I hadn't."

She said impatiently: "No, I know that. But if you need money and I've got some, why shouldn't I make you a loan? When can I see these designs of yours?"

He looked at his watch. "I'll tell you what—why don't we go along to the studio now? I can show you enough to give you an idea, and I can explain anything you want to know."

He looked so much like a little boy with a new

plaything that Mim could not help laughing. She raised her glass to her lips.

"Do you think I might just finish my wine?" she asked.

"My dearest Mim, you can have champagne, if that's what you want. Loads and loads of champagne, and my undying gratitude into the bargain!"

...From the outside the studio was not much to look at; nor was it particularly impressive inside, either. It was a large room which, from the fact that there were mirrors ranged on two of the walls, and bars, Mim assumed had once been a dance studio. The place was draughty; and there were a number of unpacked boxes, a drawing-table, one long table pushed against one wall, and a pile of old newspapers in a corner.

"The flat's back there," Richard said, pointing to a door at the far corner of the room, "but it's a mess, so I won't bother showing you that. I know this looks pretty grotty right now, but I have sketches somewhere, showing what it will be like eventually. I'll let you see them when I've dug them out. But the important things are the designs for the fabrics. I'll get them now."

He went into the flat, and came back carrying a large portfolio. Taking a deep breath, Mim watched as he undid the strings, and prepared herself for what was to follow.

She needn't have worried. The designs were magnificent—exciting and alive, and fully warranting all the enthusiasm he had shown.

She looked at every design before she spoke. Then: "Richard, they're fantastic! This is indeed your field. Thank goodness you've found out—it would have been such a terrible waste otherwise."

He grinned proudly. "They aren't bad, are they? Something suddenly clicked when I was in Europe. Know what I mean? All of a sudden, I knew that what I had been doing was all wrong, and that this was really me."

Mim nodded, her eyes still on the designs. "I know exactly what you mean," she said. "They're tremendous. And it's obvious that they come from the depths of you." She looked up at him, her face full of admiration. "Or does that sound silly?" she asked.

Richard swept her into his arms. "Not silly at all, my dearest love. Very astute, in fact." He gave her a quick, tight squeeze. "Well, what do you say, then?"

She was perplexed for a moment. "About the drawings, you mean?"

An impatient look crossed his face, but it was hidden from her.

"I mean about the money. Would you like to invest in my work, or not?" He felt her stiffen slightly in his arms, and held her even more tightly to counteract the reaction.

"I'll need a bit of time, Richard," she said slowly.

He held her away from him. "Time? Why, for goodness' sake? You yourself said that the designs are good, didn't you?"

"Yes, of course. They're wonderful."

"Well, then? Do you think that we are the only two people in the world who are going to feel that way?"

"No. I'm sure that everyone will like them. It's just..."

"You don't think I can pull it off, is that it?" he asked, almost pouting. It was a ploy he had used

before, and Mim had hardly ever been able to resist
it. Now she fought against it, remembering those
old days, and the hurt she had suffered.

"I'm sure you can, Richard," she said. "But it's a
lot of money, that's all."

"I'm well aware of that, my love. But I'm not
asking you to give it to me. It will be a loan, an
investment. You'll get every penny of it back, and
then some, I promise. And you'd be helping me, too.
Isn't that enough of an inducement?"

It took all her strength to fight against him,
especially when he was being at his most charming
and persuasive. The plain truth was that she knew
beyond doubt that she was, and always had been,
completely in love with him.

And yet, she could not submit completely. He was
asking so very much. Perhaps it was simply that it
was too soon. If he'd waited a bit, shown her that he
was really serious about the project . . . She could not
deny that what he had shown her proved beyond
doubt that he had the talent, the creativity, to take
this venture to the very top. And yet, what proof was
there that he would continue with it? Could she be
quite sure that he would not do as he had done
before—just chuck everything up, and disappear
without a word for months on end? Then where
would she be?

Without her money, her man, or even her dignity.
That's where she would be. And, dazzled and
delighted by the nearness of him, as she undoubtedly was, she was fully aware of the fact of possible
loss.

He put his finger under her chin and tilted her
face up to meet his eyes.

"Well, precious one?" he asked, smiling so

confidently, so lovingly, that it almost took her will-power away.

"Richard...just give me a little time, will you?"

"Darling," he said deliberately, almost harshly, "time is just what I don't have. If I want to make a go of this thing, I have to begin now. Don't you understand that?"

Mim nodded. "Yes, I do. But what if I hadn't had the money? What would you have done then? I mean, you didn't know I had it, did you?" she asked, a sudden doubt creeping into her mind.

His eyes widened in hurt astonishment. "How could I know? Really, Mim, that's unfair. When I first told you I needed money, I was just stating a fact. I had no idea that you could possibly help me."

Immediately contrite, she said hurriedly: "No, I know that you weren't asking me. I know that. And, as I say, if I couldn't have helped you, you would have had to find the money somewhere else, wouldn't you? Oh, Richard, I'm sure I'll be able to let you have it. I'd just like a little time to think it over, that's all. Please?"

The frown on his features softened. "I'm sorry, love. I'm being a beast. Of course you must have time. Think it over carefully. I know in the end you'll see that it's the wisest move you ever made." He took her face in both his hands, and kissed her at first tenderly, then more passionately. Then he broke off suddenly, and almost roughly pushed her away from him. "This is no good," he said, his voice husky. "I'm going to take you home now, darling. Just hang on a minute while I get my jacket."

He left her, and Mim stood where she was, the touch of his lips still burning on hers. How had she possibly managed to refuse him anything? she wondered.

She went back to look at the portfolio for a moment, and was thrilled anew by the drawings. Then she discovered a large envelope which she had not noticed before. Opening it, she discovered more drawings, smaller ones. She looked at them carefully, puzzled by what she saw. These were totally different from the others. They lacked the sparkle, the excitement of the larger ones. The colours were all wrong, and the designs themselves lacked imagination and interest.

"What are these, Richard?" she asked curiously, looking back into the envelope.

"They're nothing," he said, almost self-consciously. "They're the very first things I did. They're pretty awful, aren't they?"

"No, not awful. But certainly not like the others." She smiled at him. "You really did have some kind of metamorphosis in Europe, didn't you?"

Richard laughed out loud. "Yes, I think you could call it that." He took her arm and linked it with his. "Come on, my love. You've got a lot of hard, serious thinking to do, and you have to get your rest so that you can give it all your attention."

He walked with her out of the studio, down the stairs and outside, where he left her on the pavement while he hailed a taxi.

CHAPTER TWO

Mim heard from Richard frequently in the next few weeks, although she saw little of him. He said that he had no free time, as he was trying to raise a bit more money, making arrangements for getting the studio renovated, and looking for a car for himself.

"It's not a luxury, love, it really isn't," he said. "I'm not thinking of buying anything showy. Just a little car which will get me around, and convince people that I'm a man of some means."

She sighed, hoping that she could believe him. The old Richard, she knew, would have rushed out

and bought himself the most lavish, sumptuous
model he could afford. Maybe this new, more settled
man would have the wisdom to get something
which would do the job he required it for, use as little
petrol as possible, and cost him something less than
a fortune.

It was during one of his telephone calls that she
took her courage in both hands and ventured to ask
him: "When am I going to see you, Richard? It's
been such a long time."

"It's only been two weeks, my angel," he said,
almost scornfully. Then he became contrite. "But I
know what you mean. I miss you, too. You know I
do." There was a short silence, and then he
continued: "I'll tell you what. Why don't you come
and meet me at the studio tomorrow evening? Quite
frankly, I'm just about skint at the moment, so I
won't be able to take you out. But we could have
something here."

Her spirits rose immediately. "I'll tell you what—
how would you like it if I brought some food, and I
could cook it there for us?"

"Perfect! It's about time I got another sample of
your cooking. About seven?"

"Lovely," she said warmly. "I'll be there."

It was going to be a meal to remember, Mim
promised herself as she went shopping next day.
For starters she planned to have a concoction of
eggs, butter and sour cream, with a topping of real
caviare. For the main course she bought the most
expensive steak fillet, which she would serve with a
sauce of tomatoes, mushrooms and wine. French
bread, and—yes, asparagus. Tinned, if she couldn't
find fresh. Camembert and biscuits to follow.

She took her shopping home, and prepared the

first course and the sauce for the steak. Then she found suitable containers for them, put them into a strong bag, and went to have her bath and change her dress. It was going to be a perfect evening, she could feel it in her bones.

She had planned it carefully, and arrived exactly on time. With her heart pounding, she rang the bell.

She heard footsteps on the other side of the door, took a deep breath, and put on her most loving smile.

But it was not Richard who opened the door. Instead, she was looking into the eyes of a rather attractive man with a bland, questioning expression on his face.

"Yes?" he said.

"Is Richard Carlson in?" she asked.

"Not at the moment, no."

Mim frowned. "Is he expected back soon?"

The young man shrugged his shoulders. "I don't know, really. He wasn't here when I got in about an hour ago, and there was no message."

"He's expecting me," Mim said, fighting back a sudden feeling of disquiet. "May I come in and wait for him?"

Again he shrugged. "Nothing to do with me," he said, stepping back to let her pass.

She walked ahead of him into the studio, conscious all the time that he was right behind her. Who was he, for goodness' sake? He obviously wasn't an intruder whom she had surprised; he acted as though he had every right to be there.

She turned and faced him. "I'm Miriam Evans," she said. "Perhaps Richard has mentioned me."

He shook his head. "Not that I recall," he said slowly. "I'm Andy Thomas."

Mim smiled faintly. This was certainly not at all how she had pictured her evening beginning.

"Do you work with Richard?" she asked.

Andy smiled mirthlessly. "You could say that," he said.

She looked around her, not quite knowing what to do next. Where on earth was Richard? She found it acutely embarrassing to be facing this strange man whose eyes seemed to be questioning her very existence.

"Are... are you staying here, with Richard?" she ventured.

"No. I do some work here occasionally, that's all." He indicated the carrier bag with his eyes. "What have you got in that?" he asked.

Mim laughed nervously. "I've brought dinner." Suddenly her heart sank. "Will you be here this evening?" she demanded.

He smiled at her, and Mim tried to figure out what it was about this man that made her feel so uncomfortable. He had not been discourteous, but she got the distinct impression that he was laughing at her, mocking her in some way.

"Don't worry," he said. "I'm just holding on until Richard gets back, because there's something I want to discuss with him. I won't stay long."

"I didn't mean..." Mim began, but he held up a hand.

"Not to worry. It's a meal for two. I understand." He gestured to a chair. "Why don't you sit down? Richard might be a long time."

"He should be here soon. He said I was to come at seven," Mim said.

Andy looked at his watch. "If you know friend Richard at all, you'll know that his timekeeping is erratic, to say the least. Would you like a drink? As I say, it could be a long time."

This strange man, whom Richard had never even mentioned to her, was a bit free and easy with Richard's things, wasn't he? Even so, Mim approved of his suggestion. Her nerves hadn't been all that calm when she had arrived, and a drink would help. At least, she hoped it would.

"Yes, thank you. Is there any sherry?"

He laughed. "I doubt it. Richard's stock usually runs to lager, whisky and gin. I'll check, though."

He opened the door that Mim knew led to Richard's flat, an action that made her even more uneasy. Had Richard given him the right to move around like this?

It was just as Andy was returning that she spotted Richard's portfolio lying open on the table. She looked up with a growing feeling of unease and suspicion.

"I was right, I'm afraid. And the gin's pretty low, as well," Andy remarked.

"That's all right," Mim said slowly. "I'll have a small whisky and water." In truth, she was not very fond of whisky, but she wanted a bit more time to think.

Those designs were the most important things that Richard owned. And it looked as if this young man had been going through them. Why? And how had he got in? With a key, presumably, but how had he obtained one? Mim was quite sure that Richard would not willingly allow anyone such easy access to the designs he prized so highly.

Andy came back, carrying two glasses filled with amber liquid, one darker than the other. He handed her the weaker drink.

"To your health," he said, raising his glass to his lips.

Mim sipped her drink slowly. Finally, suspicion making her bold, she asked him straight out: "Why were you looking at Richard's drawings?"

He looked directly at her, his gaze not wavering, as she had expected it to do.

"I was just checking on something," he said, without a hint of embarrassment.

There was no sign of guilt in his gaze, that Mim could detect. More a feeling of challenge, she thought.

"I don't suppose you were thinking of copying any of the designs, were you?" she asked. There was something about Andy Thomas that made her uncomfortable, and she reacted with anger and the feeling that she had to score over him in one way or another.

But he only smiled lazily at her veiled accusation. "You're absolutely right in your assumption. I was not trying to steal any of Richard's designs," he said.

"What were you doing then?" she demanded.

"Look, Miss..." he began, then hesitated.

"Evans," Mim supplied coldly.

"Miss Evans. If I were doing anything under-hand, would I be sitting here, calmly drinking? Especially as you've already told me that you expect Richard at any moment. Would I even have opened the door to you? Use some sense, Miss Evans. If someone is out to steal, they take pains not to get caught. Right?"

Mim nodded grudgingly.

"Fine. Anyway, Richard will be back soon, and will vouch for my honesty, I'm sure."

Mim opened her mouth to speak, but thought better of the idea. There was something about Andy that put her on her guard, made her feel decidedly uncomfortable. She prayed silently that Richard would soon be back.

At that very moment they both heard the scrape of Richard's key in the lock. Neither of them moved.

He was whistling when he came in, and Mim ran to him and threw her arms around him out of sheer relief. As soon as he saw them, however, Richard's carefree expression changed immediately to that of a small boy who had thought he had got away with something, but had been caught just when he was feeling quite safe.

Mim noted the look, and felt a sudden stab of discomfort. Which one of them, she wondered, had he not expected to see?

"Ah, our forgetful host, at last," Andy said. "Richard, do explain to this good lady that I'm not here to steal your precious ideas, will you? She was on the point of calling the police."

Richard regained his composure immediately. "What's all this?" he asked, grinning at Mim.

"She thinks I'm trying to copy your fabric designs," Andy said before Mim had the chance to say anything. "She firmly believes I'm a rival, out to do you dirt. Ironic, isn't it?" he added, his voice almost teasing.

Richard frowned for a second, then began to laugh. "Is that it?" he asked. "Mim, my love, you've got it all wrong. Andy's my partner. We met in Brussels, purely by accident. Andy's got a lot of connections which are going to be extremely useful, and I've got the designs. So we formed a partnership. Isn't that right, Andy, old lad?" Richard asked the younger man.

Andy did not answer at once. Finally he did speak, looking directly at Richard.

"That's right, old man," he said slowly, drawing his words out. "That's it, exactly."

"I hadn't expected you today," Richard said. "Was there anything special?"

Andy nodded. "I wanted a word with you. It won't take long."

"Good," Richard said. "I'm starving. Did you bring the food?" he asked Mim.

It took her a second to realize that he was talking to her. She had been listening carefully to the dialogue between the two men, trying to understand it. There was something in the tone of their voices, rather than their words, which made her even more uneasy than she had been before.

"The food? Oh, yes, of course. It won't take long to cook."

"Lovely. I'll tell you what, pet. Why don't you go to the kitchen and get things started? Then Andy and I can have a short chat. I won't be long."

Without waiting for her answer, he gave her his hand and helped her from her chair, then began steering her towards the kitchen. He put the carrier bag on the table and kissed her on the cheek. "I'll only be a few minutes," he whispered. "I'll get rid of him as quickly as I can."

Mim unpacked the bag carefully and searched round the kitchen for the utensils she would need. The place was ill-equipped—Richard obviously ate at home rarely—and she had to do a lot of improvising. By the time Richard came to join her, the meal was almost ready.

"Sorry, darling," he said, putting his arms round her waist and kissing her on the tip of her nose. "I wish I had chosen a profession where normal office hours were taken for granted."

"It doesn't matter. You're here now. And we can eat as soon as you like."

Richard was effusive in his praise of the meal. He was so complimentary, in fact, that Mim had to choke back a rising doubt as to his motives.

It was over coffee, after Richard had filled her in completely about what he had been doing with regard to the studio, that Mim asked him:

"Who is this Andy, exactly? Is he really your partner?"

Richard looked at her suspiciously. "Why? What has he been saying?"

"Nothing," Mim answered, slightly puzzled by his tone. "It's just that you never mentioned him before, and I ... Are you absolutely sure that you can trust him, Richard?"

He relaxed visibly, and laughed, taking her hand in his.

"I'm absolutely sure I can trust him, love. Actually, it was Andy who got me started on textile design. When I met him, he had been trying to sell some of his designs—without any success, I have to add. He has no imagination, no flair. But he did have a bit of money, and, as I told you, a number of good contacts. It was then that I tried my hand at designing, and we decided that we should get together."

"I see," Mim said, not absolutely sure that she did.

"Don't worry. Andy's a bit of a nuisance, I'm

afraid, and a bit of a bore, but he's going to be very useful indeed."

"He has a key, I assume," Mim said, still dubious about the wisdom of this.

"Why not? After all, he's my partner."

Mim said abruptly: "Richard, those drawings in the envelope at the back of your portfolio—are they Andy's?"

Richard leaned back on his chair and tipped it so that it was resting on two legs.

"Andy's drawings?" he said after a few seconds. "Yes, I suppose you might say that. Why?"

"You were trying to cover up for him the last time, weren't you? When you told me that they were yours, your early ones. Don't you remember?"

"Oh, yes, of course. Well, I knew they had no merit, and I didn't want you to get a bad impression of him before you met him, that's all."

Mim laughed shortly. "I'm afraid he managed that all by himself. I don't think I like your friend, Richard."

"He doesn't have all that much going for him— and it wouldn't help me any if he pulled out now," Richard said gently.

"Well, I don't suppose I'll be seeing him all that often, will I? He's not living here, is he?"

"That's true. No, I don't suppose you'll be seeing much of him," Richard said.

... But they were both wrong. The very next time Mim saw Richard, the following week, she saw Andy as well.

Richard had begged off going out, saying that he was really too tired to make the effort.

Against her better judgement, Mim said quickly: "Could I come round after dinner, then? Just for an hour or two? It's been so long since I've seen you, Richard."

In the end he relented, saying that there was something he wanted to discuss with her, anyway. When he suggested that she came over about nine, she hid her disappointment, and said brightly that that would be fine.

Richard opened the door to her, and she forgave him everything when he bent his head to give her a loving kiss. She stiffened immediately, though, when she opened her eye and saw Andy Thomas sitting on a chair behind Richard.

The situation was made even more uncomfortable with Richard's first words.

"I was just telling Andy about the money you're going to lend me," he said. "He thinks it's great of you."

Andy looked at Richard blandly. "Is that what I said, Richard?" he asked.

"Yes, of course you did. Anyway, love," he went on quickly, turning back to Mim, "what would you like to drink? Coffee, or something stronger?"

"Coffee would be fine," she said, wishing she could ask him why Andy was there. He had known she was coming, couldn't he have told Andy to come back another time? They saw each other so seldom, surely it would not be too much to ask that they could be alone when they had the chance.

"How have you been?" Andy asked when Richard had gone to see about the coffee.

"Fine, thank you," Mim answered, immediately hating the cold sound of her own voice.

"Good." He looked at her steadily, but said nothing else. Then suddenly: "Are you really going to give Richard the money?"

"It's not a gift, exactly. Richard has made it clear that it's to be a business arrangement. I'll be getting it back, plus interest."

Andy kept looking at her, his expression thoughtful. "It's just..." he began, but at that moment Richard came back, and Andy quickly changed the subject. "I was just about to ask Mim if she's seen your car yet," he said.

"Have you got it already?" she asked, surprised.

Richard laughed. "Didn't I tell you? I got it yesterday. I'll take you home later, and you'll be able to see it then."

The conversation was stilted after that. Mim was wondering why Andy didn't leave. It was obvious that she had come expecting to be alone with Richard. Did the man have so little tact that he was just going to sit there all evening, when it was patently obvious that he was not wanted?

The mystery was solved when after a long, unpleasant hour, during which they talked in clipped sentences and forced themselves to be polite to each other, Andy excused himself for a moment, and Richard said that he really would have to take Mim home and get to bed.

"What about Andy?" she asked him, as he helped her on with her coat.

"Andy? What do you mean?"

"Well, is he just going to stay here now? Or are you going to take him along with us for the ride?" she asked, not very successfully hiding the bitterness she felt.

He did not notice it. "Oh, that!" he said, laughing. "He's staying here now, didn't I tell you?"

"Where is he going to sleep, then?" she asked, anger building up inside her.

"In the studio. There's no room in the flat itself. Honestly, Mim, what else could I do? He told me that it was getting too expensive for him to stay in a hotel. After all, every penny he spent there was one less that he could give to me...to the business, I mean. You aren't really angry, are you?"

She was about to give in to him again, she could feel it. It was more than she could do to resist him when he looked at her in that way.

It was at that moment that the telephone started to ring.

Richard squeezed Mim's arm distractedly. "Hold on a minute, love. I'll get rid of whoever it is in a minute."

Andy came out of the flat just as Richard was about to go in. Andy stood back and Richard passed by him as though, Mim reflected, he thought it was no more than his due for people to make way for him.

"Are you leaving," Andy asked, noting her coat, "or just cold?"

"We were on our way out when the phone rang," she answered.

"May I talk to you for a moment, while our host is unavoidably detained?" he asked her.

"Yes, of course."

Andy smiled ruefully. "I don't know how happy you're going to be when I've said my piece, but I'm going to say it anyway." His face became serious. "Don't lend him the money, Mim."

She felt anger rising within her again, and clenched her fists to keep from losing her temper altogether.

"How dare you?" she said, her voice low and dangerous.

"Simply because I know that you'll never see a
penny of it again. It's none of my business, I know,
but you're a nice girl, and you haven't a clue as to
what our Richard's really like. And I couldn't have
lived with myself very happily if I hadn't warned
you."

She took a deep breath to steady herself. Then:
"In the first place, you're absolutely right. It is none
of your business, and I resent you interfering in any
way. And in the second place, it's rather funny
advice, coming from you, isn't it? I don't know how
much money you've lent Richard, but it must have
been a pretty tidy sum, I would imagine."

There was a slight frown on his face now.

"Is that what Richard told you? That I have lent
him money?"

"Of course. He doesn't keep secrets from me, and
he has told me all about your partnership."

She would have said more, and very likely she
would have hated herself for it afterwards. At that
moment, however, Richard came back, smiling and
sure of himself, and she had promised Richard to be
nice to this tiresome man.

All thoughts of Andy were dispelled as soon as
Richard showed her his new car, however. As she
had feared, he had gone for the most flashy,
impractical vehicle imaginable.

"Not bad, eh?" he asked.

"It must have cost the earth," she said hesitantly.

"Not at all. Second-hand, of course, but it won't
half impress my clients. Speaking of which," he
said as he opened the door for her, "that was one of
them on the phone just now." He got in and started
up the engine with a roar. "Quite a feather in my
cap, actually. A big business, and he's definitely

interested." He did not go on to explain why the ma
had rung at such an odd time.

When they reached her place, Richard switche
off the engine, then leaned over and swept her int
his arms.

"We're going places, sweetheart, we're reall
going places," he said gleefully.

Mim knew that this was not the time to burs
Richard's bubble by bringing him down to eart
with her objections. Then he drew her closer, and hi
kiss was everything that she had ever dreame
about, all rolled into one: tenderness, passior
affection, and a deep need of her, as well. It literall
took her breath away, suffocated any logica
thought she might have been capable of. Nothin
else seemed to matter one jot in that ecstati
beautiful moment.

She felt Richard stifle a yawn, and her heart wa
filled with an even deeper love for him, a carin
protective love.

"You'd better get back," she said quietly, afrai
that the sound of her voice might somehow ruin th
beauty of that moment.

"I'm afraid I must," he said, holding her awa
from him. "I'm really just about asleep. I d
apologize."

"I know." She took his hands from her shoulder
and started to open her door. "When shall I see yo
again?" she asked.

"I'm not quite sure," he said, then added quickl
"But soon. Very soon, I promise. Oh, and Min
darling," he went on, almost as though it was
trifle, a tiny afterthought, "you will let me kno
about the money, won't you? I hate to nag, love, b
I'm getting to the point..."

He let the sentence die in the air, and Mim felt her heart turn ice-cold just for a moment. There was a worried frown on her face which he could not see, as he promised that she would give him a definite answer very soon. Then she closed the car door, and before she had reached her flat he had started up the engine and was away.

... Mim woke up angry on the following Saturday morning. She had been dreaming about Richard, and while she could not remember anything about the dream, her anger upon waking was due to the fact that not only had she not seen him for the past week, but he had not even bothered to telephone.

She almost hoped he wouldn't ring again, would give her a chance to get over him by disappearing as he had done before. At the same time, she knew that she was straining her ears at every noise, hoping it was the telephone bell.

And finally, in the afternoon, he did ring.

"Mim, love? How about coming out with me tonight? I've got something to show you."

Just like that. No excuses, no mention of the fact that he had neglected her. And, despite her resolve to tell him exactly what she thought of him if he did bother to ring again, Mim succumbed, as she had secretly known she would.

He took her to a new, very fashionable restaurant. With its romantic lighting and soft music, she could imagine many proposals being made and accepted there. Richard had forestalled any objections on her part by telling her that it was a wickedly expensive place, but that, after all, he had not taken her out anywhere for some time, so she deserved it.

After such an introduction, Mim could do nothing

but sit back and enjoy the surroundings, and she would have thought herself a fool not to make the most of it.

All through the delicious meal Richard spoke of people he had seen, of ideas he had been having for the business. It was only when they were sipping their brandies afterwards that he produced the ring.

It was incredibly beautiful, and must have cost the earth, she knew. It was in the shape of a flower, the petals made of garnet, with a cluster of tiny diamonds in the centre. It was a magnificent ring, and after giving her a chance to take in its beauty, Richard slipped it on her finger.

"I couldn't resist it," he said, watching her closely, enjoying her pleasure and astonishment. "I saw it in a shop window, and it seemed so right for you. You do like it, don't you?"

"Like it? Oh, Richard, it's magnificent. But honestly, it's far too..."

"Not another word," he said softly, covering her lips gently with the tips of his fingers. "The only thing to say about it is that it's not nearly good enough for you."

It took her a few moments before she could trust her voice. Then she said: "It's absolutely perfect Richard. I could never wish for a more wonderful present." She looked into his eyes, seeing him through a mist of happy tears. "But you needn't have done it, you know."

He smiled and took her hand. "I've been neglecting you, my love, and I'm fully aware of it. It couldn't have been helped, of course. I've been so very busy... but even so, I feel guilty about it. And I just wanted you to have the ring to let you know that, even when I'm not with you, my thoughts are there. You do mean so very much to me, Mim."

Never in her life had she been so happy. She wished the evening could go on for ever.

"Well, what shall we do now?" Richard said abruptly, looking at his watch. "Would you like to go back to the studio?"

Mim frowned. "I don't think so," she said. "To be quite honest, I've had enough of your friend Andy for one month."

Richard laughed softly and took both her hands in his. "I know what you mean," he said. "But there's no problem tonight. He's gone away for the week-end. So we'd be completely alone."

She brightened instantly. It had been so very long since she had been completely alone with Richard.

"I'd like that very much, then," she said. "I would indeed like that very much."

He signalled for the waiter and helped her on with her coat, allowing his hands to linger for a few seconds on her shoulders. Then he had paid and they were outside, walking slowly, dreamily, their arms around each other, to his car.

But when they reached the studio, Mim had a shock. There was a woman in front of Richard's door, sitting disconsolately on a suitcase.

Richard had been looking for the right key, and so did not see the woman until Mim nudged him. Then his expression was almost comic. At first he frowned, then his eyes opened wide, and then he frowned again.

"Jan!" Richard said, his voice a mixture of surprise and displeasure.

She looked up then, and smiled.

"Richard! Thank goodness you've come. I was

beginning to wonder if you'd gone away for the week-end."

"But what are you doing here?" he asked her, hardly concealing his annoyance.

"What a fine greeting!" the woman answered, totally unmoved by his obvious coldness. "I wanted to surprise you."

He laughed shortly. "You've done that, all right." He turned to Mim, and the look in his eyes was plainly apologetic. "Mim, this is my sister, Janice. Jan, this is Miriam Evans, a very good friend of mine."

Janice held out her hand to Mim. "Hello, Miriam," she said cheerfully. "It's good to meet you."

Richard opened the door, and bent down to pick up one of the two cases that Janice had brought with her. He snapped on the light, and put the case on the floor.

"You still haven't told me why you're here," he said.

"Just a visit, Richard," Janice said as she peeled off her gloves. "My oldest friend's getting married, and I'm here for the festivities. The only trouble was that the hotel had mucked up the booking, and there wasn't a room to be had anywhere. So I thought I'd take a chance and see if I could stay with you. Just for the night, of course. Tomorrow I'll see about finding something else. But quite frankly, after the flight, and the rush beforehand, I was just too weary to drag from one hotel to another, hoping to find something. I am sorry, love, honestly."

Richard shrugged his shoulders. "Can't be helped, I suppose. I have a friend staying with me, but he's away for the week-end, so you can use his bed. And now I suppose we could all do with some coffee, couldn't we?" Without waiting for an answer, he went into the flat.

Left alone, the two young women smiled at each other shyly.

"I'm sorry about this, Miriam," Janice said. "I did try to phone Richard from the airport, when I got in, but there was no answer. I hope I haven't ruined your evening completely."

"No, of course not," Mim lied. "And please call me Mim. I hate the sound of Miriam."

Janice smiled broadly. "Oh, good. And you call me Jan. I don't know why Richard went so formal all of a sudden. He hasn't called me Janice since we were teenagers."

There was an awkward silence then, and Mim broke it by saying: "Did you have a good flight?"

"Yes, not bad at all. I confess that I hate flying, which is why I rarely come back. I'm living in the States, in New Jersey. I went out there five years ago, just on a holiday. Then I met Jack, and that was that. We were married within a month, and I've never looked back."

Mim smiled. How marvellous it must have been, to meet your man, and know that he was yours within such a short space of time. Long courtships, she was beginning to think, were hard on the nerves, if nothing else.

Janice was friendly and easy to talk to. Mim was almost sorry when Richard came back. He was smiling now, and Mim saw that he had regained his usual composure.

"I've been trying to work out why you, who pop in and out of people's lives like a jack-in-the-box, should be annoyed because I turned up without announcing myself," Janice said to her brother.

Richard put his arm around her and squeezed her shoulders. "I wasn't annoyed, Jan. Just surprised, that's all. You usually give fair warning. How are Jack and the kids?"

"Flourishing. Jack sends his regards, and both Mike and Sue told me to tell you that they want you to come out for Christmas this year. They feel cheated, having an uncle they've never met."

He winked at Mim and released Janice. "You never know, love. I might just make it this year. If things go the way I've planned . . ." He allowed the sentence to trail away.

Janice looked questioningly at her brother. "What's that supposed to mean?" she asked.

Richard shrugged. "Just that, for once, I might have the money this year."

"Does that mean you're planning to rob a bank, get an honest job, marry a rich widow, or what?" Janice demanded.

"I'm in business, sister dear," he said cheerfully. "At least, I shall be very soon. I'm going in for textile design."

Surprised, Janice looked first at her brother, then at Mim, and back at Richard again. "This is something new," she said sceptically.

"New, different, and very exciting," Richard went on. "Would you like to see some of the preliminary designs?"

"Yes, of course. Are they here?"

Richard nodded. Then he turned to Mim. "Would you get the coffee, love?" he asked her. "It's almost ready. I'll show Jan the drawings in the meantime."

As soon as Mim had gone, Richard steered Janice over to the portfolio and opened it. One by one he removed the drawings and sketches and handed them to his sister.

Janice was impressed. She had seen examples of Richard's work in the past, and had never thought much of them. What she was looking at now, however, was something altogether different. The sketches showed quite remarkable talent.

"They're marvellous, Richard, they really are," she said, handing him back the pile of drawings. "I'm most impressed. When did you decide to take up textile designing?"

"While I was in Europe. It just came to me, you know? I suddenly felt that that was where my talent could find the best outlet. I'm just getting started, of course."

Janice was looking thoughtful when Mim came in with a tray. She put it down on the coffee table and handed out the cups.

"Well, what do you think?" she asked Janice. She glanced at Richard, and just had time to catch a warning look from him. But what was he trying to convey to her? That she shouldn't mention the money, perhaps. She decided to say little, and take her cue from Richard.

Janice smiled at her. "I think they're marvellous."

"I couldn't agree more," Mim said, relieved. She hadn't really thought that Janice would dislike the designs, but it was good to hear her say how much she admired them.

"To be honest," Janice said teasingly, "I didn't think you had it in you, Richard. You must have a number of hidden depths."

"Oh, many more than that, I assure you," he said with a grin.

"Would you like any help?" Janice said, serious again. "I mean, I have a feeling that those designs would go over extremely well in the States. I know a few people who are in that field in one way or another, and I think they'd not only be very interested, but would know what would be the best thing to do about them. What do you say?"

Richard beamed. "What do I say? My dearest sister, I say yes, yes, yes! Anything that will help me to get started will be gratefully accepted. You just say which ones you want, and I'll copy them for you."

The evening was turning out well after all, Mim thought. Of course it would have been better still if she had had Richard to herself; but Janice was a pleasant out-going young woman, and she somehow made Mim feel almost like a part of the family. She had realized, without having been told, that Mim was more to Richard than merely a date for the evening, and she seemed to approve.

When they had finished their coffee, Richard announced that he was sure that Janice must be tired after all the travelling, and anyway, it was time he took Mim home.

"Let's get together, while I'm here," Janice told Mim as she was leaving. "I'll tell you what—I've got to do some shopping before I leave, so why don't you come and spend the day with me? We could have lunch together, and maybe come back here in the evening. Can you arrange to take a day off?"

"Yes—I've some leave due to me," said Mim.

They arranged it for the following Wednesday, and then, unexpectedly, Janice reached out and gave Mim a warm hug. "I'll look forward to that, then. We'll meet at the Oxford Street tube at ten o'clock."

Richard hardly said a word on the drive home, merely nodding when Mim enthused about his sister. When they arrived at her house, however, he invited himself in for a minute. This was unlike Richard, and she had learned to be slightly wary whenever he did anything out of character.

As soon as they were in the living-room, he took her hands in his. "I'm sorry, love," he said, "about having to share our precious time with Jan. She's a good kid, and I'm fond of her, of course, but I did so want to be alone with you."

"It didn't matter," Mim said. "There will be many more times. Anyway, I liked Jan so much. I'm glad I met her."

"The thing is," he went on, "I'd be just as happy if...if you didn't tell her about the engagement."

"But...but you never said..."

"Do you honestly mean to say that you didn't know that was what I meant? Why do you think I gave you that ring?"

"I don't know, really. I thought it was just—just a present."

He laughed, low and deep. "You silly girl. Of course it was to be an engagement ring. You do want to be engaged to me, don't you?"

"Oh, Richard, you know I do. I've wanted that for as long as I can remember. But why don't you want Jan to know?"

He pulled her to him, and hugged her tightly. For a moment he said nothing.

"It's just," he began, "that I'm a little frightened, I think. The one thing I've learned throughout my life is that when you want something badly, you mustn't tell anyone about it. Because then, somehow, it goes wrong. And this is something that I don't want to go wrong, Mim, darling."

"Oh, Richard, neither do I!"

"Then do me this one favour, will you? Don't tell anyone, not just yet. Let's wait until we're absolutely sure."

"All right, darling," she said. "I won't say a word until you tell me it's all right."

He sighed and held her even more tightly. "Thank you, love. I can't tell you how much better it makes me feel. It will be our secret, something for just the two of us to share. And when we're sure, when we know that it's the one thing we both really want, I'll be the proudest man on earth."

He bent his head and kissed her. "I'd better be getting back now. I'll ring you tomorrow, all right?"

"Yes, all right. Drive carefully," she said as, her arm around his waist and his around her shoulders, she walked him slowly to the front door.

When the door was opened and he had kissed her good night, he hesitated before he actually left her. Then:

"Oh, Mim, darling, one more thing," he said, as though a new thought had suddenly struck him. "Would you be upset if I asked you not to wear the ring? Just until Jan goes back home."

She felt something inside her going cold. "But why not?" she asked. "She won't know what it means."

Richard smiled. "She's a very perceptive lady, is my sister. And she knows my taste. Knowing her, she'll put two and two together, and I don't want her asking any questions until I'm ready to answer them." He kissed the tip of her nose and smiled. "I know it seems mean, but it won't make that much difference, will it?"

Mim sighed. Once again she was beaten, and she knew that even if she tried to argue, he would talk her out of it.

"Okay," she said. "But only for two weeks. I love that ring, Richard, and I can't wait to wear it."

After he had gone, Mim tried hard not to let all the little doubts intrude on her state of happiness. He had asked her to marry him, after all. He had given her a ring, to seal the bargain—even if he had asked her not to wear it, not to mention it...

True to form, Richard did not ring on the following day. Nor did he manage to contact her on Monday.

She made arrangements to take Wednesday off, and looked forward to seeing Janice again. If nothing else, being with Richard's lively sister would take her mind off Richard himself. At the same time, she hoped that Janice might tell her something about Richard's background, and fill in some of the gaping holes in the scanty knowledge that she had about his life before she had met him.

She and Janice met at the appointed place, and Mim knew at once that it was going to be a good day. They walked along Oxford Street, wandering in and out of the shops. Janice had decided to indulge herself—her husband was a successful lawyer, earning plenty of money even by American standards; and he had given Janice enough cash to go on a real spending spree.

By the end of the afternoon, Janice had got so many things—for herself and her family as well—that they could not possibly have got home on the Underground.

"I've got a few pennies left," Janice said cheerfully. "I think I'll treat us to a taxi."

They went straight to the studio. Janice told Mim that she would have Richard drive her to her hotel later on with all her parcels.

"Are you sure he'll be in now?" Mim asked. "I can't see it being much fun standing in the hallway with this lot, if he's not."

Janice smiled and rooted in her bag, lifting from it a key. "I'm not as dumb as I look," she said. "I made him give me this on Saturday. Even though I'm not staying there, I knew that times like this would arrive, and I know of my brother's erratic life-style from way back. Anyway, Andy will probably be there, even if Richard isn't."

Mim stiffened suddenly, and Janice noticed the look on her face.

"What's the matter, don't you like Andy? I think he's awfully nice, myself."

"I... I just wonder if he's the right person as a partner for Richard," Mim said.

Janice said forthrightly: "I think Andy's just the right sort to keep Richard as much on the straight and narrow path as anyone could. After all, he's got an investment to protect, so he'll do as much as anyone can to make sure that Richard doesn't go off at a tangent and ruin things for himself. He's liable to do that, you know, if no one watches him closely."

As it happened, Janice had predicted correctly. Richard, although knowing that the two young women were expected at that time, was not in, and had left no word as to when he would be. Andy was there, though, and Janice greeted him cheerfully.

"Whew!" she said. "I think we bought all of

Oxford Street. I did, anyway. How are you, then? Busy?"

"No, I've finished for the day," Andy said, and Mim wondered what he did with his time.

Richard had said that Andy's greatest value lay in the fact that he had many contacts in the textile world. And yet, from what she could see, it was always Richard who was out, talking to people, making arrangements, while Andy spent his time at the studio. What on earth did he find to do there?

Janice asked the question that had been on Mim's mind.

"What have you been doing all day, contacting people, or what?"

"Oh, just...this and that. You know." Then, seeing that Mim was looking at the drawing-board, he added: "I was just going over Richard's new designs. Would you like to see them? I think they're rather good, myself," he said, an expression on his face that Mim could not understand.

They all went to the board where the new drawings were pinned. Andy had been right. They were excellent, certainly as good as the former ones, and perhaps even more exciting.

"He's really hit on something, has my brother," Jan said proudly. "To be completely honest with you, I would never have credited him with the imagination for this kind of thing. But he's really come out on top."

Mim looked up suddenly and caught the same expression in Andy's eyes as she had seen there before. Now she understood what it meant.

Pure, unadulterated jealousy. And she could not blame him when she remembered the drawings that he had done himself, pale imitations of Richard's beautiful creations.

Suddenly she felt terribly sorry for Andy. She knew how he must feel, knowing that he did not possess anything like Richard's gift, and yet having to be reminded of that fact every day. And yet, at the same time, he had had the good grace to be able to show off Richard's drawings with pleasure, praising them as they deserved.

She found herself able to see Andy through Janice's eyes as they talked and waited for Richard to come home. There was an easy, pleasant rapport between Richard's sister and his partner, and Mim began to revise her ideas about the young man.

Andy fixed them drinks, and whether it was the sherry, the atmosphere, or a combination of the two, Mim did not know, but it suddenly felt very nice indeed to be talking to these two people.

Time went by almost without any of them noticing, but finally Janice announced that she was getting hungry. When they looked, they saw that it was eight o'clock.

Where on earth was Richard? Mim started to worry, but Janice laughed it off.

"He's probably just got involved in something, and lost all track of time. What would you care to bet that he'll come waltzing in at about midnight, having had a gorgeous dinner, and having forgotten that we were going to be here? And now I suggest we raid the fridge and feed ourselves," she said. "If Richard does show up, he can join us. If not, he can fix himself something later on. That is, if he hasn't eaten. But I, for one, am not going to wait any longer."

Richard came home just before eleven, delighted

with the world and all it had to offer him. Instead of apologizing to Mim and Janice for being late, or holding them up, he simply described the splendid meal he had had with a prospective client.

Janice insisted that Richard must drive Mim and herself home.

"But I've just got in," he wailed, obviously thinking that his sister was being extraordinarily unkind.

"That's your problem, lad," Janice replied unfeelingly. "We've both got to get home, we're both exhausted, which is basically due to sitting here for hours waiting for you. Come on, old boy, up on your feet. The chariot awaits."

If Mim had hoped that Richard would take Janice home and then spend a few minutes alone with her, she was disappointed. He dropped her off first, without even kissing her on the cheek.

"I'll ring you tomorrow," he said.

CHAPTER THREE

Since Nancy Batsford had left London for Paris over a year ago, Mim had had no really close friend. It was amazing how quickly Janice closed that particular gap in her life, and how soon she felt she could talk to her new friend as frankly as she had earlier confided in Nancy. So, one day when they were lunching together and Janice asked her about her friendship with Richard, Mim told her that he had asked her to marry him.

Janice nodded. "I thought so. But why the big secret? He could have told me, surely."

"I'm not quite clear about that myself. He said

something about being afraid to talk about it until it was absolutely sure."

Janice smiled a little doubtfully. "Well, let's just hope he comes to his senses quickly, and does something about it. He'd be even more of a fool than I think he is if he allowed you to slip through his fingers."

Mim laughed. "Oh, I don't think there's any fear of that. To be honest, Jan, I'm nuts about him. I've never loved another man, not really loved him. And if Richard wants me, I'm his for life."

Janice reached out to squeeze Mim's hand. "I think you'll be the best thing for him that's ever happened. Have you got as far as setting a date, or anything like that?"

"No, not yet," Mim admitted, frowning slightly. "I have a feeling that Richard wants to get the design business off the ground before he does anything definite. And I don't blame him, either. At the moment, it's taking all his energy and concentration, and that's as it should be."

"Granted. But it might take some time, you know. And he's going to need a lot more money, as well."

Mim was not sure if she should admit to her own involvement in this direction, but finally decided that there was nothing wrong in it. After all, what was more natural than that a woman should try her best to help her fiancé in every possible way?

"To be honest with you, Jan," she began slowly, "I've got a hand in that aspect of it, as well. You see, my father died some months ago, and left me a little money. Not a fortune, you understand, but enough to help Richard get started, anyway."

Janice hesitated before she spoke. "I see," she said, her voice slightly strained. "And you're going to give it to Richard, are you?"

"Well, of course!" Something in Janice's tone made Mim feel suddenly defensive. "It's the natural thing to do, isn't it?"

"I suppose it is," Janice agreed. "I was just wondering if you'd gone into this thoroughly. I mean, are you going to do it through lawyers? I'd advise you to make it an absolutely legal proposition, Mim. For Richard's sake as much as for your own."

Mim looked at her friend. "What do you mean?"

"Simply that it's time that Richard began to grow up a bit. He's always had things easy. And if he doesn't begin to learn soon that the world is a harsher place than he thinks it is, he'll be in for a very hard, very unpleasant fall. If he had a legal arrangement with you—whether he's married to you or not—then he'd be forced to do things the right way. If it was a choice between paying you an instalment, or buying himself a new toy, he'd have to think twice. And that's what he's never had to do before. He's always done exactly what he wanted, and then charmed his creditors out of wanting to murder him. Do you see my point?"

Mim didn't want to, but she had to admit that what Janice was saying made sense.

"Yes, all right. I'll tell you what—I'll have a word with my solicitor, see what he says. And I'll take his advice, whatever it is. Will that satisfy you?"

Janice beamed. "Perfectly. And now let's talk about something else. For instance, have you any ideas about your engagement ring?"

Mim considered. Don't wear the ring, Richard had said. Not until Jan goes home. But she was sure that Jan would never give her away to her brother.

Besides, she simply couldn't keep it to herself any longer.

"Can you keep another secret, Jan?" she asked.

Janice's eyes lit up. "Of course I can. What is it?"

Mim reached into her bag and extracted the ring. "I've already got it," she said, her eyes sparkling.

Janice examined the ring slowly, carefully, with a frown settling on her face. She did not speak for some moments. Then:

"It's quite beautiful," she said, but there was no warmth in her voice.

Mim was baffled by this lack of enthusiasm, but she decided to ignore it. There might be any number of reasons why Janice was not as excited by the ring as she was, including the possibility that she simply didn't care for it.

After that, Janice carefully avoided mentioning Richard at all.

When they had finished their lunch Mim suggested that they might have dinner together, but Janice declined.

"I'm going to be spending a few days with my mother, starting tomorrow, and I have to pack yet. But we'll get together when I'm back in town, I promise."

When Janice got back to her hotel, she had a quick bath, applied fresh make-up, and then went downstairs to the lobby. She rang Richard, made sure that he would be in, and ascertained that Andy was out. Then she hailed a taxi, and went to see her brother.

Richard was smiling when he opened the door, but even his monumental self-approval was not strong enough to hide from him the fury in his sister's eyes.

"What have I done?" he asked her as soon as he had closed the door behind her. "I haven't stolen the Crown Jewels, I promise."

Janice was in no mood for jokes. "No. But what you've done is almost as bad."

Richard was more than surprised. "You'd better come right out with it, little sister. What is the great grievance?"

"As you know, I had lunch with Mim," Janice said. "And she told me that you had proposed to her."

Suddenly he, too, was angry. "She promised she wouldn't say anything," he stormed. "She swore blind that she would keep it to herself for the time being."

"That's not the point," Janice said, refusing to be sidetracked. "What happens between the two of you is none of my business—except that, if I were you, I wouldn't let her know that I've told you. That little girl is the best thing that ever happened to you, Richard, and if you're not careful, you're going to lose her. It's too much to ask, telling her that she isn't supposed to mention your engagement to anyone. And another thing, dear Richard—she showed me the ring you gave her."

"How dare she? She promised, she promised faithfully..."

"But she broke her promise. Shame on you for ever asking her to keep quiet about it. Of course she wanted to show it off, to let the world see what you'd given her. Oh, don't think that she was wearing it. She didn't have the nerve for that. But, since she could not for the life of her understand why you had asked her to conceal it, she saw no reason for not displaying it, if only for a moment. The thing is, I know very well why you told her not to wear it, and that's why I'm here."

"All right," he said, sitting down heavily in the armchair, "so you've seen it. I hadn't wanted you to, because I thought you might be jealous."

"Jealous?" Janice echoed incredulously.

"Exactly. I knew that you'd be upset because it was given to me, instead of to you."

Janice smiled sadly and shook her head. "It won't work, Richard. That was Mum's engagement ring. She wouldn't have given it to anyone, not while she's alive. Ever since her fingers got too gnarled for her to wear it, she's kept it in the jewellery case by her bed. She wouldn't have parted with it for anything."

But Richard showed no sign of guilt. "That's where you're wrong, I'm afraid, Jan. As it happens, she did give it to me. I told her all about Mim, and how deeply I care for her. When I mentioned that I was looking for a ring, and that it had to be a very special token, Mum said that I must have hers. She offered it, I didn't take it. You can ask her yourself, if you don't believe me."

Janice looked at her brother. He was bluffing, and she knew it.

"All right, I will. As it happens, I'm going to be spending a few days with her from tomorrow. And I most certainly will ask her if she gave you her precious ring so freely."

Mim was having a bath when the telephone rang the next morning. Moving quickly—she would never have forgiven herself if it had been Richard, and she had missed his call—she threw a towel around her and ran to the phone.

"Good morning, darling," Richard said. "Are you busy this evening?"

"I think I might just be able to fit you into my schedule," she said. "Would you like to come to my place for dinner?"

There was a momentary pause. Then: "No, why don't you come here instead? I'm a master at beans on toast."

"What about Andy? Will he be there?" she asked.

"No, he's gone away for a few days. Not back until tomorrow some time."

"Fine. I'll be there at seven, if that's all right."

"That's perfect."

It was Saturday, and Mim got on with the chores reserved for that day. When she had finished them, she decided to give the bedroom a really good clean. She had been promising herself for months to sort out all the papers that had collected in the cardboard box that she kept beside her bed, those things that she never knew quite what to do with at the time, and put in the box for future sorting. Well, today would be the day.

At the very bottom of the box, she came across her first play. She had written it months before, sweated over it during her evening hours; and she had been immensely proud of it when she had finished it.

But then she had not known what to do with it. So she had finally consigned it to the cardboard box, where it had lain ever since.

But all that was before Richard had come back. Now he was here, and he had shown her that the way to get things done was to do them, and not waste time considering. Without waiting to deliberate another second, she wrote a short letter to a theatre which she knew was looking for works by new authors. She put this with the play, weighed it, added a pound note for the return postage, and parcelled up her work. Then she posted it before she had time to think things over...

At seven o'clock exactly, Mim rang Richard's bell. The door was opened almost immediately, and he flung his arms around her.

"Hello, my precious girl," he said. "How reliable you are—and how beautiful. I am a very lucky man, truly I am."

Mim said nothing, but simply beamed at him. For the moment, her heart was so full that her mind was robbed of any coherent thought.

He served her a meal of cold chicken and coleslaw, bread and crisps, washed down with tins of lager. Mim thought it one of the most delicious dinners she had ever had.

Afterwards, Richard refused to do the washing-up, and would not allow her to do it, either.

"I can do that any time," he said, taking her hand and leading her to the settee. "What I don't seem to be able to do very often is be alone with you. So I intend to take advantage of this extraordinary circumstance while I'm able to."

Mim didn't argue. It was good to be there, cradled in his arms, talking of nothing in particular. Richard told her about what he had been doing lately, and she mentioned her work briefly. Then they were silent for a long, lovely moment, and Mim revelled in just being close to her man and feeling the strength and warmth of his arms around her.

Richard cleared his throat almost self-consciously.

"Darling," he said, "I know you're going to think that I'm being a nuisance, but there is something we simply must discuss."

"You mean the money," she said evenly. "I

haven't forgotten about it, I promise. As a matter of fact, I've been giving it a lot of thought."

"You mean you'll let me have it?" he asked, his smile irresistible.

Mim nodded. "Yes, I will. But it's got to be a proper, legal business deal."

He shrugged his shoulders. "Look, love, would you want it to be a 'proper business deal' if we were married?"

"No, but..."

"Exactly. And we're almost married, aren't we? We're engaged. It's just a matter of taking that final step, isn't it? So why do we have to go all formal on each other?"

She felt more unhappy than she had for some time. She had handled it badly.

He lifted her chin so that their eyes met, and he was smiling.

"Don't worry about it, sweetheart," he said gently. "It doesn't matter. The important thing is that you trust me enough to promise the rest of your life to me. We'll work something out. Now get that worried look off your face, and kiss me."

And it was so much nicer that way. Mim wasn't quite sure where they had got to in their discussion, but she didn't care. He was holding her to him, kissing her, whispering how much he cared for her, and she wouldn't have minded if the world had come to an end in that very moment.

Suddenly, breaking this magical spell, the door was flung open and Andy was framed in the doorway, holding a suitcase and looking embarrassed.

Richard pushed Mim away and stood up. He turned his back to Andy and ran his fingers through his dark hair.

It was almost comical, Mim could not help thinking. After all, they had only been kissing; and yet, there was Andy looking stunned, and Richard behaving as though he had been caught in a very nefarious act indeed.

"I . . . I'm terribly sorry," Andy stammered. "Honestly I am. I'll go away again, all right?"

"You said you weren't going to be back until tomorrow," Richard said, his voice grating.

"I know. My business was finished sooner than I thought." Andy looked directly at Mim who, for some reason that she was not quite sure of, was on the verge of bursting out into laughter. "Mim, I swear I had no idea you would be here. Look, I'll go now. I'll . . ."

"Don't be silly," Mim said, rising from the settee. "It doesn't matter. Come on in, for goodness' sake, Andy. It is your place, too, after all."

Andy picked up his suitcase and came inside, closing the door behind him.

"Actually," he said, "I needn't disturb you at all. I'm dying to have a bath, and . . ."

Mim did laugh then. "Don't worry about it, Andy," she said. "You look as if you could use a coffee. Right?"

He looked at her for a second, and then he, too, began to smile.

"As a matter of fact, that does sound just the job. The last cup of coffee I had was this morning, and it was absolutely vile."

"Good. I'll go and make it, then. As for food—we had a cold meal, and there's plenty left over. I'll get you some and put on the coffee. Then, when you've had a cup, Richard can drive me home." She turned to her man. "All right, darling?" she asked him.

He said hotly: "No, it is not all right. I had looked

forward to a night alone with my girl, and I had no intention of sharing it with anyone else. If you find Andy's company so much more interesting than mine, he can ruddy well drive you home himself!''

With that he strode furiously out of the studio, slamming the front door behind him. Andy and Mim stared after him for a moment, and turned to each other, amazed. Then, without another word, Mim went into the kitchen to put the kettle on.

...It was oddly comfortable, being alone with Andy and talking with him as he ate. It occurred to Mim that when she was with Richard she was always tense, always worried that she might do something wrong, fail to please him in some way. With Andy there was so such feeling.

It was natural, of course. She didn't really give two hoots what Andy thought of her. Still, it was pleasant to be able to relax, to talk freely and not keep a close watch on her every word.

By unspoken agreement, Richard's name was not mentioned during their conversation. Instead, Andy began asking Mim about her job and her hobbies. He was most interested when she mentioned her ambition to be a writer.

"So?" he asked. "Have you done anything about it?"

"I've written reams, if that's what you mean. One novel—very autobiographical, and very bad— dozens of short stories, a few dreary poems. And,'' she added, the tone of her voice slightly altered, "three plays.''

Andy nodded. "And the plays are really your thing, I take it.''

She turned to him in amazement. "How did you know? Did Ri...did anyone tell you?''

He smiled. "You did. When you mentioned the plays, it was almost as if you were talking about your own children. And from that I deduced that they meant something more to you than the others."

"What a perceptive man you are, Andy Thomas," she said with a little smile. "As a matter of fact I sent a play off only today. To one of the small companies, which says that it's interested in finding new writers."

"Good for you. The one thing I've learned in life is that if you want something, you have to go out and get it. No matter how good you are, you'll never get anywhere unless people know about you and what you can do."

Mim was about to agree with him, until she suddenly realized that he was talking about himself, and the memory of his poor, lifeless sketches flashed across her mind's eye. She felt a new and disturbing sympathy for this young man. How galling it must be for him to have to witness Richard's success, to listen to the excited comments of others about Richard's work, when he must know that he, himself, would never have the same flair.

But she did not have long to dwell on these thoughts. Andy had changed the subject, and was talking about Janice.

"I like her very much," he said. "She's got something. Perhaps it's just that she's a thoroughly nice human being. But she's fun to be with, too, and I like her attitude to life. She's almost always smiling."

Mim looked directly into his eyes, but found something there that made her turn away.

"You mean, in comparison with me," she said quietly.

"No, I hadn't even thought it. But now that you mention it, I don't often see you happy, Mim. Or is it just that you don't always show your feelings?"

She drew herself up. "That's not true. I've been very happy these last weeks, and I do show it."

He smiled almost sadly. "Then I can only assume that it's my presence that causes the frown. I'm sorry, Mim. It must be a bit of a trial for you, always to find me here. I'd find somewhere else to stay, but Richard says he'd rather have me here, on the spot."

Unwilling to explore the implications of that remark, Mim ignored it completely. "I think we're both a bit to blame, to be quite honest. I must admit that I haven't been exactly friendly towards you."

"No, you haven't. But in the circumstances, I'm willing to overlook it."

Mim wondered about that, too, but decided that now it was her turn to change the subject.

"It's getting late," she said, "and there's no sign of my hero returning. Do you think he'll be back soon?"

Andy shrugged. "You know Richard," he said.

Mim laughed. "I wonder if I do. About the only thing I could say about Richard with certainty is that he's thoroughly unpredictable."

"Exactly. Which leaves us with a problem. All I've got is a pushbike, and I doubt if you'd enjoy riding on that. So are you going to wait for the great man to return, or should I ring for a cab?"

She looked at her watch. "A cab, I think. Richard may sulk for hours, and it's a long walk to my place from here."

While Andy was on the phone, Mim heard her last words echoing in her ears, and wondered what was happening to her. If anyone else had said anything about sulking in connection with Richard, she would have bitten his head off. And yet, as soon as she had said it, she knew that it was true. Whatever she felt about Richard, she could not deny that he was, in some ways, very childish.

That night she found it difficult to get to sleep. But it was not Richard who kept her awake, it was Andy. Now that she knew him better, she could not imagine why she had disliked him so on first meeting him. Tonight she had discovered a warmth in Andy Thomas, a depth of understanding which Richard so sadly lacked.

CHAPTER FOUR

When the telephone rang early the next morning, and Mim jumped out of bed to answer it, there was a tender, happy smile on her face. Richard had realized how childishly he had behaved, and was ringing to apologize. It pleased her to know that he could sometimes see the error of his ways.

But it was not Richard. As soon as she lifted the receiver and heard the pips at the other end, she knew that it could not be, especially at that hour on a Sunday morning.

"Hello, Mim?"

"Speaking," she said, stupidly angry at the as yet

unknown caller, for having so cruelly raised her
hopes.

"It's Nancy, love. Nancy Batsford."

It took some time for the name to register on
Mim's consciousness. Then:

"Nancy! Where are you? Oh, it's good to hear
from you."

"I'm at Victoria. Any chance of having lunch
with you?"

"Yes, of course," Mim said, collecting her
thoughts. She hadn't heard from Nancy in months.
When her friend had gone to Paris over a year ago,
and got herself a job there, the two girls had written
to each other quite frequently. But then Nancy's
letters had taken longer to arrive, and finally had
ceased altogether. "Are you staying in a hotel, or
what?"

"A hotel, I think. I'm going to try and book myself
a room right now."

"Don't be ridiculous. Get over here right away,
and stay with me. I've got plenty of room. How long
are you going to be in London?"

"I'm not sure. But it might be as long as two
weeks," Nancy said.

"Great! Look, it would be silly to pay all that
money for a hotel room. Grab a taxi and get yourself
here straight away. I'll have breakfast waiting for
you."

Mim flew around the flat, making sure that it was
tidy, getting out sheets for the spare bed and rooting
through the fridge to see what she could find for
breakfast. She was delighted at the prospect of
seeing Nancy. Three years ago the two girls had
shared a flat, fresh from the cloying comfort of their
respective homes. Nancy was a freer spirit than

Mim, more willing to do new things and sample different experiences. Mim owed her a great deal for showing her that life had more to offer than work and the occasional visit home at week-ends. It was very much due to Nancy, in fact, that Mim had been able to cope with things when first her mother, and then her father had died, leaving her to fend for herself. Without Nancy's support, she had often thought, she might have gone under.

How marvellous it would be to have her here now! It would be like old times, even if it did only last for a few days. And just at the moment, Mim felt an overwhelming need for a friend. Someone to talk to, discuss things with.

As she put the coffee on to percolate, she admitted to herself with a slightly sardonic smile that the main 'thing' she wanted to talk about, of course, was Richard. And then, with a jolt that surprised her, she realized that the need to talk was not, after all, so urgent. Thinking back, she knew that Richard's behaviour last night hadn't disturbed her nearly as much as she would have imagined.

After all, he had walked out on her. And he had done it in a most childish, petulant way. Yet, here she was, almost twelve hours later, and the memory of his actions was not throwing her into a whirlpool of misery, guilt and self-chastisement, as so many of his tricks had done in the past.

Tricks? What a funny word to use, she thought. And what a strange idea to occur to someone who is deeply in love—as I am with Richard.

She had no time to dwell on this new idea, and she thought, as she went to answer the bell, that it was probably a good thing. Then, like a breath of fresh, clean air, Nancy was hugging her, a dear friend, a more than welcome guest.

"I've come for a holiday, quite on impulse," Nancy told Mim over breakfast. "It was just yesterday that I decided, and before I had the chance to change my mind, I booked the flight. So here I am, but where I'll be tomorrow remains to be seen. I want to do whatever strikes me, and hang silly things like plans and schedules. If that's going to make things difficult for you, say the word and I'll move out, love."

Mim laughed and poured out more coffee for both of them. "It sounds just right," she said. "I'll give you a spare key, and you can come and go exactly as you please."

They made up the spare bed together after they had eaten, and Mim sat and watched with awe as Nancy unpacked. Out came evening dresses, trouser suits, jumpers, skirts, boots, shoes—enough clothing, in fact, for months, by Mim's standards.

"You must be doing all right for yourself," Mim said, without envy, "to be able to afford all those."

Nancy nodded. "I'm doing all right," she agreed.

"Still with the same designer?"

"Wouldn't change for the world. I started there as a typist, as you know, and now I'm in charge of publicity. Not bad for a year's work, is it?"

"Not bad at all. Richard's in design, too, now. Fabric design." She said it casually, trying to sound completely matter-of-fact.

"Richard?" Nancy said, surprised. "Richard Carlson, you mean? I thought he'd gone out of your life many moons ago."

"He did. But he came back in. And he's designing

fabrics now, as I said. Just about to set up in business for himself."

"I see," Nancy said. "And how involved are you in all this?"

Mim cocked her head to one side and grinned broadly. "Can you keep a secret?"

"I'll make an effort. Come on, what's up?"

"We're engaged," Mim said.

But Nancy did not rush to her and congratulate her, as Mim had hoped. Instead she said:

"Are you really?" And there was something in the tone of her voice that made Mim jump. "I can see that I've come back to London at just about the right time," Nancy went on.

Mim said hotly: "What's going on around here? Everyone seems to have the same reaction to my news—and you haven't even met Richard!"

"No, that's true. But you did write to me about him. And I've heard about him from other people, too," Nancy said slowly.

"Have you indeed?" Mim asked, thoroughly put out. "Well, whatever you've heard makes no difference. He's quite a changed man since he got back. He's settled down, and he's really got something good going now. His designs are marvellous."

"Okay," Nancy said, "have it your own way. And invite me to the wedding, because I won't believe it until I actually hear him saying the words."

A few days after Nancy's arrival, Richard telephoned Mim. He was as warm and charming as ever, and apologized briefly for not getting in touch sooner, pleading once more the pressure of work.

"But let's get together soon," he said. "I don't

want to make a habit of being without you, love."

Mim explained that she had a guest, but said that Nancy was going to be out that evening, and that might be a good time to see each other. Richard agreed, and suggested that she come over straight from work. Then they could decide where they wanted to go.

She arrived at the studio, and was just about to ring the bell, when the door opened. Richard was obviously on his way out.

He told her as he kissed her fleetingly on the cheek: "I was hoping you'd get here before I left. The thing is that I've got to see someone straight away, but it won't be for long. Half an hour, that's all. And then we'll go out and have a slap-up meal. Anyway, Andy's inside. Tell him to fix you a drink, and I'll be back before you know it." With that he gave her arm a squeeze, and was gone without a backward glance.

Shrugging with resignation, Mim closed the door behind her. Andy looked up as she came into the studio.

"Hi," he said. "It looks like it's just us again, doesn't it? Let me get you a drink."

Mim took off her coat and draped it over the back of a chair. "A glass of white wine, if you've got it," she said.

"Oh, yes, it's here. The first thing I did once I was installed was to stock up on the booze. Right, one white wine coming up. Not chilled though, I'm afraid. Is that all right?"

"Fine." She wandered around the studio reflecting that in spite of Richard's fine schemes, the only difference to the room, since she had first seen it, was the addition of Andy's bed, and a curtain which hung from a railing in the corner, and presumably acted as his wardrobe.

Andy came back and handed her the drink, then raised his glass of beer.

"Santé," he said. "Now tell me your news."

So she told him about Nancy, and he said that she sounded great fun. After that a somewhat awkward silence developed, and Mim found suddenly that she did not want to meet Andy's penetrating dark eyes. She again felt slightly uncomfortable in his company, but this time it wasn't a matter of not liking him. It wasn't that at all.

"Mim, could I ask you something?" he said suddenly.

"Yes, of course," she said.

"Would you go out with me?"

She felt as though she had just had a not-so-gentle punch in the stomach.

"I...I don't think that would be a good idea, Andy. But thank you for asking."

"Why wouldn't it? We're both free agents, aren't we? So what would be the harm? Just come out with me for a drink or a meal, something like that. Richard wouldn't mind, I'm sure, if that's what you're worrying about."

Oh, why on earth had Richard asked her to tell no one about their engagement? It made things so difficult, having to keep it a secret.

Andy was smiling almost bitterly. "I don't think you know our Richard as well as you think you do. He wouldn't bat an eyelid if you came out with me, I promise you."

"Andy, the truth of the matter is that Richard and I are engaged," she said quietly. "So you see..."

"Engaged?" he echoed incredulously. "He never said a word."

"I know. And he asked me not to say anything, either. So I'd be more than grateful if you didn't let him know that I told you."

He got up abruptly and went into the flat, coming out with a fresh glass of beer. He looked almost angry, and Mim was at a loss to understand why.

"You're a fool," he said, his voice low and controlled.

"I beg your pardon?" she asked, completely taken off balance.

"You heard me. I had a better opinion of you than that." He looked down at her, and his eyes were hard and cold. "Look, lovely lady, do you really think he'll go through with it? He'll string you along with sweet words and honeyed promises until he gets your money and then he'll leave you as flat as a pancake. That I promise you."

"That's not fair," she said with quiet fury. "You have no right to say such a thing. Richard's not a cheat."

She stood up abruptly and jerked her coat off the chair. She shot him a look of contempt, and turned to the door.

"Tell Richard that I'll be at home if he wants me," she said, without looking at him. Then she opened the door and walked out.

How could Andy talk like that, she thought furiously as she rode home in a taxi. Of course Richard was going to marry her. And wasn't that the one thing that her heart desired? Well, wasn't it? Of course it was, and she hated Andy even more for planting a small, insignificant seed of doubt where before there had been complete confidence. No one had ever suggested, least of all Mim herself, that life with Richard would be easy. But by the same token, she had never said that what she wanted was an easy life. All she wanted was Richard.

When Mim reached her flat she found that Nancy had decided against going out, after all.

"Oh, there's a letter for you," she told Mim. "Let's hope it's good news. You look as if you could do with some cheering up."

It was only after the second reading of the letter that it got through to Mim's conscious mind.

The theatre company had liked her play, and wanted to produce it. Not right away, of course, schedules being what they were, but they were actually saying that they liked it, and were anxious to put it on.

She could hardly believe it. Everything else went out of her head at that moment, and she felt the tension lifting from her like a dark cloud.

"Tell me," she said, handing the letter to Nancy, "does this really say what I think it does?"

Her friend skimmed over the single sheet, then threw her arms round Mim and hugged her.

After that they had a drink to celebrate, and then they got together a scratch meal. They were too excited to eat very much.

Just as they were clearing away the phone rang.

"What happened to you, sweetheart?" Richard asked. Mim was feeling far too happy to remember why on earth she had left the studio, let alone still be angry.

"Richard," she began, "guess what was waiting for me when I got home?"

"I haven't the faintest idea," he said impatiently.

"The thing is, when am I going to see you? What about tomorrow night? Are you free?"

"Yes, I suppose so," Mim said. "But Richard..."

"Darling, I'm really too tired to talk about anything tonight. Leave it till tomorrow, okay? Be here at about seven, then we'll discuss it." He rang off.

...The next evening Mim rang Richard's bell with some trepidation. She only hoped that Andy would have the good sense to be out.

She was in luck. Richard opened the door and said that Andy would not be back until very late. Then he took Mim's arm and linked it with his, announcing that the restaurant he had in mind was not far away, and it would be nicer to walk than to bother with the car.

"Now," he said as they swung along, "what was the news you were so excited about last night?"

"I may not have told you about it," she said, "but I sent off a play of mine to a theatrical company, and the letter I tried to tell you about was their reply. They want to do the play, Richard. They actually want to put it on the stage."

"Really?" he said. "That's nice. How much are they going to pay you?"

"I have no idea," she said after a slight pause. "Nothing, I should think."

He laughed. "Nothing? What's the use, then? I'd tell them to take a running jump, if I were you."

"But that's not the point, darling, quite frankly. I'd be willing to pay them, just for the thrill of having it put on. Don't you see, this is the first tickle of success I've ever had. And it might lead to other things."

"What's it going to lead to—more occasions on

which people will take advantage of you? No, you'll have to be firm and insist on being paid. If your play isn't worth money it isn't worth anything."

They continued in silence to the restaurant. Mim felt totally deflated. She had been so looking forward to telling Richard her news, sharing with him what was to her a moment of triumph and exhilaration, and his attitude towards her announcement had been like a slap in the face.

Feeling as she did, she was not in the best frame of mind for what he said next. He did not speak again until they were installed in the restaurant, and he had ordered the meal, tasted and approved the wine.

"Well, my love," he said then, "the time has come for you and me to have a bit of a serious talk."

Mim's heart sank.

"You know what the situation is with me," Richard went on. "The plain truth is that I need money now, sweetheart, and I need it rather desperately if I'm going to go on with the business. So what do you say? Can we come to a decision, do you think?"

She looked at him dispassionately. He was smiling his most winning smile, but for once Mim did not see it as charming. She was still hurt by what he had said to her earlier.

"I'm sorry, Richard," she said slowly. "I ..."

His face fell, and Mim thought that she saw, for a fleeting moment, a look of pure loathing in his eyes.

Then the moment passed, and he was smiling once again—but now, she felt sure, the smile was less genuine, more forced.

"Look, love," he said, the tone of his voice that of an adult talking to a wayward, and perhaps slightly backward, small child, "I just don't have the time for more consideration. If I don't get that money now, I'm going to be in real trouble. Don't you understand that?"

This was a new Richard, Mim was thinking, and not a particularly likeable one. Or perhaps it was really the old Richard, the man she had hoped he no longer was.

"I know you've got a lot on your mind," she said. "But I myself have a good deal to think about. And at the moment, what is most important to me is this play. I've been asked to make some changes, alterations which will make it more suitable for the company that will be doing it. And that, whether you like it or not, is what is uppermost in my scheme of things."

His eyes narrowed, but at that moment the waiter arrived with the food.

The meal was eaten in silence. When they had finished, and without bothering to ask her if she wanted coffee, Richard signalled that he wanted the bill. He paid, and then stood up. As Mim was putting on her coat he said, with controlled calm:

"If what you need so terribly is time, I suggest you might like to have some tonight. I trust you can find your way home alone. I'll be at the studio tomorrow evening. I suggest that you stop by after work, and that by then you will have done some serious thinking. That is, if you want to go ahead with the engagement."

He turned and left her without another word, but his meaning was clear: the marriage that she so desperately wanted was to be had at a price. She stood where she was, staring after him, rooted to the spot with shock and dismay.

The next morning Mim woke up knowing exactly what she would do. Richard's love, she had decided, was not worth being blackmailed for. To her, the loving was far more important than the money, and if it was not like that for Richard, then he would have to lose them both. Yes, she loved him, and yes, she wanted to be married to him. But she was simply not willing to buy his love.

Richard had suggested that she should come to the studio on her way home from work; and she had thought that this time he would have made a point of being there when she arrived. But it was Andy who opened the door to her.

"Is Richard in?" she asked.

"Sorry, no," Andy said. "And I don't know when he'll be back. I was out this morning, and when I returned he was gone. Was he expecting you?"

"Yes, he was," Mim said.

"You might as well come in and wait for a while," Andy told her, stepping back to let her pass.

She looked undecided. "No, I think I'll go home. If you'll just tell him..."

"Look, love," Andy said, with a sad, tired smile, "can we call a truce? I'm sorry I upset you the other night, I really am. And if we're both going to be involved with Richard for some time, it's a bit silly for us to be at odds with each other, isn't it?"

She answered his smile with a weak one of her own, and gave in as gracefully as she could.

"All right. But honestly, Andy, if you ever say such things to me again..."

He held up his hand to silence her. "Not another word, I promise. Okay? Am I forgiven?"

The fact was that, even if she had wanted to, Mim

could not resist him. There was something extremely appealing about Andy Thomas; indeed there was no denying that he was a most attractive human being.

Impulsively, Mim held out her hand and Andy shook it.

"I've just made coffee," he said. "Want some?"

"Yes, thanks. I could do with a cup."

He looked directly at her. "Things been rough at work, have they?" he asked tactfully.

"No, not really. But I haven't been going out for lunch the last few days, as I usually do. And I miss my walks in the open air."

He told her: "You don't look as fit as you normally do. I suppose I shouldn't ask, but is anything worrying you?"

She regarded him thoughtfully for a moment, and felt moved by his concern. But she could not talk to him about Richard, and she knew it.

"No, nothing's wrong," she said lightly. "Indeed, I've had a bit of luck. A play of mine has been accepted by a theatre."

"That's great, Mim, really marvellous! What kind of theatre is it?"

"Oh, just a small one," she said. "More of an experimental group, really. They're not going to be paying me anything," she added.

"Well, you mustn't let the copyright out of your hands," said Andy. "But the main thing, surely, is that it's going to be done. That really is good news, Mim. Please let me know when it's on. I'd love to see it."

She accepted the cup of coffee that he gave her, with gratitude. She no longer blamed Richard for his reaction when she had told him about the play;

but it was very pleasing to know that someone else could be enthusiastic about what was important to her.

"Janice is back, by the way," Andy said suddenly. "She's been staying with her mother for a while; and she rang when she got in, but Richard wasn't here. She did mention that she wanted to talk to you about something, as a matter of fact."

"Oh?" Mim said. "Well, I suppose I'll see her before she leaves. And now, do tell me about Richard's designs—has he got any firm orders?"

"I think he's got a number of promises," Andy said in a somewhat strange tone. "But I can't be sure. He doesn't discuss such things with me."

Mim laughed. "Honestly, this is the strangest partnership I've ever heard of. You don't know what Richard's doing, and he doesn't seem to know much about your movements, either."

"Yes, it is strange, isn't it?" Andy agreed, but then he was silent, and obviously had no intention of explaining anything.

Mim did not want to let the subject die there.

"Well, tell me about what you're doing, then," she persisted. "Or do you think that I shouldn't be allowed to hear about the inner workings of this business?"

"No, of course I don't think that," he said with a self-conscious laugh. "I'll tell you what I do think, though. My cup is empty, and I'm still thirsty. Want another coffee?"

"No, not particularly. Andy..."

"I'll just go and make a fresh pot," he said as he stood up. "Won't be long. Browse through one of Richard's expensive magazines, why don't you?"

He walked quickly into the flat, giving Mim no

chance to question him further about the business.

All right, she thought, let him try to evade the issue. I'm not going to be put off quite so easily, however.

She glanced at one of the glossy magazines, then threw it aside and began to walk idly round the big room. There was a large scrapbook on the bed and, without thinking, she picked it up.

What she saw inside at first shocked her, and then made her absolutely furious. What she had found inside the book confirmed her earlier suspicions—there were more designs, in the same style as the ones Richard had shown her, but they were signed with Andy's name. Proof positive, Mim was convinced, of his guilt and treachery. There was no getting away from it now, no denying the evidence: Andy was, and had been for some time, stealing Richard's work.

How on earth he expected to pass them off as his own, Mim could not think. How, too, he could expect to sell them without Richard finding out was equally a mystery to her. But neither of those considerations mattered one whit, as far as she was concerned. What was important was that Andy was stealing, and stealing from someone who had tried to help him, who had given him a place in which to stay.

When Andy came back with his freshly-brewed coffee, she whirled round and faced him, the book open in her hands. He made straight for her, his hand extended.

"That's mine, Mim," he said quietly. "Nothing to do with the business. May I have it back, please?"

She gave him a look of pure loathing, and made no move to relinquish the book.

"I wonder at your gall," she said. "I really do. This book is yours, you say?"

Andy nodded. "That's right. May I have it, please?"

"Even though the contents are not yours in any way?"

"Please, Mim. I don't want to argue."

She laughed. "No, I don't imagine you do. You have stolen something precious, something to which you have no right, and yet you stand there and tell me that this is yours, and you don't want to argue about it. No, I certainly don't imagine that you do. But I want very much to argue about it, and to let Richard know at the earliest opportunity that he has been harbouring a viper beneath his roof."

Andy laughed, and the sound served to harden Mim's heart even more.

"That's a bit old-fashioned, isn't it?" he asked. "Come on, now. Whatever you think, this is between Richard and me, and for us to sort out between ourselves. In the meantime, that book belongs to me, and I would like to have it back. Say whatever you like to your precious Richard, but do me the kindness of returning my property to me. Please." Again he held out his hand.

Almost childishly, Mim held the book behind her. "You won't get it," she told him. "I think it would be far better if I kept it, until Richard returns." She shot him a look of contempt. "You know, you really amaze me. What goes on inside your mind, while you sit and talk to me about this and that, knowing full well that you're a cheat and a thief? Quite frankly, I just don't know how you do it."

Andy sighed with exasperation. "This is ridiculous, Mim. I assure you that Richard knows all about those drawings..."

"I'm quite sure he does," Mim said.

"...and that if you'd let me have them, Richard will be able to put your mind at rest when he comes back." He looked at her for a moment, and his features softened, though his gaze did not wander. "Look, love, you know how erratic Richard is about time-keeping. We could be standing here for hours, waiting for him. Put the book down and have a coffee. Or a drink, if you prefer."

She would have liked to defy him, but even she could see that it would get sillier as time went on. Finally she brought the book out from behind her back.

"All right. I'll put it back where I found it. But don't you dare try to remove it before Richard returns."

"Promise," he said quietly. "Scout's honour."

She put the book on the bed, watching him as she did so. He nodded, satisfied.

"But this doesn't mean that I think you're any less of a traitor," Mim said, not being able to resist getting in another dig.

He turned quickly, a look of fury in his eyes. Then, suddenly, he was standing in front of her, shaking her.

"You have no right to say such things to me," he said between clenched teeth. "A man can take only so much..." He pulled her to him. "Traitor, you say? I'll show you how much of a traitor I am."

Then, before she could stop him, he had crushed his lips to hers, fiercely, hungrily. His arms around her were like steel, his passion demanding.

Struggle as she might, Mim could not free herself. When he finally released her and she could move, her arm shot out instinctively and she slapped his face as hard as she could.

The sound was grotesquely magnified in the large, almost empty room. For an instant they simply regarded each other without moving. Then as if brought back to life, Mim jerked away and ran to where her coat and bag were lying on a chair.

She did not hear the phone ring or notice that Andy went to answer it. It was only when she reached the door and the words: "Yes, she's here" intruded on her blind anger that she stopped, the need to talk to Richard stronger even than the desire to get away from Andy Thomas.

"When did he contact you?" Andy was saying into the phone. Then: "I see. Where are you, did you say? Yes, all right. We'll be there as soon as we can." He hung up and turned to Mim. "Richard . . . it seems he's had an accident," he said.

CHAPTER FIVE

They were able to get a taxi almost immediately, and on their way to the hospital Andy had a chance to explain what little he had learned from Janice.

"Richard rang her when he was out, evidently," he said. "He wanted to see her, and they arranged that he would pick her up at her hotel. She was waiting in the lobby when she heard the crash. He was hit from behind, I think. Anyway, we'll learn more when we get there."

"And Richard ... ?"

"She didn't know. He's still alive, though. That's the important thing."

They didn't speak again until they found Janice. Andy had paid off the taxi and taken Mim's arm. In her misery, she hardly noticed, and did not have the strength to object.

"How is he?" she asked Janice frantically as soon as she saw Richard's sister.

"They're not sure yet, but they think he's out of danger. He's got no internal injuries, thank goodness. We'll just have to wait and see."

Luckily, they did not have long to wait. A middle-aged Sister, who looked tired and overworked, approached them before many minutes had elapsed.

"Mrs. Holmes?" she asked.

"Yes," Janice said anxiously. In answer to Sister's questioning look at Mim and Andy, Janice went on: "These are friends of my brother's, Sister. Please, do you have any news?"

"Mr. Carlson is in the ward now. He's been X-rayed, and the doctors are quite satisfied that there is no internal damage. He has broken three ribs, however, and has a slight concussion."

"What will happen to him now?" Janice asked.

"He'll have to stay here for a while, of course, for observation. And it's important that he be kept quiet for a time. Probably about a week."

"May I see him?" Mim asked, both worry and relief showing on her face.

"Miss Evans is engaged to my brother," Janice explained.

Sister shrugged her shoulders. "He's heavily sedated at the moment, so you won't be able to talk to him at all."

"I realize that," Mim said. "But I'd like to see him. Just for a few minutes."

Sister looked at Mim for a moment, her expression blank. Then she turned away.

"If you wish," she said curtly. "Follow me, please."

Mim looked helplessly at Janice.

"Go on, love," Janice said gently. "I'll take Andy for a coffee over the road. You come and join us when you're ready."

They watched her walk quickly behind Sister, and then turned to each other.

"Nasty business," Andy said evenly.

"Yes, but it could have been a great deal worse. Come on," Janice said, linking her arms with his. "You look as if you could use a coffee. And I know for sure that I could."

It was a small, not particularly attractive café, but the coffee was hot and good. Andy bought them a sandwich each; they were both hungry and welcomed the food.

"Poor Mim," Andy said, his eyes seeming to take in every detail of the spoon that he twisted between his fingers.

"Yes. Richard will have a great time, I'm sure of it. But she'll suffer far worse."

Andy looked up at her questioningly and she went on:

"Richard will have the time of his life, and I'd be willing to be quoted on that. It couldn't have come at a better time. He can lie back and collect all the sympathy that will undoubtedly be his, and he doesn't have to do a speck of work in the meantime."

Andy looked sharply at Janice during this speech, and noted the way the expression on her face changed.

"That's a strange way to talk about your own

brother, isn't it? Especially at a time like this," he said mildly.

Janice snorted. "I imagine it must sound horrid, and I certainly wouldn't be saying these things if Richard had been badly hurt, you must know that. But then, it was foolish of us ever to have thought that he might be seriously injured. Richard is one of those chosen people, who go merrily through life, never being touched by it in any unpleasant way, but using it consistently for their own ends." She looked up at him then and, seeing his penetrating, too understanding gaze, glanced down at her coffee cup. "Sorry, Andy," she said. "It's just that I've learned a few things about my dear brother these last few days that haven't pleased me much."

"I see. Is that why you wanted to see him, when you rang earlier?"

Janice nodded. "And why Richard was so anxious for once to see me." She looked up at him and smiled. "I trust I'm not shattering any dearly-held illusions," she said, and it was more of a statement than a question.

He was about to protest, then he raised his shoulders in a gesture of defeat.

"I don't think it's much of a secret that I'm not one of your brother's greatest fans," Andy said matter-of-factly.

"No. I was aware of that almost from the minute I met you."

His eyebrows went up slightly. "I'm sorry about that. I mean it. Whatever I think about Richard, I had no right to let you, of all people, know about it."

"Don't worry about me," Janice laughed. "Oh, I'm fond of my brother, in a way, and probably always will be. The thing is that, few though they may be, I know his good points. But they don't blind me to his faults, and they're legion. I have a theory, you know, that the world needs people like Richard, so that the rest of us are always kept on our toes, just a wee bit. The trouble is, for every Richard there are a number of people who get taken in. Until now, that's never bothered me particularly. Those whom he's conned in the past have usually been conners themselves, so it's a matter of tit for tat. And his girl friends have been the type who look after themselves, and give as good as they get. But Mim's different. I like her tremendously, and I don't think she deserves the kind of treatment that Richard intends to give her."

"Intends to give her?" Andy said, his fists clenching under the table. "He's said something?"

Janice shook her head and smiled. "No. It's just that I know him. He'll keep her on a string until he's got every penny that she's got to give him, and then he'll drop her quicker than you can blink your eyes."

Andy scowled. "I know," he said. "I know exactly what you mean. But what can we do about it?"

"There's only one cure, when a woman's in love with a man. And that's to find another man to fall in love with."

"Marvellous!" Andy said sardonically. "Do you have any candidates in mind?"

Janice nodded. "I think you'd do very nicely, as a matter of fact."

"Me?" he asked. "Whatever makes you think..."

"That you're head over heels in love with her? Just about everything. The way your eyes light up when her name's mentioned. The way you looked at her tonight, in the hospital. That solicitude wasn't for Richard, no indeed."

He grinned at her. "It's not much use trying to hide anything from you, is it? I have a feeling it's a very good thing that you're going back to New Jersey in a few days' time."

"I'm not all that bad," she said.

"No," Andy agreed, "in fact, I think you're a rather super person. Just not particularly bright, that's all."

"Oh?" she said, a trifle coldly.

"Not if you can think of lining me up as the new love interest in Mim's life. The fact of the matter is that she can't stand the sight of me. So if you're looking for someone to save her from herself, you'll have to try someone else. Because I've tried to warn her a number of times, and only gained her steadily increasing dislike of me each time."

"Have you ever tried telling her the truth?" Janice asked gently.

"You mean, the way I feel about her?"

"No. I meant about the designs. That they're yours, and not Richard's."

He looked at her, completely stunned.

"Richard never told you that," he said, perplexed.

"No. He didn't have to. As I told you, I know my brother. At first he had me fooled, I must admit. I had never thought of Richard as being particularly talented, but I was able to convince myself that he had finally discovered a hitherto dormant creativity. I began to get suspicious, though, when I never saw him at work. Richard's a show-off, if nothing else, and it would have given him the greatest kick to have people watch him produce more designs. The final thing was your fault." She saw his face drain of colour, and laughed. "Oh, don't worry, it wasn't deliberate, I know that. I was at the flat one day when you were on the phone. There was a pad and pencil there and, quite unconsciously, you were making little sketches. And of course I recognized the style at once." She sat back with a measure of satisfaction, like a detective in a novel who has just explained to a room full of people who the murderer was, and how clever he has been in discovering the truth. "So," Janice went on, "I know, you see, and you know that I know. Which means that we can now begin to be honest with each other."

Andy had not taken his eyes off Janice all the time that she had been talking. His expression had undergone a number of changes: worry, fear, slight annoyance. Now he smiled easily—and a trifle sadly, at the same time.

"I had a feeling that you'd be trouble, Jan."

"Really? Why on earth? You're not going to deny that what I've said is right, are you?"

"Not at all. But the next obvious question is why I let Richard get away with it, and I can't tell you that. But being a typical woman, with a normal, active, curious mind, you're not going to want to let it rest there. Are you?"

Now Janice was serious. "I don't want to, no. And I have the feeling that I shouldn't." She leaned forward, with an air of intensity. "Look, Andy, I know a bit about creative people. Most of the time, and rightly so, they want credit for the things they do, and they deserve it. The only possible reason I can think of for you sitting back and letting Richard get all the acclaim for work that you've done is that Richard is blackmailing you in some way. I'd like to help, and I don't mean just you. It's time that my brother got a taste of his own medicine. If he's allowed to walk over people all his life—well, I fear for him, that's all. He's rapidly turning into a man I find difficult to like, and that saddens me. At the same time, I've become rather fond of you, and you don't deserve this kind of treatment." She reached out her hand and covered his. "Please, Andy," she said, "let me help."

He sat back in his chair. "You can help, as a matter of fact," he said. "But not in the way that you think. I'm grateful for your offer, Jan, I really am. You're a very nice person. But the only thing I ask is that you say nothing. Especially to Mim."

"To Mim? But why not, for goodness' sake? Surely that would be one way to make her see what kind of a man Richard is."

He nodded. "Perhaps. But I don't want her to know." He went on, in an obvious attempt to change the way the conversation was going: "You really are amazing. Why are you going all out to break up this romance between Mim and Richard? Nice as you are, you're not going to sacrifice Richard's future for her sake, are you?"

She grinned. "All right, so we can see through each other. I'm not saying that what I said before, about worrying about Mim, is untrue. I do worry about her, and I think that she stands a very good chance of being crushed completely by Richard. We both know that he has no intention of marrying her and, to be honest, if he did go through with it, for some reason, that would probably be even worse. For both of them. Life with him would be pure hell for her. At the same time, Richard stands to do badly out of this as well. If he does manage to get her money, and then drops her, it will be one more incident to convince him that he can go on like this for ever. And if he marries her, that will finish him off. He doesn't need a woman who will let him treat her like dirt. He needs a strong person, someone at least as strong as himself. Someone who will stand up to him and make him take a good look at the man he's become. You do agree, don't you?"

Andy nodded, and then got up and took their cups to be refilled. When he returned he sat down heavily in his seat and began stirring his coffee thoughtfully.

"Yes, I agree with every word," he said, carrying on the conversation as though there had been no break in it. "But I'm afraid that you've hit on the wrong solution if you think that I'm the person who can do anything about it. First of all, Mim would never believe me if I told her that I did the designs. She already thinks I'm a thief, and such a statement would just convince her of my villainy. Richard would swear blind that I'm lying, and we both know whom Mim would believe. Then, too, I have to go on doing designs for Richard—maybe one day I'll tell you why—and the atmosphere at the studio would be something less than delightful. So I'm afraid, Jan, that we'll just have to let things take their natural course, and hope that before disaster strikes, Mim gets some sense into her beautiful, delicious head. I don't think I could bear it if she showed more scorn for me than she does already. And if she were to be told the truth, I'm sure that she would remember only those parts of it where I come off rather badly. So for everyone's sake, Jan, please keep your pretty mouth shut, and go back to your nice husband and lovely kids, and leave us here to sort everything out."

Janice watched Andy's hand as it guided the spoon round and round his cup. Finally she reached

across and gently took it from him, laying it down in
the saucer.

"I'll tell you what," she said. "You tell me what
this is all about, and I promise you I won't say a
word."

He looked up at her and raised his eyebrows.
"Feminine curiosity?" he asked her.

Janice nodded. "That, too. But mostly for your
sake. Whatever threat Richard is using, it's eating
you up, that's plain to see. It might help if you could
tell someone. And I've got a well-deserved reputation as a good listener."

Andy smiled. "You're a very nice lady, Jan.
But..." He picked up the spoon again. When he
looked up at her again he had obviously made a
decision. "All right, why not? I was working in
Brussels, living off the money I had been left by my
parents. They had died when I was very young, and
the money had been held in trust until I was of age.
It wasn't all that much, but enough for me to do
what I wanted for a while. I had grown up with a
succession of aunts and cousins, being shunted
from this one to that. I struck off on my own as soon
as I was able. I never had any formal art training,
but I always knew that it was the one thing that
satisfied me. When I had my first job, I met Jon
Levke, a German who was in England getting his
degree in business studies." He looked up at Janice
questioningly. "Am I boring you?"

She shook her head. "Go on," she said gently.

"Right. Jon and I became good friends, and when
he left England he told me that he was going to
Brussels, where he had a house. If ever I was there,
he insisted that I must stay with him. So one day,
about two years ago, I decided that I was going. I

was twenty-six, too old, I thought, to start studying art, but too young to throw my life away just getting by with this job and that. I hadn't touched a penny of my parents' money, so I drew most of it out and just took off. I wrote to Jon, asking if I could stay with him for a while. He wrote back immediately, telling me that he wasn't going to be there, but enclosing a key and begging me to make use of the house and to stay as long as I liked.

"So I packed my bags and went. I still had no idea what I wanted to do, but it felt good just being free. And then, one day, I hit on the idea of textile design. I don't know, perhaps if I had had any training, I wouldn't have thought of it, but as it was, the idea stimulated me tremendously. And I had the feeling that I might be good at it."

He stopped talking suddenly, lost in private musings. Janice watched him for a while, trying to read from his expression what he was thinking.

"Don't stop," she prodded him. "Tell me all of it."

He looked up at her and nodded. "The next part isn't quite so pleasant," he said. "Just about that time, I met Erika. She was a few years older than I was, but it didn't matter at all. I fell passionately in love with her, almost at first sight. I'd never known a woman like her before—sophisticated, worldly, exciting. Beautiful and fascinating. She knew so much more than I did, knew about the right places to go, about an exciting, glamorous side of life that I'd never realized even existed. She was staying with a friend not far from where I was living, so it was perfect. We were together always, with her friends, at Jon's house, everywhere. I thought that I'd found perfection, and I couldn't believe my luck."

He paused again, and Janice said gently: "It

stopped being quite so idyllic, I gather."

Andy nodded. "After a while, yes. You see, Erika stirred all the romantic cravings inside me. I was only happy when I was with her, and could think of nothing but her when we were apart. So I wrote letters to her. Passionate letters, outpourings of a very immature heart that had become intoxicated with feelings I didn't know how to cope with."

"And she wrote back to you?" Janice asked.

Andy laughed. "No, not once. And that, if nothing else, should have given me a clue. Things went on like that for a few months. I wanted nothing more from life than to marry Erika and settle down, and see what I could do in the field of fabric design.

"One day I got a letter from Jon to say that he was coming back. I thought that now my happiness was complete. I knew what I wanted to do with my life, I had met the woman of my dreams, and now my dearest friend was on his way home. I had told Erika about Jon, of course, and now I informed her that he was coming back. And she said nothing."

"Should she have?" Jan asked.

"It would have helped. Because I discovered, as soon as Jon arrived, that she was his wife."

Janice stared at him, open-mouthed. "I don't understand," she said.

"No, neither do I. Oh, I understand full well that she was just having a good time while her husband was away, and that she had no desire to ruin the fun by telling me she was married. But if she had confessed when I told her that he was coming back, at least she would have spared me the horrible embarrassment of that moment when Jon walked into his own house and greeted his own wife, saying that he hadn't realized that she was back in

Brussels, and showing pure delight that she and I
had already met."

Janice looked confused. "I don't quite understand," she said. "Hadn't they been in touch with
each other?"

Andy nodded, smiling twistedly. "They wrote.
Erika had posted her letters to a friend she had been
staying with in Italy, and had her send them on to
Jon from there. So as far as he knew, she had been in
Italy all the time, and had only just returned."

"It must have hurt you terribly," Janice said
quietly. Poor Andy, he seemed to be the loser in
every situation.

"For a while," he agreed. "But somehow, once I
knew the truth, the love faded rather quickly. My
only thought was to ensure in some way that Jon
never found out. He adored Erika, and I had no
desire to be the one to inform him that she wasn't
the angel he assumed her to be. And then I
remembered the letters."

"Oh, yes," Janice gasped. "I'd forgotten about
them."

"That makes two of us. As soon as I remembered
them, of course, I asked for them back."

"And she wouldn't give them to you?"

"Right the first time. She seemed to think that it
was all a great game, and it amused her to have this
hold over me. She threatened to show them to Jon, if
I ever crossed her in any way."

Janice nodded. "So what did you do? Did you ever
get them away from her?"

"Someone did," Andy said. "About that time, I
met Richard. He was in Brussels, looking for
something to do with himself. I told him all about
the ideas I had for textile design, and he was

extremely interested. And then, one night when I
had had too much to drink, I told him about Erika.
With a great pretence of friendship, he laughed and
told me not to worry. He'd get the letters back, and
all would be well."

"I see," Janice said. "Yes, it's just the kind of
thing Richard would say. I can almost hear him
now. It would give him yet another opportunity to
show a woman that he's superior to her, and make
himself a hero in your eyes at the same time."

Andy smiled wanly. "You do know him well,
don't you?" he said. "Anyway, he was successful, of
course. I don't know how he did it, but within a week
he had every single letter that I ever wrote to Erika.
The only trouble that once he got them, he decided to
hold on to them."

Janice said nothing, but her eyes narrowed in
anger.

"By this time, you see, Richard had got really
interested in the designs I was doing. So interested,
that he tried some himself."

"The ones I saw stuck behind the others," Janice
said with conviction. "The meaningless, dull ones."

"That's right. He recognized the fact that he had
no flair in this line, but still the idea fascinated him.
So he decided that he could use my idiotic letters, in
exchange for some work from me. Ten designs, he
said, fully worked out with a variety of colour
schemes. He would sign them, and I was never to
admit that they were mine. Then, when those
conditions were met, he would return the letters to
me."

"And?" Janice asked suspiciously.

"Yes, you're ahead of me, aren't you? Your

rother is really a very predictable person. I did the
en designs, and then Richard decided that he
ieeded more. And there's very little that I can do
bout it."

"You could call his bluff," Janice said.

"And risk hurting the one person in the world I
we most to? I couldn't do that."

"Maybe it would be a kindness, in the long run,"
Ianice suggested. "After all, if she's that kind of a
voman, it might be the best thing if he found out
iow. Anyway, if she is like that, he probably knows
lready."

Andy nodded. "I wouldn't be at all surprised.
Iowever, he does not know of the part I played in
Irika's life."

"But you didn't know who she was!" Janice
rotested.

"Even so," Andy said quietly, "I'd prefer to go on
vorking for Richard for the rest of my life, rather
han have Jan find out. That, I'm afraid, is that."

"Maybe not," Janice said cryptically.

Fear showed in Andy's eyes. "Look, Jan, don't
et involved. This is between Richard and..." He
tood up suddenly. "Hello," he said. "How is he?"

Janice turned to see Mim approaching the table.

"He hasn't woken up yet. I would have been
appy to sit there all night, but they told me that he
vould probably sleep through until the morning,
nd I got the feeling that I was rather in the way. So
said I'd be back tomorrow."

"You look all in," Andy said gently. "Do you want
omething to eat?"

Mim shook her head. "I'm not hungry, thanks.
ut I could use a coffee."

"Richard will be all right," Janice said comfor
ingly. "If they had been at all worried, they woul
have said."

Mim nodded, but Janice wondered if she ha
heard what she had said.

"He looked so helpless, Jan," Mim said. "I ju
wanted him to open his eyes for a moment, just
see that I was there, that he wasn't alone."

"I know," Janice said, resting her arm affectio
ately across Mim's shoulders. Anger was rising i
her, threatening to choke her. How unfair it wa
that this sweet girl should be upset about a man wh
was clearly playing her, and everyone else, false

As Janice had told Andy, she had learned a fe
unpleasant things about Richard when she ha
been with their mother. The ring, of course, ha
been taken without her permission. Not that Jani
actually told her mother about what she had seen
but she worked the conversation round to the rin
one day, and asked where it was kept these days. I
the jewellery box beside her bed, Mrs. Carlson ha
said. She liked the idea of it being with her at a
times, even if her hands were too misshapen to wea
it any more. It seemed to bring her dead husban
closer to her.

She had confessed that Richard had talked he
into giving him a great deal of money—all he
savings, in fact, leaving her to manage on he
meagre pension.

"Oh, I get by," she had assured Janice, but th
younger woman wasn't fooled. She could see f
herself the numerous signs of small deprivation
that her mother had had to put up with. The ve
next day she had wired Jack in New Jersey an
asked that he send a substantial amount of mone

to her mother's bank. At the same time, she made arrangements at the bank for a certain amount to be sent to her mother every month.

There were other incidents, too, smaller but equally unpleasant tricks that Richard had played on his mother to get something out of her, and which Janice learned about from neighbours.

And yet, somehow, he managed to win the love of a nice, unsuspecting girl like Mim. It seemed so terribly unfair.

Andy returned with the coffee and some biscuits, which Mim proceeded to eat without thinking. She spoke about Richard, about how he had looked, and how she had felt while she sat beside him. Once or twice Janice turned to look at Andy, and each time she caught a look of pain on his face.

"I've made up my mind, though," Mim said suddenly, forcefully. "I'll marry him as soon as he's out of hospital."

There was a shocked silence from the other two, but Mim was too wrapped up in her own thoughts to aware of the significance of this.

"But ... do you think Richard will agree?" Janice asked hesitantly. "He was never willing to be pinned down to a date before, don't forget."

Mim looked determined. "I know. But this time he will. I'll see to that."

Janice looked desperately at Andy, but he was staring beyond her, his thoughts in some private place which she could not enter.

"Mim," she said slowly, "you must give it more thought. You can't ..."

But Andy had put a warning hand on Janice's arm.

"I don't think this is any time to do any serious

thinking of any kind," he said. "We could all use
some rest." He stood up and asked Janice: "What
happened to the car, do you know?"

She snorted. "Hardly a dent," she said. "And
Richard wouldn't have had one, either, if he'd been
wearing a seat belt. It was only because he wasn'
that he was thrown forward, and hit his head. The
car is still at the hotel, I think."

"Right. Let's take a taxi there, and then I car
drive Mim home. Is that okay?" he asked her.

Mim nodded, but it was obvious that she was
hardly aware of his presence—and that hurt him
immeasurably. At least, when she was angry with
him, inherent in that anger was recognition of his
existence. But this was no time for self-pity. He went
outside and hailed the first taxi he saw.

Janice insisted that Mim took a tablet that night
to help her sleep, but she herself found that her
eyelids refused to close when she got into bed. What
on earth was she going to do? What would be for the
best? All she knew was that she couldn't let things
drift. Mim could not be allowed to make any plans
about her wedding, because Janice was positive
that it would never take place—and if it did, that
would probably be far worse for both her friend and
her brother.

Somehow, she knew, Mim would have to change
her mind. And it would have to be soon. Richard was
likely to be in hospital for a week at the most. The
only thing Jan could think of doing was to confront
Richard with her knowledge of the blackmail threat
he was holding over Andy's head. But what good
would that do, if Richard still had the letters? She
knew him to be a devious man, and it was no

beyond him to turn spiteful. There was every chance that he might, just out of pique, send those letters to Andy's friend on the spur of the moment. Nor could she tell Mim about the situation. Andy had asked her not to, in the first place; and besides it was not likely that Mim would believe her.

No, the most important thing, as she saw it, was to find where Richard kept the letters, and give them back to Andy. And she would have to do it quickly. Not only was Richard going to be back soon, but she, herself, was due to fly back to America in a few days. She could extend her visit, of course, but she was not terribly keen to do that. She missed her husband and children desperately, and wanted to get back to them as soon as possible.

It seemed that the only possible course, then, was to turn the flat and the studio upside down, in the hope of finding the letters. Richard might have hidden them somewhere else, of course, but she hoped that such a necessity had not occurred to him. At any rate, it would give her something to do, which would be useful in itself.

CHAPTER SIX

Mim was at the hospital long before visiting hour the next day, and she was the first in the ward when at last she was allowed in.

"How are you feeling, darling?" she asked, pity and love shining in her eyes.

Richard managed a weak smile. "Not one hundred per cent," he told her, "but they assure me that I'll live. Thanks for coming," he added.

"Are you kidding?" she asked him, horrified at the suggestion that she could have stayed away. "I hardly slept a wink last night, worrying about you. I couldn't have stood it if I couldn't have seen you today. You look a little bit better than you did last night, anyway. You've got a bit of your colour back."

"You're a good girl," he said, but his eyes were closed, and Mim could not really tell what lay behind his words.

She sat down on a chair next to the bed, longing to touch him, to be closer than she was. "Richard," she said, "I've been thinking and thinking, and I've come to a decision."

"Have you now?" he asked disinterestedly.

"I have. And it's this: we should be married straight away. There's no point in putting it off any longer, is there? And then, if we were married, I could take care of you. When you get out of hospital, you'll need a lot of attention, and I want to be the one to look after you."

"What have you envisaged, a bedside ceremony, with the nurses as bridesmaids?" he asked.

"No, idiot," she said fondly. "Not in here. But as soon as you come out."

"A good idea," he agreed sarcastically. "No need to waste the taxi, then. Straight from here to the registrar's office."

"Richard, don't talk like that," she said. "It means so much to me."

He stared up at the ceiling for some moments before he spoke, and then his voice was even and steady, lacking any of the warmth that was so evident in Mim's tone.

"All right," he said at last, "maybe you're right. But there's one proviso."

Mim looked at him wonderingly.

"I want the money first," he said. "You've been stringing me along for ages, Mim. If you love me, you should be willing to prove it."

She sighed heavily. "All right, darling, if that's what you want. It seems a bit pointless to me, since it would be just as much yours as mine once we married, but if you want to do it this way, I don't mind."

For an instant a look flashed across his features, a look of the cat who has managed to get the cream, and not have a drop on its whiskers to give it away.

"That's my girl," he said more warmly. He closed his eyes. "I'm terribly tired, Mim," he said. "If you wouldn't mind..."

"No, of course not," she said, standing up. "Sleep well. And don't forget that I do love you very much."

He watched her walk down the ward, but closed his eyes when she got to the entrance, knowing that she would turn and look at him, and not wanting particularly to have to pretend any more for the moment. It was tiresome enough having to do so when he felt well, but now he found it a particular trial. Never mind, he thought with satisfaction, it would be over soon...

When she returned the next day, Richard was in an irritable mood. He sulked when she said that she had not brought the money, and was hardly mollified when she reminded him that it was Sunday.

"Besides," Mim said, "I wouldn't carry around such a large sum of money, would I? I'll see about it tomorrow, during my lunch hour, and make arrangements to have it transferred to your bank. Is there anything you want in the meantime?"

"My dressing-gown and slippers," he said without a hint of gratitude. He was finding her presence more irritating than usual, and wished fervently that she would go away and leave him alone.

Mim sensed something of this, and put it down to the fact that he must be in pain. She left him soon afterwards, feeling let down and dissatisfied, even though she tried her best to make allowances for his behaviour. She promised him that she would be back the next evening with the things he had requested, and then kissed him lightly on the forehead. His eyes were closed, and he appeared to have fallen asleep.

On leaving the hospital she went straight to the studio. She would have no time tomorrow to pick up the things Richard had asked for, and it was important to her that she please him, now of all times.

"What a nice surprise," Andy said when he opened the door. "Have you come from seeing Richard?"

Mim nodded. "He's doing fine," she said without enthusiasm. "I didn't stay long, because I know that he needs rest more than anything. But I've come to collect a few things that he asked for."

"Can I help with anything?"

"Just his dressing-gown and slippers. If you wouldn't mind getting them for me."

Andy grinned. "I think I might be able to manage that. Hold on a second." In barely more than that he was back, carrying the things she had asked for. "How about a coffee?" he asked. "Do you have time?"

She hesitated for a moment, and then relaxed. At that instant, when her nerves still felt raw from her visit to Richard, a coffee with a friendly human being sounded very close to heaven.

"How was he?" Andy asked as he put the kettle on.

"Fine, I guess," she answered absent-mindedly. "He wasn't on top of the world, but I don't suppose that's difficult to understand. After all, he must be in pain, and he seems to be utterly exhausted."

Andy nodded, keeping his thoughts to himself.

Mim laughed slightly shrilly, her need to talk outweighing her loyalty to Richard.

"He's so worried about that silly money," she said, trying to make it sound as if she wasn't particularly bothered by Richard's attitude. "I don't imagine that's so strange either, really. After all, there he is, flat on his back, and about the only thing he can do from where he is, is try to see that he's solvent." She avoided Andy's eyes as she went on: "Besides, once we're married, it will be his anyway, so I can't imagine why I'm even thinking twice about it."

Andy poured the coffee into the cups that Mim had set out on the table. He did not look at her when he spoke.

"And yet you are, is that it?" he asked quietly.

She did look at him then, and there was a plea for understanding in her eyes.

"It's terrible of me, isn't it?" she said. "I mean, in the circumstances, I should be willing to give him that money freely, and not hesitate for a minute. And yet it's been ages since he first asked me. So what's wrong with me? Why am I dithering like this?"

Andy ran his tongue round his lips, trying to think of the best way to say what he was thinking.

"You're just being sensible," he said at last. "Let's face it, it's a lot of money, and it's all you've got."

"But I trust Richard," she said. "And I'm going to

be his wife. So why am I dithering like this?"

"It isn't a matter of trust," Andy said, avoiding the answer he would have liked to have given, but which he knew would only make her turn away from him. "Be honest, Mim. You know as well as I do that this business could quite possibly fail. If you still had the money then, you'd be all right. So you're trying to make sure—for Richard's sake, as well as your own, don't forget—that you'll be on top, whatever happens. Besides," he added carefully, "I imagine that it's in your mind that Richard, whatever good points he may have, is a bit irresponsible in some ways."

He looked closely at her, to see her reaction. He breathed a quiet sigh of relief to find that she hadn't shut him out with an angry, defensive reaction. He went on, in the same tone: "So you're probably thinking, understandably, that it would be just as much of a help to Richard to do this the right way, legally, and give him a sense of responsibility at the same time."

Mim looked thoughtfully into her cup and nodded. "I think you're right. It would be wrong of me to just give it to him, without any strings."

"Do you have a solicitor?" Andy asked casually.

"Yes, I do. He handled everything when my father died."

Greatly relieved, Andy grinned at her. "Perfect," he said. "Then it's simply a matter of having a word with him. He'll know the best way to go about it. Now, let's talk about something else. Tell me how your play's coming along."

Mim was only too happy to discuss her play with Andy. He was interested, and made intelligent and helpful comments. As they talked, Mim slipped into an easy, friendly mood, and all the disappointment of the earlier part of the evening evaporated. By the time she left, she was wondering once again why she had so disliked Andy at first, and was more than glad to have him as a friend.

The next day, Mim rang her solicitor first thing in the morning, and made an appointment to see him at lunch-time. With that done, she felt easier than she had for some time, and was able to concentrate on her work and the matters on hand.

Meanwhile, Janice had been busy, too. Knowing that Mim would be at work, and therefore would not be able to disturb her, she went early to the studio. She had telephoned first, and ascertained that Andy would be busy during the morning, so the studio would be empty. Using the key that she still had not returned to Richard, she let herself in.

The flat was the obvious place to start her search. Richard most probably would not have left the letters in the studio, where Andy would have easy access to them.

She did not have to search for long. Hidden away at the back of the wardrobe, she came across a small, locked file. She was just wondering how she could open it without breaking the lock—and hating herself at the same time for what she was doing—when she remembered that she had been given Richard's personal effects when she had been at the hospital. As she retrieved his keys from her handbag, she was grateful once again that Andy was not there. Much as he wanted to have his letters back, she had the feeling that he would never have sanctioned what she was doing. On the other hand, Richard stood a good chance of ruining a number of lives, and there was no way that she was going to stand back and let him do it. Not without a fight of some kind.

She found the right key and opened the box. On the very top was a packet of letters still in their envelopes, all addressed to Erika Smiele. She removed the packet quickly, with a feeling of profound relief.

She replaced the relocked file in the wardrobe, tidied the room, and let herself out of the studio. Now it was up to Andy...

When lunch-time came, Mim took a taxi to her solicitor's office. Mr. Spiro was anything but happy about the proposition that Mim put to him. He thought it extremely unwise of her to use all her money in this way, and he did his best to talk her out of the scheme, or at least to agree that she would use only half her money as an investment in Richard's business.

Mim could see, of course, that, to his mind, she was being extremely foolish. This was all the money she had in the world, and it would have been unprofessional, she assumed, for him not to try to dissuade her from such a risky investment. But she was adamant.

At last, but with grave reservations, Mr. Spiro agreed to make the necessary arrangements. It would take a few days, he told her, but he would ring her as soon as the papers were ready for her signature.

They shook hands as she left the office and Mim went off feeling almost light-headed.

During the afternoon, she found it difficult to concentrate on work. She had realized something as she was coming back on the bus, and what she had discovered had shocked her. The fact was that, once she had seen her solicitor, she felt much better. But she was not thinking about the enjoyment of telling Richard that she had finally taken steps to arrange what he wanted. What made her feel so buoyant was the prospect of informing Andy that she had done it in the way he had suggested. It was his face that had been before her eyes as she travelled back to work, not that of the man she was going to marry.

And last night, she remembered, when she had been alone, with no distractions to keep her from being completely honest with herself, she had had to admit that Andy's kiss had done more to her than she liked to believe. She could not help recalling that, despite her anger, she had experienced something in Andy's arms, something that Richard's nearness had failed to stir in her.

And that, she knew, was the real reason why she had been so angry. Not because he had kissed her— even if it had been disloyal to Richard, it had been a compliment to her. And had she been totally unmoved by it, she knew that she would have been embarrassed, upset and vaguely unhappy; but she would not have been angry. She had hit out at him because he had made her realize, in that instant, that there was something missing when Richard kissed her, something vital and necessary.

And here she was now, having finally done something for Richard, something that he had been begging her to do, and yet the only person she could think of was Andy.

What was happening to her, for goodness' sake? Didn't she love Richard? Of course she did. If not, why would she be returning from having arranged to give away all her money, all her security? And she was going to marry him. If she had had any doubts about that, they had been completely dispelled when she had seen him in that hospital bed, vulnerable, and needing her at last.

This thought made her even more unhappy. Could it mean that it was only when her heart went out to him in pity that she was truly stirred?

During the rest of the day, Mim got very little done. Her mind was a turmoil of disturbing, unsettling thoughts. For the first time since Richard's return from Europe, she began to think about their relationship dispassionately, and it occurred to her now that her loving was a feeble, unreasoning thing.

She knew, of course, that love was not reason, it was an emotion. Didn't one always hear people saying that they couldn't imagine why A loved B, or what C saw in D? It had very little to do with what was sane and understandable.

Still, she could no longer deny that her relationship with Richard left a great deal to be desired. He cared nothing for the things that were important to her. It had been Andy who had been excited about her play being accepted by the theatre, not Richard. And the business about the engagement, and the ring. Why was it that Richard had denied her the pleasure, one which most young women were allowed, of parading her happiness, sharing her joy with her friends? And then, too, she was always being let down by him, always expecting to see him when he simply forgot to show up or phone her. That was bad enough now, but what would it be like when they were married?

In fact, did she really love him? That was what it boiled down to, and Mim knew it. The more she analysed the situation, the more she saw that her affair with Richard had been a matter of more disappointment than pleasure, of loving him when they were apart, and feeling let down and dissatisfied when they were together.

She had been stirred and moved to excitement and fulfillment only once, and then by another man.

Was she in love with Andy? Was that the truth of the matter? Or was it more a case of being in love with love, and not having had enough experience of life to know what she really wanted?

When the end of the day arrived, Mim knew only one thing. That she was totally confused, and needed more time. Time to get to know herself.

Suddenly she was afraid. She had committed herself totally to Richard, in every possible way. She had promised to him everything that she had to give. And now she was in no way sure that she was doing the right thing.

Instead of going directly to the hospital, she went home first. She needed more time to think, perhaps to talk to Nancy, so that she could sort out her feelings. In her troubled, unhappy state, she knew only one thing for certain: that she wanted to put off for as long as possible the moment when she would have to see Richard...

When Mim got home, she found Nancy in the middle of packing.

"Are you going back to Paris?" she asked forlornly, the thought of Nancy's leaving adding to her depression.

"That's it. I'm glad to see you. My flight leaves in two hours, and I wanted to say good-bye in person instead of just leaving a note propped up in the kitchen."

"Why are you going? It's a very sudden decision, isn't it?"

Nancy nodded. "I know, love, but quite frankly, I'm homesick for Paris."

Mim studied her friend thoughtfully for a moment. This obviously was not the whole story.

She sat down wearily on the bed. "Nan, please tell me," she said. "I just haven't got the energy to wheedle it out of you. Please?"

Nancy sighed. "Okay, I will. But you're not going to like it."

Mim gave a wry little laugh. "I don't suppose I shall. But we've been friends for too long for you to hold back now."

"To be honest with you, one of the reasons that I came here at all was because I was having a problem in Paris." Nancy grinned. "Boy-friend troubles, of course."

Mim nodded encouragingly. "Go on," she prodded.

"His name is Pierre, and I love him to distraction. He has asked me to marry him."

"He did? But how marvellous! What's the problem, then?"

Nancy laughed. "Me, I guess. The thing was, he was unwilling—unable, really, I suppose—to give me the kind of love I wanted. You know, the all-encompassing, all-attention kind of love. I resented the fact that his work was so important to him, and that quite often, if the choice was between me and work, I would lose."

"Yes," Mim said with understanding. "I know all about that."

Nancy shook her head. "No, you don't, and that's

what I've learned since I've been here. You see, love, Richard doesn't just put you in second place from time to time; he simply ignores you altogether. With me, it's a matter of now and again having to accept the fact that other things are important to Pierre; but whenever he can he sees me, and when we're together he treats me like a queen. Until I came here, I wasn't satisfied with that, and I had to get away for a while to think things over. But now, seeing how you're neglected, and how miserable you are, it makes me realize how very lucky I am. You probably think it's terrible of me to say this to you, but..."

"No," Mim said quietly. "I don't, as a matter of fact. More than that, I agree with you. I'm beginning to have a number of doubts—and it makes me feel awful."

Nancy jumped up and clasped her friend's hands. "Oh, my love, you shouldn't feel awful, not at all. Maybe you're finally coming to your senses. Sweetie, it's none of my business, I know that, but now that I've started, I'm going to get it off my chest. Mim, Richard isn't right for you. To be honest, I'd pity any woman who was stuck with him."

Mim shook her head as though she were trying to clear it. "I didn't say I've turned him down, Nan. Just that I was having second thoughts."

Nancy knelt down beside Mim and looked up into her eyes. "Mim, you've got to throw him over. I know it's not going to be easy, and I don't envy you. But your whole future depends on it, love." She stood up. "Look, you know as well as I do that you can't marry him. Isn't that true?"

"I'm not sure," Mim said wretchedly. "For a long time now I've thought of my future in terms of being

Richard's wife. How can I suddenly just turn my back on him?"

Nancy looked at her watch. "That's up to you, I'm afraid. And I've got to get on with my packing, or I'll never make the flight."

"Can't you get a later one?" Mim asked. She didn't want to be left alone at this stage.

"Can't. I rang Pierre and told him which plane I'll be on, and he'll be meeting me. I wouldn't be able to reach him now, to tell him my plans have changed. Anyway, love, I want to be with him. I so desperately want that."

That was something that Mim could understand, and she only wished that she felt the same way about someone. Instead, she was dreading the visit to Richard at the hospital.

Still, she could put it off no longer. She hugged Nancy warmly, and promised that she would give the matter of her engagement serious thought before she made any definite decisions. Then she gathered up the things she had collected from Richard's flat, went out and hailed a taxi.

Janice was just leaving the hospital when Mim entered, and her face was like thunder.

"Have you seen Richard?" Mim asked.

"I have," Janice answered between her teeth.

"I see. Any trouble?"

Janice smiled and patted her hand. "No, not really. I'm just in a bit of a temper, that's all."

"I probably won't be long. Richard gets tired so easily. So if you'd like to wait, maybe we could have a meal together afterwards," Mim said.

"Yes, why not? That seems a very good idea. I'll walk back with you to the ward, and then I'll wait outside for you."

As she approached him, Mim thought that

Richard's smile was a trifle forced, but she put that down to the fact that he was probably still in some pain.

"Hello, Richard," she said. "I've brought you the things you wanted."

"Good girl. What about the other matter, though? Have you done anything about that?"

"The money? Yes, I saw my solicitor at lunchtime. He's going to arrange everything."

"Your solicitor?" Richard cried so loudly that people in the beds near his all turned to look. "What on earth did you do that for? Don't you trust me, for goodness' sake?"

"Yes, of course I do," she said, keeping her voice low and calm. "It's just that this seemed the best arrangement to make."

"Who told you so? My dear sister, was it? Talk about disloyalty, she takes the cake."

"A number of people have advised me to do so," Mim said, looking down at her hands. "It doesn't matter anyway, does it? You'll have the money, and that's the important thing, surely."

"How much?" he asked quickly. "All of it?"

She looked at him carefully before she answered. He seemed different tonight. She could see nothing in him now of the sweet, gentle man she had known. Or was it simply that her eyes were finally open so that she could see the truth for once?

"Yes," she said at last, her voice hardly above a whisper, "if I do lend you the money, it will be the amount I mentioned before."

He reached out and grasped her hand.

"What do you mean, 'if'? You said you've made all the arrangements."

"Yes, I have. It's just..." She looked directly at

him, and there were tears in her eyes. "Richard, I don't think I can marry you."

Had she expected him to be upset, she would have been disappointed by the look of unconcern on his face. But a light had begun to dawn in her mind, and his words hardly surprised her at all.

"That's all right by me," Richard said evenly. "But that's not what we're discussing."

"Isn't it?" Mim asked. "Funny, I had thought we were, one way or another." She sat up straight now. "You hadn't meant to marry me at all, had you?" she asked him. "All you wanted from me was my money. Why don't you admit it? I might respect you a bit more if you did."

"Darling, that's not fair," he said pleadingly. "Of course I was going to marry you. But that's something different. We're talking about an investment, one that makes sound business sense. And don't forget, you promised that I could have the money long before there was any talk between us of marriage."

Mim nodded bleakly. "That's true," she admitted.

"So will you still be lending it to me? Don't take any notice of what I said before. If you want to do it through solicitors, that's okay. What do you say?"

"I don't know, Richard. I just don't know. I'll have to think about it."

"There's nothing to think about," he snarled, and Mim was suddenly frightened. If he had been able, she knew, he would have struck her at that moment. "You made a promise, and you can't go back on it now."

"Richard, I..."

"No more talk!" he snapped. "You made a promise, and I expect you to honour it."

She looked at him in horror, and then stood up abruptly and almost ran out of the ward. It was not until she got outside that she remembered that Janice was waiting, and went back to meet her.

The two of them walked in silence to the café over the road, and Mim sat down while Janice ordered coffee. Neither of them felt like eating at the moment.

"You had the same kind of time with him that I did, I take it," Janice said.

"It wasn't pleasant, no," Mim admitted.

Janice sat silently, twisting her wedding ring for some moments. Then: "Mim, there are a few things I have to say to you, and since I'm going back to the States in two days' time, I might as well get it over with."

Mim laughed. "You're about to advise me not to marry Richard, aren't you?" she asked.

Her eyes widening, Janice said in surprise: "How did you know?"

"Everyone seems to be telling me that these days. Well, Jan, I may as well tell you that I've..."

"No, let me talk first. It's going to be hard, because he's my brother, but I can't hold it in any longer, Mim. There are two things, really. The first is that I'm quite convinced that Richard has no intention of marrying you. It sounds hard, love, but I'm sure it's only your money he's after. But if he does marry you—and he might just do it—then that would ruin his life, as well as yours. But yours, mostly. He'd make the most terrible husband for any woman, but he'd be impossible for you in particular. And if, for some reason, he decided that it would be to his advantage to go ahead with it, then I'd never forgive myself for not speaking out now."

She stopped for breath, and looked closely at Mim to see how she was taking the lecture. Strangely enough, it seemed to her that Mim was actually smiling.

"You said there were two things, Jan. What's the other one?"

Janice bit her lower lip thoughtfully. "This is harder still to say, because I promised that I wouldn't. But you've got to know, Mim. I may not be thanked for it, but someone's got to tell you."

"Go on, Jan. Let's clear the air, and get everything into the open," Mim said firmly.

"Right. The thing is, those beautiful designs of Richard's..."

"He didn't do them," Mim finished for her.

Janice stared at her in amazement. "You knew?" she gasped.

"I guessed. I only admitted it to myself last night, but I think I must have known all along."

"You must know who did them, then," Jan prompted.

"Andy, of course. It couldn't have been anyone else. How did you know? Did he tell you?"

"I guessed, too. I simply couldn't believe that Richard could produce such work, and Andy seemed to fit much better. I had to worm the truth out of him, though. And he made me promise that I'd never tell you."

"Why? Surely he would have been much better off if he had told me. And why did he allow Richard to tell everyone that he had been the artist?"

Janice shook her head. "No, that I can't tell you.

You'll have to ask Andy himself."

Mim wanted to question her further, but knew that she could not. If it meant anything to her—and she knew now that it did—she would have to probe deeper herself.

"Are you angry with me, Mim? For telling you all this?" Janice asked her cautiously.

She smiled. "No, not at all. I'm very grateful in fact. But it was quite unnecessary, in the event. I tried to tell you before, but you stopped me. The fact is that I've just broken the engagement with Richard."

Janice said very soberly: "You've done the right thing. But it must have been difficult for you, just the same. How did he take it?"

Mim laughed. "Quite calmly, to be honest. Which further enhances your suspicion that he never intended to go through with it in the first place. No, his only concern was for the money."

Janice nodded. "What are you going to do about that?"

"I'm not sure. Richard said one thing that was true, that I had promised to lend it to him, and that was long before any thought of a close relationship between us."

"True. But it was under false premises, wasn't it? I mean, it was on the basis that he was a talented textile designer. Well, he's not—and he won't have Andy around any more."

Andy was going away! The thought shouldn't have bothered Mim in the least. But there was no denying that it did.

"Why? Where's he going?" she asked Janice a trifle too quickly.

"I don't know that he's 'going' anywhere," Janice

said, observing the look on Mim's face, and being somewhat amused by it. "It's just that he owes no allegiance to my brother any more, that's all."

"Yes, I see, Jan, does Richard know about Andy?"

Janice shrugged her shoulders. "I don't know that, either. Why don't you ask him yourself?"

"You're right. There have been enough misunderstandings about this whole thing already, haven't there?" She cocked her head to one side and looked penetratingly at Janice. "Tell me one thing, though. Richard's your brother. Why have you set about ruining him?"

Janice shook her head sadly. "No, Mim. All I set out to do was to make him see that the way he's been going about things is the worst possible. I know that he's done some mean things, and one part of me hates him for them. But the other part still cares for him a great deal. If something isn't done pretty soon, he'll go on and on, cheating and using people, until every scrap of humanity is drained from him. And I just don't want to see that happening."

Mim reached across the table and covered Janice's hand with her own. Then she began searching in her bag. Taking out the ring that Richard had given her, she handed it to her friend.

"I think he should have this back, Jan. Would you mind if I asked you to return it for me?"

Janice took the ring and held it in the palm of her hand.

"No, I wouldn't mind at all returning it to where it belongs," she said...

Mim spent the next hour walking aimlessly. She and Janice had parted when they had finished their coffee, and Mim had promised to come to the hotel to see Janice the next evening, before her friend returned to her husband and family.

Now, however, Mim's mind was too full of chaotic thoughts for her to be able to relax. And so she walked. She hardly thought about Richard—her chief emotion, with regard to him, was relief and a sense of blissful freedom. She had decided that it would have been foolhardy to lend him any money. She knew how it would be spent—on high living, fast cars and other women.

She would ring Mr. Spiro in the morning and tell him that she had changed her mind. She smiled to herself when she thought of how pleased he would be by her decision.

So Richard wasn't her worry, and it was not thoughts of him that filled her mind now. As she walked, staring idly into shop windows and seeing nothing, Mim was thinking only about Andy Thomas.

How could she turn round now and say that she loved Andy? Would he believe her? Or would he be scornful, and tell her that she seemed to pass her affection around very easily, and what guarantee was there that her 'love' for him wouldn't evaporate as easily as her feelings about Richard had done?

Feeling thoroughly dejected and deflated, Mim hailed a taxi and went home.

She went to Janice's hotel the next evening after work, as she had promised, and they had a meal together. Mim felt quite drained by the time it was over.

Janice hugged her friend warmly and kissed her on the cheek. "Good-bye, dear Mim. You will write to me, won't you?"

"Yes, of course I will. And you, too."

"You have my address, do you?" Janice asked.

"Yes, I do," Mim answered with a smile. "And thanks for everything. You've been marvellous." Then, afraid that she would no longer be able to control her feelings, she turned and walked swiftly out of the hotel...

Mim sat in her flat, her dressing-gown belted tightly round her, a cup of hot cocoa in her hands. She had been wondering how she could contact Andy.

Just at that moment the doorbell rang, and Mim jumped up and went to the door.

Andy stood outside, looking sheepish and dishevelled. He was the most welcome sight she had ever seen.

"May I come in for a minute?" he asked her.

"Yes, of course. Come on in."

He looked about him as she ushered him into the living-room.

"This is nice," he said. "Very nice indeed."

"Of course—you haven't been here before, have you?" She stood awkwardly, aware of her dressing-gown, and the fact that she could not think of a thing to say to him.

"I've moved out of the studio," Andy said suddenly.

"Yes, I know."

"Do you? Oh, I suppose Richard told you."

Mim looked at him, trying to decide how much she should tell him. Finally: "No, I haven't seen him since yesterday."

Andy shook his head. "He didn't know until today."

"I see. Have you got another place?"

He nodded. "A small bed-sit in Earl's Court."

An embarrassed silence followed.

Suddenly Andy looked directly at her. "How did you know, then? About me moving out?"

"I wanted to contact you," she said. "I wanted to tell you..."

He waited for her to continue. Then he said: "Yes?"

"Just that I've broken it off with Richard. I thought you'd be pleased to hear it."

He frowned. "I think it's the best thing," he agreed. "Are you very miserable?"

Mim thought for a moment, and then shook her head. "I'm not, quite frankly. I just feel that a great weight has been lifted."

Andy grinned. "It sounds marvellous. What about the money?"

Mim began to find the situation quite amusing. They were both trying to tell each other something, and to find out a great deal more, and neither of them knew exactly how to go about it.

"No, I'm not doing that, either. He doesn't have a business any more, you see."

Andy frowned. "Really?"

"Really. It seems that his designer has left. So he'll have to find another project—and another backer, as well."

He cleared his throat awkwardly. "Just what has Janice been telling you?" he asked her, avoiding her eyes.

"Nothing more than I had already guessed. That the real artist was you, and that Richard has been conning everyone right and left, and me in particular. But she didn't tell me why, or how he was able to get you to sign yourself away like that. Was it something so terrible?"

"It wasn't particularly pretty," Andy said quietly.

"I don't believe it could have been anything bad. I won't believe it—not about you. Won't you tell me?"

He opened his mouth, but then closed it again. Then he looked directly at her and, with only the hint of a smile, said: "I think I love you, Mim."

She gasped involuntarily. This was not what she had been expecting, not at all! Then she, too, began to smile.

"Isn't that funny—because I think I love you, too."

"Then do we need to talk at all?" Andy asked her.

"Oh, yes, I think so. I think we've got a great deal of talking to do. But I think there's something else we've got to do first."

As if by a prearranged signal, they both stood up at the same instant. They began walking towards each other slowly, almost fearfully. When they met they stood looking at each other for a moment, and then before she knew how it had happened, his arms were around her, his lips were on hers, telling her, wordlessly, so many of the things she wanted to know.

When at last he released her, let her come up for air, he said, as he caressed her hair and gently kissed her cheek, her eyelids, her neck: "Do you still want to talk?"

Mim laughed happily. "Yes, I do," she said. "But

there's time for that. There are years and years for that. Just for the moment, though, I want you to kiss me."

"I love you," he said, his voice deep with emotion. "I love you very much, my darling."

THE END

EIGHT THRILLING NEW ROMANCE BOOKS!
THREE COMPLETE STORIES IN EACH NOVEL
NOW AVAILABLE DIRECT TO YOU
BY MAIL AT ONE LOW, LOW PRICE

Heather Romances

You may wish to enjoy

To: Heather Books
720 Post Road, Suite 310
Scarsdale, N.Y. 10583

Gentlemen: Rush me the books checked below at $1.95 per each. I enclose $_____ plus 50¢ to help defray postage and handling.

HR-109 ☐   R-111 ☐   HR-113 ☐   R-116 ☐
R-110 ☐   R-112 ☐   R-115 ☐

NAME: _____

ADDRESS: _____

CITY _____ ZIP _____ STATE _____